PIRATES OF THE WILD WEST

BY

BRYAN CANTRELL

BRYAN CANTRELL

A PIRATE TIME TRAVEL NOVEL

Pirates of the Wild West is a work of fiction. Names, characters, places, and incidents are the product of the author's imagination and are used fictitiously other than the public figures depicted in the book. You may ask are pirates and outlaws' public figures? Absolutely. All dialog and story elements of the public figures in this novel are the work of fiction. I did an extensive search and found no public records of any pirates, cowboys or other public figures time traveling or doing the things they do in this novel such as committing theft, murder, or mayhem. Again, for the record -Fiction.

BRYAN CANTRELL

Published by Dark Gravity Studios

www.bryancantrell.com

First edition: December 2022

Contents

CHAPTER 1 - THE PARDON

NASSAU HARBOR 1718

Edward Thatch expertly lit the sweet-smelling tobacco that was packed into the bowl of his ivory pipe with the help of his tinderbox. It took a moment for his eyes to adjust back to the darkness of the night as he inhaled that first hit of head-clearing nicotine. The jolt to his heart rate felt satisfying, and he exhaled slowly and deliberately, watching the smoke dissipate into the night air. He carefully closed the tinderbox, waited a moment, then opened it again to ensure the mix of cotton and wax was completely snuffed. He knew all too well the consequence of carelessness when it came to fire management on a 200-ton frigate made almost entirely of wood. Even cooking in the galley required the exercise of great caution on a ship with forty cannons, a hoard of gunpowder and many gallons of flammable tar and oil that was used to waterproof the hull and sails. One had to be incredibly careful and have their sea legs about them to construct a meal using hot oil and grease while constantly accounting for the roll and pitch of the unpredictable Caribbean Sea. Edward was well aware of the ban on smoking aboard ship, as he was the architect of the rule, but as captain of the *Queen Anne's Revenge*, he allowed himself a few liberties. There was also no one else aboard the *Queen Anne's Revenge* to hold him accountable for breaking his own rule. No one other than his first mate Black Caesar, that is, who was currently below deck preparing for their arriving guests.

The low rumble of thunder in the distance caused Edward to turn his head toward the open sea. The dark of night and the starless sky prevented him from seeing the coming storm clouds encroaching on the Pirate Republic city of Nassau. The occasional streak of lightning would illuminate the angry gray clouds covering the Caribbean like a billowing blanket. The sheeted trio of masts that lined the deck of his frigate were only now beginning to smack and clank in the wind. Thatch turned his eyes back to the small harbor as the lamp lights of several tenders carrying passengers were rowed slowly toward his anchored ship.

He took a puff from his pipe as he considered the parchment he had tucked into his belt. He had read its contents many times over, even out loud to the over two hundred men under his command. They all had listened in rapt silence as he recited the official offer of a pardon from the King of England. Most, if not all, of his crew were illiterate, and in this part of the world, most people couldn't read even a lick of the written word. Edward, however, was an educated man and a well-trained English Navy sailor. He had come to piracy after the war with Spain and France ended. Many of his ilk had taken the same path. Once the war ended and privateering against France and Spain was no longer sanctioned by the English Crown, there was no work for most of the sailors that were now stranded in the waters of the Caribbean. For many, privateering or what they now considered piracy was the only job they were qualified to do. It was truly the only job that was available to them.

Thatch unrolled the parchment to read over the details again but found it impossible in the low light of the evening. In truth, he could recite the words from memory now after so many readings. The idea that that damned German King George the First would honor the pardon was difficult to believe after an entire year of Thatch and his cohorts raiding England's merchant ships. The King of England's pardon granted indemnity from all acts of previous piracy and crimes as well as the rights to keep all plundered loot and assets obtained prior to the signing of the contract. He and his crew had quite a haul on board, as well as in the pockets of each member when they disembarked to enjoy the spoils in the capital city of the pirate kingdom. Edward smirked as he imagined the debauchery that was taking place in the lively drinking holes of Nassau. He himself would have joined his crew if it had not been for this call to parley between the reigning pirate captains. The message he had received upon arriving into the harbor from his old commander Benjamin Hornigold contended that there was some urgency to the discussion on the signing of the contract. The urgency probably had something to do with the three British Navy ships that now sat in the crowded harbor.

The heavy footfall of Black Caesar sounded behind him as the dark and imposingly large man climbed up the stairs from midships.

"Everything prepared below for our guests?" Thatch asked without turning from the vision of the small boats just moments from arriving.

"It is. And me brought your armament." Black Caesar held out the belts and holstered weapons he carried in his large hands.

Edward Thatch made short work of the buckles and straps to adorn himself with four ornate 7-inch flintlock pistols held tight against his chest, two polished and sharpened cutlasses scabbarded on each hip, several daggers clinging to various belts and bootstraps along with a prized 26½-

inch blunderbuss within easy reach hooked to his waist. Black Caesar gave a nod of approval to his captain and adjusted his own plethora of personal armaments. Thatch tapped his pipe against the railing, sending the smoldering tobacco into the warm Caribbean waters.

"Drop a ladder for our brethren and gather 'em in the main hold," Thatch said as he strolled to the forecastle.

"Aye, Captain," Black Caesar responded and made his way to the folded rope ladder waiting on the starboard side.

The first drops of rain began to fall as the tenders arrived to tie off against the *Queen Anne's Revenge*. Black Caesar watched as the first man ascended the ladder and climbed over the top of the rail. His mood darkened as he took in the broad-built form of Henry Jennings. Jennings was a coarse, self-righteous, arrogant man that Black Caesar had the displeasure of knowing for about a year now. He was a man that only smiled maliciously if at all. Jennings was a captain in the Royal Navy during the war and a plantation owner on one of the islands that Black Caesar could never remember the name of. Jennings took in his surroundings as would a cat seeking its next mouse to make a meal of, as the *Queen Anne's Revenge* was the envy of all pirate ships. He looked right through Black Caesar as though he was just another fixture of the 200-ton frigate, another tool or mechanism that was just used to operate the vessel. Henry Jennings commanded the ship named *Bersheba* and spent most of his time sailing along the coasts of Florida and Jamaica raiding shipwrecks and small merchant vessels. His sometime first mate Charles Vane followed him up, using Jennings' shoulder to steady himself. Jennings roughly brushed off Vane's hand, almost sending the half-drunk man sliding to the deck. As Vane recovered, he sent a smirk in Black Caesar's direction.

"Where's Thatch?" Jennings questioned the empty deck of the ship as he would not talk directly to a former slave such as Black Caesar.

"Probably primping in his mirror like some sort of dandy," stated a slurring Vane. Black Caesar only waited silently for the rest to climb aboard.

Next up was the young Sam Bellamy with his long coal-black hair and dashing good looks. Sam in just a few short months had become one of the wealthiest pirates ever to sail. He and his crew had captured a returning English slave ship named the *Whydah* that was loaded down with a fortune in gold and ivory. His first mate, Paulsgrave Williams, hopped easily to the deck next to Bellamy.

"Yes, where is that old sea dog?" Sam said with a flash of bright white teeth that shone even in the dark of this night. Black Caesar clasped the outstretched hand of Bellamy, then of Paulsgrave.

"He waits below deck," said Black Caesar.

Bart Roberts and Charlotte De Berry boarded seconds later. The two only knew each other by reputation before this meeting but found common tastes in their clothing and jewelry. They both had a fondness for crimson and wore waistcoats of the same shade. Bart Roberts wore an enormous diamond-crusted cross made from an unusual heavy silver metal with a pink hue that was plundered from a treasure destined for the King of France. Charlotte's mocha-colored skin was decorated with bracelets, rings, and necklaces of gold and brightly colored gemstones. The two were becoming fast friends, and Roberts offered an unnecessary hand for Charlotte to take when climbing up from the ladder.

"A gentleman pirate. How disarming," Charlotte said, accepting Bart's hand.

Roberts bowed with a flourish. "At your service, my lady. I find it best to be gracious when a beautiful woman ornaments herself with such finery as well as deadly... accessories," Roberts said, glancing at the several dirks, blades and other sharp instruments of death that adorned Charlotte's attire. Charlotte gave a knowing smile as she strolled past Roberts to join the others on deck. Bart smiled and gave Paulsgrave a wink as they watched her pass before they both followed in her wake.

Sam Bellamy leaned over the rail and whistled down at the next arriving boat.

"Be quick about it, you sad lot. Are we to wait around, becoming drenched in this rain?" Bellamy called.

The second ship to tie up held Benjamin Hornigold, Mary Read, Anne and James Bonny, Calico Jack Rackham, Stede Bonnet and several of their seconds-in-command. Once they were all on deck, their total numbers were twenty-four. Twenty-four of the most successful and feared pirates that had ever sailed the waters of the Caribbean. The deck of the *Queen Anne's Revenge* was gently swaying and becoming slick with rain under their thick leather boots. The wind was kicking up, and the raindrops were becoming larger and more consistent by the minute.

"That's all? Then follow." Black Caesar led them all down the steps to the main hold. Flickering whale-oil lanterns that lined the gangway guided them into the large hold that was lit by several lanterns whose flames danced, creating shadowy ghosts along the walls. The large hold was filled with treasures that would delight even the wealthiest merchant or duke of their age. The store held floor-to-ceiling stacks of commodity goods, chests yielding overflowing coin, jewelry, and ornate weapons. There were crates of rum and wine to tempt the thirst of the tavern-hungry sailors. Several spare cannon, pistols and long rifles also lined the walls. Though these pirate captains were jaded by their own successes, they couldn't help but stare admiringly at the impressive haul of loot crowding the hold belonging to Thatch and his thriving band of pirates.

Anne Bonny leaned comfortably against one of the polished wood beams in the spacious mid-deck hold of the *Queen Anne's Revenge*. Her husband, James, had told her earlier of the supreme craftmanship of the vessel. It was certainly a prize to be envied by all the pirate captains gathered here. She glanced with disdain at James standing beside her, gawking overtly at the open boxes spilling over with linen finery, ivory and pewter and silver items. The rich, intoxicating smell of tobacco filled the room, no doubt wafting from the collection of burlap bags shelved floor to ceiling on one side of the room. She found that her stomach had turned lately when she was so close to James. Maybe it was his weak chin, or the paunch of his middle, his smell… the smell of a coward. She couldn't help but shake her head at the thought of all the opportunities James had to lead, yet he had always chosen to follow or to fink.

Her wild eyes drifted to the dashing figure of Jack Rackham standing aloof, preening his fingernails with an ornate stiletto. Her heart now leapt at the memory of the night they spent together after they had captured the *Kingston* off the shores of Port Royal. The *Kingston* was a fine sloop with eight guns that now added to their growing fleet. Jack's thirst for adventure was only matched by her own and it twisted her heart to be married to James when her destiny was to be at Jack's side forever. The passion that had overtaken them that night was heard by the entire crew and was now etched in the legend of their bold attack on the *Kingston*, within sight of all the merchants watching helplessly from the port. Jack slyly looked up from his grooming and drank in her copper-colored hair and exposed cleavage spilling from her open-topped men's shirt. If that same look had come from James, she would have shuddered with revulsion, but she now arched her back a bit and tossed her hair to one side.

Anne's eyes reluctantly pulled away from Jack to observe the other occupants. Most were men, though beasts may have served them better as a simple description. Two other women were present within the group, though, and she gave a quick nod to Mary Read. Mary was standing next to Jack and was smirking at Anne as she clearly had noticed the exchange that had taken place between them. Mary made a rude gesture in relation to James with her ringed pinky finger, that caused Anne to stifle a giggle. The two women had been friends instantly when meeting as they found themselves so like-minded. They both adopted the dress of their male counterparts, not to conceal the fact that they were women, as was clear by their ample breasts, but for the freedom of movement allowed by men's breeches, shirts, and coats. One needed to move quickly and efficiently on board a pirate ship, especially in battle. How fierce could one possibly be with both hands hiking up skirts to run from one side of the deck to the other? Anne unconsciously laid her hand on the handle of her sheathed machete and gazed at the third woman in the room.

Charlotte De Berry barely glanced in Anne's direction. She had never been receptive to any advances that Anne ever made to her, friendly or otherwise. Charlotte's dark coffee-colored skin accented the array of bangles and bracelets that decorated her sleeveless arms. She too chose to wear breeches like Anne but with knee-length soft leather boots. Her hair was braided long and ornamented with beads and colored glass jewels. Charlotte slouched back in a chair, tipping its front legs off the floor with the ease of a panther relaxing on a branch high above the forest. She was well known for her expertise with a blade, that was almost like watching a trained dancer performing a ballet of death and mayhem. Anne watched as Charlotte tapped the ivory handle of her flintlock attached to her waist. Her long fingers moved in rhythm as if she were tapping along to a piece of music only she was hearing. Charlotte only carried one pistol on her person, unlike the rest of the gathered pirates who were outfitted with up to ten such weapons, unwilling to risk the need to reload once engaged in a heated battle. This was most likely due to the fact that Charlotte De Berry was one of the worst shots that ever wielded a gun. Jack had commented once that it was probably because of her poor eyesight when it came to seeing anything more than a yardarm away.

Bart Roberts eyed the lusty form of Charlotte De Berry as he made his way around the hold. He ran his hand over the crates and barrels Thatch had stored throughout the crowded room. He knew Thatch had been quite successful the last several months, harassing the trading vessels coming to and from the new world. There were rumors that Thatch was known to stop at various small islands and atolls around the Carolina coast to bury portions of his plunder, careful to ensure it wasn't being stored in just one place. It was hard to believe that even more existed outside of the treasure-crowded hold in which he now stood.

A sly smile formed on his lips as he caught the eye of Charlotte while she watched him case the room. She was definitely a desire that he would seek to satisfy once they were all back on land in the port of Nassau this evening. His hand touched the cool stones of the jeweled cross that hung from a cord around his neck. He felt an odd shiver course through his body as he strode past the many chests while Charlotte squinted at him.

"Where is Thatch for God's sake!" Jennings bellowed. Black Caesar was in the process of passing out cupfuls of wine from several pitch-black bottles and held one out to Jennings who ham-fisted it from him, sloshing the dark, crimson-colored liquid to the wooden floor. Black Caesar stared momentarily as it slowly seeped between a slim gap in the floorboards as Jennings stomped away. Vane took one of the cups from Thatch's first mate and held it out for a pour. Black Caesar accommodated and in a quick gulp, Vane swallowed the wine with a grimace and held the cup for another round.

"Where the devil did this come from?" Vane asked as Caesar moved on. "It burns horribly, but with a touch of sweetness." Vane focused his bleary stare on Anne Bonny. "Just as Anne would taste, I'd say." Vane nudged his elbow into the side of Jack Rackham.

Anne retorted with a rude gesture that sent many to laugh.

"Can we get on with this meeting, Hornigold?" Jennings said, turning toward the architect of the Pirate Kingdom of Nassau. "I can only imagine what nonsense Thatch will have to say regarding the pardon in hand."

Hornigold looked around the room at the expectant faces and cleared his throat.

"We've all had a chance to read... or have the King's pardon read to us..." he began.

"Imposter King!" Thatch's deep-toned voice boomed from the doorway as all heads turned to see his figure backlighted by the brightly lit oil lamps framing the entrance. Thatch held the silence, or more accurately, relished the silence his statement initiated. He then sauntered into the grand hold and several pirates gave way as he brushed past them to stand in front of the crowd with the boxes of shimmering loot behind him. "The German-born King George offers us this weak document in hopes that some of us will jump at the chance to bend the knee once again. He claims we can keep our plunder, crimes against the Crown and its interest forgiven and forgotten. All we must do is give up piracy. We must disband the haven we've created—that Hornigold has created!—and allow the dreaded pirate hunter Woodes Rogers to ascend to the governorship of our beloved Nassau."

"You'd rather we were hunted down by the Royal Navy for the rest of our lives?" exclaimed Jennings. "We not only have the English Crown to attend to, but Spain, France, the Dutch and now thanks to you releasing the slaves bound for Virginia and the Carolinas, we have those governors wanting our heads as well! We've all become rich this past year, at least if you didn't spend all your take on whoring and drink. I say we take the pardon and count ourselves lucky."

"That's an easy choice for a plantation owner to make. Easy to retire when one has land and title," said Mary Read. There were many grumblings through the crowd as each voiced an opinion. Hornigold stepped forward, gesturing with his hands for quiet.

"It's true I had designed this republic as a new beginning for those of us who were cast aside by our beloved England…" he began.

"Not so beloved to those of us Irish!" laughed Anne Bonny, interrupting. Many joined in with the jest as some attending were Irish, African, and Scots.

"Fine, fine, beloved for some of us," said Hornigold "We were abandoned throughout the Caribbean when the three crowns made peace, while most of us sailors had no way of going home. We all saw opportunity, and we took it. We decided to continue doing what we do best. During the war we were privateers with the blessing of King George, now… now we are all pirates. Pirates that King George relished as he looked the other way while we plundered the merchants of Spain, France, and the Netherlands. This republic was to be a haven where any man or woman could raise their station. A place you could arrive without a pot to piss in and, through your hard work, cunning and grit, carve out a life with freedom and success. We've done that. Together. Look at you all. I would imagine that none in this room would have believed they would have achieved so much. But some, and I'll put my foot forward to be included, got greedy. We became tempted by the fat merchants that sailed from our beloved…" (said with a smirk and wink at Anne) "England and began to bite the hand that held the whip. We have all done well, as Jennings has said, and it is my opinion that we take our spoils and begin a new life. A life that doesn't end with our necks in a noose."

"This pardon is a Kraken!" Thatch roared. "A Kraken meant to wrap its rubbery tentacles around our hearts and drag us under the sea to a watery grave. Do you not see the fallacy of it, Hornigold? It is meant to divide us. German George knows good and well some of our rank will jump at the chance for forgiveness. Divided, we are weakened. Easy pickings. But if we stand together, we have the strength of three navies. I command over two hundred of the strongest, fiercest, best-trained sailors ever to roam these waters. Together with Hornigold, Rackham, Sam Bellamy, Stede and Jennings there is a combined total in the thousands." Thatch pointed to each man with his cup of wine. "I say we stand our ground. Retain our rights and independence! Together we could bring the Crown to its knees!" Thatch raised his cup in a toast and downed the liquor in one giant mouthful.

The divided crowd erupted in both cheers and dissent. Jennings and Hornigold shared a look together, even though there was no love lost between the two. Jennings turned to his drunken first mate Vane, who he knew had no desire to sign the pardon and give up his life of piracy. It was easy to see that Vane agreed with Thatch. Jennings' mood darkened as his life was becoming too complicated and dangerous to attach himself any longer to this lot. He desired nothing more than to disband his crew of five hundred thieves and degenerates and sail home to the Bahamas. He was in fact a plantation owner and had no more need for the treasure that had driven him into this life after the end of the war. As unwilling as he was last year to give up the command of a ship, he was now unwilling to sail with the threat of the English Navy behind every cove and squall he encountered. In truth, he avoided fighting alongside these lesser, ungodly men, choosing to pursue the easy prey that would give up before combat or to plunder the recent wrecks that occurred throughout the reefs, rocks, and sandbars of the Caribbean Sea. Hornigold, who once was his second-in-command during the war, felt the same. They had spoken days before, agreeing that they must find a way to convince their brethren to sign the pardon in order to preserve their influence on the profitable trading port that Nassau had become. If Thatch and the rest of these bastards and whores continued to pirate these waters, they would force the Crown to send a large armada to control the ports and shipping lanes to deal with them. If that happened, then his and Hornigold's hold on Nassau would be threatened.

Jennings looked over at the monster that was Edward Thatch. Wine was dripping from his long braided beard as he laughed and was patted on the back by Sam Bellamy. He despised them both. Partly out of jealously, as they were two of the most successful pirates ever known. Bellamy, he mused, was just lucky. He was an excellent sailor but did not have what it took to run a ship with an iron fist. Bellamy was a true believer of the pirate republic ideals. He fancied himself a Robin Hood, known for his mercy and generosity. Young and an idealist, that one. It was told to Jennings that Bellamy had pursued piracy in the hopes of earning enough money to win the approval of his love's father up in Cape Cod. Bellamy was a street rat that wanted to marry into a proper upper-class family and Jennings could understand exactly why the girl's father would never allow it. No matter how much money a rat could steal, a rat he would still be. Thatch, though, was something else altogether. He arrived in Nassau as a mystery of sorts. It was apparent that he was an educated man, well read, and an adept war technician that one would dread to come up against in battle. Jennings had overhead him converse in as many as six languages, yet the debauchery that he was capable of would bring a blush to the cheeks of the devil himself. Whereas Jennings' first mate Vain was a tool of violence to be used by someone with intelligence and wit, Thatch was an instrument of destruction that could not be controlled and could possibly outsmart you at every turn. Jennings knew he should not take chances when dealing with that one. Best to leave him for Hornigold to clash with, and maybe both would do each other in on their own.

Jennings was about to take a drink of the rich, dark wine in his cup when he felt the ship rise and fall from the crest of a wave. He managed to keep from spilling the liquid only from the years of experience one acquired from living aboard ships and coping with the mundane challenges of eating, drinking, and shitting without solid ground underneath your feet. The size of the wave struck him as odd as they were anchored in a bay. It must have seemed unusual to the rest of the seasoned pirates, as everyone in the room paused what they were doing and stood in abrupt silence. The noise of the rain and wind, as well as the creaking of the wooden vessel, seemed amplified by the hush that went through the hold. Then the ship rose and fell on the crest of an even larger wave that sent all of them grabbing something to steady themselves. Jennings looked over at Thatch and saw his wild eyes widen and turn to Black Caesar.

"Topside!" Thatch commanded.

Black Caesar was the first to climb the stairwell with Thatch behind him. The rest crowded the narrow exit to follow them up as another wave drove the ship high in the air at an odd angle before crashing down with a loud bang as the hull must have lifted out of the water to come slamming down on the surface of the sea. Those still left out in the open went sliding down, banging their bodies against the floor and beams. Jennings found himself knocked to the floor. The crates that hadn't been secured skidded about and one narrowly missed smashing into Jennings' legs as he quickly pulled them to his chest. He shot to his feet as soon as the ship righted itself and shoved his way up the stairwell and onto the main deck.

Thatch was shouting orders as Jennings once again lost his footing on the slick surface, wet with rain. He looked in shock as he was assaulted by the howling wind, pelting downpour, and the force of waves as they crested the frigate's railing. Jennings rushed to starboard and searched for the lights of Nassau. Blackness engulfed the horizon. He pushed his way past the frenzy of pirates arriving on the main deck. Darkness was the only thing to be seen beyond the rolling sea.

"Hoist the main!" Thatch shouted as he climbed the ladder to the aftcastle and took the wheel. He continued to shout orders that were echoed by the collection of captains and first mates, as they were all well-trained sailors who knew every job aboard a ship this size.

Stede Bonnet made his way to the aftcastle and yelled to be heard against the raging wind. "Who pulled anchor, and why?"

"I don't bloody know!" growled Thatch.

"We were God damn anchored in the harbor!" yelled Jennings, as he mounted the ladder to the aftcastle. "How the bloody hell do you explain we find ourselves in the middle of the damn ocean, Thatch?" They all were rocked when a wave slammed into the ship with enough force to throw them both against the large mahogany wheel. The water that drenched them roiled over the deck to empty out on the other side. Thatch pushed Jennings away from the wheel as they regained their footing.

"Find a job and do it," he said.

Black Caesar appeared at the top of the ladder.

"Anchor lines were cut," he told Thatch.

"Cut! By who?" Jennings demanded.

Black Caesar just shook his head.

"Who would cut the anchors? And why?" Stede questioned.

They were suddenly lifted into the air, weightless. The *Queen Anne's Revenge* was thrown completely out of the water, tossed like a twig by a thirty-foot wave. For the pirates, it seemed as though time stood still while they all hung in the air a foot above the safety of the ship's deck. The frigate hit the water below a mere second before its crew came crashing down against the hardwood flooring, soaked with salt water. Lightning cracked all around them, sending ozone and electrified droplets prickling over their exposed skin. Jennings pulled himself to his feet and was about to scream an obscenity at Thatch when he spotted an enormous shadow looming in the distance. No sound escaped his lips, but his excited eyes, haunted expression and pointed finger caught Thatch's attention.

Edward Thatch turned to see the forming of a fifty-foot wall of water closing in on them. With urgency, he spun the wheel of the ship to point the bow to face the oncoming wave head-on.

"Come about!" Thatch screamed, and the crew responded frantically, working the rigging to turn the ship into the behemoth. At first it seemed the bow had dug into the bottom of the wave and was forcing the ship down into the sea to be crushed, but as the wave grew beneath the ship, they started to climb. Thatch was the picture of a man gone mad, his hair and beard plastered back by the gale force of the wind, his eyes wild and mouth open in a half scream, half laugh. He steered the frigate up, climbing, climbing the seemingly endless wall of water. The wave towered over the ship, threatening to curl over it, and pound it to the bottom of the sea.

Anne Bonny held the rigging of the aft sail in hopes of not falling backward over the railing into the roiling sea below. Her location meant she was the last of the crew to climb to the top of the wave. From her view, it seemed the world had fallen away as the *Queen Anne's Revenge* crested, pivoted, then began its thundering decent down the other side. She searched for her new love, Jack Rackham, across the crowded deck but couldn't pick him out among the drenched figures cloaked in the darkness of the starless night. Anne fretted that he may have been tossed overboard to drown in the churning waters, as she had seen happen to several others in these last minutes of hell. Her heart ached at the thought and tears streamed down her face, mixing with the salty sea water that coated the rest of her hair and skin. The horrifying sea below caught her attention, as it looked so foreign that she didn't trust her eyes. Their ship was speeding down the back side of the monster wave they just ascended, yet it seemed there was no end to their descent. The water below them spun in a giant funnel so large that she struggled to see the other side. By all rights they should have slipped down the backside of the wave only to be tossed again by another, but there seemed to be no bottom in sight. A scream escaped her lips as the ship was caught up in the spinning whirlpool, accelerating it, around and around, sucking the *Queen Anne's Revenge* and all its passengers down into its gaping mouth and into the unfathomable darkness below.

CHAPTER 2 – THE EMERGENCE

SAN FRANCISCO HARBOR 1873

Charlotte De Berry's wide eyes blinked rapidly in the dark salt water that filled the ship's cargo hold. She was holding back panic as she swam along the ceiling looking for an air pocket to give relief to her oxygen-starved lungs. Her last breath was a distant memory now, as was her mind's image of the cargo hold since the torrent of water rushed in to fill the room from a hole created by an untethered eight-foot cannon barrel that sailed across the room to crash completely through the side of the ship. She was using that fading image of the room to navigate herself back to the entrance in the pitch-black water. She turned and moved her braided hair to see the dimmest rays of light that were coming from the stairwell now. Charlotte kicked her feet off a beam to propel herself toward that welcoming sight.

Her mind pushed back the fleeting thoughts and confusion of how she found herself in this horrifying predicament. Images flashed in her head of the enormous whirlpool that swallowed the *Queen Anne's Revenge*. The entire 200-ton ship was sucked into its gaping mouth like an ant caught in a drainpipe. The storm, with its hurricane-force winds, had brought forth the ghastliest sea that had ever been seen. Her brethren pirates were tossed and slammed about the ship's deck, some propelled over the side as if the tentacles of a Kraken yanked them over. Edward Thatch, in all his fiendish glory, faced the brunt of the storm, hands gripped tightly to the wheel with a maniacal grin on his bearded face. He had steered the ship up that wave of ungodly proportions, which seemed an impossible feat, bringing the hull fully out of the water and into the starless sky as it crested, only to plunge down faster than a raging tiger toward the bottomless depths of the churning sea. She remembered diving down the stairwell of the hold to escape being thrown from the drowning ship, which in retrospect was a foolish idea now that she was trapped in the flooded, dark compartment.

A clamorous sound reverberated through the vessel, audible even in the water, as it suddenly twisted and what seemed like up became down. Charlotte, lungs burning, scraped and clawed along the floor as her buoyancy flipped and the light faded away. She fought against all urges to breathe in the cold, salty ocean as she reached the stairwell. Working her arms and legs, she desperately traversed out of the stairwell, finally reaching the deck of the drowned ship. She achingly searched for the surface of the water and felt the force of the ship pressing down against her. She was about to let out a watery scream in frustration as she realized the ship was sinking upside down with her underneath it when suddenly the *Queen Anne's Revenge* let out a thunderous groan and once again rolled, righting itself. Suddenly, the bow of the ship pointed toward the surface like a hand desperately reaching out for a hold. Charlotte's eyes could see the dim light of the surface becoming brighter as her lungs reached their limit and began to take in the briny, cold water.

Mary Read had no time to shiver despite being plunged into the freezing water as she struggled to stay afloat. She was now regretting the years she spent at sea, never learning how to swim. Cold and fatigue were taking its toll on her legs and arms as she looked around at the bits of flotsam surrounding her. Her eyes searched desperately for something to hang on to, something large enough that would float and carry her weight. A few yards away the vacant eyes of the drowned Paulsgrave Williams, first mate of Sam Bellamy, panicked her heart. Her head went under for the fifth time, and she kicked and churned to rise again. Spitting water and sucking in air, her face crested the water's surface. She saw at that moment Jack Rackham clutching a large floating piece of yardarm. She called out to him, screamed in fact, for his help. He clung tightly with both arms wrapped around the safety of the wide cut of wood. His eyes full of fear, he turned his head away from her.

Coward, she thought. Pretty to look at, but with the backbone of a jellyfish. This was it, she thought. Here was her end. Doomed to drown in the sea in which she sought to command, only yards away from a helping hand that was selfishly gripping the only floating thing large enough to support a woman's weight.

Mary's strength waned, and she dropped under again. She made less of an effort this time to surface, giving up and letting her body sink as the gentle pull of the water enveloped her. She looked down beneath her feet into the dark sea. She could barely make out the brown ocean floor rising to meet her. My mind must be going, she thought, she was the one sinking, not the sandy floor rising. Air bubbles began to surround her as she watched the incredible sight of the *Queen Anne's Revenge* ascending to the surface underneath her. The wide deck was rapidly surging up from below her feet. She made a determined effort to kick her feet and swim her arms to match the speed of its ascent. The ship reached her, picked her up, and pressed her body to the deck of the bow as it raced to the surface.

The *Queen Anne's Revenge* broke through the water and into the night air, rising five yards out of the cold sea before settling down, listing starboard. The fifteen-degree list caused Charlotte De Berry's body to roll several times until she slammed into the rail. That impact is what most likely saved her life. The thrust of her body hitting the rail against her back caused her chest to convulse and expel the sea water from her lungs. She violently coughed and spit, gasping for breath. It took a moment, but she realized someone was holding her and slapping her on the back. A woman's voice, she thought as her head cleared. She turned her tear-filled eyes to see the smiling, soggy, wretched face of Mary Read. Mary had a gash on her forehead that leaked blood over one side of her face. Her wavy red hair was darkened by the water and clung in wild mats against her face.

"You can stop slapping me, you ghoul," Charlotte managed to choke.

Mary Read helped Charlotte sit up and then slouched down next to her.

"You're welcome," she retorted. "Next time we drown, I'll not help you if that's how you say thanks."

Charlotte looked over at Mary and then used her hands to wipe the blood from Mary's face.

"Comin' back from the dead to first see your bloody face could make a girl die again from fright," she said.

The two women looked on, exhausted, as several other figures began to rise and cough water out of their lungs.

"To hell with you, Poseidon!" the booming voice of Edward Thatch called out as his broad, panther-like frame rose from the deck of the aftcastle.

There were a few laughs as the throng of water-drenched pirates gathered themselves from the chaos. Thatch, followed by Black Caesar and Henry Jennings, climbed down onto the main deck. Emerging around them were Bart Roberts, Sam Bellamy, Benjamin Hornigold, Charles Vane, and Anne Bonny. All differences were set aside as they patted each other's backs and laughed off the danger they had all faced. Mary helped Charlotte to her feet, and they joined the remaining crew.

"Is this the lot of us?" asked Hornigold as he gazed around the deserted deck.

"I saw many drown and go over the side," Black Caesar commented.

Anne looked fearfully at Black Caesar.

"Jack? Did you see him? Did the sea take him?"

"Aye. Your husband James as well," Black Caesar told Anne, whose face flushed as she'd given no thought to what happened to James. "Paulsgrave, Stede Bonnet, others, all swept away."

The pirates looked around at one another, taking stock of the remnants of their crew.

"Ten, just ten survivors. The sea did in one night what England, France, and Spain could not," said Jennings, shaking his head.

"Help!" came a distant cry to their ears.

"Jack!" exclaimed Anne. She ran to the side, peering off into the night, searching for the source of the voice.

The rest of the pirates lined the railing, leaning out over the water, looking for Jack Rackham.

"There!" Vane pointed.

Jack was clinging to the broken yardarm with his hand reaching out just below them. His long, black, water-soaked hair hung over his face.

"You look like a drowned cat, Rackham," Thatch laughed.

"Throw me a damned rope! This water is freezing!" Rackham yelled desperately.

Black Caesar tossed down a rope and he, Hornigold, and Sam Bellamy hauled up Rackham, shivering and soaked to the bone.

Anne threw her arms around him and held him close as Rackham's teeth chattered.

"I thought I lost you, love." Anne said through tears.

"Nothing could keep your Jack away. Not even the worst hurricane the Caribbean has ever seen," Jack told her.

"I don't know what makes me want to retch more, the sea water in my belly or listening to these two," said Thatch.

"I'd drink a barrel of ocean water if given that choice," said Charlotte.

This made the crew erupt into laughter that brought on fits of coughing from a few. The ship's creaking and groaning was the only thing that quieted them down. Henry Jennings eased himself port-side and gazed off at lights on the distant shore. He was shortly joined by Thatch and Hornigold.

"Looks like all the lanterns in the entire town of Nassau are lit tonight," said Hornigold. The two other men were silent for a moment.

"The coastline looks strange. Different," Thatch said quietly.

"I've never felt the Caribbean waters so cold before," Charlotte De Berry said from behind them. Neither of the men turned around, eyes fixated on the lights.

"Maybe the storm blew us to another port? Saint Augustine, Tortuga?" suggested Jennings.

"Too far," said Hornigold.

"Aye, but that ain't Nassau," Thatch said.

"Then where?" asked Jennings.

The *Queen Anne's Revenge* groaned again and began to list even more, causing everyone to stumble toward starboard.

"Caesar, do we have an intact skiff?" Thatch called out to his first mate.

Caesar went aft to check on the condition of the two skiffs that were stored near the rear of the ship. The sounds of wood giving way could be heard as water continued to flood below decks.

"She's definitely taking on water," Rackham said.

"Observant that one," Charlotte De Berry quietly quipped to Mary Read.

"You have no idea," replied Mary with a shake of her head as she squeezed water from her long hair.

Edward Thatch made his way to the stairwell leading back to the main hold, along with Bart Roberts and Sam Bellamy.

"There's a fair amount of plunder below deck," he told them. "Let's see what we can carry."

"The main hold is flooded," called Charlotte.

Thatch looked down the ladder, seeing it was as she reported.

"Damn it all," he said.

"Captain! We have only one skiff, the storm must have taken the other," Black Caesar arrived to exclaim.

"Right then. Let's get it in the water," Thatch said, leading the motley band of pirates toward the stern.

They arrived and began quickly untying the skiff and lowering it into the water. There was no longer the need for a ladder to reach the waterline as the *Queen Anne's Revenge* had sunk low enough to have the sea lapping over the deck now. They piled into the small craft just as the ship's list grew greater and half the deck was swallowed by the bay. Bart Roberts and Charles Vane manned the ores and stroked toward the shore. Thatch stoically watched as the sea claimed the *Queen Anne's Revenge*. Hornigold sat next to him, watching the ship's forecastle disappear beneath the water.

"She was a prize," Hornigold remarked.

"That she was." Thatch took a last look, then turned toward the lighted port.

The extensive docks were crowded with ships of all sizes. Several large ships were anchored nearby. One such ship became more visible as they approached the harbor. This one held all the pirates' gaze in awestruck silence. Mary Read took in a loud breath as its details began to become clear. The ship was of massive size. She estimated it to be almost four hundred feet long and fifty feet wide. It towered out of the water like nothing she had ever seen before. Most notable was the inadequate number of sails attached to its three masts. A ship this size would need a dozen sails to move its hulking frame, she mused. She searched the sides and the deck and realized that it had no cannons or guns, no way to defend itself for such a trophy. A great wheel was placed midships like a huge wheel taken from a giant's wagon. Next to the wheel stood a large black cylinder that was slowly leaking dark smoke from its opening, that smelled of burning coal.

"What the devil?" exclaimed Jennings.

"What the devil indeed," replied Thatch.

Roberts and Vane had ceased their rowing as they coasted slowly past the ship, its name now visible along the side of the hull: SS *Great Republic*. Vane stared, mouth agape, at the enormous vessel. They all silently inspected its details in amazement.

"What is the wheel for?" asked Anne Bonny.

"Moves the ship," Hornigold answered quietly.

"What moves the wheel?"

"Don't know," Hornigold answered after a few moments.

As the pirates slowly glided upon the water, the rest of the ships anchored and moored in the harbor continued to astonish. There were many that were clearly made not of wood but entirely of metal, with some completely devoid of sails whatsoever. The crew remained silent and awestruck as they reached a small beachfront that allowed them to pull the skiff up onto the shore.

"Where the bloody hell are we?" asked Jennings of no one in particular.

They all walked up the bank to the dirt road that stretched along the beachfront. To the left were the docks lined with buildings that looked like storehouses and boatyards. There were strange, softly glowing lamps illuminating the buildings, roads and sidewalks that expanded into the main part of the large city. To the right, the buildings were sparser; most resembled homes that became larger and more grand as they crept up the hillside.

"I could use a drink to wash out the taste of the sea from my mouth," said Charlotte De Berry as she began walking toward the docks.

One by one the rest of the pirates followed her up the path. There were still men working at this hour of the night, moving boxes from ships to shore or in reverse. Groups of people could be seen walking through the streets and milling about. Horses and carriages trotted up and down the roads in the distance.

The eleven pirates, in dripping clothes, marched toward the main street that ended at the docks. A small party of men standing on the street corner smoking and talking paused in their conversation as they noticed them approaching. One of the men nudged the man next to him who then turned to take in the motley group. The men were dressed in pants, pointed boots, with buttoned shirts underneath vests and long overcoats. They wore a variety of hats that featured bowler to wide-brimmed styles. All the men sported mustaches of various lengths. They all watched in confoundment as the ornately dressed and overly armed pirates of the Caribbean Sea approached their little band.

"Ain't this a fancy bunch?" one of the men said.

"Maybe they's part of some entertainment playing in one o' them theaters?" suggested another.

Thatch was the first to speak as they stopped in front of the men.

"What town might this be?"

The men looked at each other in confusion.

"San Francisco."

"Never heard of such a town. What island is this?" asked Bart Roberts.

One of the men squinted his eyes at them and let out a chuckle.

"Ain't no island. Y'all actors in a play or something?"

"This part of the Americas?" asked Hornigold.

"Yeah, San Francisco is part of the Americas," one of the men said with a laugh and an elbow to one of his mates.

"How far is it to St. Augustine?" asked Jennings, referring to the popular Florida port of call.

The men looked at one another before one of them piped up.

"Hmm, maybe three thousand or so miles. Best get yourself some good, sturdy horses. Or maybe take the train if you're needin' to travel there."

"Train?" inquired Anne Bonny.

There was an awkward silence as the men tried to figure out if this was some sort of joke that was being played upon them.

"Why are y'all dressed like that?" one of the bolder men finally asked. "You with the theater or something?"

"No, blast your eyes, we're not," Jennings replied testily, fingering his nearest pistol. "And who might you be to presume such slander?"

"Oh, we're nobody, sir," another of the men said hastily, "don't mind us. We're just harmless cowboys, sir, passing through."

"Where can we find a drink?" asked Charlotte.

One of the men pointed up the street, and the pirates made their way along the lighted boulevard, leaving the befuddled group in their wake.

"Ever heard of San Francisco?" Jennings asked Thatch.

Thatch answered by shaking his head. He was too busy looking at the storefronts, wagons, horses and uniquely dressed townsfolk. He hadn't seen so many people in one city since his days in Europe. Even Virginia paled in comparison to this… San Francisco. They, as well, were being noticed by the many people they passed. The stares were becoming uncomfortable. The uniqueness of the faces was intriguing as well. Thatch noticed there were more Chinese faces here than he had ever seen. There were also blacks, natives, South Americans, Irish and more he didn't recognize.

They were passing the front of a three-story brick building with a waiting crowd out front when several bystanders pointed and motioned toward the pirates. The crowd was well dressed in suit coats, ties and top hats for the men, and the women sported ornate gowns and dresses. Two men were in the middle of the street with a black cloth draped behind a device standing on three legs. One of the men nudged the other and pointed at the group. Hornigold stopped, and the others paused with him to stare at the onlookers.

"Hold, hold, hold," said one of the men, holding up a hand. The other man spun his device to face the crew. Hornigold and several other pirate hands found the hilts of their swords or pistols but paused there as the man behind the device ducked his head under the black drape and the other held a light on a pole that flashed brightly. Vane and Bart Roberts pulled their cutlasses at the blinding flash but held their ground as the crowd laughed and cheered. The device men clapped and waved before gathering up the gear and moving into the building with a sign above displaying the name Wade's Opera House.

The pirates looked at one another in confusion and continued their journey through the strange streets of San Francisco.

"There," said Charlotte, nodding toward an ornate two-story building with red curtains hanging behind the windows. Lively music was emerging from inside and the sign mounted above the door frame proclaiming the name of the establishment as The Paris. Charlotte marched up the steps to the entrance. She turned back toward the group. "Come on then. Thatch, I think you owe a girl a drink after that voyage."

Thatch arched his wide black brows. Charlotte opened the door and piano music and rowdy laughter poured out from the opening.

"That I do," Thatch said with a mischievous grin. With a wide motion of his hand, he held open the door for his band of Caribbean pirates to enter the late 1800s gambling hall sitting at the end of Sacramento Street in San Francisco, California.

Chapter 3– Legends

THE PARIS SALOON & GAMBLING HALL

Brightly lit by gas lamps and chandeliers, the main room of The Paris was a feast for the eyes. A large, polished wood bar dominated the left-hand side of the room with a mirror extending its entire length, doubling the images of the multitude of bottles filled with various spirits that lined the shelves. A large indigenous man with long braids in his hair poured glasses of amber-colored whiskey for the patrons and waitresses. He moved with efficiency, never cracking his stone-faced expression as people shouted their drink orders to him.

The crowded hall was bustling with energy as cowboys, miners, gamblers, and thieves indulged themselves in the entertainment The Paris provided. A corner stage featured a piano man hammering out an upbeat tune while three women in colorful dresses danced. Several men stood at the edge of the stage and whistled and hollered whenever the women would hike their dresses to kick their legs in unison. There were tables crowded with gamblers, drinks in one hand and a fistful of cards in the other. Pretty young women moved through the crowds in dresses and petticoats, delivering drinks, offering quick dances, and engaging the patrons in laughter and merriment.

A staircase in the rear of the hall led up to the second floor that featured a long hallway balcony with a multitude of doors. Several of the doors were open with views of decorated rooms with four-poster beds and clawfoot tubs. A man and woman were sharing an intimate kiss in one of the doorways until they passionately moved inside, and the man shut the door behind them with his boot heel, never interrupting the embrace.

Philip Edward Albert was intently watching the cards that were being dealt around the table. He glanced briefly into the eyes of the dealer Colette Dallaire, who was also the proprietor of this establishment. Her pale piercing eyes bored deep into his own as she seemed to dare him to continue his task of counting cards. He felt his face flush and with great effort turned from her and began watching the cards again. This was his second night playing Colette's unique game of twenty-one. She had delighted him with the story of how she had learned to play the game from her Choctaw Indian abductors when she was just a young girl. The tribe had raided ranches and farmhouses kidnapping young women to sell back to their families. Colette had lived with them for years in semi-captivity, but eventually her family paid a ransom, and she was returned home. As it turned out, her family would later shun her, claiming she was a ruined woman and could not be properly married. It seemed those years of living with the Choctaw had brought out a wildness that didn't integrate well into the proper New Orleans society.

Philip watched players around him take cards as he stayed the course with a nine and a jack held in his delicate hand. His wife always complained that his were the hands of a woman, long thin fingers with soft, pale skin. He had to concede that next to her large plump digits his would be considered dainty, but then so would most unless one was a hardened farmhand from birth.

Philip hadn't seen her in years, barely even writing at all these days. He had little desire to sail home to London. A chemist by trade, specializing in explosives, he had carved out a nice niche working with mining companies to blast away unwanted rock to get to the precious ore they sought. Here in San Francisco, there was no shortage of companies and individuals that needed his services, as the easy pickings of gold and silver had already been had. It took a lot of digging or blasting to get down to the precious metals hiding underneath tons of worthless stone, rock, and dirt these days. He watched as Miss Dallaire drew cards turning over first a three, then a five to end her hand with an eighteen. He was delighted by his win, though the two miners next to him in recently washed clothes slapped down their cards in disgust and vacated their seats in an angry huff, slamming empty glasses on the table.

"Tough luck, boys, but don't let your luck get you down. Go have a drink at the bar on the house," Colette said, as she gave a head nod to the large Choctaw bartender, and he nodded in return as the miners approached the bar. The bartender fisted two glasses and generously filled them with whiskey as they sat down. Two smiling young women, as if on cue, approached the men and engaged them in conversation.

"Well, don't you have everything rightly in hand?" Philip said as he watched the two young girls quickly turn the mood of the men.

"I merely care that all my patrons leave remembering what a good time they had at The Paris."

Philip watched as the men laid down more money on the bar to buy drinks for the women. He watched as the bartender filled the girls' glasses from a different bottle than the one he used for the men.

"Your working girls are drinking a watered-down version of spirits," Philip said knowingly.

"It would do no good to have them walking about without their wits all night," replied Colette.

"Indeed," Philip started to say as the door opened and the most unusual-looking band of characters entered one by one. Colette turned toward the door to see what Philip's wide-eyed gaze was taking in.

Charlotte De Berry was the first to enter. Her wild and dreadlocked hair swayed as her head swiveled to survey the room. Her embroidered coat was open, showcasing her African kukri blade, with its jewel-ornamented hilt and a flintlock pistol strapped to her waistband. Charlotte's tan-colored eyes took in the scene as though she was a panther happening upon a watering hole where small animals had gathered to drink. She was followed by the raven-haired Sam Bellamy, Bart Roberts, Anne Bonny, Calico Jack Rackham, Mary Read, Charles Vane, Henry Jennings, Benjamin Hornigold, and Black Caesar, who turned and waited as his captain entered in all his glory.

The hall went quiet as, one by one, the patrons turned to take in the new arrivals. The music awkwardly stopped as the last of them entered and the door closed.

Edward Thatch's white teeth shone brightly in the midst of his bristly dark beard as his broad smile widened as he took in the saloon. The crowded bar seemed in awe of the group's grand attire, and the amount, as well as the antiquity of the pirates' armaments. Most men in the saloon would never have been seen with a sword on their side, not since the Civil War ended, that is. Now before them were eleven ornately dressed, sword-carrying pirates with out-of-date flintlock pistols crowding into the gambling hall.

"I think I'm going to like this place," announced Thatch with a wide grin. "Let's drink."

Colette recovered quickly and threw a look at the piano player and dancing girls, who immediately launched into a new tune. The rest of the bar slowly followed suit by going about their business but keeping a wary eye on the strangely dressed newcomers. Bart Roberts, Bellamy, and Vane headed to the bar while Rackham, Read, and Bonny took seats at one corner of a large table. The patrons sitting on the far side of that table hastily moved away as Thatch, De Berry, Jennings, Hornigold and Black Caesar approached to sit.

"A night at The Paris never ceases to astound," said Philip.

"It's why you keep returning, Mr. Albert."

Colette watched out of the corner of her eye as drinks were brought to the pirate table and the group began to break apart as a few went to watch, in curiosity, the entertainment on the stage. The others went to drink at the bar, enquiring about the variety of spirit bottles that lined the back counter. The one with the wild blue eyes and long black beard was standing now alongside another pirate with brown hair tied in a ponytail, his face framed by long sideburns. They conspired a moment after noticing her and the open seats at her table, then began to make their way over.

"What sort of game have we?" Edward Thatch inquired as he noisily adjusted the seat to allow himself and all his armaments to sit in the chair. Hornigold sat in between Philip and Thatch, with one lone cowboy seated at the end of the table. The cowboy looked the men up and down, scooting his chair a bit further away.

"It's called twenty-one," said Colette as she expertly shuffled the cards. "You win by having the highest total number without going over twenty-one."

Hornigold looked around the table, noticing the US banknotes that were stacked in front of the gamblers and Colette.

"We don't have banknotes, but I have these." Hornigold pulled a few silver coins from a small bag at his hip.

"Where are these from?" asked Philip, reaching for one of the silver coins. Hornigold snatched them back before Philip could take one.

"Spain, though it be no business of yours."

"May I see one? To test the authenticity of the coin," asked Colette with a hand extended.

Hornigold flipped the coin in the air, which was caught deftly by Colette. She looked it over, turning it around, checking the sides and the weight. She then flipped it back into the air to be caught by Hornigold.

"'Bout the size of our silver dollars if you'll accept them as equal," said Colette, pushing a US silver dollar across the table.

Thatch picked up the dollar and hefted its weight.

"Aye, close enough."

"Then let's wager, gentlemen," Colette said.

Philip and the cowboy sitting at the table pushed paper money in front of them. Hornigold and Thatch mimicked their move with coin and Colette dealt out two cards to each and laid two in front of herself, with one queen showing and the other card face down.

"The cards with faces are worth ten and the ace," Philip showed the ace in his hand to Thatch and Hornigold, "is worth eleven." Philip smirked at Colette over the ace in his hand.

"A kindly fellow Englishman is showing us his cards, Thatch," quipped Hornigold.

"I am English, London, and I show you because we are not in competition with each other, only with the dealer."

Thatch looked at his cards, calculated, and looked around the table. "What now?"

"Would you like another card, or are you happy with what you have? You can take as many as you want, but if your total is over twenty-one you lose," said Colette.

"I'm quite happy with what I have then, lass."

"What about you, dear sir?" she asked Hornigold.

Hornigold looked up in the air, calculating in his head.

"She has a ten," Philip said, "and must take another card until she at least has seventeen, though we won't know until the end what the face-down card is worth. If you want to stay with what you have, she could possibly draw cards totaling over twenty-one and lose the game." Hornigold only frowned at him, still not comfortable with the little man's help.

"The longer you think, the older I get, Benjamin," Thatch sighed, leaning back in his chair to adjust the blunderbuss from his hip.

"Quiet, Thatch, I'm considering my choice."

"I'll take a card if these fancy pants ain't takin' one," the cowboy said.

Hornigold looked harshly at the man, noticing the drab nature of the man's clothing compared to him and his mates. He merely wore a pair of brown trousers and a whiteish shirt underneath a vest made from sheep's wool.

"It's not your turn, Clayton, you know that," scolded Colette.

Hornigold leaned over to see the other player's cards, with the cowboy pulling his close to his chest.

"Hornigold, please!" Thatch bellowed.

"I'll take a card," Hornigold exclaimed.

Colette pulled the top card from the deck, turning it over in front of Hornigold. The card was a nine.

Hornigold paused in thought, then his face went slack.

"Twenty-four," he said with dismay.

"Truly unfortunate," said Philip. He then asked for another card and Colette delivered a five.

Colette turned over another card for the cowboy, which was a three. He then asked for another, and it was a five which elated the cowboy.

"Nineteen!" he exclaimed. Colette only smiled at him.

Colette turned her card over, and a seven sat next to the queen, making her hand a seventeen.

"May I see your hand, good, sir?" she asked Thatch.

Thatch turned over a king and an ace making twenty-one.

"Beginner's luck," said Philip as Colette paid out the winners.

"What's with your getup?" asked the cowboy named Clayton.

"It's obvious that they are actors. Costumed for a performance at the opera house," answered Philip.

"Captains, privateers, pirates if you wish! But do not insult me, you little worm," Hornigold said with a dagger quickly pulled and pressed against Philip's neck.

Colette was wide-eyed and wary. Her hand reached under the table to a short-barreled rifle affixed underneath to a hook. She clandestinely pointed it at Hornigold.

"I meant no offense, my good man. Forgive me for my ignorance," Philip stuttered out, arching his neck so it wouldn't be pierced by Hornigold's blade.

"Oh, let the little man be, Benjamin. We do seem to be in a city with contrasting fashions," Thatch said, putting a hand on Hornigold's shoulder. Hornigold slowly pulled the dagger from Philip's neck and then expertly flipped the blade into the sheath on his belt. Philip rubbed his neck and looked at his hand, relieved to see that no blood had been drawn.

"Where exactly is this San Francisco located in relation to Nassau?" asked Thatch.

"Why, I haven't heard of Nassau before. Is that where you and your friends have traveled from?" Colette said as she eased her hand away from the hand cannon under the table.

"We were in the port of Nassau when a hurricane hit and then got caught in the storm. Blew us out of the harbor and beat the ship to kindling. When the storm passed, we ended up here," Hornigold said.

"Ha. Simplified the story a bit, Hornigold. Mind you never be the one to tell me life's tale."

"You want me to tell about the largest wave man has ever seen that you steered us over, Thatch? Only to plunge the entire ship into a whirlpool that drug us to the bottom of the sea? Half our crew dead and drowned. All of us trapped many leagues below the surface. Then emerging, though not in the warm waters of the Caribbean, but in the ice-cold bay of God knows where! This… this, San Francisco," Hornigold ranted.

Thatch looked at him and stroked his beard in thought. Philip stared at the bar where Sam Bellamy, Jack Rackham, Anne Bonny, and Mary Read were sharing a bottle of dark rum. He turned back to Thatch and looked over his garments. They were ornate, yes, but a bit worn, unlike a costume, authentic. He noticed that their clothing was damp and smelled of sea water. The blade that was held to his neck was genuine, of that he was sure. The multitude of weapons arranged on these men were not props from an opera, but also authentic and deadly devices albeit antiquated.

"Thatch? Hornigold? Edward Thatch?" Philip said, staring at their weathered faces, looking them over carefully.

"That's right. You've heard our names before?" Hornigold asked.

Philip let out a chuckle that sounded like a cross between a laugh and the noise a frog would make. He looked at Colette, who just sat with a curious expression, and then at the cowboy, who was completely confused.

"Heard of you? Of course I've heard of you. Who hasn't heard stories of the pirates that ruled the Caribbean seas?"

Thatch slapped the back of Hornigold. "See that? And you were about to stick your dagger in his throat."

"I still might if he doesn't answer where we are."

"Nowhere near Nassau. Nowhere near the Caribbean nor the Atlantic," Philip said, looking manically at each pirate. "You're on the northern coast of the Pacific Ocean."

Thatch and Hornigold looked at one another. Neither were ready to believe this little man, but the waters were vastly different from the Caribbean. Any sailor worth his salt could have seen that. This strange town they found themselves in was completely alien from any other that was near their usual ports of call. Thatch looked at the woman who was dealing cards. She was quite an attractive young creature who he was sure had a weapon hidden underneath the table as her hand had suspiciously gravitated there when Hornigold had held the blade to the little Englishman's throat. She was staring at them with curiosity and a bit of wariness. Thatch had already noticed that several men in the hall were armed with small-barrel pistols the likes of which he had never seen before. The glowing lamps used to light the room were unique as well.

"You've heard stories of these men? Back in England?" asked Colette.

Philip was still staring in awe at Thatch and Hornigold. He turned and looked at the entire party that had entered The Paris along with them. His eyes took in again the authenticity of their dress and weapons. The way they moved and talked. The scars and wounds they bore, he now took notice of.

These were not actors ready to put on a show in the newly opened San Francisco opera house.

"Yes, I know all about them. But it's not possible. Edward Thatch and Benjamin Hornigold disappeared, along with the rest of the pirate captains of Nassau in 1718. Everyone knows their story. Miss Colette, you're from New Orleans. You must have heard of them. Their names are legend."

"Hornigold, Thatch, can't say those names ring any bells," Colette said.

Philip shook his head. "Maybe, maybe... maybe not by the name Edward Thatch, but this man," Philip pointed at Thatch. "This man is better known as... Blackbeard."

CHAPTER 4 – COMING TO TERMS

Colette looked quizzically at the man Philip referred to as Blackbeard. His long, wild beard was certainly black. The man had a galvanizing energy to him. His radiant eyes were penetrating with an intensity set against the deep tan of his face and dark brows. She had heard of pirates, of course, the most famous in her mind being Jean Laffite, who was both hero and villain from her home of New Orleans' past.

"Blackbeard. I'm afraid our paths have not crossed, nor have I heard of your… reputation."

"That's alright, lass, the port of New Orleans was not one of my calls. Mostly spent my time in the North Carolina territory."

Philip listened to Blackbeard's response and shook his head.

"Yes, yes, of course, but the reason you haven't heard of him, Miss Dallaire, most likely is… is that he's dead."

Philip looked around at the table. Blackbeard's eyes narrowed and Hornigold scowled at Philip. The little man gulped and switched gears.

"Well, obviously not dead, but… but rumored to be dead," he stammered. "Like I said, Blackbeard and the rest of the pirate captains went down at sea." Philip looked around at all the pirates in the hall. "They were never seen again."

Blackbeard gave Philip a maniacal smile.

"You're seeing us now, ain't ya?" he said in a low, threatening voice.

"You... you all died. One hundred and fifty years ago! Off the port of Nassau!" Philip said a bit louder than he intended.

The two pirates at the table stared in silence at Philip for a moment, then Hornigold burst into a raucous belly laugh. Blackbeard joined in and neither man could control their laughter. Their pirate mates closed in with curiosity. Blackbeard slapped the wide-eyed Philip on the back. Hornigold was laughing so hard he nearly fell from his seat.

"What is it?" Charlotte De Berry asked with an infectious grin as she arrived at the table.

"Ghosts!" Hornigold said amid his laughter. He pointed at Blackbeard. "You're a ghost, Thatch!"

"What?" Charlotte asked again, confused along with the others as all the pirates gathered around.

"Ah, you are a fine-looking corpse, Miss Charlotte," Blackbeard was able to say through gasps of laughter.

"What the devil are you two going on about?" Jennings asked in irritation.

"This little Englishman says we've all been dead for a hundred and fifty years," laughed Hornigold as he pointed at Philip.

"That's absurd," Jennings said without humor.

Hornigold and Blackbeard's laughter was contagious to Anne Bonny, Mary, and Bart Roberts as they laughed along to the joke they didn't quite understand. Sam Bellamy smiled for a moment, but it faded as he looked around the setting. His heart began beating faster, and he felt a trickle of sweat drop down his back.

"What year is it?" he asked Philip in a small voice. Philip only stared back without answering. Sam turned toward Colette and asked the same question louder. The rest of the pirates' laughter abated and they slowly all turned to Colette, waiting for an answer. Colette curiously glanced at the group before answering.

"1873."

Colette was met with stares of disbelief.

"1873," Philip confirmed quietly.

"You shut up!" Hornigold screamed at him.

"Settle down, Benjamin," Blackbeard said, laying a hand on Hornigold's shoulder. Hornigold shoved the hand away and stood up. He slammed his fist on the table in front of Philip, startling the man, then strode angerly to the bar.

"Maria. I was supposed to go back to her," Sam said in a daze.

"And you will, mate. You will. Don't believe this horse shite. 1873!" said Bart Roberts.

Sam wobbled a bit and felt the room spin. He was planning to travel within a week back to Cape Cod with a hoard of treasure to marry his love, Maria. He had left her over a year ago to find his fortune. Maria's family would never have let her marry Sam when he was just a pauper. Now, somehow, he felt the truth that he was more than a century too late. He felt his insides tighten up, and he bolted out the door before he'd be forced to empty his stomach in front of the entire hall.

The rest of the pirates watched Sam sprint out with a hand to his stomach and the other covering his mouth.

"Thar she blows," Charlotte De Berry joked and received a few chuckles.

"I'd better go look after the bloke; see to it he doesn't get into trouble," Bart said before exiting after his friend.

"Best watch he doesn't spoil your trousers with the last of his eighteenth-century supper," Hornigold quipped as the laughter slowly died down.

Jack Rackham's smile faded from his face too. He looked at Anne, who bore this odd news with no effect at all. Jack stopped a man walking past and asked, "What year is this?" The man just gave him a drunken look and moved on. Jack moved to the other patrons, asking the same question. Those that answered gave him the same date again and again. 1873. Jack spun as Anne approached him.

"Is it true? Could it be?" Jack asked her.

"It must be. Everything feels different here," Anne said calmingly. Jack's eyes darted left and right, there was genuine fear in his eyes.

"How? How is this possible?" Jack asked to no one in particular.

"It isn't possible, you buffoon," answered Jennings. He pointed his finger at Thatch. "You! You did this. Something in that wine you served us! What did you do, you sodding bastard?"

Blackbeard just quietly stared with a look of curiosity. Charles Vane, who had been uncommonly silent, slammed his fist on the table, jarring the cards and coin with the force.

"You ingrate rat! Answer the question. What did you do!"

Black Caesar moved behind Vane in response, ready to intervene if it became necessary on his captain's behalf. Blackbeard put his hands on the table and half rose out of his seat to come face to face with Vane.

"My doing? It's my ship at the bottom of this cold port. My prize. My treasure locked in its hold. God knows how many fathoms down." He looked hard at Vane, then at Jennings. "You two keep your tongues elsewise I will cut them out and keep them meself," he growled. The three men looked ready to commit violence on each other.

"Settle down, you overgrown piss pot boys," Mary said, intervening. "Have you all missed the fortunate news in this?"

"What fortunate news?" Jennings said without moving his eyes from Thatch.

"We's free now. No more price on our heads. No more damned pardon. Woodes Rogers, the dreaded pirate hunter, is dead and gone a hundred and fifty years. Spain, France, and England no longer seek our heads. King George rots in some grotesquely ornate grave in England." She turned toward Philip and asked, "What king reigns in England now?"

"Victoria. Queen Victoria. She's sat on the throne for thirty-five years now," Philip answered in a state of awe.

Blackbeard sank back into his chair. Jennings turned away and ran his hand over his bald head. Vane turned as well, surprised to come face to chest with the much larger Black Caesar. Vane sheepishly moved a safer distance from Blackbeard's second-in-command. Charlotte and Anne moved to Mary's side, with Anne taking her hand. The two women looked into each other's eyes with a fervent smile.

"Queen Victoria," Mary smiled. "A woman rules Great Britain again. This is truly a fine future. A better world. And it's ours for the taking." She smiled and raised her glass. "So, drink up! Then let's plot how we get our riches back!"

Anne Bonny stood with her elbow on the bar, her hand supporting her head while she comforted the forlorn and mildly drunk Jack Rackham. She played with one of his long, black, curly locks with her other hand while he sipped a glass of local ale. The pirates had scattered to various corners of the hall to drink, talk, or just sulk in their own thoughts. None had seen Bart Roberts or Sam Bellamy return since they had learned of their other-worldly predicament. The pirates felt no desire to leave this drinking hall to enter the new world that they were now banished to exist upon by some unknown force or sorcery. Anne glanced over at Mary, sitting on her own. No one had engaged in her enthusiasm for the situation. She had eventually taken a bottle and sat near the man playing the piano. He wasn't really playing a song per se but seemed to be working out a melody that was new to him, repeating it time and again before adding a bit more to the growing piece of music. Mary's red hair spilled from her hat as she gazed at a wall adorned with paintings of horses and cattle.

Anne's mind wandered back to a time when she was unaware that Mary was a girl disguising herself as a man. Mary had joined Calico Jack Rackham's crew under the guise of being a male, not that that was a requirement in the pirate society. Anne had comically found Mary to be an attractive young man with similar-colored hair as her own when they first met, and she sought to use their flirtations to make Jack jealous. It worked quite well until Jack became so enraged with Anne's interest that he wanted to kill Mary in a duel. Anne confided the truth about Mary to Jack and, for a time, they were the only ones who knew Mary to be a woman. Jack had boasted that he was minutes from killing Mary in that jealous rage. In honesty, she wasn't sure that Mary would not have bested Jack with either the cutlass or pistol in that duel. It wasn't that Jack wasn't skilled at both, but not many were a match for Mary, or for herself in that regard.

Anne knew full well that Mary had grown to detest Jack, mostly from Jack refusing a challenge from her now lost-at-sea husband, James. James had gone to Henry Jennings once he learned about the affair between her and Rackham. Jennings was captaining the fleet of ships that she, Jack, and James were a part of. Jennings was loth to have women on board ships believing they were an unneeded distraction to the sailors. James had wanted Anne to be housed ashore waiting on him, something that had pushed Anne away from her husband ever since they arrived in Nassau. Jennings offered to preside over a duel for the honor of Anne, but Jack had declined, claiming an injury which would make the duel unfair. In lieu of the duel Jennings had decided Anne would be punished for breaking the vows of her marriage by ten lashes that he himself would deliver. Jack was made to watch as Jennings dealt out the punishment with gusto, leaving Anne's back marred with scars from the lash.

It had broken Anne's heart to see the tears that streamed down Jack's face as he was forced to watch her take that beating. He had pleaded forgiveness from Anne and assured her that once he was healed, he would deal both Jennings and James a thrashing they'd never forget. Mary, afterwards, as she tended to Anne's wounds, remarked that she knew of no such injury to Rackham and wished that she had been present to accept the challenge in Jack's stead.

Anne stared again at Jack's handsome face. She knew that they were destined to be together no matter what the world threw at them. She had joined him time and again sailing through the West Indies and all along the ports of the Americas, and now they would find new adventures in this time, in this place, throughout the seas of the Pacific. Luck was on their side now with her husband James now sleeping in a watery grave, leaving her in the fortuitous situation of being a widow. She was free to marry and make a life with Jack, the love of her life.

An icy wind blew through the hall at this late hour as four dusty cowboys entered the saloon. They were dressed in long coats that fell to their shins. The tallest of the men removed his brimmed hat, revealing light brown hair, cut short and combed back away from a handsome face. One of the other men looked similar enough to be related and the other two were shorter, with long mustaches also looking like they could be brothers themselves. They searched the room with intense eyes and Anne noticed that the other patrons made sure to avert their gaze from the men. She watched as they made their way to the bar where she stood with Calico Jack Rackham.

The tall one moved with long, smooth strides, the shiny metal spurs attached to the back of his boots chiming with each step. He stood an arm's length from Anne with one boot planted on a brass rail that ran along the bottom of the bar. He set his hat on the counter and cracked a crooked smile at her before ordering a bottle of whiskey. One of his eyes had a slight squint, but they were both an intense blue she'd only seen presented by a clear morning sky while sailing across the calm Caribbean Sea. Her heart uncontrollably quickened, and she felt a flush upon her cheeks.

"Me crew, me ship, me treasure... all gone," Jack bemoaned.

Anne turned back to Jack with a start. She had almost forgotten he was there.

"You still got me, Jack, and Mary. All's not lost. We just need to find us a new ship." Anne pushed his shoulder playfully. "Steal us a new ship."

Jack rolled his eyes to the thick-beamed ceiling.

"I don't belong here in the future. I want to be in me own time!" Jack continued to grouse.

One of the cowboys nudged the tall one. "Get a load of this pair, Jesse."

Jesse, the cowboy who stood next to Anne, glanced over to her and Jack, looking them both up and down.

"Haven't even finished one drink and I'm not sure if I'm seeing two women or two men dressed as women," Jesse smirked.

The other three men had a laugh. Jack, drunk and in a foul mood, gave an exaggerated sniff at the men.

"Anne, I've finished all me drinks and I can't tell if I smell men who shite their britches or pigs who've wallowed in shite."

The man next to Jesse, who looked like his brother, slammed his shot glass on the table and moved aggressively at Jack. Jesse set his hand on his brother's shoulder to hold him back.

"Now Frank, take it easy. You know Momma says we shouldn't hit no woman. Not unless she's really deserving of it." Jesse took Anne's chin in his hand, tilting her face up to his. "This little one is definitely a woman." Anne swatted Jesse's hand away, stepping back a bit.

Jesse moved closer to Jack and towered over him. "This one, though, could be a woman. I can't really tell… Cole, Jim, you got any ideas on the subject?"

The other brothers answered in unison, one saying "Girl" the other said "man". They turned and looked at each then started laughing.

Jack moved Anne behind him and puffed his chest out. He set his hand on the hilt of his sword.

"I will not be insulted by your lot."

Jesse moved his long duster from his hip and hovered his hand above the grip of his Colt revolver.

"That so? You going to try poking me with that stick? Cause I'd be happy to fill your guts with a handful of lead."

Jack grinned and moved his hand from the sword to the pistol secured to his waist belt.

"Pistols it is then," he said with a drunken gleam in his eye.

The large Indian man serving drinks had silently arrived behind the bar with a double-barrel shotgun at his hip.

"Outside. No killin' in The Paris," he said in thickly accented English.

Jesse looked at the deadly shotgun pointed in his direction and smiled widely.

"Alright. Alright. Save my bottle, native," he said. "I'll be wanting it when I return."

"A duel it is then," announced Calico Jack Rackham. With a flourish, he whisked past the cowboys and toward the exit. Jesse bowed and extended his arm out for Anne. She gave a hateful look and followed Jack out. The cowboys laughed and headed for the exit.

Vane and Jennings, who had been watching the last of the exchange, got up from their table to follow and shortly after, the rest of the pirates exited along with the majority of the saloon's patrons, excited to see the drama that was about to take place.

CHAPTER 5 - DEAD EYES

Jack Rackham walked purposefully out onto the muddy street and stood in the center as several men on horseback rode by and a cold rain lightly drizzled. There were several bystanders that stopped to watch as Jack pulled out one of his pistols to check the load. Behind him, the man named Jesse that he had challenged to a duel emerged from the bar followed by his cowboys. Anne and her fellow pirates filed out to stand along the wooden sidewalk. Jack watched out of the corner of his eye as the three men with Jesse crossed to the opposite side of the street from The Paris saloon. They stood silently while Anne and several pirates yelled words of encouragement to Jack.

"Put a bullet in his belly, Jack!" Anne called.

Philip Albert stood next to Thatch and the gathering of pirates along with Colette and pulled a cigarette from a silver case. He glanced at Colette, and she raised an eyebrow at him and nodded to the case. Philip sighed and took another sweet-smelling cigarette from the ornate case and handed it to her. He struck a match and held the flame cupped in his hand while she leaned forward to light her smoke. Colette noticed Thatch watching the ritual. She took in a deep drag and slowly expelled the smoke.

"What is that that you used to make the flame?" Thatch asked the little man.

Philip stared at him, then handed over a small box that held the match sticks. Thatch slid the lid open and picked out one of the thin wooden sticks with a round tip coated in something he couldn't identify. He held it to his nose and smelled the tip.

"Antimony sulfide, potassium chlorate and gum Arabic mixed to a paste. Then, you see this here strip?" Philip pointed to the dark yellow side of the box. Thatch sniffed that as well and made a cringing face. "Sulfur. You strike the tip of the matchstick, and the friction will ignite the wood."

Thatch closed the lid of the small box and struck the match tip across the sulfur. It sparked with a bit of black smoke, but no flame ignited. He looked at Philip, who nodded his head in encouragement. Thatch tried again with success as the small stick now had a flame glowing from it. Thatch smiled at it and held it to his face. Philip pulled another cigarette and held it out to Thatch.

"Smoke?" Philip asked.

Thatch took the cigarette with a grunt and held it to his lips and lit it. He took a long drag and was immediately thankful for the stimulating jolt he received. He blew out a cloud of smoke and handed the little man back his box of matches.

"That is excellent," Thatch said.

"Yes." Philip took a drag from his own cigarette, then said, "I'm sorry about your man there." Philip nodded toward Rackham, adjusting his pistol in the street.

"No need for sympathy. Rackham is a seasoned fighter. Very quick with the pistol as well as the sword," Thatch said with a bit of bravado. He then sized up the man calmly waiting on Rackham. The man showed no fear and had the eyes of a predator underneath the brim of his unusual hat. A bit of a smirk lay on his face like he was enjoying this game of waiting for the violence. Thatch turned to Philip and Colette.

"Is that man known to you? He seems dressed as a farmer or horseman."

Colette answered without looking at Thatch. "Not a farmer. That is none other than Jesse James. The leader of the James Gang. His brother Frank stands over there. Not sure who the other two men are."

"Cole and Jim Younger," said Philip, "the other half of the thieving bank robber gang. Not that I'm bearing judgment on any man's choice of livelihood."

Thatch chuckled. "So, they are pirates as well."

"Something like that," said Philip.

"What is it that you do?" Thatch asked the little man.

"I am a scientist. I have been educated in many disciplines but currently earn a living in the chemistry of combustibles."

Thatch looked questioningly at the Philip.

"Things that go boom."

Thatch smiled in acknowledgment. "A handy man to have around." He watched the eyes of the cowboys as they took in the crowd. They seemed to be sizing up everyone gathered. Looking for intent. Looking for potential trouble. Looking for targets. The man, Jesse, who was about to duel Rackham, was staring at Anne Bonny. He had one eye that wandered a bit from the other. His manner was exceedingly calm in the face of possible death. The man's attention was more absorbed presently in the red-headed pirate woman then the scoundrel pirate standing across from him with deadly intent. Jesse James' confidence was exhibited for all to see.

Thatch took another drag on the paper cigarette. *In that case, this should be interesting.*

Jack Rackham finished inspecting his flintlock to make sure his powder and paper were dry and ready to be fired. Satisfied that his weapon was in good working order, he turned to his pirate friends standing under the overhang of The Paris waiting for his duel to commence. He looked directly at Anne and gave her a smile of confidence.

Jack nodded to Anne and turned, pistol in his hand, held down at his thigh, to face the calm yet intensely focused cowboy. Jesse's pistol was still holstered, and the man stood at an angle with his long coat moved aside, away from the hip that held the gun. He was making himself a smaller target for Jack to hit. Fat chance, thought Jack, as the man was the size of Charles Vane and at fifteen paces it would be difficult for Jack to miss. The cowboy had the hint of a smile which antagonized Jack further.

"Say when," Jesse said.

"The lady shall signal," Jack replied and glanced at Anne.

"The lady?" asked Jesse.

Anne knew that Jack wanted her to signal the start of the duel by dropping a handkerchief. She quickly searched her person, but finding none, she turned to Mary. Mary removed a scarf that held her hair under her hat and handed it to Anne. Anne took the maroon cloth and stepped forward with it raised high.

Jesse watched with curiosity and turned toward his brother, who just shrugged. Jesse refocused on the ornately dressed man in front of him holding an ancient flintlock pistol at his side. A strange lot, this crew was. They all carried similar weapons with cutlasses and knives strapped to their bodies like the pirates of old. His brother Frank and Cole and Jim Younger had ridden with him into San Francisco on a hunch that the banks in this city would be flowing with gold as the local mines continued to produce. They had spent a few months in Arizona and Nevada robbing stagecoaches and trains, but the Pinkerton National Detective Agency was closing in on them. The gang had mostly split up for the time being. Several made their way to Mexico and others headed back to Missouri to lie low. The four of them had been in town a few days and had found that the Wells Fargo bank was employing more heavily armed agents than they had in the past. Jim Younger kept reminding Jesse to be patient, but that was not in Jesse's nature. He was struggling with his desire to brazenly march into one of the banks, guns blazing, and take all they could carry.

This pompous, coiffed little pirate, dressed in a flowing shirt that looked like he stole it from a woman's wardrobe, was just what he needed to satisfy the impulsive rage he was feeling inside by waiting. Since he became a bushwhacker during the Civil War, he hadn't gone more than a few days without inflicting violence in some form or another. He watched out of the corner of his eye how the rest of the pirates sized him up and he wondered if any of them would pull their old flintlock pistols after he was done with this wretch. But Jesse knew that his brother and the Youngers had his back, so he calmly waited for the Irish redhead to drop her sash.

Anne attempted to will all her strength and fortitude into Jack as she held the handkerchief between her thumb and finger. She gave Jack a wink and then… let it fall.

BAM! BAM! BAM!

Edward Thatch watched Anne Bonny drop the cloth from her hand. Jack Rackham confidently started to raise his pistol toward the cowboy with a sneer on his lip. Three shots had rung out in the blink of an eye and smoke was wafting from the cowboy's pistol. The man had pulled his gun from his holster faster than Thatch would have thought possible. It was like a blur of violence, a lightning strike of death. Three shots almost at once. Thatch stared in disbelief as Jack Rackham's gun arm was slowly dropping, having never made it level with his opponent's chest. Jack stared down at the three red circles growing upon his shirt and stumbled back a step. He fell first to his knees, and locked eyes for a moment with Anne, giving her a weak smile that faded as he fell face down into the muddy street.

Thatch watched as the cowboy turned to the crowd, looking for anyone with fight in them. Not seeing any, he spun the pistol on his finger and replaced it with a flourish back in its holster. Thatch's eyes never left the pistol. Multiple rounds, so quick, so easy. He wanted one of those. He wanted several.

Anne watched as Jack fell. Her heart stopped beating. She was sure of it. She couldn't breathe, scream, or move. The cowboy looked at her, a hint of a smile on his lips. His hand went to his hat, and he tipped it to her. Rainwater splashed off the brim and he strode across the street to join his friends. The four cowboys then casually walked off. Several onlookers wandered off too now that the drama was over. Some made their way back into the saloon. Anne slowly found the use of her legs and she stumbled, trembling to the fallen Jack Rackham. She turned him over and used her sleeve to wipe the mud and dirt from his beautiful face. His dark eyes that she had gazed into so many nights were dull and lifeless. Her tears mixed with the rain fell onto Jack's face, washing away streaks of dirt. She gently closed his lids to protect them from the mud and rain, then she buried her face in Jack's neck and cried like she never had before.

Hornigold put his hand on his pistol after Jesse started walking away. Jennings gripped his arm, stopping him from pulling the weapon out.

"Fair duel. One that our Calico Jack initiated," Jennings said.

Hornigold steadied his hand and let it drop. He approached the sobbing Anne Bonny and stood over her and the body of Jack Rackham. Jennings and the rest of the pirates surrounded the grieving woman. Mary knelt and put her hand on Anne's shoulder. She looked up at her friend and wiped her eyes.

"I want to bury him at sea. It's where he ruled," she said.

"Yes, dear. We will."

The rain was continuing to fall, and they were all getting soaked once again.

"Caesar, carry our brother to the skiff and help Miss Bonny deliver him to the deep," Thatch said.

Black Caesar nodded and gently picked up Jack's body. He led the way for Anne, Mary, and Hornigold as they walked back toward the docks.

"You're not going?" Charlotte De Berry asked Thatch.

"I've not the stomach for such ceremonies," Thatch said.

Charlotte looked at Charles Vane and Jennings. Jennings shook his head.

"I never much cared for the man. Spearheaded a mutiny on my ship when he was just a whelp. Let him rot," Vane spit.

Charlotte turned from the remaining men and followed the small funeral procession on its journey to bury one of the most colorful and famous pirates in the dark waters of the San Francisco Bay.

Vane, Thatch, and Jennings ordered drinks at the bar. The crowd had settled in at the late hour of the night. Many had left to wander to their homes or camps in the drizzling chilly rain. Still, there were those that gambled at a single poker table, ordered drinks from the bar or from the pretty waiter girls that made their rounds to the half dozen occupied tables. The Paris was one of the several establishments that would continue to serve its patrons until the dawn of the new day.

"The man was fast with the pistol," Vane said to no one in particular. Thatch's eyes were on a young blonde serving waitress as she waited to pick up drinks at the end of the bar. Her eyes danced, and she gave a coy smile to Thatch before returning to her duties. "How many shots you think that weapon holds?" Vane continued.

"Six," the big native said as he passed them by with a bottle and glasses in his hands. The man didn't look at the pirates and Thatch was surprised that it was he who gave an answer to the question. It meant that their conversation was being noted by the imposing barkeep.

"Six?" Vane said after downing his glass. "No need to carry six guns when one can kill six men with one."

"Aye, what a future we've landed in," said Thatch.

Jennings gave a snort of disgust. "Not very sporting to have so many rounds at your disposal."

"Only, you thinks of killing as a sport, Jennings. The rest of us do it for necessity or survival."

"Don't test me, Thatch. You have spent a lifetime killing and marauding the innocent. Don't act as though you are above the rest of us and some sort of modern day Robin Hood. Your crimes of murder and debauchery are known far and wide."

"Harrumph, merely exaggerations and suppositions. I am but a misunderstood pussycat, Henry," Thatch said with a toothy grin.

"I would have been happy to take the King's pardon and live a peaceful life," Jennings snarled. "But you, and you!" He pointed at Vane. "You two wanted to continue harassing and pirating until the King had no other choice but to bring down Woodes Rogers on us."

Thatch looked at Vane, who had a worried look on his face. He knew that Vane was under Henry Jennings' thumb even though Vane also wanted to continue piracy to build his fortune. These two had been hand in hand for years, Jennings bringing his brains and influence to help Vane, Vane then being the blunt end of the hammer for Jennings to wield when necessary. Thatch supposed that Vane was a tool that would eventually be discarded by Jennings when it was broken or no longer useful. Jennings had been pressuring the pirates for months to limit their targets to small merchants, Spanish, French, and Dutch ships, but the heavily loaded British merchant ships were far too tempting, even to Vane.

"You could have signed the pardon and sailed back to your Bermuda. What did you need our consent for?" Thatch growled.

Jennings looked away. Vane stared at the back of Jennings' head, confused. The silence continued for a moment. Then Thatch smiled.

"Ahh… I see. Conditions of the deal."

"What? What deal?" Vane asked.

Jennings continued his silence, taking a sip of his drink. Vane looked at Thatch questioningly.

"Henry Jennings. Governor Jennings, it must be." Thatch laughed.

Vane turned to Jennings. "What does he mean?"

"You see, Charles, if our good captain here could deliver all our signatures on the pardon then a governorship would be in order for our hero, Henry Jennings."

Vane looked between the two men, Thatch with a big grin and Jennings wearing his scowl.

"Well, maybe I want to be governor of some place too," Vane said.

"You?" Jennings narrowed his eyes with a look of disdain. "We have not a prayer for it now, or any of it!" Jennings pointed a finger at Thatch. "You went and got us all stuck here. Where we don't belong. *When* we don't belong. I don't know if you're in league with some sort of witch, or gypsy... or the God damn devil himself, but this is your doing!"

Thatch continued to be amused. "My doing? You give me credit for moving time, Henry? Oh, I have cheated death once or twice, turned the tide of battle that other men would surely have lost, done things that would give most men nightmares, but this? I have no claim on this magic. But as I'm still alive... and if this is all real and not some opium dream, then I'm going to live as I did before. Free, answering to no one and with fire and passion!" Thatch spotted the blonde, pretty waiter girl and caught her eye. "Now, if I am to believe the date on the calendar, then it has been over a hundred and fifty years since I've been with a woman. You may be used to such things, Jennings, but that's much too long for me."

Thatch stood up, and Vane watched him approach the girl and quickly engage her in conversation. She smiled and put her arm around him. Vane followed them with his eyes as they climbed the stairs, entered a room, and closed the door behind them.

CHAPTER 6 - THE PIRATE HUNTER

Henry Jennings sat with his back against the wall on the far side of the near-empty saloon. The woman running the establishment had retired to a back room, and the music had long ago ended. None of the pretty waiter girls were left making rounds and only the native bartender was left working, cleaning glasses, and wiping down the bar tops. Jennings was either going to have to rent a room upstairs, find another inn, or sleep on the cold, damp streets like some petty vagrant. His first mate, Vane, had taken a plump wench into one of the rooms a short time ago, and Jennings was happy to be rid of him. The man was an ingrate. Jennings had allowed Vane to captain a ship or two in his fleet, but that had always ended in some sort of failure. The man was a blunt tool of violence but without the intelligence or strategical mind necessary to be a genuine leader. If the odds tilted from his favor, he would be quick to abandon his post, his men, and his ship to escape harm. Jennings imagined that Vane, as a child, was torturing small animals to satisfy some sort of wanton blood lust.

He had thought he convinced Vane to sign the King's pardon prior to the pirate captain's meeting, but he had quickly learned that Vane had no intention of giving up piracy, even after inking his signature on the document. He had been heard publicly boasting about his disregard for the rules of the pardon. Jennings had been planning on cutting Vane loose at the first opportune moment, but now all his ploys were nullified by this nightmare that he found himself in.

Jennings rubbed his tired eyes. How had this happened to him, he pondered? He was so close to closing out this stage of his life. The deal he made would have allowed him to comfortably return home with extensive finances and property, as well as the power and position worthy of his family name. Why had he allowed Hornigold to convince him that his plan to have all the pirate captains together on Thatch's ship was the right way to implement their scheme? He should have signed the damned document in Nassau and sailed home to Bermuda that day. Instead, he was tossed into a hurricane, sucked into a whirlpool to almost drown, and now he found himself stranded on the shores of a future world against all the natural laws on God's green Earth.

He looked up from his gloomy position as the door to the saloon opened. Three men entered the room, and the sight of the lead man sent a shock wave through Jennings' tired body. The three men were tall with broad shoulders and dressed in the familiar uniform of the British Navy. They wore the white breeches and unbuttoned dark blue coats with the white navy regulation shirt underneath. Each man had a sword strapped to his side. The lead man's head swiveled as he took in the room before landing on Jennings. The man's face turned devilish with a smile that accentuated the large, pocked scar that covered the left side of his face. Jennings knew the story of the scar quite well. The man had taken a pistol shot to the face in the heat of battle years back. The lead ball had lodged itself into the roof of his mouth after it had ripped apart his cheek. The wounded man had continued to fight until the enemy was vanquished, but it had cost him the life of his brother and half his shipmates while leaving him with the wicked-looking scar.

"Woodes Rogers," Jennings whispered to himself.

So, the pirate hunter had survived the same ordeal as we. He stared in disbelief as Rogers strode purposefully toward him. Rogers pulled up a chair and sat in front of Jennings at his table. The two soldiers stood at attention behind him, watching the room for signs of threat. Rogers and Jennings stared silently at one another for a moment.

"I don't suppose the good Lord has seen fit to drown that lot of scourge and strumpets, save you?" Rogers asked aggressively. Jennings only stared at the man's fiery eyes before looking away.

"No matter. It seems God has tasked me to finish this job while in some sort of state of purgatory. I don't know what to make of this place we find ourselves in, but I trust you will aid me in dispensing the King's justice on these pirates?"

Jennings looked at Rogers in disbelief.

"I lost almost twenty God-fearing sailors to the seas this night, and the righteous must be avenged," continued Rogers. "You have failed me, Jennings, and I expect you to atone for your blunder."

"Failed you? I did as you asked! They were all gathered in one location! I am not responsible for the... the sorcery or such a storm!"

"Calm yourself, man," Rogers said, shaking his head. "It seems we are being tested by the Lord Almighty to purge the heathens from the Earth in his name."

Jennings put his head in his hands, then rubbed his tired eyes. He spoke in a low tone, trying to control his temper and his voice. "Woodes, I implore you to look around you and see where we are, *when* we are. We have landed in a future world. One hundred and fifty years have passed. Our king has long since died and an unknown queen sits on the throne. The age of piracy on the seas has come and gone. You must have seen the enormous ships in the harbor. A pirate would have no hope of taking such vessels when they are encased in iron. Thatch, Bellamy, and the others have nothing left to their names. We have no ship, no crew, no treasure. Our pursuit is over. There is no point. We are all souls lost to time."

Rogers' scarred face attempted a smile as he shook his head like he was listening to the story of a child. He sighed and stood up from the table.

"You disappoint me, Jennings. Where are they?"

"Most are gone, God knows where. Thatch, Vane are upstairs. Each took a wench into a room," Jennings said.

Rogers looked up at the upstairs hallway lined with doors, then noticed the two pistols Jennings had strapped to his chest.

"I will relieve you of the flintlocks so that we can make short work of this," Rogers said with his hand held out.

Contented, Edward Thatch rose from the bed and picked up his breeches. He glanced at the bare legs of the pretty waitress girl he bedded that were partly exposed outside the sheet. She was quite fun and uninhibited, he mused. He might have to have another go at her before the morning, he thought as he made his way to the piss pot and relieved himself. There was a basin of water on the dresser, along with a sliver of soap for washing. He pulled on his breeches first and then washed up his hands and face with the cool water. He glanced at his hairy reflection in the mirror. His eyes were bloodshot from no sleep and the night of heavy drinking. Sleep would be difficult even now, he mused. The short-term distraction of sex did little to ease his mind from the reality of being stranded in this unfamiliar time and place. *At least things couldn't get much worse for you, Blackbeard*, he thought to himself.

BAM! The door to his room was kicked open and three Royal Navy men entered violently with swords and pistols in hand. Luckily for Thatch, they were momentarily focused on the bare-breasted woman who rose suddenly with a frightened start from the bed he had just been lying in. Thatch quickly picked up the piss pot and flung it at the three men, catching one in the chest and drenching all three men in his warm piss. Through the shouts of disgust and alarm, Thatch started to make a dash for his weapon stash near the bed, but one of the pistol-armed men pointed a flintlock at him and pulled the trigger. BLAM! The loud blast sent the girl diving below the bed and Thatch twisted away to avoid the shot, which went a hair wide, shattering the mirror on the dresser. He spotted the half-open window facing the street and made a run, then a dive at it, as another pistol was taking aim at him. BLAM! Thatch crashed through the window and landed on the second-story overhang of the roof in a burst of wood splinters and glass. He rolled uncontrollably off the overhang, reaching out his hands for purchase on the edge, scraping and clawing, but his momentum was too powerful. All he was able to do was slow his descent enough to control his fall to the ground without breaking his legs.

Thatch landed hard in the muddy street, rolling his body to cushion his fall. He glanced up at the window he had flung himself through to see a scarred-faced man staring down at him. The man was yelling, pointing at him,

65

but Thatch's ears were ringing too loudly to comprehend what was being said. He was on all fours and mentally took inventory of any pain his body was receiving. *Am I shot? Am I bleeding mortally from anywhere?* He rose unsteadily to his feet. No bullet wound felt present on his body. His bare chest and back felt scraped and scratched, but otherwise intact. He swung his head left and right. There was no one around at this hour on the street. His mind finally caught up to the situation at hand. Without a weapon he needed to escape; at least three men had burst into his room to kill him and there could be more waiting somewhere outside. He started with a limping gait, but as his muscles loosened, he was able to run barefoot toward the shadows of the opposite corner and continue into the night before anyone was able to exit The Paris to give chase.

From a room several doors down, Vane peered out the crack he'd opened in the door as three men in Royal Navy uniforms raced down the stairs. He had heard the shots and the window breaking and rushed to the door, pistol in hand. That room was the one that Thatch had retired to with a pretty waitress girl. If someone had come for him, then Vane could be next. He quietly closed the door and hastily dressed.

"What is it, love? That gunfire?" the wench he had bedded asked as she also dressed.

"Is there another way out of here?"

She nodded her head yes, and Vane grabbed her hard by the arm.

"Then show me," he hissed at her.

Swords in hand, the three naval men hurried into the main hall. Colette stood, robed in the hallway, Colt .36 caliber pistol in hand. The bartender moved to her side, all the while pointing a shotgun at the men. Rogers paid them no mind and strode by Jennings who was now standing.

"You. With us," he commanded.

Jennings reluctantly followed Rogers and his men from the saloon and into the street. It was empty and quiet but for the soft, icy drizzle that fell, coating the scenery with a moist sheen that reflected in the lamplight. One of the soldiers smelled the sleeve of his coat and made a cringing face. Jennings looked the men up and down, noticing the rank odor of urine that emanated from them. Rogers then noticed Jennings wrinkling his nose at one of his sailor's shirts and his face darkened when he realized he was wet as well, and not from the drizzle.

He turned toward Jennings and pointed a finger at him. "You're going to help me hang each of these rotten scoundrels no matter how long it takes, no matter how far they run."

CHAPTER 7 - BURIAL AT SEA

The pirates sat in silence as Black Caesar rowed their skiff over the calm waters of San Francisco Bay. They had decided that they would bury Jack at sea nearest to the site where the *Queen Anne's Revenge* had gone down. They were all tired and their nerves were raw, but it was only fitting that they make the best effort under the circumstances to send their fellow marauder into the afterlife with a traditional sailor's funeral. Black Caesar had spotted some flotsam from their ship and estimated where it must be lying at the bottom of the bay. He let the small craft drift as he stowed the oars, then nodded to Anne that this was the spot.

Mary held Anne's hand as the others prepared Jack Rackham's body to be lowered overboard from their skiff. They filled Jack's pockets with rocks and wrapped a heavy anchor chain that had been stored on the skiff around his waist so that he would not float or drift. Black Caesar had begun to remove Jack's weapons when Anne shouted, "No!"

"He won't be needin' these, but we will," Black Caesar said.

"He's right. Better we be well armed for this new world rather than for the one beyond," Charlotte said, while putting a comforting hand on Anne's shoulder.

Anne wiped tears from her eyes and moved over to kneel beside Jack. She put her hand on his soft cheek, then kissed his lips for the last time. She pulled two pistols and his dirk from his waistband and set them aside on the wooden floor of the small boat. Anne gave a loving smile to her Jack and guided his hands to the hilt of his polished cutlass and wrapped her scarf around them to hold them in place.

"He keeps his sword. He's a pirate captain and a pirate captain always has his sword," she said as she stood back, taking Mary's hand again.

Hornigold stood and turned toward the small group. "We don't have the prayer book, but I'll say the words best as I remember them if you'd like."

Mary nodded her head. Hornigold and the others all bowed their heads. He cleared his throat and began the pirate prayer for the dead.

"We offer our brother Calico Jack Rackham, captain of the swift sloop *William*, to the Lord and to the sea. His rich life was cut short this day and we therefore commit his body to the deep, to be turned into corruption, looking for the resurrection of the body, when the sea shall give up her dead and the life of the world to come through Our Lord Jesus Christ; who at his coming shall change our vile body, that it may be like his glorious body, according to the mighty working, whereby he is able to subdue all things to himself."

Hornigold nodded to Black Caesar, and they both lifted the body of Jack and gently lowered him into the icy waters of the awaiting bay. The pirates watched as Jack's body sank, becoming only a fading shadow as it disappeared below the dark, glassy surface.

Black Caesar gently rowed the skiff back to shore as the other pirates huddled together while the drizzle soaked through their coats and into the garments underneath. None had said a word since they had laid Jack to rest below the icy waters. Anne Bonny was done crying for Jack, as it would now do no good. Her grief was quickly turning to anger. When she found out her husband James didn't make it through the storm and they rescued Jack from the sea, she expected that they would wed at the soonest opportunity. Now another James has taken Jack away from her, but this time it was forever.

The others were adrift in their thoughts of everything they had lost and the seemingly hopeless situation they were in. Hornigold began to hum a familiar tune in hopes of turning the despair that was slowly overtaking the remnants of his pirate republic. At first no one paid him any mind, but then Anne turned her face to him and picked up the song with the rest of the small crew joining in:

> *Hang sorrow, let's cast away care,*
> *the World is bound to find us:*
> *Thou and I, and all must die,*
> *And leave this world behind us.*
> *The Bell shall ring, the Clark shall sing,*
> *The Good old wife shall wind us.*
> *The Sexton shall lay our bodies in Clay*
> *Where the Devil in Hell shall find us.*

Anne smiled at Hornigold, and Mary patted her knee affectionately.

"Thank you all for helping me bury my Jack."

"What do we do now?" Mary asked.

"We find the others and we steal ourselves a new ship," said Hornigold as they once again floated past the amazing array of ocean vessels.

"Something with sails, mind you," quipped Charlotte.

"Not me," said Anne.

They all turned to look at her. Anne pulled her damp hair back and tied it into a ponytail away from her face.

"I'll be seeking my vengeance on this Jesse James. I will not rest or sail from these shores until my dear Jack has been avenged."

They pulled the skiff up along the shore, stowing it above the tide line, and began their walk back to the saloon where they had left the others. The streets were near empty but for a few drunks and vagrants wandering the alleyways or sleeping under the shelter of the buildings' awnings and overhangs. The only sound was a sucking noise as their boots sank into and dislodged from the muddy ground as they walked. None could guess the time of morning since the dark, overcast skies blocked the moon and stars from view. They were all dragging their feet, mind and bodies depleted of energy save for Anne who walked with purpose toward her newly minted mission.

Rounding a corner first, Hornigold held his arm out for the rest to stop. He stepped back into the cover of a building and turned, holding a silencing finger to the others. He carefully looked around the corner, seeing four men outside The Paris conversing. One of the men was Jennings and the three others were wearing the blue coats of the British Navy. Hornigold let out an inaudible sigh as he recognized the tallest of the three navy men. He turned back to the impatiently waiting group behind him.

"What?" Charlotte inquired in a hushed voice.

"This night has become darker. Around that corner is the pirate hunter, Woodes Rogers."

They stared at him for a moment, then Mary moved Hornigold out of the way to have a quick look. She grimaced on seeing the men standing outside the saloon. She then turned back and ushered the group away.

"It's him alright, and he's with Jennings, that damn turncoat. How did Woodes Rogers follow us to this place?"

"If he followed us here, then maybe, there's a way back," Charlotte said.

Hornigold was silent and looked away from them for a moment. He took a few steps away from the street that led to the men and The Paris. He turned back to the group.

"We need to find another place to hole up. We all need sleep and to put some distance between us and them. Come on."

He hastily set off back toward the docks and the others looked at one another questioningly, but then followed him back the way they had come. They followed the road back to the docks and began searching for an open door to a warehouse. All were locked up tight, but Charlotte spotted one with a window high above the ground.

"You two boys give a girl a boost?" she asked of Black Caesar and Hornigold.

The two men held their hands clasped together and bent their knees for Charlotte to climb up with both feet in their palms. They counted three and boosted her up in the air toward the window. Charlotte's hands clasped the window ledge, and sure-handedly she was able to open the window and pull herself inside. A few moments later, she unlatched the door and ushered the rest of them inside. Through the dim light of the windows, they were able to see the contents of the warehouse. Lining the shelves were boxes of clothing, some open, most closed. The crew strode around, opening the cases and pulling out the articles to get a better look. Mary rubbed the unfamiliar denim material between her fingers.

"Such bland colors, but the quality is high," Charlotte mused.

"Colors be damned, they are dry," Hornigold said and began pulling off his wet clothes. He held up buttoned shirts and dungarees, finding ones that would fit his frame. The rest went through the same process and quickly changed into the new clothing. Anne stopped and looked at Hornigold in his blue denim pants and cream-colored shirt that had no embellishments or frills.

"Look at you, future man," Anne said.

"I look ridiculous, but at least I'm dry. You look like a common scallywag in that, "he replied, looking over Anne's choice of men's pants and shirt.

Mary dumped a box of shirts on the floor, then laid them out as a bed. The rest followed suit and before long, they all settled in for a few hours of sleep.

"Do you think we'll find our way home?" Mary asked no one in particular. After a moment, Mary sighed, as there was no answer.

"In the morn, we will regroup and find a way," Hornigold finally said without conviction.

"Where do you think Bellamy and Roberts got off to?" Mary asked.

"Drinking, whoring, my guess," Hornigold said, again without conviction. He didn't believe that was the case, but it came out of his mouth, as his mood was foul. Bellamy was too in love with the lass from his home for whoring. Where they were at the moment wasn't a concern of his, but he was having doubts that it would be easy to reunite with his pirate gang. The only point of reference they all had in common was that saloon. Now that the pirate hunter had found Jennings at The Paris, it was probably best to avoid the location. He hadn't seen Vane or Thatch in that group, and he could guess why. Woodes Rogers would have killed them both on the spot, so either they were dead or had escaped somehow. He needed a strategy going forward, but his head was clouding with fatigue. He had closed his eyes moments ago and now he felt himself drifting into sleep. *This all must be a dream.*

In his slumber he saw himself commanding a nimble sloop of war, eight cannons and a crew of fifty. A hot wind blew through his hair and the warm Caribbean Sea sprayed against his suntanned face. A Spanish treasure galleon was on the horizon, and he called to his mates to give chase. He smiled as around him, buccaneers manned the rigging and set the sails. Hornigold turned the polished wooden wheel with a flourish toward the galleon. All was right in the world again as he lay on his bed of soft clothes dumped on the floor from a warehouse box.

CHAPTER 8 - THE LIGHT OF DAY

Thatch opened his eyes in the fresh morning light to find an enormous rat sitting on his chest twitching its nose at him. It seemed to be searching his beard for bits of food with its clever little paws. He quickly knocked it away with the back of his hand, sending it scurrying into a pile of wood that lay to the side of his makeshift bed of straw and burlap sacks. Thatch stood and brushed himself off, his mind clearing enough to remember how he had found himself in this empty, half-collapsed old stable. He stretched his shirtless broad frame and winced at the knots and bruises that covered his body. At least he was in one piece and without holes after being shot at and falling from the second floor of a building, not to mention half-drowned and sucked into a time-traveling vortex. He couldn't remember how far he had run last night to find this dilapidated shelter at the edge of town, but it had felt a safe distance from the navy men who were hunting him. He looked around now in the light of day to find something that might be of use to him, like a coat or shoes, but the place was cleaned out of anything of value.

Thatch carefully lifted several large boards aside to exit the stable. The rain and drizzle from the night before were gone. He took a deep breath of the new crisp air that was warmed by the sun. Thatch spied several Chinese men and women pushing carts filled with goods of varying sorts through the alleyway he had found himself in. The cart pushers barely gave him a second glance, as if they were used to seeing vagrants emerging from the trash on a regular basis without their clothes. He watched as two carts bumped into one another with several pears from one falling to the ground. The two Chinese women argued and shouted at each other while a watchful young Chinese boy swiftly picked up two of the pears before they knew they were missing. He then continued his way further down the alleyway toward Thatch.

"Oi! Boy, come here," Thatch said as the boy was rounding a corner with his contraband. Thatch followed and when he turned the corner a heavy-set Chinese man in a white apron dusted with flour had a hold of the boy's arm and was yelling at him in Chinese. The boy was struggling to escape as the man slapped him hard on the head. Thatch stalked directly toward the two.

"Oi!" he yelled as he approached. The Chinese man looked up at Thatch with annoyance that turned to fright and confusion as the pirate closed the distance between them. Thatch stood almost a head taller than the portly man, who was clearly a baker, and put on his most devilish scowl to impress that he was no one to be trifled with. Without another word, Thatch grabbed the man by his thick throat and pushed him against the building. He, in turn, smacked the man on the head, sending him sprawling to the ground. The man yelled a few choice Chinese curses and then ran off.

The boy, seeing the man run off, turned around, about to run himself, then stalled for a moment seeing the towering, bearded, shirtless sight of Thatch. His eyes went wide, and he turned too late to make a getaway as Thatch was able to grab his arm. The boy was a second from yelling out when Thatch held his hand up to his face with a finger to his lips to shush him.

76

The boy was frozen with fear and Thatch held out his other hand to him. The boy looked at him, then his pears. He dropped one of the golden-colored fruits into Thatch's hand. Smiling, Thatch took a bite from the ripened pear. Juices ran into his beard, and he happily savored the sweet flavor. Without letting go, he looked at the boy's round face.

"Speak English lad?"

The boy looked hesitantly at him before nodding his head.

"I ain't going to hit you like that one. A fellow has to eat, right?"

The boy slowly nodded yes.

"What's your name?"

"Tom?" said the boy, almost like his reply was a question.

"Tom?" Thatch said with a chuckle. "Not a very good Chinese name. Alright, Tom, I'm in need of a good thief. A local. One who knows the lay of the land, mind you. You seem to be qualified in my eyes."

Tom looked frantically away as Thatch continued to eat his pear one-handed, still holding the boy's arm. He struggled a bit in an attempt to break away, but Thatch's grip was like iron around his skinny arm. The boy held up the other pear in offering to Thatch, but Thatch just shook his head.

"Pirate code. Plunder is always split evenly. You heard of pirates?"

Tom nodded his head yes.

"Well, young Mr. Tom, you are looking at the most feared and famous pirate in all the Caribbean," Thatch said, with a twinkle in his lively eyes. He tossed the finished pear over his shoulder, let the boy's arm go and wiped his hand on his breeches. The boy looked confused and was ready to bolt. Thatch smiled big and held out his freshly dried hand for Tom to shake.

"Blackbeard at your service," Thatch said as the boy focused on the immense black beard covering his face. "Can you guess how I acquired the name?" He laughed. "Heard of me?"

Tom shook his head no.

"Well, we are a long way from Nassau. No matter. Seeing how I saved your hide from that overweight bilge rat, you are now owing me a debt. I'm short on crew as of late, so I hereby anoint you with the honor of being my cabin boy. It is a very prestigious job aboard ship, running errands for the captain, carrying important messages, and relaying them to the crew."

Thatch looked around the alleyway. It seemed that Chinese people completely occupied the neighborhood he found himself in. The shops and doorways held signs in handwriting that were only displaying Chinese symbols. The men and women dressed in unusual attire that featured sandals and long braided hair for the men, as well as brimmed hats or headbands. Their slacks extended down to their ankles and most wore long-sleeve shirts similar to button-up blouses but without the buttons. These shirts overlapped in the front and were held together by a belt. The shirts had sleeves that were unusually wide at the wrists. Thatch crossed his arms over his hairy chest and looked down at his dirty, bare feet.

"I'm in need of dress at the moment, young Tom. Your first job as a new pirate recruit is to procure your captain some clothing." The boy looked around at the small Chinese men that moved about the area, then sized up Thatch. "Yeah, not going to find something to my liking here. I have a bit of a fancier taste than what I see. Any ideas, lad?"

Tom nodded and smiled. He then led the way through the twisting and turning alleyways.

Thatch stood across the street from a building that held a laundry store run by Chinese immigrants. Tom had told him that his mother had worked in this store before she was killed in a fire that had happened here almost a year ago. The store had been rebuilt, and he knew the layout of the building well as it hadn't changed once they had completed the repairs. Thatch looked around the busy street and noticed a few men coming and going from the laundry that looked to be of a well-to-do type. A few of the men were armed with the same sort of weapons he had seen last night at the saloon: pistols held in leather holsters at their hips. He even saw belted holsters that were dyed to match their outfits of black and brown colors. He longed to possess one of those pistols that had a multitude of shots contained in the one firearm.

This line of thinking brought him back to the duel between that young local and Calico Jack. Thatch only knew Jack by reputation and second-hand association. They had each sailed the same ports but had never interacted throughout the last couple of years. Jack's reputation was one of cunning and backstabbing. He had long heard that Calico wasn't a great fighter or naval tactician but did well leading men and women with his charisma. Thatch guffed to himself. These stories seemed especially true after seeing him easily gunned down by that James fellow. *I guess his charisma wasn't as big of an asset in this new age.*

Thatch needed to arm himself before he ventured back to look for his fellow pirates. Those navy men who broke into his room last night surely made off with all his weapons that he had left behind. He would need to be well prepared before he met up with them again. He could still recall the scarred-faced man that glared at him out the window after he had fallen to the street. It dawned on him at this moment who that man must have been. Woodes Rogers, the pirate hunter. Thatch had heard stories of him recently as news spread through the Caribbean that Rogers was the one tasked with offering and enforcing the King's pardon. Woodes was said to have a wicked scar from being shot in the face during a battle with a Spanish galleon. The man had made a name for himself first as a privateer, then more recently as a pirate hunter protecting the interests of merchants and the Crown.

He pushed aside the question of how Woodes and his navy men had come to be at the same time and place as Thatch and his pirates. Time… his head hurt to dwell on that subject. The idea of a new time, while difficult to believe, seemed the only logical answer to the new world he currently found himself in. This thought made him more conscious of his lack of protection. It would be folly for him to remain unarmed much longer in this violent city. Once his cabin boy returned with something for him to wear, he would set about procuring one of those advanced pistols for himself.

Thatch watched as Tom emerged from a back door in the alley of the laundry store with a satchel slung over his shoulder. The boy had a satisfied smile on his face as he approached Thatch with his plunder.

"You made that look easy, lad."

Tom set the bag down on an empty crate for Thatch to look through.

"They so busy there, no one notice me. Think I just delivery boy," Tom said.

Thatch pulled the articles from the bag, holding up each one. Ankle-length black dress trousers, white shirt, black vest, necktie, thigh-length frock coat and last to come out were polished black boots.

"You've done well, boy, very well." Thatch held the sole of one boot up to his foot and was pleased that it would be a match. "Good lad."

Thatch took several minutes to dress himself in the clothes as the boy motioned to him on the correct way to tie the necktie. Thatch straightened out his clothes and then walked around the corner of the alley to a shop window. He eyed his reflection in the window. It was a dashing outfit despite the lack of color. He would have preferred a bit of red to invoke a little extravagance, but now he didn't look so out of place. His wild hair and beard still managed to create a dichotomy of image. The boy stood next to him in his worn, bland Chinese dress and it fouled his mood.

"Oi. You are a disgraceful-looking cabin boy. Have you no pride? I will remind you that you are now part of the crew of the most fearsome and prized ship in the Caribbean, the *Queen Anne's Revenge*. And your captain, Blackbeard, will not tolerate his cabin boy looking like some scullery maid." Blackbeard looked down with a menacing look to Tom. "Now get back in there and find yourself a suitable dress before I throw you overboard to the sharks."

The light of day streamed through the warehouse window high on the wall that Charlotte De Berry had climbed through last night. But those rays of sunlight that highlighted the dust motes floating through the air were not what woke her and her pirate friends. It was the loud clamoring of the warehouse door as it was pushed open by the first workers to arrive this morning that sent them all sitting bolt upright, reaching for their pistols and cutlasses.

Three Italian men in rapid-fire conversation with each other in their native language were so shocked to see the motley group of pirates standing before them pointing various weapons of death and dismemberment that one let out the scream of a little girl and another dropped his lunch tin, spilling its contents on the floor. The men slowly raised their hands to prove that they were in submission and stood stock still.

"Gather our things. It's time to go," said Hornigold as he pointed two flintlock pistols at the men.

Mary and Anne stuffed the pirates' belongings into a couple of burlap sacks, and they all moved to exit the warehouse while Hornigold and Black Caesar guarded the workers. Charlotte picked up an apple from the spilt lunch box and crunched it as she walked past the men.

"Call out or follow and I'll have your hearts for breakfast," Hornigold said with a finger slashing across his throat to make his point before he and Black Caesar closed the warehouse door behind them, leaving the three frightened and confused men inside.

The pirates made their way down the dusty streets of San Francisco's marina district in their new clothing and only garnered a few looks because of their wild hair and strange weapons strapped to their bodies. The early hour of the morning brought in a bustle of workers, merchants and horse-driven vehicles. It brought a sense of awe to their eyes as they had never imagined such a frenzy of commerce flowing through one port of call. The scale and quantity of ships in the harbor were truly breathtaking in the light of day.

"I've never seen such plunder ripe for the taking. Hornigold, do you see cannons on any of these ships?" Charlotte asked.

They stopped to gaze out toward the crowded harbor, eyeing the iron and wooden ships that were moored at the docks or lay at anchor on the calm bay. They all scanned the hulls looking for the cylinder outlines of cannon barrels, but the portholes, if there were any, were empty of any armaments.

"Not a one I see," Black Caesar commented.

"There! What in the Lord's name is that beast?" Mary pointed at a metal hulk moored to the dock whose deck was a mere eighteen inches above the waterline. There was a round iron turret ten feet high and fifteen feet in diameter that rose from the middle of the low deck and featured two 15-inch guns protruding menacingly out of holes in its sides. The guns looked enormous in comparison to the 3- to 4-inch guns that you would find on the typical sloop of war. There were two men on the deck in uniforms consisting of white pants, blue vests, and jackets, with a blue cap on their heads. They each held a long rifle in their hands and stood ramrod straight with watchful eyes as workers passed them on the dock.

"What kind of ship is that? It has no room for cargo or crew," Anne commented. "A floating cannon is all. With munitions of the like I've never seen."

"Could be more to it below the water line? Built to sink ships, that one," said Hornigold.

"How does it move with no sails?" asked Mary.

"It has one of those chimneys like the other iron ships…" Hornigold didn't finish his thought.

"Look!" Mary called out, pointing further past the docks.

They turned toward Mary's gaze, spotting the back of a lone Charles Vane with his head on a swivel searching the streets. They quickened their pace to catch up.

"Vane!" Hornigold called out.

Charles turned, and a note of relief crossed his face. He stopped and waited for the others to catch up with him.

"Aye, wasn't sure I'd see you scallywags again," Vane said as they reached him.

Vane looked them all up and down, noticing their new, but drab, attire.

"Decided to give up piracy and work in fields, have you?" Vane laughed and tugged on Hornigold's shirt.

"Where have you been? What happened after we left last night?" Hornigold asked.

"I found me a nice pretty waitress girl to lay with. Thatch did as well. Jennings, the pious bastard, sat and drank in a sour mood. Well, then later, after I delivered my graces to the girl, there was a shot rang out from the hallway. I looked out my door and seen the wretched face of the pirate hunter Rogers and several of his navy men come from Thatch's room. I don't think they got him because Woodes had a face of rage, not that his could ever look pleasant. The girl showed me a back way out and I escaped. Came down to the docks and slept in a skiff. Where did you lot get off to? Besides burying poor Jack Rackham?"

"When we came back from laying Jack to rest, we'd seen Woodes and a few navy men out front of The Paris looking fairly friendly with your Captain Jennings," Charlotte said.

"Jennings wanted the King's pardon. That is already known. He'd be happy to sign and retire back to his fancy plantation. Not me. I'm not done pirating. What did the Crown ever do for me? He knew I wouldn't sign that

84

damn document. He'd been meeting with that pirate hunter for a few days before all this." Vane spit.

"Then Thatch lives?" asked Hornigold.

"In the dark night he lived. Not sure if he still walks the light of day," Vane said with a shrug of his shoulders. "We should steal ourselves a ship and sail away from this dreadful place."

"What of me, Captain?" Black Caesar said. "I cannot leave him here to face the pirate hunter and his men alone."

Vane began walking off toward the marina, with the others following.

"He ain't my captain," Vane said.

"We need more than the six of us to take a ship and sail her out of here. We have no idea where Bellamy and Roberts are, either," Hornigold said.

"Six of us can take one of these small ships," Vane said. "We don't need them. Besides, should we stay here and risk Woodes Rogers and his navy finding us?"

Charlotte stopped and put her hand on Black Caesar's shoulder and the rest stopped as well.

"We need to vote on what we do next. Pirate code," Charlotte said.

"Aye, let's put it to a vote," Hornigold agreed.

Vane rolled his eyes skyward and let out a sigh of frustration. "We are not on a ship, and we are not members of the same crew. I'll be damned if I will let my fate be decided by the soft hearts of your lot. We have been drowned, stranded, and pursued to the end of the world with the pirate hunter and his navy at our heels. It's time to escape while we can rather than stay here to search for three scurvy lost souls in a strange city that's near the size of London herself!"

"We will vote, as is the pirate way. Ship or no ship!" said Mary. "Who votes to stay and find the others at all costs?"

Hornigold, Charlotte, Mary, and Black Caesar raised their hands while Vane stood fuming. Mary looked around quickly with surprise on her face.

"Where's Anne?"

They all turned and looked around the crowded streets, searching for the red locks of Anne Bonny.

"Anne!" called Mary.

Anne was nowhere to be found as they looked desperately to and fro. She had disappeared somewhere in the crowd. Black Caesar hopped up onto a parked carriage and looked around from his high perch. He scanned the streets and docks for a sign of the young woman but was unable to spot her. He leapt down and shook his head.

"This godforsaken place will swallow the rest of us if we don't leave now!" Vane bellowed. "First Bellamy and Roberts, then Thatch and now Bonny. Should we lie here and wait for our doom? I call for a re-vote!"

CHAPTER 9 – SHANGHIED

Bartholomew Roberts groaned and opened his eyes with great difficulty. They felt crusty and sore as he rubbed them with his hands. His tongue felt too large for his mouth as he tried to swallow and lick his dry lips. His eyes had trouble focusing on the metal ceiling that was inches above his pounding head. He reached out and touched the cold gray metal and immediately noticed his naked fingers. It had been years since he had looked at his knuckles without the adornments of several layers of gold and silver rings. *Funny that vanity brings me back from a stupor*, he thought to himself as he realized that it wasn't the ceiling that was within touching distance but the bottom of a bunk bed that hung over the one he was lying in. Carefully, he swung his heavy-feeling legs to the side and bent down underneath the low-hanging bunk. The entire interior of the room was metal and lined with more than a dozen other bunks, several of which were occupied by sleeping men. His hands went to his chest in search of his prized diamond-laden cross and he cursed to find it gone.

Roberts rose to his feet and quickly grabbed hold of the side of the bunk to keep himself from falling. His head swam as a moment of dizziness enveloped him. Swaying and taking a careful step forward, he turned to scan the room. Two bunks down, he noticed the long dark wavy locks that belonged to Sam Bellamy. He grabbed the sides of each bunk to remain stable as he made his way toward him.

"Sam. Sam, wake up, matey."

Sam was slow to stir, but as his eyes opened and focused on Roberts, it was clear he was experiencing the same disorientation and dizziness that hung over Bart.

"Where are we? What happened?" Sam asked as he slowly sat up, stooping below the low-hung bunk above him.

Roberts sat down on the floor next to him and rubbed the sides of his head to ease the ache he felt there.

"Was it all a dream? Are we in Nassau? Is this some sort of prison?" asked Sam.

"Don't know but feels as though we are on a ship. One of the metal ones we'd seen. So probably not a dream, I'm afraid."

Sam settled a bit and noticed the slow rise and fall of the ship he found himself in. Sure enough, he knew what it felt like to ride the open ocean, and he knew they were indeed at sea. He rose on unsteady feet as Roberts had done and looked around at the room. Strange bulbs hung from wires, creating soft light without heat or flame. He stared and wondered what sort of magic could create such light. He knew in the back of his mind it must be a technology that was of the time they had found themselves thrown into. There were several other men in bunks, a few of whom were waking from their slumber because of the sounds of the pirates' voices. They all turned toward the heavy metal door as it opened and a large man with a thick red beard stepped through. He stooped his enormous frame through the opening and grinned at the groggy group of men.

"You all had a good night's rest?" he said with a thick Scandinavian accent. "I am Vern, the quartermaster. You all can call me boss, sure enough." He turned and looked at each of the eight men having trouble standing or getting out of their bunks.

"This here ship is the *Lurline*, and the captain thanks you one and all for volunteering to work on this great voyage." Vern gave a devious grin.

"Ain't never been on a ship in my life," one of the men said, practically falling out of his bunk trying to stand up. "I sure as shit didn't volunteer to work on one!"

"Ha! Well, volunteer you did. Why else would you be on my ship?"

Sam Bellamy's stomach was turning as he looked around at the other men, then at Bart Roberts, who looked like he was partly recovered from whatever affliction they all were affected with.

"I would remember volunteering for ship work, especially as I've been a captain meself for many years," Roberts said.

"Captain? Ha! You'll be lucky to make cabin boy on *Lurline* dressed like that," Vern said, looming over Roberts and eyeing his seventeenth-century pirate clothes.

"You God damn shanghaied us, you bastard!" said an older man with a long mustache that curled at the ends.

"What does that mean? Shanghaied? What's that?" asked Sam.

The older man shook his head in disbelief and cursed under his breath. "The bastard drugged us. Stole us off onto this damn ship and we're… God knows where. Forcing us to work on this ship!"

Vern smiled and crossed his arms. It was then Bart noticed the pistol on Vern's hip. It was in a black holster with a black handle grip. He remembered seeing that type of thing on men in the saloon and walking around town. Bart had a feeling of vulnerability wash over him as he realized both he and Sam had been stripped not only of their jewelry but of all their weapons. He tried to remember what happened that would have put him in this predicament. He and Sam had wandered the streets of the strange city called San Francisco trying to make sense of their circumstances. Sam was completely broken-hearted once he realized he would never be able to return to his love, Mary. Bart had felt a kinship to the young man, mostly through Sam's reputation in the Pirate Republic. He was impressed that Sam had been able to become so successful in his pirating career in such a short time while maintaining and even expanding upon the pirate code of conduct. He saw a fresh version of his younger self in Bellamy.

Vern nodded to two hardened men who stood in the doorway. Neither man looked as if they had smiled since childhood. They entered the room and stood beside Vern.

"This here's Max and O'Farrell," Vern said, indicating Max as the lanky, bald man on his left and O'Farrell as the barrel-chested shorter man on the right. "They're going to give you your work duties and I expect their orders to be followed to the letter, lest I have to deal with you."

"I demand to talk with the captain!" one of the men yelled out.

"The captain is a busy man. Too busy to deal with the likes of you all. You'll just be dealin' with me. Consider my words as those of the captain's. I'll have no disagreements and no dereliction of duty from the crew," Vern said.

"What if we refuse to work for you?" the older man with the curling mustache asked.

Vern menacingly approached the man and growled, "If you ain't going to work, then no need for you to be on my ship. Maybe you try swimmin' back to San Francisco. Max, how far we from San Francisco now?"

"Hmm, maybe only a hundred or so miles. Easy swim... for a dolphin."

"Can you swim like a dolphin?" Vern smiled viciously.

The old man averted his eyes from the icy smile.

"I thought not. Well then, it's been decided. We've all got jobs to do, so let's have at it." With that, Vern turned and exited, leaving Max and O'Farrell to assign the group to their respected jobs on board the *Lurline*.

The temperature was stifling in the boiler room where Sam and Bart found themselves stationed along with a dozen or so men. The heat and steam permeated from every pipe and piece of metal that twisted and wove throughout the stern of the ship. The two pirates were in awe as they were led through the enormous ship, never imagining that such a marvel of advanced technology could exist. They had barely said a word to one another, not that it was easy to hear each other over the loud churning and droning of the engines. The two men were toiling, feeding the burners with coal while monitoring the temperature gauges as they were showed how to do by the stocky O'Farrell.

Sam wiped his drenched brow with his sleeve and was shocked to see it come away black with soot and coal dust. He looked over at Bart Roberts and saw that he, too, found himself coated with the same black muck. They had shed their coats and scarves prior to starting their tasks. He couldn't imagine there was a worse job on this ship. Sam would need to find a way to escape this fate with his new friend Bart.

91

He found himself wondering again if he was truly dead and hell was where he had really ended up. The intense heat only added to the viability of his nightmare. He was sinking into an abyss of despair as he continued to shovel the black coal into the mouth of the burner. Thoughts of his lovely bride-to-be began to bring tears rolling down his soot-covered cheeks. He had been so close to sailing back from the Caribbean to marry her. He had had a ship, crew, and many chests full of gold to prove to her family that he wasn't just some bilge rat wanting her hand with no means of support. Now all that was gone. He was back to doing the dirty work of a common simpleton in another time and place, with no hope of going back.

The older man they had met earlier with the long mustache was moving a cart full of coal when he passed by a burner that was loaded too heavily with fuel. It coughed up a burst of flame. The man shoveling coal into the burner jumped back, accidentally slamming his shovel into the side of the mustached man's head and sent him falling hard into a bulkhead. Bart was first to react and rushed to the man's aid. Sam also dropped his shovel and went over to assist the fallen man. They each took a side and pulled him to his feet. The man's head and arm were bleeding from deep gashes.

"You alright, mate?" Sam asked.

The man looked a bit dazed and put his hand on his head. He pulled his hand away to see the blood covering it and then started to sink to the floor again. Sam and Bart held him up from falling again but carefully lowered him to the floor so they could look him over. The head wound looked worse than the arm to Bart.

"It's pretty deep, mate," he said. "Might need some sutures. I'm going to wrap it to quell the bleeding."

Bart took off his shirt and tore the sleeve from the garment. The outside of the sleeve was filthy from soot, so he pulled the sleeve inside out and tied it around the man's head to stop the bleeding.

"Thanks. I'm Chester." The older man held his hand out for Bart's.

Bart shook the man's hand firmly.

"Bart. This here is Black Sam Bellamy."

Sam and Chester nodded hellos.

"What the devil is going on here!" bellowed O'Farrell as he came running up. "Why are you men sitting around on the job?"

The three men stared at the red-faced Irishman now holding a billy club in his hand, pointing it aggressively at them.

"This man is injured. Do you have a surgeon on board?" Sam asked.

"I don't give two shits if he's got bones poking out of his skin! Get your arses back to work," O'Farrell screamed at them, raising the club to strike one of them.

Sam and Bart looked ready to fight, but the frightened and bruised Chester held up his hands.

"I'm alright. I can work," he said.

O'Farrell looked hard at each of the men, daring them to challenge his authority.

"Then get to work, you shit sacks!"

O'Farrell watched as the men went back to their respective duties then stood leaning against a bulkhead, cleaning his teeth with a thin piece of wood while they worked. The noise of the engine was so loud that Bart and Sam were able to ask Chester questions about the workings of the ship without O'Farrell hearing. Chester had worked on other cargo ships doing maintenance and repairs for many years. He was able to explain the propulsion method these steam-powered ships operated under. Surprisingly,

Chester had never learned to sail nor worked on a sailing vessel in all his years. He spent most of his career on riverboats that were steam-powered and that used a paddlewheel to move them about.

Chester had traveled to San Francisco to become a miner but was unable to secure a claim for himself. He had worked off and on repairing ships docked in the harbor for about a year now. He told them it was becoming more and more common that men would be shanghai'd into working on cargo ships as it was difficult to find men to do these filthy and sometimes dangerous jobs.

Chester told them he had heard of this ship they were on, the *Lurline*. She was a cargo ship that made runs between San Francisco and the Hawaiian Islands delivering farming equipment and textiles, then bringing back pineapples, coconuts, sugar cane and native hardwoods to be sold at the San Francisco markets. The pirates surprised Chester by never having heard of the Hawaiian Islands before, as well as with their lack of knowledge regarding steam ships. He found their ignorance very odd, as they both claimed to be captains of sailing ships based in the Bahamas. Chester explained how the six boilers they were continually shoving forty-two tons of coal into each day powered turbines that turned the screw, moving the ship at a rate of seventeen knots. It took almost a hundred men working in four shifts to power the craft. The travel time to cover the entire 2,500 miles to Hawaii was just under a week, depending on the Pacific Ocean's conditions. This time of year, it wasn't uncommon to have to pass through a typhoon or smaller storm while on the journey. It wasn't a worry though with this size vessel, it just delayed their arrival.

The hard labor was taking a toll on Sam's back, and he stopped his shoveling to stretch it out as a new group of sad-looking men entered the engine room. It looked like the next shift was coming to relieve them. Sam glanced at Bart, who was covered in black soot with one sleeve missing from his shirt. Bart too was watching the new group enter, with Max trailing them. O'Farrell capped a flask of drink that he'd been sipping on and pushed himself up from the bulkhead he'd been leaning against. He approached Max, and the two conversed for a moment before O'Farrell walked to the center of the engine room to address the workforce.

"Alright, ladies, shift's over. Go get yourselves fed and rested."

Sam and Bart followed the line of men toward the exit. There were basins of water for the men to wash off the coal dust and grime the best they could. What Sam would give for the ability to dive into the warm, clear waters of the Caribbean right now.

Once they were as clean as they could get using the same dirty water as the other men, they followed the group through the various hallways and stairs until finally coming to a crowded mess hall. Sam remained in awe of the size of the ship. Even this kitchen and dining area impressed him with its ability to feed and sit a hundred men at a time. There was a counter that was serving plates of chicken, potatoes, vegetables, and bread. Sam and Bart both looked at the metal plates, forks, and knives to eat with and couldn't believe the fare that was served to the general crew.

The two pirates stood in line to fill their plates behind Chester. Once their turn arrived in front of the food servers, they were shoved aside by the stocky O'Farrell.

"Give way, you lot," he growled.

Bart held Sam back from confronting the foul man and they waited for him to have his plate filled by the cook and leave to sit with a small group of uniformed men in the far corner of the mess hall. Bart and Sam held their plates out next and watched with mouth-watering impatience as the food was dished out for them. They took their trays and searched the room for a space to sit.

Sam's stomach was growling like a hungry wolf from the smell of the hot food wafting to his nose as they made their way to a couple of empty seats. He and Bart sat at a long table across from their new friend Chester and a few other men that had worked their shift in the engine room. Sam savored the first bite he took of the seasoned chicken, then began to quickly devour the rest of his food. He glanced over at Bart to find him doing the same. He was quickly forgetting the fact that they had forced him to work on this ship, as his stomach was now in control of his mood. *Strange how basic needs can outweigh your sense of pride and freedom of choice*, he thought to himself.

"I don't think I've had a better meal," Bart said as he used his bread to wipe up the remaining potatoes and juices from his plate. His eyes hooded as he popped the piece into his mouth.

"The pay is bad, if any, but they will keep you fed. Otherwise, you wouldn't have the strength to shovel all that coal," Chester said.

"Just imagine what they are feeding the paying passengers," another man said as he shoved his mouth full of potatoes.

"What do you mean, paying passengers?" Sam asked.

"The top level has room for two hundred or so folks that are traveling to Hawaii," the man said.

"Two hundred people not working on the ship?"

The man looked quizzically at Sam. He pointed his fork around the room.

"Lower levels are for us, workers. Top level is for passengers. We live and eat down here; they live and eat up there."

"Mate, are you telling us there is more than one galley on this ship?" Bart asked.

"Some ships have several," Chester answered. "The larger ones that cater to first-class passengers have dining rooms to rival anything you'd find in a city like San Francisco. This one is mostly cargo, but they built it to carry passengers as well. Not as fancy as some, but a lot better living conditions than we've found ourselves. This route has become very profitable for the shipping company over the last couple years. Probably charge a couple months' wage for a ticket. Add in the five thousand tonnage of goods and you're talking quite a haul."

The two pirates looked at each other with interest. This ship and its contents could be the single greatest plunder that ever existed.

"Five thousand tons? We'd seen such ships when we… arrived in the harbor, remember, Sam?"

Sam nodded his head, deep in thought. He was still coming to grips with the idea of this all being real. The idea he and his pirate cohorts had been drowned into the late 1800s. Drowned was the only way for him to describe what happen to them. Drowned to reawaken with no hope of going back. He was going to have to live his life without his lost love in a strange new time, where ships could sail the ocean without sails or paddles. A world with advanced weapons that could fire many rounds, one after another without reloading. A time where giant ships crossed the ocean in weeks, not months, carrying enormous amounts of cargo in holds made entirely of metal. England and the Crown would have long ago forgotten their names and the crimes they committed. They were free again. Free from the pursuit of the pirate hunters. Free to pursue whatever course and desires they fancied.

"How many cannon she carry?" Sam asked.

Chester laughed and shook his head. *Who are these men?*

"No cannon. You expecting pirates?" Chester continued laughing, and a few other men at the table joined in.

CHAPTER 10 - THE JAMES GANG

Jesse led his brother Frank and the Younger brothers, Cole and Jim, into the alleyway behind the Wells Fargo Bank located on the corner of California Street and Montgomery Street. The building was a two-story red and brown brick structure with a small second-story balcony overhanging the front entrance. There was a heavy wooden door that served as the rear entrance to the bank and the cowboys stood watchfully outside. The entire backside of the building was windowless, so Jesse had chosen this location for them to ready their heist without being seen. The four men double-checked the load-out of their pistols and the double-barrel shotguns each of the Younger brothers carried.

"Frank and I will go around the front and force the guard inside the bank and lock the entrance. You two wait here in back for one of us to open up this rear door for you once we're inside," Jesse said.

"Them streets are more crowded than yesterday. We won't have much time before someone knows what's up," Cole said.

"We'll be quick, no safe unless it's open. Then make for the horses," Frank said.

The men nodded at each other, and Jesse and Frank made their way out of the alley with their heads on swivels.

Frank scanned the street for any sign of extra law enforcement while Jesse focused on the guard standing by the door of the bank. Jesse had a dollar coin in his hand that he began to flip up in the air, catching it then flipping it again. The guard noticed the two James brothers as they approached the bank, and Jesse continued to flip the coin. Jesse deliberately missed the catch as they approached and the guard, distracted, watched the coin fall to the walkway. He bent down to pick up the coin, and Frank and Jesse manhandled him through the door of the bank. Jesse grabbed the guard's pistol from its holster and a clubbed him in the head with the butt. The two brothers quickly pulled their bandanas over their noses to conceal their identities. Frank's pistol was already in his hand as Jesse closed and locked the door behind them and he pointed it around the room as all heads turned toward the commotion.

"Get your hands up or get shot!" Frank yelled out to the startled patrons and employees.

Jesse stuffed the guard's pistol into his belt and pulled his own from its holster, threatening each person in the bank. There were three patrons making transactions and three employees behind the barred counter. Jesse quickly crossed the room, pointing his gun at the nearest teller.

"Open the door," Jesse said with menace.

"I… I'm not supposed to," stuttered the teller.

"Are you supposed to die today?"

Jesse was pointing his pistol through the bars at the man. He pulled back the hammer of the gun, cocking it audibly. The man was sweating and looked faint.

"Open it!" Jesse yelled.

The man practically jumped and with his hands in the air, he moved to the locked door and fumbled a moment with his keys as Jesse followed with his pistol pointing at the man's head. The moment the key turned in the lock, Jesse slammed the door open, knocking the man off his feet.

"Everyone inside and have a squat over there!" Frank said as he ushered the patrons and employees against the wall inside the teller's room.

Jesse made his way to the rear of the bank and unlatched the door for Cole and Jim to enter. The three cowboys rushed back into the teller's room, where Frank stood guard.

Jim roughly tossed a bag to the first patron and brandished his shotgun at him.

"Empty your pockets into the bag, then pass it down. I better not see a speck of jewelry on you that doesn't go in the bag lest I fill your gut full of lead."

Jesse and Cole went through the teller's drawers, pulling out cash, coin, and a few gold nuggets to put in their saddlebags. Jesse looked back at the safe sitting closed and locked against the far wall. He licked his lips and looked over at the teller with the keys. He strutted over and pulled his pistol from its holster and placed it against the man's head.

"Open the safe."

Jim looked questioningly from the safe to Jesse.

"I thought we were going to leave the safe if it was locked."

"We got time," Jesse said.

Jim looked out at the front door. Just then, a jarring noise could be heard as a patron stood outside and tried to open the locked door. The man then put his face up to the window to peer inside the bank.

"We ain't got time!" Jim said.

"We got time! Now open the safe!" Jesse yelled at the teller and grabbed the man's shirt, pulling him up. Jesse forced the now crying man to the safe and held his pistol to the back of his head. "Open it."

"God damn it," Jim muttered under his breath. "Cole, watch the front. We could have law here any minute."

The teller fumbled and shook as he tried to turn the dial for the correct combination, while Jesse continued to threaten him.

"Come on, come on," Frank said.

CLICK. The safe's lock opened, and the teller leaned back. Jesse pushed the man out of the way and swung the safe's door open, revealing neatly stacked bills and a tray full of small gold nuggets. The four cowboys stared at the contents of the safe from where they stood. A broad smile formed on Jesse's face. He looked at Cole and raised his eyebrows at him.

"Alright, you can gloat later. Let's pack it up," Cole said.

"Drop yar weapon, bastard!" Anne Bonny yelled as she entered the room from the back.

The entire crowd turned in surprise to see the fiery-haired woman holding a pair of flintlock pistols, one pointed at Jesse, the other in the direction of Jim, Cole, and Frank. Jesse immediately knew who she was, and a sly smile crossed his lips.

"Someone forgot to lock the back door," he said.

"You took my love from me, you bastard!" Anne spit out her words.

"Now that was a fair draw, miss. Nor was it my idea to have it in the first place."

"You started it with your insults. Jack was honor-bound."

"Maybe that's partly true, but he asked for pistols," Jesse said, raising his hands a bit but still holding his pistol in one.

"He could have just punched Jesse in the eye instead," Jim Younger said.

"I'm honor-bound to avenge his death, so we's be having a duel as well," Anne said.

"We're kind of in the middle of robbing this bank, girl, so maybe this can wait," Frank said.

There was a loud knocking on the front door. A quick glance by all showed a small crowd out front trying to peer inside through the windows. Anne glanced at the contents of the safe, eyeing the gold and stacks of bills.

"Open up this door!" A shout came from outside the front door, along with more pounding.

"We gotta go!" Frank yelled.

"Why don't we finish here, then you and I can finish our issue after? That way, all this money doesn't go to waste," Jesse said to Anne.

Anne looked again at the safe, then back at Jesse. A moment passed without any talking or movement other than the pounding on the front door. Jesse took her silence as acceptance and nodded to Cole. Jesse remained with his hands up, and Cole emptied the contents of the safe into his saddlebag, that he then hefted to his shoulder. Jesse indicated the back door with his head to Anne and she watchfully backed up toward the rear exit. A smile crossed Jesse's face, and he slowly put his hands down. Anne and the four cowboys exited into the alleyway behind the bank and stood facing each other. Seconds later, two men with rifles and metal stars on their chests burst into the alleyway.

"Drop 'em!" one of the lawmen yelled.

The four cowboys turned toward the lawmen and opened fire, sending the pair into cover behind the corner. A chaos of bullets erupted from both sides and the cowboys started down the alley in the opposite direction to the lawmen. Anne was at a crossroads with her two pistols. One still trained on Jesse but the other she pointed at the lawmen firing in her direction indiscriminately. She could shoot Jesse now, but the odds were that she would be the next one shot, either by the lawmen or the cowboys. She cringed as a bullet from the corner of the alley whizzed by her cheek, narrowly missing her. Two more lawmen entered the fray. One stood his ground out in the open, firing his rifle in her direction. Anne made her decision by firing both pistols at the man, scoring each time, hitting the man in his chest, sending him falling back onto the hard ground.

"Let's go!" Jesse yelled to her, and she turned and followed Frank, Cole, and Jim further down the alleyway, with Jesse covering their exit. More men were pouring into the chase behind them as they took a few turns on their escape route and continued running for a few blocks. The crew stopped for a breather a short way from a main street. Anne pulled an empty pistol from her belt along with a powder case and ball. Jesse watched as she expertly filled the muzzle and loaded the shot. He shook his head and pulled from his own belt the pistol that he took from the guard and spun it so that the grip was out toward her. She glanced at the revolver, then into Jesse's captivating eyes before shoving her own flintlock back into her belt and taking the revolver. Jesse smirked at her, then nodded for the group to continue out into the street.

"Stop! Hold it!" Several armed men shouted at the group when they emerged onto the open street. The lawmen were advancing toward them, pointing rifles and pistols. Pedestrians shouted and ran from the scene. Several wagons pulled away and sped in the opposite direction as the threat of violence arose from the two groups. Anne pointed her newly acquired revolver at the oncoming lawmen and opened fire, sending the men in search of cover. The men began to fire back as the bandits made a right-hand turn down the next street.

"Behind that church over there!" Jim shouted.

The crew made a dash for the white-painted wooden church that stood on the next corner. Just as they were arriving at the building, a lawman on horseback emerged from the street in front of them, pistol in hand. The lawman fired a couple rounds at them and successfully clipped Jim in the arm, sending him spinning to the ground next to a horseless wagon parked near the church. Jesse fired back at the lawman but missed, and the bandits took cover behind the wagon.

"You hurt bad?" Cole asked his brother.

Jim was holding his hand over his wound and grimacing in pain. Frank pulled Jim's hand from his arm and looked at the damage.

"Ah, he'll live. If we can get out of here, that is," he said.

Jesse stuck his head out from behind the wagon to take a look and almost got it blown off by the lawman on horseback, pacing on the other side.

"Damn, more coming up the road. I'll cover you. Count of three," Jesse said.

Anne nodded at Jesse and looked over at the church. It was about twenty yards away. Jesse stood to one side of the wagon as the others readied their escape on the other.

"One, two... three!" Jesse spun around the wagon and started giving covering fire.

Cole, Jim, Frank, and Anne darted toward the church. They got about halfway when Jim tripped while holding his bleeding arm and went down in front of Anne. She stumbled on top of him and rolled off into the dirt. She turned from her position on the ground to see Jesse backing up toward them while in a shoot-out with the horse-mounted lawman. Jesse's pistol went CLICK after he had used up all the ammo. The horse reared up, then settled down on all fours, giving the lawman a clear shot at Jesse standing there. The lawman took careful aim and pulled back on the trigger. BLAM! Jesse stood there, not knowing if the man had missed or if he just didn't feel the shot yet. He watched as the lawman's gun slowly dropped from his hand, then he followed it to the ground, dead from a wound in his chest.

Jesse turned to see Anne there next to Jim, holding the pistol he had given her, smoke swirling around the barrel. Anne and Jesse stared at one another for a beat.

"Let's get the hell out of here," Jim said, gathering himself up.

Frank and Cole arrived from the back of the church on horseback, each holding the reins of an additional horse. Jim painfully climbed onto one of them. Jesse looked back to see several lawmen rushing down the street toward them. He mounted his horse, then circled it around Anne. Jesse held his hand out toward her. She looked at his outstretched hand, then glanced at the lawmen.

"Come on!" Jesse shouted at her.

Anne turned and looked up at Jesse. He had that crooked smile on his face. She quickly made her decision and grabbed Jesse's hand. In one fluid motion, he swung her up behind him. Anne pointed her revolver at the lawmen running toward them and fired her last two rounds.

"Yaa!" Jesse yelled at his horse, and the bandits took off at a fast gallop out of town.

Anne held tight to Jesse's waist while her thoughts raged at her. They had been riding fast for over thirty minutes, and the horses were foaming with exhaustion. She had contemplated reaching for her knife and slitting Jesse's throat in revenge several times. It would be easy to kill him, slide him off the horse and take the reins herself. This man had killed her poor Jack just yesterday. How did she wind up riding on the back of his horse, saving his life and robbing a bank alongside him and his gang of cowboys? Anne was no stranger to the rough and wild life that men like Jack and Jesse lived. She herself could be judged as a dangerous and deadly woman. Anne was only thirteen when she stabbed one of her father's servant girls, after she squealed on her for a tryst that she'd had with a young man who was a sailor on one of her father's merchant ships. Anne's father had quickly sent that man on a year-long voyage to the Orient, never to return.

She had married her husband, James Bonny, at seventeen. James had bragged about being an accomplished sailor and a well-known pirate. He had promised her a life of adventure, but she found out years later he was a coward, known for double-crossing other pirates. He turned out to be a poor sailor and a worse pirate. Anne's father had seen through James' lies and exaggerations. He disapproved of Anne secretly marrying him and disowned her, kicking her out of his plantation homestead. Homeless and cut out of any inheritance or family money, Anne and James decided to move to the pirate haven of Nassau, but not before Anne, in a drunken rage, burned her father's plantation house to the ground in retaliation.

How life can change in the falling of a knife. In a matter of days, Anne had lost both her husband and her lover. She chuckled to herself with a moment of self-loathing as she held the muscular torso of the man who successfully dueled Calico Jack Rackham, her fallen sweetheart. Her quest for vengeance was already beginning to fade. She recalled a saying from her best friend Mary: *Bury the dead, before they get in the way of the living.*

Anne was brought out of her musing as Jesse slowed his horse by pulling the reins. The four horses stopped just off the trail in front of an old,

106

abandoned mine-shaft. She slid down from the horse and looked around at the broken tools and piles of rocks and lumber. The cowboys dismounted their horses and Jim went to sit, exhausted, holding his injured arm with his back against a fallen tree.

Frank looked over at Anne and asked, "You got any skills at tending to wounded men?"

"I ain't no nursemaid," Anne said sourly as she toured the site.

Cole and Frank walked over to look at Jim's arm. It was still weeping blood, and Cole helped his brother remove his bloody shirt. Looking closely at Jim's arm, he could see the bullet went straight through, missing the bone in his upper arm. He ripped the other sleeve from the discarded shirt and used it as a bandage to tie around the wound, which would hopefully stop the blood from flowing out.

"Going to need to be cleaned and stitched up," Cole said.

"Why don't you boys head to San Pedro, find a doc to patch Jim up?" Frank said to the brothers.

Anne was fiddling with her new revolver and managed to open the spinning chamber. She pulled out one of the discharged rounds and peered at it, turning it over in her hand. Jesse watched while he tied his horse to the branch of a tree. Anne popped all the rounds out and was examining them as Jesse walked up.

"They're spent. Can't load them the way you do your flintlock." Jesse pulled a live round from his belt, which had small loop holders for about a dozen bullets. He held the round out and Anne went to grab it, but Jesse pulled it back and closed his fist around the bullet. Anne looked up at him with furrowed brows.

"I'll reload you if you promise you aren't going to use them on me or my boys."

Anne put on her performance smile and said sweetly, "Now why would you have such evil thoughts about me?" She held out her hand for the rounds.

"Don't trust that girl, Jesse," Cole said as he went to his horse to grab his loaded saddlebag of loot from the bank. "Let's divide this up and separate as usual. We'll meet back up in San Francisco after I get Jim patched up in a maybe a week."

"Yes, lads, what's the take… and what's my share?" Anne asked.

"Your share?" Cole asked. "You don't get a share. You ain't part of the gang."

Anne aggressively approached Cole and poked at his chest while her other hand held the hilt of her dagger. "You wouldn't have gotten away with the loot if it weren't for me. You'd be dead." Anne turned to Jesse. "You'd be dead for sure. It was me that saved your skin from being shot by that horseman. Seems I'm entitled to an equal share of this here plunder. Twenty percent and I'll be on my way." Cole burst out laughing and, quick as a flash, Anne had her knife at his throat. Frank quickly drew his pistol and pointed it at Anne, but Anne's eyes never left Cole as he raised his chin high to keep her blade from piercing his neck. Cole slowly raised his hands.

"Drop the knife, woman," Frank said.

"Not until we agree on the split," Anne said as she slid her loaded flintlock pistol from her belt and pointed it at Cole's belly.

"God damn it, Jesse, do something with her!" Cole stuttered, still craning his chin higher.

Jesse shook his head, and a bit of a smile crossed his lips. He raised his hands in the air and approached Anne and Cole. "Alright, little miss, alright. You've made your point. You did aid a bit in our getaway, even if your first goal was to put a bullet in me out of revenge. Now you ain't part of our gang, nor did you take part in the planning or the robbing. The way I see it, we could part with five percent of the take to you."

"What the God damn hell are you talking about, Jesse?" Frank asked.

Jesse continued to approach Anne and Cole and waved his brother off, motioning with his hand for him to cool down.

"Fifteen," Anne responded without looking away from Cole's face.

"Ten," Jesse countered.

Anne considered the offer for a couple of seconds. She pulled the knife from Cole's throat but kept her pistol ready. She re-sheathed the blade and turned to Jesse with her hand out to shake. "Deal." Jesse shook her hand with a grin and head shake.

"Who are you?" Jesse asked.

"Anne Bonny. Co-commander of the sloop, *William*." The cowboys just stared at her with questioning looks. "Well, now that I think of it, since you went and killed Jack, I would be the only remaining commander of the *William*. So, there you have it. And who are you lot? I heard your name is Jesse James."

Jesse nodded his head. He pointed his chin at Frank. "My brother Frank, that one you rudely had a knife to be Cole and his now gimpy brother over there is Jim."

"I ain't no gimp. I'll be fine," Jim said, standing up.

"Alright then, let's divide the take, give Miss Bonny her share and be on our ways," Jesse said.

CHAPTER 11 - LOCKED & LOADED

Edward Thatch stood across the street from the storefront with a sign in the window that said ROY AND SONS – GUNS, AMMO, AND FISHING GEAR. As he gazed at the wooden, one-story building, he let a smile cross his lips. He could hardly contain his excitement at what marvels he might find behind that door. Thatch didn't see himself as an overly violent man, surely no more than the average pirate. He wasn't one to be cruel without justification. Thatch relied more on fear and intimidation to achieve his goals. He found that with enough fear, he could plunder without harming, sinking, or destroying the treasure he sought. Many pirates made the mistake of taking things too far. It's much harder to pull gold from a ship that you sunk than one that has surrendered to you. Most sailors didn't want to die protecting some merchant's goods whom they hadn't and most likely would never meet. If you started with violence, you left them with little choice but to retaliate with violence. He had learned the lesson that showing more guns, bigger guns, usually won the day, even without having fired a shot.

"Not good place to steal from," Tom said.

Thatch looked down at his cabin boy, now dressed in dark blue pants, a white shirt, and a brown waistcoat.

"Sound advice, boy. We won't be stealing from them."

"You have money? You had no pockets."

"I have these," Thatch said, showing Tom his rings as he moved his fingers like he was playing a harpsichord. Several rings were adorned with gems and others were thick gold bands with artistic details. "I'll pocket a few so they don't get too greedy." He stuffed a few rings in the pocket of his pants and crossed the street after a horse-drawn wagon noisily drove by.

They stood in front of the shop's door, and Thatch waited.

"Door, boy."

Tom jumped in front and opened the door for Thatch to enter. As Thatch stepped inside, a whistle escaped his lips.

There was a counter at the rear of the store and shelves lined the side walls. Behind the counter, the wall bristled with rifles of varying lengths that covered the entire width of the store. The shelves along the sides were inventoried with fishing gear, holsters, belts, ammo knives and hats. Two men were behind the counter, both about thirty years old, bearded, and bald headed. *These two are definitely related*, thought Thatch, probably the sons of Roy as the sign outside telegraphed. One of the men was sitting in a chair busily working at a desk behind the counter. The other watched Thatch and Tom enter with interest.

"Welcome, friends. What can we help you with?"

Thatch approached the counter, eyes roaming around, admiring the array of weapons displayed.

"I'm looking for pistols, the ones that hold many rounds," Thatch said.

"Well, we have plenty of revolvers to choose from. You fancy a Colt, or a Remington? I've got your standard six shooters, but I did get this foreign model that is a seven shot. It's got some heft to it." The man began pulling several pistols from behind the counter and laying them out in a row. Thatch picked up the first one and held it in his hand, marveling at the workmanship and moving parts. He fumbled a bit with the chamber, turning it to see how it moved.

"Here, let me show you how this works. You look a bit green with guns," the man said to Thatch, taking the pistol from his hand. Under other circumstances Thatch would have throttled him, but he was interested in how it operated, so he tolerated the man's insolence. Thatch watched as the man expertly ran through the spinning chamber, the trigger, the sights, and loading procedure. He then handed the unloaded pistol back and Thatch worked through all the mechanisms that the man had shown him.

"That there is the Colt 45. Excellent firearm with quick action and heavy stopping power."

Thatch spent time looking over each pistol that lay on the counter. He turned and eyed the shelves that displayed holsters and belts. Some of the belts had small loops that would hold spare bullets. He glanced at Tom, who was looking closely at the pistol that held seven rounds. He was trying to make out the writing that was in another language on the bottom of the grip. Thatch recognized the writing as Russian, though it was a language he hadn't studied.

"Well, what do you say? Any of these seem the right one for you, mister?"

Thatch turned to the man and pointed at each pistol. "I'll take two of the Colts, one Remington, the Russian, some of the belts and holsters." Thatch looked at the wall with fishing gear that also held many knives. "And several of them blades."

The man stared for a moment, dumbstruck, and then looked over at his brother. His brother had finally got his nose out of the paperwork on his desk at Thatch's verbal list and raised his thick eyebrows in return.

"Well, then... I trust you have funds for these purchases?" the brother sitting asked.

Thatch removed several of his rings and set them on the counter. The second brother got up from his chair and came over to look at the rings. He took in his hand one that had a large ruby in the center. His eyes went up to his brother, then focused on Thatch.

"That ruby real? Ain't glass, is it?"

"That is a question I will not stoop to answer," growled Thatch, taking offense.

The second brother found a jeweler's loupe and examined the ruby as well as the other rings on the counter. The first brother waited along with Thatch and Tom for the other brother to approve the trade while he weighed, then bit with his teeth on the gold rings. He finally looked at his brother and nodded his head.

"Fair trade, friend. Let's get you locked and loaded up," the first brother said.

Thatch looked down at Tom, who was still examining the Russian pistol.

"You got something for the boy?" Thatch asked. Tom's face lit up with a smile.

A few minutes later, Thatch and Tom exited the shop and walked side by side down the wooden sidewalk. Passersby openly gaped and steered clear of them. Thatch caught a glance of his reflection in a store window he passed, and it pleased him greatly. He wore a holstered belt lined with bullets around his waist, which held the two matching Colt 45s against each hip. His chest held two more holstered belts on the outside of his waistcoat, each holding the two other pistols. On his right lower leg, he had a hunting knife strapped in a leather sheath, one on his waistbelt in front and one more attached to the chest mounted pistol belt. He looked down at his cabin boy, who held his gleaming new pistol in both hands, turning it with admiration. It was small and compact, with a polished pearl grip.

"What did the man say yours was called?"

"Derringer"

"It's a beauty. First one?"

Tom nodded his head. He repeatedly holstered it and pulled it out from a chest-strapped holster under his jacket. Two older women who were sitting in chairs out front of a clothing store saw this and scoffed, making faces while they watched him draw the small gun and wave it around. Thatched noticed this and shot them a devilish grin. "He's a wild one, ladies. Best watch out before he shoots those ratty wigs right off your heads." Thatch let out a hardy laugh as he passed by. Once they passed around the corner, he put his hand on the boy's pistol.

"Let's keep it safe and stowed for now. If it's your first, I'll teach you how to use it, aim it, clean it. Treat your weapons right and they'll be in good working order for when you need them. That's another pirate code. You remembering them codes as I tell you?"

"Yes, Captain."

"That's a good lad." Thatch stopped at a street corner. He looked down each way. "Time to find me mates. You ever heard of a drinking place called The Paris?"

Tom nodded. "Everyone has."

"Well then, lead the way."

Colette Dallaire shuffled the single deck of cards with nimble fingers, flipping them gracefully between each other like they were performing a choreographed dance. The young ranch hand directly across from her was watching with an awed expression on his face. She glanced at his eyes, then realized he wasn't paying so much attention to her card skills as the cleavage visible above her fitted dress. She smiled back at him, not because she liked the attention, but she now knew he was an easy mark. This was the kind of man who would sit at the table until all his money was gone and cause no trouble, despite the outcome. It was the fellers that had eyes only for the cards she worried most about. Twenty-one was a game that wasn't overly difficult to increase your odds if you were good at counting cards. This was something Colette had excelled at for as long as she could remember. A good head for numbers was what her dad had called it. Something her mother wasn't so proud of. *A girl's head should get fuzzy when it comes to numbers. Just remember your posture and poise Colette*, her mom had always said to her. *That's the way to find a good man.* She looked over at the other two men seated at her table. One was a supply store owner who was on his way to being drunk as a skunk by nightfall. The man seated at the far right was the one she would have to watch. His eyes never left the cards. He wasn't counting, that she knew. His name was Gabriel, one of the sergeants in the police force. He made his rounds each week, gambling at different halls, mostly losing his money. Colette did her best to guide him in choosing the correct play so that the damage was minimal or that he would walk away with a little more than he came in with. Best to keep the law on her side, or at least not against her. Gabriel stared so hard at Colette's hand that she was sure he was trying his best to see through to the other side of the cards.

"You boys ready for another round of drinks?" Colette asked.

The men just nodded or grunted assent. Colette smiled and motioned to one of the waitress girls, who then busied herself at the bar preparing drinks. The Paris was already lively this afternoon with drinkers and gamblers. Colette sometimes marveled at her own ability to grow her saloon's business as fast as she had. In just under two years, The Paris had become the premier saloon and gambling hall on the Barbary Coast. San Francisco was the fastest growing city in the United States and at this rate, she would need to expand into a second location or add to the building she currently owned. Colette saw opportunity everywhere she looked. She just needed to keep investing her profits. She had been quietly buying plots of land and several buildings along the waterfront for the past several months. Soon she would not have to sit in front of these men dealing cards, smelling their foul breath, and having to put up with their leering eyes. Colette would promote one of the ladies working for her to manager and let them run The Paris. She was growing tired of dealing with the troublesome cowboys, gangsters, thieves, and politicians that blew through her door.

She looked up at that moment as the door swung open and the picture of the devil himself entered. It was that wild man from the other night with the giant black beard twisted in braids. He stood momentarily in the doorway, surveying his surroundings with his sharp blue eyes that existed in contrast below the heavy black brows. Gone was the ornate old-fashioned clothing that he had worn soaking wet from his last appearance. Now he was elegantly dressed in pants, white shirt and fitted waistcoat. His antique weapons were replaced with an excessive number of new pistols and knives strapped to his body. Colette imperceptibly shook her head. The man had a flare for the grandiose. His name, Thatch, popped into her head as he turned his gaze on her. His eyes bored into hers and that cat-that-ate-the-canary grin of his formed on his face. Colette immediately chastised herself as she felt an uncontrolled blush rise in her cheeks. She felt sure that he had noticed because he strutted, self-assured, over to her table, and elegantly bowed, then in a roguish fashion sat in the vacant seat of her table. Once he was seated, she noticed a small Chinese boy, similarly dressed, standing behind him.

"Good afternoon, Mr. Thatch. Welcome back to The Paris. We were sorry to see you leave in such haste last night," Colette said.

"It was rude of me to depart without saying so much as a goodbye. I hope that you could forgive my manners, Miss Dallaire."

Colette began the dealing of the cards to the other three men as she spoke with Thatch.

"I suppose you have returned to claim the belongings that you had left behind."

"That, and if you might know the whereabouts of me friends."

Colette smiled and flipped one of her cards over for the players to see. It was a six which put a smile on all the players' lips.

"I have put aside your clothing, but you should know that the strange military men that... interrupted your evening confiscated your weapons," Colette said.

"That is of no matter, I was able to acquire new armament," Thatch said with a wave of his hand.

"I can see that." Colette motioned to the players if they would like additional cards, and all declined. She flipped over her second card that showed a ten, giving her the total of sixteen. She dealt herself an additional card that showed a seven. A muted round of cheers emerged from the players as Colette busted and gave them winning hands. She paid out the men and gathered the cards.

"The men and women that had accompanied you had mostly gone their separate ways after that poor young feller you were with was killed in the gunfight. The only two who remained once you went upstairs were the older bald man and the angry-looking feller that also took a pretty waitress to a room. He then escaped out the back during your scuffle. The bald man seemed to be on better terms with the military men than you had been. They left together shortly after and I haven't seen them since, nor any of your friends."

Thatch leaned back in his chair. "Jennings. It's as I thought. I never did trust the man. It makes more sense now that he'd be in league with the Royal Navy."

"Royal Navy?" asked Gabriel. He looked Thatch up and down. "You some sort of outlaw?" Thatch looked over at the man, noticing the badge clipped to his vest.

"A misunderstanding. I'm just a humble trader from England. I assure you I have broken none of your laws in this fine town," Thatch said with a smile.

"See to it that you don't," Gabriel said after setting his money down for his next bet.

"I'm thirsty, Captain," Tom said from behind Thatch.

"Aye, Tom. Acquire us a bottle of rum." Thatch motioned the boy to the bar and Tom quickly made his way over.

Colette shook her head gently. "We don't allow children in The Paris, Mr. Thatch."

Thatch turned and looked at Tom standing at the bar trying to get the attention of the large native barkeep and gave a hearty laugh.

"Child? Old Tom there is part of me crew. He may be small, but he's twenty years old, I assure you." He smiled at Colette and the men at the table and then leaned in conspiratorially. "We all know these Chinese are of a small stature. I heard it's because of their strange diet. Don't let him hear you talk about his size, though; he has a fuse to match his height and the nastiness of an angered cobra. He joined me crew two years ago after we captured a sloop en route to New Providence from the Orient. Turned out old Tom was quite the tailor and skilled at repairing worn and damaged sails." Colette ignored the obvious lie and continued to deal her game. She nodded consent to her large native bartender to give the boy the bottle of rum.

"Are you going to play a hand or just continue to flap your gums?" Gabriel asked.

"Hmm, I do remember enjoying the winnings from my last round playing Miss Dallaire's clever little game," Thatch said.

"Do you have any money to wager, Mr. Thatch?" asked Colette.

"Were there any coins left in my discarded clothing I left in your room last night?"

Colette once again blushed against Thatch's stare. She watched his lips turn the slightest bit up beneath his braided black beard as he played with the insinuation that she had shared that room with him. "Let me ask the waitress who entertained you." She turned to look around the room.

"No matter, I happen to have several paper notes I exchanged earlier." Thatch removed bills from his pocket and set them on the table. Tom arrived with the bottle of rum, an empty glass, and a glass filled with water. Thatch poured a healthy portion of the caramel-colored rum into the tumbler and drank the contents. "Ahh, that is fine." He looked over at Tom, who had finished off his water and held out his hand for Tom's glass. Thatch poured a few fingers of rum into the glass and handed it back to the boy. He then poured himself another helping. He looked at Colette as she gave a slight scowl toward him, and he only raised an eyebrow in response.

"Are we playing cards?" Gabriel moaned.

"We are," Colette said and began to deal the hand, while watchfully eyeing the young boy sip tentatively on his glass of rum.

Several card hands and half a bottle of rum later, the saloon door opened, and the booming voice of Black Caesar rang through the hall. "Captain Blackbeard!" he said, and his long strides quickly brought him to the gambling table where Thatch sat.

Thatch rose and clasped the big man's arm in greeting.

"In the flesh," Thatch said as Hornigold, Charlotte, Mary, and Vane each greeted him as well. "Let's find a table to talk in private." Thatch pushed a small stack of bills toward Colette. "Food and drink for me mates, Miss Dallaire, if you please." He then led the pirates to an empty back table with Tom trailing behind. They all sat and then stared in question while Tom took a seat at the end.

"This here's Mr. Tom, me new cabin boy. He's proven to be of great value in this unfamiliar port. He hasn't taken the pirate oath but been living the life for a long time, so treat him as one of our crew."

Vane rolled his eyes and sighed audibly. "We ain't a crew."

"We are all pirates, maybe the only ones left, so we need to stay together crew or not," Hornigold said.

Tom sat silently, watching the adults with his brow furrowed. Charlotte looked at the boy while cleaning her fingernails with a cut-throat dagger. She squinted one tan eye at him. Tom squinted an eye at her in mimic.

"Does your cabin boy talk?" Charlotte asked.

"When appropriate. Now fill me in on what has happened since you laid poor Calico Jack to rest," Thatch said.

CHAPTER 12 – OUTLAWS

Anne steadied herself with a fistful of the cloth from the back of Jesse's jacket while the horse carrying them trotted along. Anne had been talking Jesse's ear off for an hour now about her travels and boasting of all the battles she took part in and ships she had plundered. Jesse, somewhat amused, asked a few questions during her dialog while his brother Frank periodically sighed with exasperation as he tried to remain stoic and uninterested.

"How many banks have you raided?" said Anne.

"I don't rightly know. Frank, how many banks you figure we robbed?" asked Jesse.

Frank shook his head in annoyance as he rode next to them.

"I don't know why we can't just leave this girl on the side of the road and continue on our way," Frank grumbled.

"Maybe about twenty or so robberies if you count stagecoaches and trains among the total," said Jesse.

"Twenty? That all! Jack and me and Mary took so many ships we lost count. Though, thinking, with just the four of you, makes it hard to plunder anything of real size. Can't man a sloop with such a small crew. We had eighty men under our command. What's a train?"

"You don't know what a train is?" asked Jesse.

"She's from the seventeen hundreds, remember? The girl's done crazy! Jesus! Pirates, cannons, swords. This ride would be a lot more peaceful if we could at least gag her and tie her to the back of your horse," Frank said.

Anne whipped a dagger from her side and brandished it in Frank's direction.

"You just try it, ya bilge-sucking dog!" she growled.

"Now, now, Miss Bonny, old Frank just has no imagination," Jesse said. "Can't blame him for that. He don't believe the world has secrets that it keeps from the likes of simple men like him."

"You saying you believe one word out this loon's mouth?" asked Frank.

"I ain't lying. Few days ago, we was in the port of Nassau in the Caribbean Ocean. King George was on the throne, and it was the God damn year 1718. We was all aboard Blackbeard's frigate discussing the King's pardon when the devil of a storm hit, never seen anything like it. The anchors was cut, and we were pulled out of the harbor by the tide. We came on deck to see fifty-foot swells. Blackbeard, like a madman, drove us up and over those monsters. Many of the crew washed over the side to rest in Davy Jones' locker. An then the sea began to swirl, and swirl. We was caught in it, spinning. The sea opened up like the mouth of a Kraken and swallowed the ship an' all of us whole. I seen my Jack get swept overboard, and Mary too. I just remember the water surrounding us and the darkness closing is as we was pulled to the bottom. And then... then..." Anne felt a tear form in her eye.

"And then you wind up here, in the future," Jesse said.

Anne nodded her head. Frank shook his in disbelief. They rode for a few moments in silence.

"So, is this... Blackbeard's ship still in the harbor? Got any treasure chests on it?" Frank asked.

"I think I heard of that pirate. Maybe from a dime novel? He was richest, right?" Jesse asked.

"Yeah, it's got treasure on it. No, he ain't the richest. That be Black Sam Bellamy. Black Sam, he captured one Spanish galleon with more than five tons of treasure on it. Blackbeard... I'd say he's the fiercest pirate. Most ships just surrender when they know it's him looking to plunder their holds. But his treasure, it's still on his ship. Problem is, his ship is at the bottom of that cold bay. It sunk just after we got here. Storm ripped holes in the starboard side."

"Blackbeard, Black Sam, what was your man's name... Calico? You all sure have colorful outlaw names, I'll give you that. Maybe you need a name like that, Jesse. You got your Billy the Kid, that young cattle rustler that everyone asks you about. There's old Wild Bill too." Frank looked Jesse up and down. "You do dress real nice... how 'bout Gentleman Jesse?" Frank gave a laugh.

"Yeah, you'd like that, wouldn't ya?" Jesse said.

The three were cresting a hill when they spotted a stagecoach stopped on the opposite side of a rocky creek. The coach was leaning to one side as one of the spoked wheels was off, resting on a pile of rocks. Two men were leaning over the wheel, attempting to repair it. There was a heavy-set balding man in a dark suit fanning his sweaty face with his hat as he sat on a large, flat river rock. The suited man looked up at the sound of trotting horses and alerted the two men working on the wheel. They each looked up with concern at the two oncoming horses. The two men stood up and their hands rested on their holstered pistols.

"What have we here?" Jesse whispered.

"Opportunity," Anne breathed.

Frank glanced at the couple riding beside him, noticing a shared yearning for adventure and a hint of restlessness etched into each of their faces. He slowly shook his head as he was now becoming accustomed to doing since being introduced to this fiery young woman. He held up a hand in greeting to the three men now standing next to the disabled stagecoach.

"You boys having some troubles with your coach?" Frank asked as they rode up.

"A bit," said one of the men holding a large wrench in one hand with grease covering his arm.

"Need a hand with your repairs, friend?" Jesse asked.

The three men eyed Jesse and Frank suspiciously.

"We're nearly done. You folks heading into San Francisco?" the sweaty suited man asked.

"That's right." Frank eyed the large luggage compartment on the back of the coach. "Been traveling far?"

"Not so far… started out in the Arizona territory. I have some business to attend to in San Francisco."

"What sort of business are you in?" asked Anne as she slid off Jesse's horse. The three men stared at Anne, taken aback by her beauty and the fact that her shirt was showing more cleavage than the men had ever seen outside a brothel. Anne approached the luggage case and ran her hand over the top, noticing the padlock securing it closed.

"Liquor distribution," the man said, wiping a fresh sheen of sweet from his forehead.

"Rum?" asked Anne, rolling the r.

"Kentucky bourbon. Finest you'd taste anywhere."

Anne pulled on the lock to test its latch mechanism, making the man nervous. The two other men who were hired as driver and shotgun glanced from Anne to the two cowboys watching from horseback, dusters pulled away from their holstered pistols.

"Bourbon, you say? Turns out Jesse and Frank over there are connoisseurs of bourbon. What do you say we put your claim to the test?" Anne glanced at Jesse. "You boys want to sample this man's gut rot to see if it lives up to being the finest anywhere?"

"Well, I don't…" the balding man started to protest.

"I could use a drink 'bout now," Jesse interrupted. "Frank, care for a swig?"

"No James ever turned down Kentucky bourbon," Frank said through squinted eyes that never left the three men standing near the wagon. The balding man stared at Frank and swallowed hard. He then looked at Jesse and the color went out of his face as the last name of James rang a bell.

"You two Jesse and Frank James?"

"Mhmm," said Jesse with the slightest grin.

"How 'bout you open up that trunk?" said Anne.

The man patted his shirt pockets and jacket.

"I, I may have misplaced my key."

Anne, in a flash of steel, held a dagger to the man's crotch, tapping it with the broad side of the blade.

"Maybe check your pants before I use me blade to check for you," she said.

The two other men drifted their hands toward their pistols but froze when Jesse and Frank fast-drew their guns. The two men each quickly raised their hands above their heads. The balding man slowly felt his pants pockets, gently moving Anne's dagger to the side, and removed a key.

"My mistake. I have it here." He held the key out for Anne. She smiled and stored the blade in her teeth while she took the key and opened the lock of the trunk. She tossed the lock to the side and pulled up on the lid. Inside were five dozen fancy bottles of alcohol. She sheathed her blade and pulled one amber bottle out and admired the label.

"Ballard & Lancaster," she read from the bottle. She uncorked the bottle and took a swig of the bourbon. "Ahh, that is fine." She walked behind the three men standing there and tossed the bottle up to Jesse on his horse. He caught it and took a pull himself before passing it to Frank. Anne leaned against one of the men with his hands in the air and put her arm around his shoulder.

"What do these bottles fetch in the city?" she asked.

"Well, this is just a trial sales trip," the man with the hat said. "The bulk of the inventory is in Arizona. But the bottle sells for three dollars. This inventory is for the saloon owners to try out." He gestured with his hat. "You boys, and um, ma'am, could have a bottle for yourselves. Grateful for you stopping to help us an' all."

"Oh! An entire bottle? Your generous nature is touching." Anne leaned into the man she had her arm around. "Did he promise you a bottle as well?" The man just shook his head, not taking his eyes from Frank and Jesse. Anne sauntered over to the balding man and took his hat from his hands. She popped it on top of her mane of red hair. "We's be takin' a few extra bottles... an' one of them horses." Anne pulled a gold pocket watch from the man's jacket pocket and gave a toothy smile. "An' a wee bit more of ye valuables."

Minutes later, Anne, Jesse, and Frank rode away with saddlebags full of bourbon bottles, a few pieces of man's jewelry and one of the wagon's horses that Anne was now perched upon.

"I'm warmin' up to this firecracker that you've burdened us with," Frank said to Jesse. "She's still crazy as a loon, but not without some value."

"She's entertaining, I'll give her that. A real outlaw," Jesse said.

Anne rode silently as she looked over her new pistol, opening and closing the chamber, as well as sighting down the barrel.

"Bet you one of them bottles of bourbon she's still going to kill you while you sleep," Frank said.

Anne smiled and then spun the revolver into her holster like she had seen Jesse do several times.

Henry Jennings stood outside the San Francisco City Hall building alongside Woodes Rogers and his two navy men. The structure of the building was as impressive as any castle or monument to rival those in London or Paris. A large rotunda was still under construction above the enormous complex of buildings arranged on a triangular plot of land at the end of Market Street. Tall columns lined the building's exterior with arches in between. The area was a hive of activity where workmen, suited businessmen, bankers, and merchants all blended together in the frenzied activity of the day. The building was the location for the office of the mayor of this strange future city. Jennings had attempted to explain to the pirate hunter what he had learned about their new existence more than a hundred and fifty years from when they were swallowed by the sea. Rogers would hear nothing of it. He still claimed that once they fulfilled their obligation to King and country, they would be released from their purgatory and be able to return home.

Rogers had decided to approach the governmental leadership of the city so that they could be on notice that a number of infamous pirates were being harbored in this jurisdiction. The mayor, William Alvord, they were told, had his offices within the newly constructed City Hall. Rogers was going to seek out the assistance of the local authorities in apprehending Edward Thatch and his cohorts. Jennings was reluctantly along for the ride.

"Do straighten your clothing, Jennings. You look disheveled and common," Rogers said, leading the way into the hall.

There was nothing Jennings could do about his appearance. He had yet to procure a new change of clothes, but he made a show of smoothing his shirt and jacket to appease the pompous pirate hunter.

Once inside the building, they inquired the location of the mayor's office, then strode through the high-ceilinged hallways to arrive at the open door of a busy waiting chamber. There were several desks with secretaries tapping away on noisy machines that fed paper through a wheel mounted at the top. Jennings had never seen such devices and was unsure of what they were doing. As they entered, they saw three men in suits with holstered weapons enter a large office with a man sitting behind a massive polished wooden desk. "Shut the door," the man said without looking up from the papers he was examining. Rogers paused for a moment to glance around the office before heading toward that door, assuming it led to the mayor in charge. A young man in a crisp blue suit noticed them as they entered and approached with a bemused expression on his face.

"Are you fellows from the playhouse?" he asked.

"I am Captain Woodes Rogers, the Governor of the Bahamas. I need to speak with your mayor at once."

"I see. Governor of, where did you say?"

"Bahamas."

The man looked quizzically at their attire from boot to head, stopping on the scarred, stern face of Rogers. "The mayor is a very busy man, and he doesn't have time to trifle with some sort of… performance."

"I am a busy man as well, and nor do I have time to trifle with underlings. I serve the King of England and demand to be heard by this mayor. The news I bring him is of great importance. Now move aside, knave." Rogers pushed the man aside and strode confidently toward the office door of the mayor with his sailors in tow, Jennings following behind.

"Sir! Sir! You can't barge in there. There has been a bank robbery, and the mayor is meeting with the Wells Fargo men!" The young man headed them off and blocked the office door with his arms wide apart to fill the doorway. Rogers slammed his fist into the man's belly, sending him bent over in pain. One of the secretaries screamed in alarm and Rogers shoved the doubled-over man aside and opened the door.

The armed, suited men pulled their pistols as Rogers burst through the door and into the office. He stood in the doorway, unalarmed at having the guns pointed at him. The man behind the desk rose to his feet. He was large and heavyset with a dense mustache and receding hairline. A lit cigar sat smoldering in a glass ashtray next to a tumbler half full of whiskey.

"What is the meaning of this?"

"I am Captain Woodes Rogers of the Royal Navy and Governor of the Bahamas," Woodes said as he confidently strode into the room with his men following behind. "I have been sent here in pursuit of the most vile, criminal swine that has ever sailed the seas. The true scourge of the Earth. A blight of humanity brought about by the devil himself."

The mayor looked at the men with vivid irritation.

"Is that so? Well, unless these criminals are the same ones that robbed one of my banks yesterday, your theatrics will have to wait..." the mayor said.

"They may very well be the same."

Rogers approached the desk, passing by the men holding pistols at him and took a seat across from the mayor. The navy men stood at the ready alongside Jennings waiting to see what was going to happen. The mayor glanced at all the men, then back to Rogers. He then motioned for the Wells Fargo men to lower their weapons. The mayor sat heavily in his large leather chair and leaned back.

"Alright, you have my attention. Explain yourself," the mayor said and picked up his cigar to puff some smoke.

"These pirates came to your shores after their vessel sank in the harbor a few nights ago. I have been pursuing them from the ports of Nassau after King George offered them a pardon that they maliciously defaulted on. I had trapped the reigning leaders, men and women of the worst sort, on board the frigate belonging to one Edward Thatch, a vile man sought for murder and mayhem by the Crown. A hurricane that blew us off course to your shores unfortunately beached us. This dozen or so men and women will no doubt continue their debauchery and criminal behavior within your town. If you will lend your aid to my cause, we can make quick work of their capture and deliver the Lord's justice upon them."

"You said men and women?" asked the mayor. Rogers nodded. The mayor looked at one of the Wells Fargo men. "Didn't you say there was an oddly dressed woman who participated in robbing the bank?"

"Yes, Mr. Mayor. That is what the witnesses described. The other men were thought to be a few members of the James-Younger gang. Jesse James in particular."

Jennings' eyes narrowed as he recognized the name Jesse James, but kept quiet.

"Seems mighty far west for Jesse James to be involved. Reports of him robbing banks have been mostly out of Missouri and Kansas," the mayor mused. "You work for the Crown of England, you say? Well, if these are your people, then we might be in agreement that we could use your assistance in apprehending these outlaws."

"These are not **my** people. Some don't even hail from England. Irish, Scots, former slaves, truly the lowest class of wretch," said Rogers.

"Fine, fine. Be that as it may." The mayor turned toward a shorter, bearded Wells Fargo man and introduced him. "This is Bill Cooper. He's the head of security at Wells Fargo. You can assist his men with tracking down the outlaws."

"Mr. Mayor, we can handle our own affairs," Cooper objected.

"Handle your own affairs? Clearly that is not happening, Mr. Cooper. The bank in which I sit on the board has been robbed several times this year and though you've caught half the culprits… half had gotten away! If these foreigners can help retrieve the stolen gold and bank notes, then we are going to damn well let them help! Are we clear?" And the mayor slammed his fist on the desk.

"Yes, Mr. Mayor," Cooper said.

"Good! Now all of you get out of my office and get that money back!"

The three men from Wells Fargo stood outside City Hall with Woodes Rogers, Jennings and the two navy men, after all being introduced.

"We should interview the staff at The Paris and see what they know of your… pirates," Cooper said.

"Yes, capital idea. They might be using that den of indecency as a base of operations. These pirates are drawn to whores and rum like flies to dung. Isn't that right, Jennings?" Woodes said, looking at Jennings accusingly.

"Don't lump me in with that lot. You know good and well my allegiance to the Crown. Privateer was what I was, with official marques to plunder the enemies of King George. Never once did I attack a ship of our brethren!" Jennings almost spit.

A tight smile crossed Rogers' scarred face.

"Yet you associate with Vane and the rest of them while picking the bones from sunken English ships."

"Salvage is not a crime! And my association with them served your purpose just fine when gathering them all on one ship for you to arrest. I delivered the entire lot for you!"

"Botched! You delivered me nothing." Woodes moved inches from Jennings' face.

"I… can't… control… nature, damn you," Jennings said, tightly controlling his temper.

"Alright, let's be off then, shall we?" Cooper said, breaking up the tension between the two men. "Where are your horses?"

"We are navy men. We have no horses," Jennings said, turning to face Cooper.

Cooper sighed and turned toward his two associates. "Fine then. You fellers get our horses and a carriage for these navy men, so we don't have to walk all the way to the Barbary Coast."

CHAPTER 13 - ROBERTS' CROSS

Bart Roberts observed the quartermaster's movements closely as the big man pushed past the line of workers on their way to the engine room, where Bart stood at the tail end. Vern had given Bart a snide wink as they passed each other. He was wearing several of Bart's ornate rings on his fingers. Bart turned his head to follow the large Icelandic man as he dipped his head below each bulkhead while striding down the metal hallway. Roberts now knew exactly where all his jewelry had gone when he had been shanghaied aboard this vessel and lay in a drug-induced stupor. His life seemed to be on a downward slide this last week. Forced into hard labor in hot, dangerous conditions for twelve-hour days was taking a toll on his body. The threat of violence had stopped him each time he sought to go topside of the ship. Sam had been bludgeoned with what he later learned was an instrument called a sap by Max, the lanky enforcer, when he demanded to talk with the captain about the poor working conditions. his eyes glared at the receding quartermaster who was now also assuredly in possession of his prized diamond-encrusted cross as well. He vowed to himself that before this ship reached its destination port, he would cut out Vern's heart and retrieve all that the man had stolen from him.

"How many men stand in our way of a successful mutiny?" asked Sam Bellamy in a low, conspiratorial voice.

Roberts turned toward the young idealist pirate and smiled. It was as if Sam was reading his thoughts.

"Three. Three men and three guns is all I've seen. Just Vern and his two mates."

"There must be several more above decks guarding other parts of the crew," said Chester.

Sam, Bart, and the rest of the engine crew were restricted to the engine deck, the crew galley, and their bunks. None had seen more of the ship, nor had they been allowed to see the sun or breathe fresh air since they had been shanghaied into working on the *Lurline*. The men made their way to the engine room, following in the wake of the stocky enforcer O'Farrell. The clanging noise of the engines grew louder as they approached the entryway, and the heat of the boilers could be felt rising as the men moved through the hallway like they were approaching the gates of hell itself.

"Get to work, you sad-looking scum," bellowed O'Farrell as he stood in the doorway pointing at the fiery coal boilers. The crew that was currently working looked up at the new shift arriving and their faces blackened by coal dust and streaked with sweat barely showed signs of relief that their workday had ended. The men were so beaten down by the harsh working conditions and long hours that they couldn't even take pleasure in the end of their day's work. They just set their tools down for the next man to use and slowly shuffled out the door. O'Farrell barely gave them a glance as they passed him on their way to either bed or chow. *The enforcers were becoming lax as the trip drew on*, thought Bart as he watched.

"How long before we arrive at the Islands?" Bart asked Chester loud enough for him to hear over the engine noise, but not so that his voice would carry to O'Farrell.

Chester thought and counted on his fingers for a moment before answering, "Three days, give or take."

Bart looked around at the men toiling in the engine room. *Not a long time to organize a mutiny, but the longer we wait, the more tired and beaten down we will become.* You could see the weakness in the eyes of the men who had been conscripted into servitude aboard this ship for a longer time than Sam and Bart. They had lost their resolve and given in to the idea that this was just their life now. There was the promise of pay at the end of each voyage, but Bart had been told that each time the boat docked, Vern had withheld pay by deducting the men's food, uniforms and whatever else he could come up with to avoid giving the men their wages.

Bart stared at the revolver shoved into the front of O'Farrell's pants. If he could get possession of that gun that fired six shots without reloading, he would have a chance to take over the ship. Looking around at the tired men toiling around him, he wondered how many would fight for their freedom against the enforcers of the *Lurline*. Bart had been involved in a few mutinies throughout his career and he knew that once the tide turned in a specific direction, the majority of the men would follow that tide. That gun stowed in the waistband of the cocky Irishman was the key to turning this tide.

Once the twelve-hour shift was over, the engine-room men made their way to the galley for their dinner. The quality of the food had lost its luster for Bart and Sam, now becoming just fuel to shovel into their mouths to keep their own fires burning. They sat across from Chester at the table crowded with workers that they had come to know over the past several days.

"Bart and I been planning something…" Sam said in a hushed voice to Chester.

The older man with the long mustache looked up from his food at Sam, focusing on the day-old bruise blackening the right eye of his handsome face. He glanced around the room and then at the men eating at their table for a moment.

"I know it. Going to get someone killed, likely." Chester looked hard at the two pirates. "It's a big ship. There'll be more enforcers on the upper decks, plus the captain, and I'm sure he's got men and guns." He pointed his fork at the other men at the table, who were beginning to listen in on the conversation. "Some of these men will follow you for sure, but it probably ain't enough. You also got a hundred or so regular folk up there. You going to be responsible for them too? What if they resist? You going to kill 'em?"

"These men… and their captain, took our freedom. You said so yourself, they ain't going to let us off at the Islands. They'll work us till our backs break, then feed us to the sharks. Look at Sam's face. Look at your arm. It ain't healing properly. It's growing rot and if it don't get treated, it's going to have to come off," Bart said.

Chester looked at his bandaged arm that was hiding discolored skin underneath.

"Tomorrow, at the start of our shift, we take O'Farrell," Sam said. "We stop the engines and Vern, or Max will come to check, and we take them too. Then we have two, maybe three guns and we go straight to the pilot deck and take the captain. Once we have him, the ship will be ours. No more fighting. Trust me, I know how the dynamics of ship and crew works. The civilians can join us or be secured until we reach the Islands. No harm will come to them. They'll have their freedom when we dock."

"Which one of you becomes captain then?" asked Chester.

All the men at the table were listening now, watching them. Bart smiled and leaned into the crowd.

"We vote. Everyone gets a vote. All men equal shares, each able to rise above their station. It's the pirate way."

Bart Roberts awoke to the rise and fall of the ship. The sea must have become bigger while he had been sleeping. He knew from his long years at sea that it meant there was a storm brewing out there. The swells must be quite large to move a ship this size in this way. Would he be able to see the storm's direction if he was topside? It was difficult to judge whether it was day or night this far below deck. He had slept for four or five hours, he judged, and it would soon be time to set out for another day working, shoveling coal into the ship's infernos. Today, though, would hopefully be the last of that. He wasn't sure if the rest of the engine-room men would follow him and Sam into an act of mutiny, but hoped that once they made their move, they would join in the fight for their freedom. He stretched in the bunk, joints audibility creaking in the process.

"Do you think our pirate mates are faring any better than us this last week?" Sam quietly asked from the bunk below him.

"Probably gambling, whoring and drinking."

"Think we'll ever see them again?"

Bart pondered that question before answering.

"Don't know. I would like to see that Charlotte De Berry again…" Roberts sighed and laid back with his hands under his head, staring at the metal ceiling.

"Did seem like there was some bewitching between you two. I hope you get a chance to find her again." Sam let a silence pass between them. "I don't understand what has happened to us, but maybe there is a reason we were all thrown into this together. If we can get back to them, we can figure it out. Maybe find a way back to our home in 1718 or find a new purpose in this place. I'm not certain that piracy can survive in this place. It's too modern. Ships made entirely of metal. Men everywhere carrying pistols that could kill you six times over. No need of a sword or a dirk, can't get close enough to use 'em anyhow. Get yourself shot well before."

"I'd give an arm for my sword or a dirk today. Make quick work of a red-faced Irishman, I would. Don't you worry, Sam. We will take back our freedom and find our mates. If we're stuck here in this world, then we will adapt and persevere. We bested the most powerful nations the world had ever seen, owned the waters of the Caribbean and created our own rules, never to be controlled by the Crown of England or Spain or the likes. We started with nothing then and we can start with nothing again. But as God as my witness, we will thrive and carve our way to riches and glory and have our freedom after this bloody day."

A clanging could be heard down the hallway and then the door opened, with the colossal form of Vern filling the space.

"Wake up, ladies. Storm's coming. You lot are actually going to need to work today. Need the engines running at peak."

The men all slowly started to get out of bed and dress for the day.

"Get to it, you lazy bastards!" Vern shouted and struck one of the men in the back of his head for not moving fast enough. The man went tumbling to the ground, taking Sam with him. Bart turned aggressively toward Vern to be stopped by the look of murder on Vern's face, as well as the hand grasping the grip of the holstered pistol.

"You looking to lodge a complaint?" Vern said smugly.

Sam helped the fallen man up and they finished dressing. Bart stood down from the threat of violence. Vern smiled and waited as they all pulled on their boots and filed out of their racks. They stumbled down the passageways and stairs to the engine room as the ship rose and fell with the increasing swells, Sam and Bart having less trouble than most because of their long experience with rough seas. Most of the men working on the ship had spent little time aboard sailing vessels before being shanghaied onto the *Lurline*. Some had been farmers, some miners, others just drunks and gamblers that just had the poor luck of being in the wrong saloon or opium den before finding themselves stolen aboard this very ship.

O'Farrell and Max were waiting in the engine room with the earlier shift when they arrived.

"They're all yours, O'Farrell. Make sure the engines run smooth until we get through this weather," Vern said.

"Aye, aye, sir. I'll make sure they don't sluff off any."

Vern and Max led the other shift of men out the door to their meals and bed.

Sam, Bart, and the others began the tasks of feeding the six burners and monitoring the engines. They were now all familiar with the workings of the two engines turning the sixteen-foot-tall four-finned propeller that moved the giant ship across the ocean. Sam and Bart waited out the time, calculating in their heads when Vern, Max and the other workers would be sitting in the galley eating their meal before making their move.

Bart kept glancing back at O'Farrell as he slouched against a bulkhead, steadying himself against the rise and fall of the ship cresting the growing swells. O'Farrell caught one of the glances and glared back at Bart while straightening himself up. Bart and Sam then looked at each other with an unspoken decision that it was time to act.

Sam pushed a cartful of coal toward another boiler, shoving another man to the side. The man who was in on the game shoved Sam back, yelling at him to watch where he was going. Sam grabbed the man and roughly shoved him to the floor.

"I'm tired of you getting in my way, bilge rat!" Sam yelled at the man who had started getting to his feet. They began shoving each other again and knocked over the cartful of coal.

"Hey! Enough, you scum! Get back to work," hollered O'Farrell.

Sam and the man continued to shove and pull their blows as they tussled with each other. O'Farrell had had enough and strode over to the pair, billy club in his hand. The man Sam was fighting with saw an opening and shoved Sam into O'Farrell, knocking them both back and sending them down to the floor.

Bart rushed over with his shovel, wielding it above his head to smash it into O'Farrell's head. Just as he reached him, the ship rolled to port, hard, causing everyone to stumble and fall. Bart crashed into a bulkhead with his shoulder, knocking the shovel out of his hands.

Sam rolled on top of O'Farrell and delivered a blow to the man's face. The barrel-chested man elbowed Sam in the jaw, then threw the lighter man off him into the toppled coal cart. The man Sam had been fighting with struck out at O'Farrell, but the blow was dodged. O'Farrell was a man who grew up brawling in the Irish port town of Wexford and was no stranger to violence. With a backhanded swing of his billy club, he sent the man sprawling to the metal floor. Chester threw a hammer at O'Farrell's head, but his aim was too low. It landed with a thunk against his chest, surely to bruise but nothing more.

A few of the other men rushed toward O'Farrell but were sent dodging back as O'Farrell swung the club, striking one and missing another. Bart recovered his shovel and brandished it toward the enforcer. Sam was on his feet with a large wrench in his hand, ready to strike.

"Enough play time!" O'Farrell bellowed and pulled his revolver from his waistband and pointed it from one man to the next. "How 'bout I just shoot you all and bring back the first shift?"

The men continued to stand their ground, but the fight was going out of them in the face of the big iron gun pointed at them. O'Farrell stalked forward, and the men retreated behind Bart and Sam. Just then, the burner that O'Farrell happened to be standing in front of belched out a blast of heat and smoke from being unattended, causing the man to flinch and cover his face with his arm from the heat. Bart Roberts jumped into action and swung the shovel, catching the hand that was wielding the gun.

CRACK! O'Farrell felt several bones in his hand break from the blow and the revolver flew across the room. He stumbled back holding the injured hand, hate filling his eyes that matched the hate coming from Roberts.

"I'm going to kill you for that, scum," O'Farrell spit out.

Roberts narrowed his eyes at the man and swung the shovel as hard as he could at O'Farrell's head.

Vern did his best to eat the stew that was slopping out of his bowl with each hard pitch and roll of the ship. He hated these Pacific storms that were so common this time of year. Not so much for the violent motions of the ship, but more for the bellyaching and complaints he would hear from the passengers and crew. He grew so tired of the lack of hardiness people displayed these days. Grown men grumbling about too much work, not enough sleep and the food not satisfying enough for their taste. He scoffed to himself, thinking none of them would be able to endure a single winter in his beloved home in Iceland. Vern stabbed a chunk of potato with his fork and popped it into his mouth, glancing at the rings that now adorned his thick fingers. He had taken them off that dandy named Roberts. Roberts and the one called Sam came on board with quite a bit of gold and silver jewelry that was now stored in a pouch under his mattress. One of the items was an enormous diamond cross necklace that would fetch a small fortune on the Islands. Probably a large fortune if he held off selling the loot until he returned to San Francisco.

Vern smiled to himself at the thought of cashing in his take from this voyage. If he played his cards right and sold the jewels for the right price, he could travel back home, rich as a duke and purchase a large piece of land, so big he would be able to hunt all the game he wanted on his own property. He could raise cattle, horses and never set foot on another boat again. Those two men were going to have to find an accident when the *Lurline* arrived at the Islands. It didn't go unnoticed by him the way the two looked at him. Ready for murder, those two. He didn't want to keep looking over his shoulder, waiting for one of them to pounce. For now, they seemed cowed, but he knew their type. It wouldn't be long before they would strike. His need for them only lasted as long as this ship took to arrive at port. He could find two more willing or unwilling sods to fill their shoes once they reached Hawaii. Maybe tomorrow night he and O'Farrell would take them above deck and shoot them. Then feed their bodies to the sharks.

Vern spilt a bit of stew on his shirt as the ship lurched beneath a swell. The feeling of the lurch felt odd. Something was wrong, he knew immediately. He rose and abandoned his meal, snapping his finger at Max to join him. The pitching of the ship had suddenly reached an extreme. He and Max exited the galley and started toward the engine room. A young sailor named Beau was hurrying toward them from the upper decks.

"What's going on?" Vern shouted.

"Engines stopped!" the man yelled back. "We need power, or the swells'll roll us!" The man kept running past them.

Vern and Max looked at each other in worry then took off at a run after the sailor and toward the engine room, both ducking under the low bulkheads as they went. The three men shouted to each other as they ran.

"What's happening down there? Captain wants to know!"

"Damned if I know! I left O'Farrell there to run the boilers," Vern hollered.

"We need that propeller turning again or we'll all be finished!" the sailor said just before being slammed against the metal wall by the motion of a wave hitting the ship. Vern picked the man up by the back of his shirt and onto his feet again.

"I'm going to strangle every damn one of them if this is sabotage!" Vern yelled to himself. The sounds of the engines should have been loud at the moment, but the ship was silent except for the creaking and groaning of metal being tested for strength by an unforgiving sea.

The three men slid down a ladder leading to the entrance to the engine room. Beau was the first to rush through the doorway, only to be blasted back from a blow to the head, knocking Vern down with his unconscious body. Vern saw *that damn rogue Roberts* standing in the doorway brandishing a now bent shovel. Vern struggled to push the sailor off him and draw his gun. Max beat him to it, firing from his own pistol, but his shot went wide as Roberts dived out of the doorway. The other one, Sam, emerged firing two shots into the hallway from what he could only assume was O'Farrell's weapon. The first shot clanged and ricocheted down the hall, the second found its mark in the thigh of Max's right leg. The man shrieked and spun down to the floor, firing another wild round toward the engine room.

Vern, now on his feet, took partial cover behind a steel girder in the narrow hallway. He took a shot at a shadow moving in the engine room as Max pulled himself up against the other side of the wall next to the ladder leading back up.

"A mutiny is it, Roberts? Best be getting those engines started again or we will all be headed toward a watery grave," Vern called out.

"You toss those guns to us, and we'll get them back started." Roberts hollered back.

"There's thirty armed men between you and the captain, couple of pistols ain't going to do it. They'll cut you down like sheep," Vern said.

Bart and Sam looked at Chester to see if he thought Vern was telling the truth about the number of men. Chester just shrugged. Sam looked around at the ten men standing ready with shovels, wrenches, and other blunt weapons. He then looked hard at Bart and quietly said, "We're committed now. We don't win this, they hang us for sure."

146

Bart nodded agreement and saw resolve on the soot-blackened faces of the men standing ready.

The clanging of running footsteps could be heard above Max and Vern. They looked up as two more sailors armed with rifles stormed down the ladder. Bart took a glance down the hallway to see them arrive to back up the enforcers. The workmen were definitely outgunned now.

"It's over now, Roberts!" Vern yelled into the engine room. "The rest of you men in there give up and we'll just hang Roberts. You'll all be free to go. Give up the gun and end this now!"

Sam held the pistol with both hands behind the doorway. Bart looked over at the closest boiler, then smiled.

"I've got an idea," he said as he started toward the burning coal.

"I'll give you the count of five. Then we're coming in killin'," Vern said.

He motioned toward the open engine-room doorway. He and the two soldiers crept toward the room, guns raised and pointed, ready to fire at any movement. Max followed them, leaning against the wall with one hand, the other pointing his pistol.

"One," Vern called out and stepped forward.

"Two." The enforcers peered over their gun sights.

"Three," Vern said as they moved within ten feet of the doorway.

"Four." Vern nodded at the two sailors, and they all cocked their weapons.

Vern paused just a few feet from the doorway, unable to see what was happening beyond. It was quiet, quiet like the forest would become while he was hunting game in the heavily wooded Icelandic forests. His memory recalled that the moments right before the violence of killing exploded into the air would always be devoid of sound. He was in his element now. Hunting again. The deliverer of violence.

"Five!"

When Vern reached the doorway, it was as if hell itself had been unleashed. Burning coal bombarded the sailors and enforcers, sending them screaming and stumbling back as coal and embers from the boilers burned through their clothing and seared their skin. Vern dropped the pistol as his hands went to his face in an attempt to tamp the licking flames that burst into his beard and hair. The other men spun and dropped to the ground, screaming, and rolling to escape. Bart, Chester, and three of the men continued to shovel burning coal at Vern and his henchmen. Vern got to his feet and stumbled toward the ladder leading upstairs. He used it to right himself as Bart stalked him down the hallway. Vern turned his burnt and ruined face as Bart approached. He reached into his boot and pulled out a knife and pointed it at Roberts.

Roberts swung the shovel at Vern's head, but the big man was quicker than the pirate anticipated, and it clanged against the metal ladder. Vern ducked underneath the next swing as well and took a swipe at Roberts with the long knife. It missed his skin but sliced clean through Bart's shirt. The two men took swipes at each other with their weapons in the narrow hallway. Roberts' shovel banged into the bulkhead, breaking, sending its metal blade spinning down the hall. He held up the broken wooden handle just in time to deflect a knife blow from the seared and smoking man that was now barely identifiable as Vern. He now looked like a demon drug up from the depths of hell. His shirt and pants were full of holes that still burned hot from the coals. His skin, welted and pockmarked, emitted heat and smoke. One eye was burnt completely out, unseeing, yet the man defied logic, refusing to lie down and die.

Vern advanced on Bart, looking for an opening, stabbing at him, just out of reach. Bart held fast to the wooden handle, its sharp splintered end the only thing between him and the knife in the hand of this beast. The men behind him had dispatched Max and the sailors with their shovels and wrenches while Bart and Vern battled. They had picked up the fallen men's guns but couldn't shoot Vern without possibly hitting Bart, so they only watched and retreated away from the duel.

Vern frantically stabbed out with his longer arms and sent Bart reeling back. The bigger man roared like an animal and rushed at him just as the ship crested a swell, sending all of them motionless into the air for what seemed like minutes. Vern was towering over Bart, knife pointed down at Bart's chest. There was nothing for Bart to do but fall back underneath the man and point his broken shovel handle up at him.

The ship and all its occupants landed hard a second later with a loud bang and groaning of metal. Sam rolled over from his side and pointed his pistol toward the mound of scorched flesh that lay atop of Bart Roberts. Sam slowly got to his feet and approached the bloody scene. No one made a sound as Sam held his pistol pointed at Vern's back. He grabbed his shoulder and pulled the man off his shipmate. Roberts was covered with blood and Vern's knife fell clattering to the floor as he rolled onto his back. Sam looked down at the wooden handle of Roberts' broken shovel protruding from deep inside Vern's chest. Roberts moaned and painfully sat up, resting on one elbow. He looked over at the men staring on.

"Let's get the engines started up and gather the weapons. We need to take control of this ship," he ordered.

"You heard the man. Let's get to it!" said Chester.

The men went into action while Sam helped Bart to his feet. Bart bent down over Vern and took his rings back from the dead man's fingers. *I'm going to pay a visit to old Vern's cabin and retrieve my damn cross as well.* He then sheathed Vern's knife in his belt and took the dead man's holster and revolver. Sam and Bart turned quickly in unison and pointed their weapons as they heard the heavy footfalls of several running men above them making their way to the ladder, then they came sliding down. It turned out to be the engine men from the other shift that they were already acquainted with. The newcomers paused and smiled to see how the tide had turned. Roberts tossed the man in front an acquired long rifle that was caught with one hand. The sound of the engines starting erupted through the hallway. Roberts shouted to be heard over the noise.

"Let's go and pay a visit to the former captain of this here ship!"

CHAPTER 14 - A GRAND PARTY INDEED

Riotous laughter roared throughout The Paris. The saloon was crowded with miners, cowboys, farmers, gamblers, and pirates. The piano player was a portly lady with blonde hair piled high. She was pounding out a fast-paced, high-energy tune while a lit pipe hung from her red painted lips. She glanced up at the stage where several dancing girls were spinning a very drunk cabin boy, Tom, around and around in what almost looked like a choreographed dance. Pirates and cowboys lined the stage, cheering and laughing, some even joining in the dance to spin the girls around, their dresses whirling with captivating colors. Tom slid under the skirts of one dancing girl to emerge on the other side. Dancing nearby, Mary Read handed the boy a mug of beer half of which he chugged down before handing it back and resuming his dancing. Mary raised her glass in the air, cheering, before finishing off the rest of the warm, golden-colored brew. She spun in place next to Charles Vane while he danced a jig shirtless and barefoot on the polished wood floor.

Black Caesar, Thatch, and Hornigold cheered each other at a table of twenty-one that was being dealt by Colette Dallaire. The three men were so drunk that they thought it was necessary, and also more entertaining, to make

151

wild bets and lose handedly. Black Caesar had just taken another card after already having a jack and a queen showing, equaling twenty. Hornigold and Thatch chanted, *ace, ace, ace!* They all fell over laughing when Colette pulled a seven to add to Black Caesar's hand, ending in a bust. Colette only smiled and shook her head as she pulled the house's winning to her growing pile. Black Caesar put his long, muscled arms around Hornigold and Thatch, then broke into a song that the two other men drunkenly joined in.

> *Of all the pirates I've heard or seen,*
> *The basest and bloodiest is Captain Green,*
> *To treat our merchant ships at such a rate,*
> *After robbery, his crime to aggravate,*
> *Under pretense of setting them a shore:*
> *Our merchant men them to devour*
> *Which clearly is proven to be very true,*
> *He deserves to be hanged and all his crew:*

Charlotte De Berry leaned against the corner of the long bar counter, occasionally fending off the advances of ranchers, cowboys, and sailors. She watched her drunken pirate brethren revel in what could only be described as a celebration of life and freedom. She sipped from a bottle of Vinicola Madeira wine that the Indian barkeep said was imported from Spain. Charlotte had sailed into the ports of Spain a few times over her ten-year career on merchant ships. Her father was a quartermaster with a merchant fleet out of France that had transported slaves from the Bight of Benin to the Caribbean and the Americas. He had fallen in love with her mother, whose family were swordsmiths in Porto-Novo. Once her father had taken an African for his wife, he could no longer stomach playing a part in the slave trade. He retired from the fleet to become a fisherman, settling into a quiet life in his newfound home. He taught Charlotte sailing skills, while her mother's side of the family introduced her to the benefits of a sharp blade. Charlotte had taken to both sets of artistry with gusto, never finding a match to her expertise with a sword. Her favorite weapon was her kukri, with its 12-inch inwardly curving blade and 6-inch rosewood handle. Her grandfather had engraved intricate African symbols of strength and courage into the forged iron blade.

Charlotte had known a few of these men and women pirates before their meeting on the *Queen Anne's Revenge*, but most she knew only by reputation. She was content to keep these captains and first mates of competing ships at arm's length. The two women, Mary Read, and Anne Bonny, she had found immediately tiresome. She was, though, warming up to Mary since their near-death experience, but that Bonny woman was gratingly arrogant and infantile. Charlotte was happy to let her go off on her own, seeking revenge for the death of her lover. What had driven the girl into the arms of that worm, Rackham, God only knew. Maybe it was to escape her poor choice in husbands, the fink, James Bonny. Clearly the woman had terrible taste in men. This thought brought her to Bartholomew Roberts.

Charlotte took a sip from the ornate wine bottle to hide her smile. Roberts was an intriguing figure, dashing and handsome. His dark hair and thin mustache framed his perfectly angular face. Whereas Anne ran off seeking violence, Charlotte desired to comb this strange port seeking love. *What a little dove I've become over a man I hardly know.* She glanced around at the pirates she was now tied to in this strange place. This looked to be a long night of festivity and once it was done, there would be a long interlude while all the rum and gambling was slept off.

De Berry picked up her bottle and made her way to the door. *I can walk the streets in hopes of spotting Roberts and Bellamy.* There were many saloons and halls in this port town and inevitably she would find the one that Roberts was holed up in. She pushed away from the bar and made her way to the exit. She shouldered the door open and stepped out into the early evening air. The chill of the night hit her, immediately calling to mind that she was no longer in the Caribbean. She stood beside the open door as two men shuffled past her on their way into The Paris. Charlotte looked left and right down the busy street with indecision on which direction to start her search. She raised her wine bottle to her lips for another drink, then spotted a carriage arriving across the street. Through the window of the carriage, she caught sight of the blue and white uniforms that she was very familiar with. The uniforms of the British Navy. Lowering the bottle, she watched as the carriage was joined by three horses ridden by well-dressed gunmen. Her gut felt a squeeze as Woodes Rogers, Henry Jennings, and two navy sailors exited the carriage.

Charlotte didn't wait to see any more. She knew why these men were here. Quickly turning back, she re-entered The Paris. Looking across the crowded bar, she decided to go straight to Blackbeard and Hornigold. She shoved several men out of her way in her haste.

"Rogers is outside!" she exclaimed, slamming her wine bottle onto the gambling table with a stern look on her face. Colette practically jumped out of her seat in surprise.

Thatch, Black Caesar, and Hornigold looked at her with heavy drink in their eyes. The three turned toward each other in confusion. Thatch smiled and picked up her wine bottle and tilted it to his lips to take a swig. The red liquid dribbled into his braided beard.

"The Jolly Rogers is outside?" Thatch asked with slurred speech. This sent all three men laughing and Hornigold fell out of his chair, which sent the laughter into higher pitch and uncontrolled fits. Thatch flipped his two playing cards over, revealing a three and a two. "I'll take another card, love, and make it a sixteen."

This sent the laughter over the edge for the men, and Black Caesar put his head on the table and stomped his foot. Charlotte was exasperated and pulled her dirk from its sheath. She slammed the blade into Thatch's two cards and right through the wooden table with an audible THUNK.

"The pirate hunter! You damn fools, he's coming here!" She yelled loud enough for the whole saloon to hear and interrupt what they were doing. The piano stopped playing mid-tune, and the dancing came to a halt, all turning to look at Charlotte. This outburst sobered the men up quick. Hornigold turned toward the door and stood up.

"Out the back!" Colette said, pointing to the hallway past her own office room. Thatch's chair fell back behind him as he bolted up. The three men started to rush toward the back of the saloon with Charlotte pointing the way. Thatch, in a moment of impulsiveness and opportunity, turned back as he passed Colette and took her in his arms and kissed her deeply. He then turned without looking back and ran toward the rear exit. Colette was flabbergasted that the man had taken the liberty with her like that. Her fingers went to her lips as she watched him run. Then her hands went to her hips as she watched people rush by her in their haste.

The miners, sailors, and cowboys were leaving in droves out the front door and some by the back exit even though they themselves were in no danger from a pirate hunter. Woodes, Jennings and the other men tried to come through the front door of the saloon, but the crowd of drunk men caught up in the frenzy the pirates created pushed and shoved them aside in their urgency to leave the saloon.

Mary and Vane were the first to exit the back, as they were closest to the rear of the saloon. Young Tom stood watching the crowd as they rushed past him, pushing, and shoving one another. Thatch handedly picked up Tom by his belt and carried him under his arm as he followed Hornigold and Black Caesar. The saloon was almost completely cleared out of patrons in a matter of seconds. The only ones left were the working men and women, Colette, and a handful of drunks who were too blasted to know what was going on.

Woodes, Jennings, Cooper and their men finally pushed their way into the now near-empty hall. Cooper looked around the room and his eyes landed on Colette, who was stacking the house's money from the gambling table. She shook her head at them.

"You boys can really clear a room," she said as she sauntered over to the bar.

Mary Read and Charles Vane ran through the alleyway to emerge onto the lightly peopled avenue. The streetlamps were giving off a yellow-tinged glow that haloed around them in the mild evening fog. Vane looked back to see the rest of the pirates slowing behind him. It seemed that they were not being pursued at the moment, so he too began to slow. Mary turned her head back as well and almost collided with a trio of horses that rounded a corner in front of her. The lead horse reared up as the rider jerked the reins to come to a stop. Instinctively Mary raised her arms to protect her head from being kicked by the horse's front hoofs.

"Mary!" The rider shouted.

Mary looked up to see a cowboy hat-wearing Anne Bonny atop the brown- and white-quarter horse. She rode side by side with two cowboys, one of them the man that had killed poor Jack Rackham in the duel.

Vane and the other pirates strode up to stand next to Mary and stare up at Anne and the two James brothers.

"Anne?" Mary looked up in confusion.

Anne shrugged her shoulders. "It's a long story."

"Best save it for now, Woodes Rogers and several men came looking for us at that tavern," Charlotte said.

"Interrupted our grand party," Vane quipped.

"You know a quiet place we can all talk?" Anne asked Jesse.

"I do. Follow me."

Jesse turned his horse down a side street and led the group a few blocks away to a stable. A young man in overalls was finishing his work of watering horses when they arrived. Jesse dismounted and handed the man a few coins.

"Wyatt, why don't you go get yourself a drink while we stable our horses for the night?" Jesse said as the man looked from the coins to the strange group. He kept his mouth shut and nodded his head, then strode off without looking back. Jesse watched him go, then motioned for the rest of them to follow him into the stables. Frank shut the door behind them after they and the horses were all inside. The group stood sizing each other up in awkward silence. Frank and Jesse couldn't take their eyes off the imposing figure of Blackbeard. Jesse lost count of the weapons strapped to the body of the stylishly dressed man.

Anne smiled through the tension that permeated the hay-littered room. She went to one of the saddlebags and pulled out a bottle of the Kentucky bourbon. She handed it to Anne who looked at the artistic label before taking a swig. She winced before passing the bottle to Charlotte. Anne pulled out another couple of bottles and tossed them to Hornigold and Jesse.

"So, ye made nice with the locals, have ye?" Thatch said after the bottle was passed to him.

Anne looked at Jesse, who had a curious look on his face waiting for her answer. "I have granted a stay of execution, but as a woman, I be entitled to change me mind with the tide."

Frank snorted and shook his head. "Don't know how you all are related to this wildfire, but you let us know when you want her back. Be willing to give you all this bourbon to take her off our hands."

"Throw in a stable of horse and maybe we have a deal," Vane joked. The group laughed and the tension began to ease.

Introductions went around and they all found boxes, haybales and crates to sit upon.

"So, who's this Woodes fellow you all running from?" Jesse asked.

"Woodes Rogers. He's that pirate hunter I told you of," Anne said before turning to her mates. "Woodes is here, in this time spot too?"

"He is indeed. Nearly killed me a few nights ago," Thatch said.

"Well, now he has help," Charlotte told them. "He and his men were travelling with Jennings and several locals that looked to be constables of some sort. Dressed like Blackbeard over there." She pointed out Thatch's fine waistcoat and clothing.

"Like him?" Frank asked, then turned to Jesse with a knowing look.

"Could be Pinkertons," Jesse said.

"Yeah, or government types. Maybe Wells Fargo men. You all rob any banks?" Frank asked.

"Not yet," said Vane and they all had a laugh.

"Where did you find this one?" Jesse asked pointing at Tom sitting next to Thatch.

"He's me cabin boy. Helping us get the lay of the land. Found him living the pirate's life on the streets of this here town, San Francisco." Thatch stood up and stretched his lanky frame. "We need to find the means to acquire a new ship, so we can sail away from Woodes, Jennings and whoever else he's convinced of his cause."

"Anne tells us you have treasure aboard your ship. Why not dive down and retrieve it?" Jesse asked.

"The *Queen Anne's Revenge* lies in waters of at least a hundred feet," said Black Caesar. "Too deep for a man to go, and too cold."

"They got them divers with helmets now that could do it. Jesse, you remember seeing 'em at Lake Superior? They had on that metal helmet and all them hoses sticking out. An' the water in Minnesota is even icier than here."

"Yeah, hell, I think they can even fix your boat and raise the whole damn thing up nowadays. Bet you can find a company or crew at the port that does such work. Going to cost ya though. God only knows how much," Jesse said.

Black Caesar stood up and approached the pacing Thatch. "If this is true, Captain, we must find a way." Thatch turned his back to the group while he thought.

"We'll all help… for a share of your treasure," Vane said with a smile.

"Right. Then we all sail out of this port. Back to the Caribbean," Hornigold added.

Thatch turned to Jesse. "This can be done?"

Jesse shrugged his shoulders. "I've seen it done. Smaller boat than what Anne says you sailed, but concept is the same. Probably just need more men, more equipment, more money."

Thatch paced again in thought.

"What do you say, Blackbeard?" said Mary. "Want some partners in salvage? All that treasure isn't rightly yours anyway. You'd have been splitting it with your crew, who's all dead now a hundred and fifty years. There was a grand lot more of them then us, mind you. You only need to split with us six now."

"Eight," said Frank.

"Nine... Captain," said Tom.

Thatch looked down at the young cabin boy. He smiled and roughly tussled Tom's hair.

"Thar's a boy thinking like a pirate! Alright, you lot, we raise up the *Queen Anne* and split the treasure. One share for each of you, two for the captain of course." Thatch said, raising a bottle of bourbon and savoring a long swallow.

CHAPTER 15 - THE SMART ENGLISHMAN

Philip Edward Albert fumbled with his cigarette case and matches as he walked through the lobby of his hotel. The pocket on the breast of his tweed jacket was just a bit too narrow for the case to slide out easily and he seemed to be all thumbs this morning as he sought the elements to satisfy his dire craving for nicotine. He used his shoulder to push open the hotel door as his hands were in the process of opening the case and retrieving a pre-rolled cigarette. He popped the smoke between his lips and struggled to restore the elegant case while looking down at the pocket in frustration. Philip turned left to walk down the wooden sidewalk without bothering to glance up. He was finally successful in pocketing the case, and then looked up, and skidded to a startled halt in front of two imposing men that he immediately recognized as the mythical pirates of the Caribbean, Benjamin Hornigold and Edward Thatch, aka Blackbeard. They were both dressed differently than the night of their first meeting, Hornigold in current-day workman's clothes and Thatch looking like an obscenely well-armed banker. Philip then eyed the small Chinese boy, matchingly dressed with Thatch, standing to the right and slightly behind the tall, spare pirate of another era.

"There's your smart Englishman, Edward. Looks like your cabin boy has come through again," Hornigold said crossing his thick arms as he hovered in front of Philip blocking his way.

Philip looked up at the two men with alarm, unlit cigarette hanging from his open mouth while it clung to his lip.

"Aye, I've been looking forward to reuniting with our new English scientist friend, Mr. Albert." Thatch said taking the box of matches from Philip's hand, striking a match, and holding it to the man's cigarette. It took a moment for Philip to recover his wits and use the flame Thatch held to light his smoke. "You do remember Benjamin and me, do you not Mr. Albert?"

Philip nodded his head yes. "You two men strike a figure that is hard to forget."

"Ah, good to hear. We'd be liking to have a talk with you," Thatch said.

"Well... I must inform you that I have an important meeting with a mining company that I'm pressed to attend," Philip said while attempting to pass them by. Hornigold stepped in front of Philip, blocking his way.

"Our meeting is more important," he growled.

"Not to worry, my good man. We won't be taking up too much of ye precious time." Thatch smiled warmly, but laid his arm around the smaller man's shoulder, leading him to walk with them down the sidewalk in the direction of the docks. "We have us a bit a problem that a man of science, such as yourself, might be able to assist with."

Thatch led Philip with Hornigold and Tom hovering behind them. Philip couldn't help looking anxiously back at Hornigold's stern face.

"Now then, you remembering the story I told you 'bout the fate of me frigate, the *Queen Anne's Revenge*?"

"Yes. Your ship sits at the bottom of the bay."

"That is correct. Not much could be done about such a predicament where we come from, but it has been told to me that currently there might be a solution to raise her from the icy depths so that she could sail once again."

Philip looked up at Blackbeard to see the seriousness of his question. He was able to pause their walk and take a drag from his cigarette to think a moment. The two men and the boy watched him with stone faces as he pondered the dilemma. He did understand the mechanics that were used to repair and raise vessels that had sunk. If the ship could be repaired, such as a hole patched, one could use flotation balloons to raise it to the surface. The *Queen Anne's Revenge* was a 200-ton vessel, but that was calculated as cargo capacity not it's actual weight. *Maybe 100 feet in length,* he reckoned, *25- or 26-foot beam, with a depth of 10 or so feet below the main deck, creating an area below deck with a volume less than 25,000 cubic feet. Lining the main hold with a large bladder or balloon that could be pumped with air should raise the ship to the surface where repairs could be made, depending on the extent of the damage.*

"What is the damage to the vessel that caused it to sink?"

"A hole, you worm, what else would have caused it?" Hornigold retorted.

"One hole? Several? A gash, a rip, a tear, a laceration, a crack? A round shot maybe?" Philip sarcastically listed.

Thatch held his hand on Hornigold's chest as the man made an aggressive move at Philip.

"Our dear Charlotte De Berry would be the one with the answer. She was down in the hold when it became flooded. Is there a solution if the hole could be repaired?"

Philip took a long, thoughtful drag on his cigarette before blowing out the smoke in a steady stream. "It would be costly, but I think it could be done."

"How costly?" asked Hornigold.

"You'd need skilled divers, a salvage boat, a large waterproof flotation balloon, several pumps, possibly a crane… several thousands of dollars. Four thousand most likely. There would be my fee of course."

Hornigold again needed to be held back by Thatch.

Thatch grinned at the small man as he nervously smoked and stared up at the two pirates. "Put the plan together and we'll meet you here in two days with the money. Don't fail us, Philip Albert. We are not men to be trifled with." The two men turned their backs to Philip and continued down the sidewalk. The Chinese boy stood glaring at Philip, tapping the butt of his Derringer peeking out of his shoulder holster before turning and following in the pirates' wake.

"Do you really think your science man can raise the *Revenge*?" Hornigold asked Thatch as they continued on their way.

"Raise it we must. I have little desire to labor while such treasure is within our grasp."

"We need four thousand of this city's dollars for the job. How do you propose to find that?"

"We will enlist Anne Bonny's new friends in our endeavor. They seem capable men of the sort to know where this money could be had," Thatch said.

"Yes, Anne told me of the coach they plundered. A nice booty of spirits and jewelry. We'd must find several together to achieve our goal for that much loot. Might take some time to fence the booty from them coaches as well. Better if we find one carrying gold or silver."

"Train," Tom said from behind them.

Hornigold and Thatch stopped and turned to the boy.

"What's that, boy?" asked Thatch.

"No moving gold by coach no more. Train," Tom said.

"I've heard talk of this train. It moves without horses. Steam, like the ships without sails," Hornigold said.

"Then it is time to see this marvel for ourselves," Thatch said then turned to Tom. "Oy. Take us to this… train."

The two pirates stood in awe of the fantastical mechanical beast that stood in front of them with its four giant slotted wheels mounted on the engine standing taller than a man. Those wheels rode upon rails of metal that stretched in either direction for as far as the eye could see. There were four small wheels on the front of the large cylinder-shaped engine car that had an open cabin in the rear where two men went about their work checking dials and levers. Black smoke was billowing from a large exhaust tube that jutted out from the front as the engine coughed while it was being shut down. Behind this car was an enormous cart overflowing with coal. Their gaze continued to take in each additional car that was attached behind the engine with some featuring curtained windows and ornate doorways with steps leading inside. The area around the train was crowded with passengers disembarking with luggage and bags. They were in the process of greeting relatives and friends as they had just arrived moments before.

Blackbeard was disappointed that they had been too late to see the arrival of the train. He slowly moved down the wooden walkway past each car, peering inside, catching glimpses of the interior. The cars began to show signs of added elegance as he moved toward the rear of the train. He noticed that between the cars there were also doors, so that one could walk from one car to the next without disembarking. Near the end of the train, he was taken by surprise to see one that also served as a dining room. He hopped up onto the steps, holding the siderail and gazed inside. There were indeed tables and chairs inside, complete with linen and silverware. A bar on one side was tended by a man sporting a fashionable suit and hat. The bartender looked up at Blackbeard from his work of cleaning glasses and Thatch slid back down the stairs to stare dumbstruck back at the length of the vehicle.

"What wonders…" Hornigold said quietly.

"Indeed," was all Thatch could say.

Young Tom was looking around, watching the passengers hurry along their way. He watched men beginning to unload cargo from cars further up near the engine. There were dozens of workers along with riflemen that were busy emptying out the contents of the train. This activity finally caught Thatch's attention.

"Train carries sometimes gold, silver… always people. People with money," said Tom.

"It is like a ship at port," Thatch said.

"Aye. How do we take such a beast as it travels?" asked Hornigold.

"It only travels by way of these rails?" asked Thatch.

"Yes, Captain," said Tom.

"We could construct a blockade so the vehicle would have to stop."

Hornigold looked down the long length of the train and counted the men and cars with his fingers. "There will be a great many people on board. Very difficult to control such a large group with just…" He looked down at the Chinese boy. "Just us nine. Maybe most on board will be just travelers and unwilling to put up a fight. But if men such as those with long rifles are on board or nearby our piracy could come to a swift and violent end."

"Aye, Benjamin. But we must meet this train far away from help and prying eyes. We will need horses and a wagon or two for our loot. Let's conspire with Miss Bonny's new friends on the best plan. We need to be quick about it since our smart Englishman will be expecting us in two days' time."

CHAPTER 16 - CHARLOTTE'S FORTUNE

In the early light of dawn, the seas had calmed, and the sky became clear, the emerging sun glowing orange as it reflected off the waters of the Pacific. The main deck of the ship was crowded with tussling patrons and weary crew members. The crew of the *Lurline* found themselves with a hard choice to make that morning as the mutinied pirates and sailors rounded them up along with the passengers to announce the change in leadership. The captain of the ship and several high-level officers knelt in front of Bartholomew Roberts, shackled and bound atop the deck of the forecastle. Roberts paced behind them, holding his new revolving pistol as the crowd on the main deck watched and waited for him to speak.

Roberts hid his glee as he thought of how surprised Captain Hilgard was to see armed sailors burst into the pilot room to take command of his ship. The man now knelt with a fearful expression on his trimmed gray-bearded face. Once they had secured the captain and any holdouts, he and Sam had toured the ship. Their awe in the workmanship of the vessel grew as they found it to be enormous and elegantly appointed. Bart had never seen such finery as well as engineering in his life. Light, he was told by Chester, from electricity was utilized in many of the public areas of the *Lurline*. No fuel from oil was used and it seemed magic to the two pirates. Flipping a switch up and down allowed all the bulbs to flicker off and on in an instant. *Incredible*, thought Roberts. He and Bellamy had just taken the greatest prize a pirate had ever thought to exist.

Black Sam looked revitalized and practically galvanic for the first time since their near drowning on the *Queen Anne's Revenge*. Nothing like a bit of piracy to break the mood of being marooned in a new century, a hundred and fifty years from your lost love. He and Sam had paid a visit to the dead Vern's cabin and retrieved their belongings. They both adorned themselves with their old weapons, clothing, and jewelry, though Sam also held a weapon of the current day, a long rifle with a cartridge of eight rounds. Roberts' exquisite cross hung comfortably around his neck, cutlass at his waist, hair tied back in a knot, every bit the figure of a pirate captain once again.

"I am Bartholomew Roberts, voted captain of this ship by the crew. Your former Captain Hilgard has surrendered his ship to my command. He has accepted my mercy as have several of his officers. They have declined to join us but will be released unharmed upon our arrival at the Hawaiian Islands within a day's journey. As passengers on this voyage, you will be confined in your rooms until we arrive. No harm will come to you if you obey my rules. Crew members will show you back to your cabins where you will remain until we arrive in port."

Roberts motioned with his hand to the armed crew on the main deck who then began to escort the passengers to their rooms. He then looked about at the sailors and workmen that stood with him. He looked to Sam then to Chester.

"Sam Bellamy, do you agree to serve as first mate?"

Sam nodded his head.

"Chester, I need a capable quartermaster. Will you serve?"

"Yes, Captain."

"Go get that wound looked at by the ship's doctor then report for duty," Bart told Chester.

He looked at the bound, kneeling men and furrowed his brows. He pointed at a few armed sailors. "Find a secure place to hold these men until we reach port." He then sat on his haunches in front of the former captain. "Why don't you show us what's in the hold, see what kind of spoils we be carrying. And get me a list of all the passengers you're ferrying."

Sam and Bart smiled at each other, then Sam grabbed Hilgard's arm and yanked him to his feet. "Lead the way," Sam told the captain as he pushed him forward, hands bound behind his back.

Bart, Sam, Chester, and several men in charge of running the ship, along with the navigator, who had needed some convincing about continuing his duties, stood watching the first island of Hawaii emerge in the distance. The navigator stood over the map of the area, holding his gauze-wrapped hand that had been beaten with the butt of Bart's pistol, and confirmed they were on the correct course. The largest Hawaiian city of Honolulu was their destination. Bart was told the city sat on Oahu, the sixth island in the chain. They would arrive at the port of Honolulu late that evening.

Bart and Sam had conversed with Chester for hours over the possible value of the goods that were stored in the hold. Some items Bart and Sam hadn't a clue as to their purpose. Machinery parts, Chester had told them. The three men had grown tired of opening boxes and crates that contained items such as clothing, grains, farming equipment and the like. Chester had said that it may take them weeks to offload and sell the items to the parties waiting for them to arrive. Some may not be keen on dealing with pirates, but these issues Bart and Sam had delt with many times.

Bart had enlisted several sailors to go room to room and relieve the passengers of their valuables, deciding all should be left with a distributed sum of thirty dollars. This would allow them a room and meal at their destination. It was a custom that served him well in the past and furthered his reputation as a pirate of fair dealing. Sam had taken to this idea, deciding that it completed the mythology of them being Robin Hoods. The passengers for the most part were wealthy and offered up quite a haul to be split equally among the crew members, who were all now pirates themselves.

Sam had suggested that Bart allow the crew to drink in celebration of their change in circumstances, but Bart had a general rule about drinking while on board ship. The rule stated that one drink of rum was the limit unless fresh water was being rationed. This was certainly not the case on board the *Lurline* which was furnished with thousands of gallons of fresh water stored in metal tanks. Though the passengers had engaged in constant merriment during their voyage the bars and galleys were still well stocked. Once they arrived in this new port and dealt with the prisoners and selling of goods there would be ample time for celebration. It was Bart's plan to offload several of the captured officers to alert the local government that he was requesting a parley. He would negotiate the release of the passengers and the captain for a fee. He might even be able to bargain with the government for the goods stored in the hold so that the deal would have expediency and he could be on his way back to San Francisco to rendezvous with the other pirates. He smiled to think of their shocked faces when they looked upon his prize. The ship had no way of defending itself, but he would remedy that. They had found a good number of small arms aboard; some were even found crated in the hold. These were most likely destined to arm a militia in the town of Honolulu. If the town's defenses included cannon, then he would have them for this ship before too long. A ship this size could probably hold more than a hundred twelve-pounders. *Imagine the look on Blackbeard's face once he sees this prize.* In truth he was only wanting to impress Charlotte De Berry. His thoughts had remained cluttered with visions of the exotic woman throughout his ordeal on board the *Lurline.*

Lurline. Obviously, the name of the ship owner's love, daughter, or wife. It will not serve me though. Bart looked to one of the sailors who had joined his crew with little hesitation. The man, whose name was Francis, had been a low-level mate who had jumped at the chance to raise his station aboard this ship. He had a crooked nose, most likely from a life of brawling in grog houses. "Find me some paint and someone good with their letters."

"Aye. I can read and write," Francis replied.

"Then we will be renaming this ship before we arrive," said Bart.

Sam looked over with a sly smile. "What be her new name?"

"*Charlotte's Fortune,*" Bart said without taking his eyes off the majestic cliffs of the Hawaiian island they were passing. *Oh yes. He did have it bad for this lass.*

Sam only smirked. He knew that Roberts had an affinity for the name *Fortune.* Each ship Roberts had commanded had been christened with it. There had been the *Fortune, Good Fortune,* and the *Royal Fortune.* He also knew that the man was smitten with the African pirate queen, but now he knew just how much. Sam turned toward the sailor. "You heard your captain. Anywhere you see the name *Lurline* it is to be changed to *Charlotte's Fortune*. Get to it."

Charles Bishop's thinning gray hair blew in the wind as six men rowed the large skiff toward the ship previously named *Lurline*. He stroked his white beard out of a nervous habit that would arise when he was under undue stress. He could make out dozens of figures lining the rail of the *Lurline*, lighted in the dark of night by oil lamps that he knew from personal experience decorated the main deck of the grand ship.

It had been just over an hour since he was awakened by a servant banging on his bedroom door. A greenhorn harbor watchman had alerted all the King's cabinet members of a band of pirates seizing the steam liner while en route to Hawaii. The ship had arrived near midnight and anchored in the harbor, sending out a boat to deliver the ship's battered first mate with a message to send an official to negotiate the ransom and release of the captain and passengers. Charles had been quick to accept the job because of his position as the foreign affairs minister as well as other more personal reasons.

The six men rowing the skiff, as well as the four other men accompanying him, were members of the United States and British marines. They were armed and trained in warfare on land and sea. King William

Lunalilo had inconveniently disbanded the Hawaiian army months ago after an attempted uprising when he had been the first elected King in Hawaiian history, so a formal Hawaiian military didn't exist any longer. Bishop was an American businessman who married a member of the Hawaiian royal family. He had recently grown to distrust the motivations of the Honolulu police force that was made up of so many of the disbanded army, so he took comfort with a portion of his escorts being members of the US marines and the other portion being British. That comfort was slowly dissipating as his crew of ten men brought him closer to the starboard side of the ship that now, in the flickering light, revealed forty to fifty armed men sighting down their rifles and pistols at him. He took note of the name of the ship, freshly painted to say, *Charlotte's Fortune*. Charles told the marines to leave their rifles in the boat and only take side arms when they accompanied him in boarding the ship. If it came to a fight, it was not going to be one they would win with ten rifles. He was now confident that they would be disarmed for the meeting, as they were greatly outnumbered, and he wasn't confident that those arms would be returned when the meeting was over.

Charles struggled up the rope and wooden ladder as his 51-year-old body strained to maintain its balance against the gentle rise and fall of the anchored ship. He followed up two marines with four more behind him over the railing of the *Lurline*. He waved off a hand of assistance from one of the marines as he lifted himself from the ladder to the deck. Once they were all aboard, he straightened his attire and stepped forward to the two men in sailors' uniforms that stood waiting behind the line of rifle men ready for action. A sailor with a bent nose strode forward to greet him.

"You a government type?" the sailor asked.

"I am the foreign minister. A ranking member of the King's cabinet."

The man looked him up and down, then turned to lead him away with a bored, "Follow me."

Charles sighed and nodded his head to his escorts and stepped in line to follow the man. His marine escorts were indeed disarmed by three of the sailors and then prodded along behind him by two dozen of these so-called pirates. He was led up to the premier deck of the forecastle where several men were gathered in an outdoor lounge area. There was a man on his knees dressed in a captain's uniform, bleeding from a gash on his forehead, to the left of a large wooden dining table. The man had his hands bound behind his back and a gag tied in his mouth. Most of the ship's men were standing, including a young man dressed in the costume of a seventeenth century pirate, complete with a cutlass strapped to his hip. He was a handsome fellow with long black curly hair. There was a similarly dressed man seated at the table, enjoying a meal of baked fish and potatoes. This man was a bit older, maybe mid-thirties, with a thin mustache. The man had dashing good looks and smiled broadly with a white-toothed grin as Charles was brought in front of him.

"Ah, who have we here?" Roberts asked.

"Says he's the foreign minister," the sailor with the crooked nose, Francis, said.

"Charles Bishop. Whom do I have the displeasure of dealing with on this dreaded night?" Charles asked with as much disdain and bravado as he could muster. He felt that he needed to put on a brave face and show that he wasn't intimidated by these men even though all he wanted to do was escape with his own hide intact.

"Join me, Charles Bishop. The fish in these waters are as succulent as I've ever tasted," Roberts said while continuing to eat from his plate.

"I do not dine with murderers and thieves."

"Sit, Charles," Roberts ordered. Charles was pushed forward and into the seat across from Roberts. Once sitting Charles noticed the large-barreled revolver lying on the table next to the pirate's plate. Roberts looked over at his new mate and nodded his head slightly. Francis turned and disappeared down a stairwell.

"Straight to business it is then," Roberts said wiping his mouth with a linen cloth. "My name is Bartholomew Roberts, our good Captain Hilgard has resigned his ship and all its possession into my custody. We also hold several of his crew and hundreds of passengers in confinement until an agreed-upon ransom is delivered to us. We are also willing to sell the contents of the ship's hold to the highest bidder, in which time we will release the weary travelers and crew to your care. I have taken the liberty to list the terms and costs for you in this report." Roberts pulled out a folded sheet of paper and slid it across the table to Charles. "You have until sunset this very day to agree."

Charles stared at the pirate for a long moment before picking up the paper and unfolding it to read the contents. He did his best to mask his emotions as he read the terms. The pirate wanted $100,000 in gold, provisions for *his* ship, 200,000 pounds of sugar, 100 small firearms with 5,000 rounds of ammunition, and 100 cannons along with 1,000 round shot.

Bishop was a wealthy businessman and banker who could quickly calculate the values of trade items in his head. He needed to determine if Honolulu could meet the demands of these thieves without the need for loss of life. This island was becoming a booming destination for trade and travelers. It would do no good to have tragedy come to these passengers in their harbor. He also knew that the ship's hold carried many items destined for local companies that were needed for Hawaii's growing economy, but these terms were outrageous. He was tasked with finding a quick end to this disturbing development and deal a harsh punishment to these pirates once the passengers and cargo were secured.

Charles leaned forward and steepled his hands. "Before I take your demands back to the King let me enlighten you on a few details from your list, that way we will be able to come to an agreement without too many boat trips across the harbor for my tired bones."

"Far be it from us to discomfort you, Mr. Bishop." Roberts chuckled and the other men joined him in laughter. "Please do enlighten us as to our demands."

Charles cleared his throat. "We are not a wealthy island, my good sir. One hundred thousand dollars in gold would not be attainable from our meager coffers. It's possible that we could scrape together twenty thousand. I would though, be able to provide you with a good amount of sugar and other provisions for your stores. We have no need of small arms and ammo in our peaceful town so one hundred is out of the question. A few, possibly a dozen, could be rounded up from the constable's office, but cannons are something we just don't have. The fort you see above the harbor is not in working condition and hasn't been for over fifty years. No munitions or ordnance remains. It was built by the Russians back in 1817 and had only been in service a few years. Now, we must come to a much more realistic, shall we say deliverable, ransom than what you have written on this list."

Charles slid the report back toward Roberts. Just then Francis emerged from the stairwell and approached Roberts to whisper something in his ear. Roberts nodded and the man went to stand near the doorway.

Bart smiled at Charles as he leaned back in his chair. "Ah, a negotiation is what you're after. I see." Roberts turned toward Black Sam Bellamy. "Seems we need to come up with a new offer for this gentleman, Black Sam."

Charles glanced over at the other ornately dressed man. This Black Sam fellow pulled a dagger from his belt and with a malicious grin he walked over to a door just off the lounge area. Charles watched as the man exited through the door but left it ajar.

"You seem an amenable fellow, Charles Bishop," Roberts said, standing up, "so before you take back our demands to your King, I'd like to give you a parting gift."

Charles practically jumped out of his chair when Sam Bellamy brought his wife out from behind the door with a gag in her mouth. Sam had a firm grip on the woman's arm with one hand. Bernice Pauahi Bishop was an attractive woman in her early forties. She was of Hawaiian descent with short, dark hair and dark eyes that were wide with fright. Those eyes pleaded with her husband for help as the two stared helplessly at one another. Bernice had booked passage on the *Lurline* for her return trip to Hawaii after a month-long trip to San Francisco. Charles was poised to bolt over to her when two sailors pushed him back into his seat and others held guns at the ready against his marine accompaniment. Bernice was brought to Roberts by Black Sam and Roberts took out his dagger to hold near her bare neck. Charles could only sit across the table and watch in horror as Roberts gently stroked his blade against Bernice's cheek.

"Since we're negotiating, let me adjust the deal a bit to fit the circumstances we find ourselves in… Sam, hold out Mrs. Bishop's hand."

Sam looked shocked at Roberts, his eyes wide.

"I'm sure Mr. Bishop understands his position here," Sam said.

Bart looked hard at Sam. "I'd like to illustrate that for him so that we are perfectly clear. Chester?"

Chester stepped forward and forcibly grabbed the woman's hand and pinned it to the wooden table. Charles attempted to rise out of his chair again but was held down by two men.

Roberts stood over Bernice. He spun the knife expertly in his hand then slammed the tip of the blade into the table between two of Bernice's fingers. The woman winced and a muffled cry escaped her gagged mouth.

"Bartholomew, we don't…" Sam started but went silent from a harsh look from Roberts.

"What a beautiful wedding band you have on your finger," Bart said as he held his blade to her digit just below the ring. He rocked the blade back and forth over the finger, lightly pressing against the flesh. Bernice's eyes leaked tears as she watched in panic.

"I mentioned a parting gift for you, Charles, and I thought you would like this ring. I'm sure it has some sentimental value to you and would go far in persuading you to deliver on our demands."

Roberts looked up from the ring to Charles' tearing eyes. "Why don't I just send you back with her finger as well? Seems a shame to separate the two." Bart made a quick move to chop off Bernice's finger.

"Stop!" Charles screamed.

Roberts stopped just before the blade touched skin.

"I'll agree to your terms! Don't hurt her, damn you!"

Roberts looked at the distraught man and smiled. "If you change your mind or wish to bargain more…" Roberts pulled his knife from the table and glided it up her arm to her throat.

Charles swallowed hard and with a grim face said, "You will get what you ask for, but I am being truthful in regard to the cannons. Hawaii has none."

"We'll need to be compensated for the loss of the cannon. How much per cannon, Sam?"

"One thousand each," Sam replied, not looking at him.

Roberts roughly handed Bernice back to Sam and approached Charles. He lifted him out of his seat by his collar.

"Hmm, that makes another one hundred thousand dollars, making the total in gold two hundred thousand dollars." Roberts then moved within inches of Charles' face. His voice became low and quiet. "If our terms are not met by sundown, I will be sending the passengers back to shore in pieces, one by one. Starting with your wife."

Charles' eyes were wide with fright. He nodded his head and gave a last look to his wife's tear-stained face before he and his marines were led away, back to their boat.

Chester and the other men took Bernice back down to her cabin and Sam stood watching the shoreline from the window. Roberts approached the young man.

"Would you have cut off her finger?" asked Sam.

"It's a tactic that I've used many times. Fear is a great motivator. Fear not only of one's own life but the lives of others. The man clearly loved his wife and most likely had little concern about the money for ransom. He was only a negotiator. But, as we found out, a negotiator with the unfortunate luck to have his wife in our possession."

Sam was silent and made no move to ease the tension in the room.

"Your reputation as a merciful pirate, generous even, has served you well," Bart Roberts said as he stood next to Sam watching the small boats move about the harbor. "But one must be able to adapt and overcome all obstacles. Hard choices are sometimes the one a captain must make. We are pirates, Sammy. We must show strength before our men. When the coffers are full the crew are happy as clams, but when there are hard times… they will mutiny should you seem too soft."

"You still didn't say whether you'd have severed her finger," Sam said solemnly.

Bart Roberts smiled. "Nine fingers can play a harpsichord almost as well as ten."

CHAPTER 17 - THE 8:12 FROM ST. LOUIS

Charlotte De Berry despised horses. Putting aside the smell and tedious maintenance they required, riding on the back of one was a painful and jarring experience. Give her the calm to wild motion of the seas any day over this constant, backbreaking clomping of hoofs. They had all secured horses with the help of the James brothers as well as the two wagons being driven by Black Caesar and Mary Read. Anne Bonny rode side by side with the younger of the James brothers, Jesse. Hornigold, Vane and Thatch rode confidently as all had experience at one time or another with horses. The Chinese boy that Blackbeard now conscripted to the role of cabin boy of his lost ship rode on the wagon beside Black Caesar. They rode through the sparse landscape following the rails that allowed the trains to move quickly across the ground. They had seen one such train from a distance as it traveled out of San Francisco to some unknown destination. It was quite a feat of ingenuity. The steam-powered engine moving all that weight faster than a horse could run, weeks' worth of travel passing in mere days.

The train they sought was coming from a city named St. Louis, two thousand miles away. The train would make many stops along its route and one of them was a stop in Nevada where it would be picking up transfers of silver bars from Virginia City. This information was purchased by Hornigold from some source that he kept to himself. Maybe it was from some character that he had met while drinking at The Paris. The James brothers seemed to think that this was an opportunistic venture as they were quick to loan their own funds to purchase the horses, wagons, and extra firearms to replace the pirates' flintlock pistols. The older James, Frank, seemed an untrusting type but he was resolved to follow his brother Jesse on whatever adventure the quick-handed cowboy decided to go on. Charlotte watched as Jesse flirted with the uncharacteristically blithesome Anne. She had either found a soulmate, or she was soon to slit his throat for killing Calico Jack.

The sun was near setting when they found the desired location for their trap. The incoming train would have a mile-long path to reach them before arriving at the entrance to a canyon where the tracks traveled between steep-walled cliffs. Frank James checked a winding pocket watch and announced the time to the group. They moved one of the wagons that was filled with wood and hay to block the tracks and unhitched the horse which was then mounted by Mary Read. Black Caesar passed out several torches and as the sun slowly faded behind the hills, they lit them ablaze.

The pirates and cowboys gazed off into the distance from atop their horses, searching for signs of the train's arrival. Thatch casually worked waxed wicks into the long braids of his beard. Frank raised his eyebrows at Jesse as the two men curiously watched him. Once Thatch was finished Frank shook his head in confusion but was in awe of the dark look that came over the black-bearded pirate. He watched the man's face change to something deadly and dangerous.

"Train!" Tom shouted as his young eyes were the first to spot the black smoke being emitted in the darkening sky far down the tracks.

Thatch turned to Vane and bellowed, "Now!"

Vane kicked his horse over to the wagon parked atop the rails and used his torch to set the hay and wood on fire. In moments the entire contents of the wagon were aflame.

The horses became restless around the smoke and fire and it took the bandits some doing to regain control. The mounted group circled and stomped as the train grew into view.

The train whistle blew several times as the conductor saw the fire in their path from his distance.

Frank's horse danced around in anticipation of what was to come.

"Ready yourselves!" Thatch yelled.

Frank turned to see the pirate and his eyes went wide. The crazed man had lit the wicks woven through his beard. His dark face was surrounded by red flames sparking and spitting. Frank couldn't take his eyes off the devilish vision. Jesse was transfixed by the scene as well. Indeed, all eyes were on Blackbeard as the fiend gave a horrifying grin and his horse reared up, kicking its hooves into the air.

The night was blasted with the sounds of the train whistle and the squeal of brakes. The conductor was desperately trying to slow down before colliding with the burning obstacle blocking the path. He hung his head out the window to get a better look as he pulled back on the sparking brakes with all his might.

Blackbeard pulled out one of his pistols and fired it into the air. "Bring hell and fury and fire upon them!" He led them galloping toward the barreling train.

The conductor let off on the brakes in horror as he watched a fiery man riding a large black horse toward him. The madman's face was afire, flames licking and dancing around his head as he passed by the engine. The train was slowing but not fast enough to avoid the burning wagon. The conductor turned toward the front just in time to see the grille of his train collide with the blazing object. Heat and fire radiated up into the cab as the train was rocked by the crash. The front grated scoop of the engine exploded the burning wagon in all directions, sending fiery debris into the dirt and bushes as the train finally came to a stop due to the small front wheels derailing from the iron tracks.

The conductor reached for his stored rifle to protect himself from the bandits that seemed to be emerging from the gates of hell. He had a childish flash of wonder that maybe bullets would have no effect on the beasts he had seen riding past. He was about to exit his cab when he turned toward the opening to see the grim face of Charles Vane and a smoking pistol pointed at him. It was only then that he felt the searing pain of the bullet that entered his chest mere seconds before.

The cowboys and pirates galloped past the terror-filled faces in the windows, continuing to fire their weapons in the air. Two armed men jumped from the train and started shooting. Jesse and Anne riding side by side took aim on the men and fired repeatedly until the men lay dying in pools of their own blood.

Black Caesar and Hornigold dismounted and entered the first passenger car. Each man held two pistols at the ready. The people cowered behind the benched seats, fearing for their lives. Young Tom appeared behind the pirates holding a large, empty potato sack.

"Money and jewelry into the boy's bag 'less you want to bleed 'til ye dead!" Hornigold yelled at the passengers. Tom, guarded by the two men, held out the sack as the men and women dumped their belongings inside, fearing for their lives.

Mary, Vane, and Frank rode to the rear of the train and started going car by car robbing the passengers as well. Their plan was to clear the cars from each direction until they met in the middle with Hornigold and Black Caesar.

Thatch dismounted and entered the cargo car near the front with Jesse, Anne, and Charlotte. Thatch's beard still emitted smoke as he kicked open the door. Three men hiding behind cover hesitated instead of shooting at the tall, strange man that swirled smoke around him. That hesitation was their downfall. Jesse and Anne stalked down the aisle past Thatch, firing repeatedly at the men until the three were dead. Thatch moved toward the center of the car looking over the crates and boxes with Charlotte bring up the rear.

A loud scream sounded behind them as a man who broke from his hiding spot ran toward them firing wildly from a pistol. Charlotte with a blaze of speed threw a knife that slammed into the man's forehead with a loud THUNK, causing him to fall over backward, dead. Thatch turned to see the man lying with the knife protruding from his head, smoking pistol still held in his hand.

"That one is a worse shot than you," he quipped to Charlotte.

Jesse found a pry bar and wrenched up the top of one of the crates. Shiny silver bars glimmered inside. Thatch walked over to stare into the crate. He smiled wide then looked to Jesse and Anne.

"The *Queen Anne's Revenge* will sail again."

It took several minutes for them to load the remaining wagon with the silver and loot. The passengers stole frightened glances out the windows as the pirates and cowboys made off with their belongings. Several cursed them but none had the courage to challenge the bandits after the death and destruction that they caused. They mounted their horses and circled around the wagon as Black Caesar and Tom climbed aboard. Jesse nodded to Black Caesar and with a crack of the reins the wagon began to move back through the canyon. Jesse reared up his horse and gave a hearty *yeehaw*. Frank joined in on the cheer as well as Anne. Vane looked at them and gave a rare smile, then tried his own version of *yeehaw* that may have sounded too British. With that they all started after the wagon leaving the sitting train behind.

They made good time over the darkened trails on their way back to San Francisco with just the moonlight to illuminate the way. They talked amongst themselves about the loot, their plans, and the success of their plot. Jesse looked back at Blackbeard riding several lengths behind him. The man's braided beard was remarkably still intact after being set aflame with wicks and wax. The vision of the pirate's demon-like presence during the robbery was etched into his mind. Jesse wouldn't be surprised to find the man the subject of a few nightmares for days to come. Certainly, those poor bastards on the train would never forget the experience. He watched for a moment longer as the man smoked on a thickly rolled cigarette.

"Don't think I saw him kill," Jesse said quietly to Anne. She turned and glanced quickly back at Blackbeard.

"No," Anne said, then rode a moment in thought. "His is a reputation of murder and mayhem, feared throughout the Caribbean. Most ships give up without a fight when his black flag flies. Though, never heard a story 'bout him killin' anyone. His crew, yes." She nodded toward Black Caesar driving the wagon. "His first mate kill'd. Kill'd his best friend, Walter Key. It was over a girl they both loved. Took poor Walt's head in a duel. Calico Jack told me of it…" Anne's eyes wandered off with a tear for Jack Rackham after she mentioned his name.

Jesse watched her face sadden. He looked down and away for a moment as they continued riding.

"I am sorry 'bout what happened. Wish I could take it back," Jesse said quietly as Anne looked away. "The 'way of the gun' will furnish a man… or a woman, not with a reward for surviving but with the punishment and misfortune of loneliness." Jesse sighed. "Miss Bonny, I am truly sorry for your loss."

Anne wiped away the fallen tear as she steadily rode. "Thank you for that," she replied without looking at Jesse.

"Might even have become friends with the Calico feller if things had gone different," Jesse said a moment later.

Anne chuckled. "That was never going to happen."

"You're probably right."

They emerged from the canyon and started to follow the trail alongside the empty railway tracks. It was slow going with the wagon in the dark. They needed to be cautious not to throw a wheel on the bumpy path. The goal was to be back in San Francisco way before dawn.

Frank was the first to crest the next rise and he reined in his horse as he stared off into the distance. He could make out twenty riders heading toward them. He turned his horse back toward the others and stopped them.

"Trouble ahead! Looks like a posse."

They stopped the wagon keeping it out of sight and moved the horses up to take a look. Vane looked hard at the riders approaching. They rode with purpose; it was plain to see. He watched as one of them pointed in their direction and they all picked up the pace.

"They're coming for us," Jesse said.

"How would they know?" Mary asked.

None spoke but it was clear they were going to be pursued.

"We need to split up," said Thatch. "Caesar, take the wagon north, meet the scientist and get him started. Vane, Mary, Charlotte, go with them. The rest of us will lead them away. Go!"

Thatch kicked his horse and rode west with Anne, Hornigold, and the James brothers in his wake. He made sure the posse would see them and stole a glance back to be sure they would take the bait and follow. Sure enough, the entire team of twenty mounted men were galloping toward them across the plains.

Thatch was skilled at horseback riding, but Jesse and Frank were beyond measure. They overtook Thatch and led the group with ease through trees and over hills. They were able to look over their shoulders, riding at full speed and monitor their pursuers while not missing a beat. Anne was keeping good pace, but Hornigold was beginning to struggle and fall behind. Thatch glanced back at his old friend and former captain, his face in a grimace of determination. Hornigold looked back at the posse gaining on them, which caused him to throw his horse off balance.

Thatch slowed a bit to allow Hornigold to catch up but that in turn caused Hornigold to further slow.

"Ride, man, ride!" Thatch bellowed. Hornigold leaned forward in his saddle and was able to reach Thatch and they rode side by side. The pursuers were close enough now to begin to fire on them. BLAM! BLAM! They were wild shots but nevertheless the danger was real.

Thatch watched as Anne and the brothers reached a tree line and raced through, angling between cover as they rode, increasing their distance from Thatch and Hornigold. Thatch looked back and could now make out a few of the faces of his pursuers, determined, hardened men. They took aim while riding and tried for lucky shots. Thatch pulled a revolver and emptied it behind him not bothering to see if he hit anything.

When they reached the tree line Thatch steered his horse left to place trees in the way of their pursuers and Hornigold stayed right beside him, galloping full speed past branches and over logs. The posse began to spread out, widening their net and soon Thatch could see several men riding almost parallel to them only twenty or so yards away. He no longer knew the location or the direction that Anne and the James brothers had taken.

Hornigold was grunting as he rode at Thatch's side. He seemed to be struggling with the control of his horse as the trees went whipping by. Suddenly he was too close to Thatch, their legs bumping against each other. Hornigold's horse collided with Thatch's and the world seemed to go off kilter. Both men and horses slammed together again, and all went tumbling into the dirt and pine needles. Thatch rolled with the fall, letting the momentum carry him off and away from the falling nine-hundred-pound beast.

He was quick to his feet, but the enemy were already upon them. Thatch rose and was facing four circling men on horseback pointing pistols in his direction.

"Get them hands up!" a bearded man ordered.

Thatch spun around as more men arrived and he reluctantly raised his hands. He looked over at Hornigold who was still on his knees attempting to stand up while three armed men hovered around him. He was surrounded and a fight would only end in his own death. He watched as more riders arrived and dismounted. It was then he saw two familiar faces emerge out of the darkness.

"Even the devil will be damned, as God bears witness," said the pirate hunter, Woodes Rogers, as he smugly approached Thatch to stare up at the man's bearded face with Henry Jennings at his side. Jennings plucked the pistols, one by one, from Thatch's holsters, smiling the entire time.

"No surprise to find you two rat finks as bedfellows," Thatch said.

Woodes smacked Thatch's face with a backhand that was absorbed with barely a movement.

"I've been dealt harder from a scullery maid, my dear Woodes, and here there's been such talk of the dreaded pirate hunter. Seems just another story 'bout a fish this big." Thatch held his hands wide then smiled and brought them in to show just his fingers an inch apart.

"Tell your musings to the hangman, Blackbeard." Woodes spit. "Bind them both, and gag this one."

"With pleasure," Jennings said, grinning.

CHAPTER 18 - PIRATE BOOTY

Mary Read rubbed her aching back from the saddle of her brown and white speckled horse. They had ridden hard and fast through the night to arrive with the sun on the outskirts of town, thankfully unpursued after their train robbery. She was now casually riding alongside the wagon driven by Black Caesar and young Tom. Charlotte and Charles Vane, whose head was on a swivel, rode in front while watching for danger on the lightly crowded streets of San Francisco as they made their way to the stable acting as their base of operations. The James brothers had paid off the stable owner along with the purchase of the horses and wagon they were riding. She had a bad feeling about the outcome of the chase their brethren had embarked upon that had allowed her and the wagon to escape. She was worried about her dear friend Anne, that she may be captured or killed by the twenty horsemen that pursued them.

Mary glanced back into the wagon at the tarp-covered booty and a smile slid across her face. During her time pirating with Calico Jack and Anne Bonny she had helped capture many ships, but few could rival the haul of precious silver and loot that they had just seized. Unless you had the luck, ships, and manpower to overtake a Spanish galleon, you would need to be content with a booty of commodities and maybe a small bit of jewelry and other spoils. Once you added in the seventy or more fellow pirates that would be splitting the haul with you, you then realized your share would support you on land for mere months at a time, even less if you engaged in the partying and gambling that most pirates succumbed to upon reaching the shores of Port Royal, Nassau, and other such havens.

The amount of silver in the wagon split between just the few members of their land crew would be a fortune. Then, if they were successful in raising the *Queen Anne's Revenge* and splitting Blackbeard's treasure, Mary would be able to retire from this life, or buy her own ship. She could even move back to London and buy a ladyship if she wished.

They had not seen any signs of Anne, Blackbeard, Hornigold or the James brothers since they parted ways. She had worried all night about Anne's welfare knowing that the posse chasing them was too big to fight. Her only hope was that they could outrun them and lose them under cover of darkness. She vowed to free her friend if she was captured, either by force or by using a portion of their booty to buy her freedom. She looked over at Charlotte and Vane and was convinced that those two would be no help in the matter. Charlotte's face was unreadable. The woman was slowly becoming a trusted partner as they navigated this strange world, but still the bond was nowhere as solid as the one she shared with Anne.

Black Caesar on the other hand was completely loyal to Blackbeard. The story about their relationship was that when Blackbeard seized the *Queen Anne's Revenge* it had been a French slave ship called *La Concorde* and Black Caesar had been one of the captured slaves on board. It was a pirate custom to offer all on board a captured ship the opportunity to join the society of pirates and Black Caesar jumped at the chance to change his fortunes, quickly rising to the role of first mate on the newly renamed *Queen Anne's Revenge*.

Black Caesar was rumored to be a tribal chieftain from West Africa, known for his immense strength and height but also as a man of keen intelligence, which is why he became Blackbeard's second-in-command. Anne knew that Black Caesar would stop at nothing to free his captain should he be caught and jailed.

Maybe they have already arrived at the stables. Their horses would be much faster than the wagon I'm accompanying. Mary was hopeful that this train of thought would come to pass and when they arrived it would be to a celebratory reunion for all. But alas, the stable was empty and after waiting for a few moments in silence they began hiding a portion of their booty underneath a large stack of hay. Black Caesar, Tom and Charlotte would take enough silver to pay the scientist and his team to raise the *Queen Anne*. She and Charles Vane would guard the remaining treasure and wait for the others to return.

Once Charlotte, Black Caesar and Tom were on their way Mary found one of the bottles of whiskey Anne and the James brothers had acquired and used her teeth to uncork it. She sat heavily on a stool and passed the bottle to Vane.

"If no one returns tonight we would be smart to take the treasure and find us a ship, sail away from this cold dreadful place," Vane said after taking a long pull of whiskey.

"No honor among thieves, Charles? They've been gone only moments and you're planning to make off with their shares."

"Oh, come now, dear Mary, those half-wits are never going to raise Blackbeard's ship. An' Blackbeard himself is either dead or headed to the gallows along with Hornigold, Bonny and those cowboys. Are we to wait here to fall to the same fate?"

Mary sat silently then stretched out her hand for the bottle, which Vane handed over.

"You know this is all a fool's errand," he went on. "We have been dragged into their schemes time and time again. Now, when we've finally tasted some success, we have to part with a fortune in treasure for the impossible task of raising a 200-ton vessel from the ocean floor? Mary, this strange place will eat us alive if we stay, just like Black Sam and Bart." Vane feigned a sad look. "And poor Calico. Do you want to end up like him? We need to take this booty, even if it's just our share, and sail home."

Mary stared at Vane for a moment, then took a drink and wiped her mouth on her sleeve. "We have no home, Charles. Take your share if you like, but none more. Together we are strong. Together we can survive. Divided we surely will end up like poor Jack. I'm staying. Maybe the *Queen Anne's Revenge* can be raised. Consider the wonders we've seen in the past days. If these people can make a carriage like that train we went and robbed, then I believe they have a way to raise up a ship. Even a ship like Blackbeard's. We've both seen with our eyes the immense ships they can make, ships powered not by sail, but by engines of steam. You go on and leave, Charles. Me, I'm staying. I pledged my loyalty to my pirate brethren and to the pirate republic. My oath stands whether it's 1718 or, or…"

"1873," Vane finished her sentence.

Mary took another swallow of the whiskey and set the bottle down. She pulled her revolving pistol and opened the cylinder. Seeing that two rounds were empty she pulled two more from a pouch on her belt and began reloading the gun. "Besides, I have a fondness for this Kentucky whiskey and little desire to go back to drinking the wretched grog in Nassau."

Vane harrumphed at her comment but picked up the whiskey and sat himself on a hay bale. Mary used a rag to clean up her pistol the best she could. Vane watched for a moment before pulling out his handgun and doing the same. Mary hummed a song while she worked.

"It would be quite grand to see the *Queen Anne* sail once more," Vane said.

Mary continued to hum her tune and soon Vane picked up the vocals mid-song:

> *Four Chiviligies of Gold in a Bloody Field,*
>> *Environ'd with green, now this is my Shield;*
> *Yet call out for Quarter, before you do see,*
> *A Bloody Flag out, which our Decree,*
> *No Quarters to give, no Quarters to take,*
> *We save nothing living, alas 'tis too late;*
> *For we are now sworn by the Bread and the Wine,*
> *More serious we are then any Divine.*
> *Now this is the course I intend for to steer;*
> *My false-hearted Nation, to you I declare,*
> *I have done thee no wrong, thou must me forgive,*
> *The Sword shall maintain me as long as I live.*

Mary smiled to herself as she knew Vane would stay... at least for the moment. *Men are fickle beasts, and this one can switch directions as fast as a school of fish.*

CHAPTER 19 - THE RUSE

Black Sam Bellamy watched the four barges depart from the wharf of Honolulu Bay through the spyglass he had found in the pilot house of the *Charlotte's Fortune*. It was a fine instrument made of brass and polished wood, English in origin. The device had a single draw that extended over three feet in length. The optics were crystal clear and allowed Sam an enhanced view of the men and large crates that were loaded and crowded on the four boats. It seemed that the cabinet minister, Bishop, was living up to the bargain they had struck. He wouldn't know for sure until the crates were brought aboard and opened to reveal their contents. Sam adjusted his view to examine the sailors that rowed the boats, six in each. He saw no signs of weapons on the men, but it wouldn't be difficult to hide a pistol or blade under their garb. He handed the spyglass to Chester after having his fill. The older man stared through the glass, moving from boat to boat to make his own assessment.

"Looks like we are about to become very rich," Chester said.

"Aye but keep an eye on them and watch the docks for any trouble."

Sam moved quickly over the deck that was crowded with armed men with greedy looks in their eyes as they too watched the approaching boats.

He took the stairs two at a time to reach the pilot house where Bart was leaning over a nautical map, studying it, and making notes.

"They're on their way. Looks like Bishop came through. The goods from the hold are on deck waiting to be offloaded. Should I bring up the prisoners?" Sam asked.

"Keep them out of sight. Let's make sure the gold is counted. They can start taking the cargo from the hold first."

"Aye. Seems easy pirating in these waters. With a ship this size none would give trouble," Sam said.

Bart looked out the window at Honolulu Bay. There were many ships with sails though most were small fishing vessels. He did see a few sloops and several steam ships much smaller than the behemoth they had arrived on. He could see an approaching rain cloud hanging over a dormant volcano. They would be wet in less than an hour. The daily rains in this Pacific Ocean were similar to the Caribbean, rain would fall hard several times throughout the day for mere minutes before moving on.

"She needs cannon, Sammy. We have yet to see a warship, but they are out there. Captain's log tells of two iron-built ships with steam engines and turrets which he describes as rotating cannon mounted on the fore and aft deck. He saw them on his last voyage from Hawaii to that San Francisco." Bart brought over the logbook that was accompanied by several drawings of ships the previously named *Lurline* had encountered. Sam looked closely at the detailed drawings. "This one is English," Bart pointed out as they both stared at the sketch of a three-masted frigate with two steam stacks in the center of the deck. Sam wasn't sure as he stared at the drawing if the size ratio of the armaments had been increased for effect or were true to scale. If they were true, they'd be the biggest guns he'd ever seen.

"She looks fast as well," he said.

"Aye. One thing at a time though, Sammy. Let's take this King's gold an' be on our way back to our mates."

The two men left the pilot house and watched from the forecastle deck as the barges approached one by one. As the first one was tied off to the *Charlotte's Fortune* Bart started down the stairway with Sam following.

"Stay alert, lads," he said to the waiting men peering over the rail. "No one likes to give up gold without a fight so look sharp."

The ship had a large, well-engineered hoist to move heavy loads to the deck of the ship from docks or in this case other vessels. Bart and Sam waited while the first load was secured to the hoist and began rising to the deck. It contained the smallest of all the crates. Two men boarded the ship from the barge and Chester had them searched for weapons. He then turned to Bart and shook his head. Bart approached the two men.

"Your boat be the one with the gold?" he asked.

"Coming up now," said one of the men.

They turned and watched the crates crest the railing. Sam looked around at their crew, seeing all eyes were now on these crates.

"Quit your gawking! I want eyes on the other boats. Watch for trouble!" he yelled.

As one they all turned their attention to the barges, some readying their rifles, but all was calm, and no threat was perceived.

Chester and three men guided the hoist to set the crates on the deck. They worked to untie the netting and then using a pry bar Chester began to open the wooden boxes. Sam, Bart, and others made their way over to peer inside. The open wooden boxes held a mixture of gold and silver coins and paper money. Bart picked up a few stacks of paper money and looked it over. He gave a questioning look to Chester. Chester took a handful and began to flip through the currency.

"Mostly American, but some from England and Mexico. Can't say what the exchange is but there is enough gold and silver here that it's probably about what you asked for," he said.

"It's all there. Mr. Bishop said to assure you," one of the men from the barge piped up.

Bart looked at the man, then looked again at the money. "The rest of them crates our supplies?"

The man nodded.

"Bring up the rest and move the treasure to the forecastle to be counted. Sam, you and Chester make sure it's all there best as you can."

The money was moved from the deck and the barges began to unload the rest of the larger crates aboard the ship. Once one barge was emptied it was then loaded with the imports that had been in the *Lurline*'s hold. That cargo filled up most of four barges. While that was happening six longboats with just four rowers each approached the *Charlotte's Fortune* to pick up the passengers being held hostage. Bart watched them as they waited for the last of the cargo to be lowered onto the barges, then as it pushed away from the ship the longboats arrived to tie off.

"Send down the passengers!" a man on the first longboat called up.

Bart looked around the deck crowded with large unopen crates; his men were just milling about discussing what they were going to be doing with their share of the loot. He frowned and shouted at them. "Bring 'em up and get those passengers off my ship!" The men quickened their pace to bring up the passengers from where they were crowded below deck and Bart wandered through the maze of crates that were as tall as him. He looked at the company labels on their sides as he strode past. Most were Hawaiian-sounding names. The passengers were boarding the longboats as quickly as they could as most were scared for their lives.

Bart turned to watch them as they pushed and shoved to be next to disembark his ship. He was glad to be rid of them. None had had any skills he was needing for his crew. Most looked to be soft, well-to-do-folk that he was glad to relieve of their valuables. He longed to get the *Charlotte's Fortune* back on the open sea, heading for the mainland. Back to San Francisco. Back to Charlotte De Berry. He smiled at the thought of the other pirates' faces when they saw the prize he and Sam had taken with just a handful of men. Bards were sure to write songs of this adventure. Within a few moments almost the entire lot of passengers had boarded the longboats.

COUGH. Bart quickly turned toward the large crate behind him. The cough came from inside the crate. Bart pulled his pistol from his belt and slowly took a step toward it. The crate was well made but still there were knotholes and spaces between the boards. Bart stopped and stared hard at one of those knot holes. *Movement*, he saw something pass behind the hole.

"Enemy in the crates!" Bart yelled and then fired a round from his pistol at the knot hole. A man screamed in pain from inside. Bart fired again.

Suddenly armed men burst from many of the crates, firing as they came. The whole side of the crate that Bart had fired into came crashing down as four men rushed out with rifles and pistols. Bart pulled a second pistol from his waist and met them head on, firing round after round until the chambers were empty.

His crew were shocked as bullets exploded around them. They returned fire but were untrained combatants and haphazardly scattered about. Bart could feel the sizzle of rounds miraculously only grazing his body as he strode at the one man remaining alive from the crate he was in front of. Their pistols were both empty and they grappled and spun back into the crate. Bart was slammed into the back wall by the man dressed in a military uniform of white pants and long blue jacket that featured white chest straps in the shape of an

x. The man slammed his fist into Bart's cheek and pulled it back for another blow. Bart was able to move his head just in time and the man's hand landed hard against the wooden wall of the crate.

Bart twisted his body away from the man, then spun back with an elbow strike to the man's jaw. He stumbled backward, and Bart was able to catch his breath for two seconds before the man pulled a knife and lunged at him. Blocking the man's knife hand, Bart was able to shoulder underneath him and hold on to the man's wrist, barely keeping the blade from slicing into his chest. He pressed the man against the back wall of the crate, one arm under the chin against his throat, the other keeping the knife from stabbing into his flesh. Their faces were so close Bart could smell onions on the man's breath. Roberts knew that the knife was getting closer to him. He felt the tip of the blade against his linen shirt. He needed to do something quick before it skewered him like a piece of meat. Bart tilted his head back then smashed his forehead against the man's nose. He felt and heard the crunch of cartilage and when he opened his eyes the man's face was filling with blood. The blow stunned and took the fight out of the man long enough for Bart to strike him several times with his knee. Bart wrestled the blade from the man's hands and stuck it into his gut several times before letting him slide down to the floor of the crate in a pool of blood.

When it was over Roberts noticed the frantic yelling and booms of gunfire happening around him. He quickly knelt and began to reload his pistols. The mechanics of opening the chamber, dropping out the spent rounds and replacing them with live ones was quite simple, but it was still unfamiliar to him. Also his hands were shaking from the adrenaline leaving his body after the fight for his life. A uniformed man appeared suddenly in the opening of the crate. He held a rifle, which he quickly brought to bear when he saw the pirate. Roberts braced for the impact of a bullet and cringed when a shot rang out. The soldier slumped over and crumpled to the planking, dead. Bart looked up and the saw his crooked-nosed mate, Francis, smiling at him with a smoking rifle at his hip. The two men then moved from cover to cover to get back on the side of the friendlies while the enemy hid behind crates and in an organized way took potshots at the pirates.

Bart saw where Sam and others were gathered on the forecastle. It was good they had the high ground, but these enemy soldiers were fine shots, and the deck was littered with the bodies of his crewmen. They made it to the hoist and were in a good cover spot, but to run across the open deck to the staircase would be suicide. He looked over the railing into the bay. The longboats with the passengers were a hundred yards away and were passing several boats loaded with more rifle-carrying soldiers heading to join the fight. It would only be minutes before they would be overrun. Bart desperately looked around for a solution. He spotted the oil lamps that sat on top of poles to light the deck in the evenings. He pointed them out to Francis, who looked back confused.

"We burn them out of their hiding spots," Bart said.

The man looked back at the wooden crates scattered about the deck the soldiers were hiding behind and understood what his captain was thinking.

"Send the bastards to hell," he said, nodding.

They took down as many lamps as they could reach without getting shot. They lit the lamps and Bart was the first to launch his to a distant crate. It crashed into the wooden box and flames burst from the oil as it splashed over it. Bart turned and smiled at this new mate and then they continued to target the crates, spreading fire throughout the deck. Smoke and flames continued to grow, and the soldiers knew that fire aboard a ship was a horrifying situation. The pirates and their crew watched as the frantic soldiers left the cover of the burning crates to be shot by the pirates, or launched themselves over the railing into the bay.

Sam and his crew came down the stairs firing rifles and pistols at the soldiers as they tried to escape the burning deck. Chester directed several men to get a water pump to start battling the fire once their enemy was dead or overboard. In a matter of minutes, the deck was aflame and the soldiers left alive were swimming toward the oncoming boats filled with more armed men. Those men sent covering fire at the pirates and attempted to rescue their swimming companions.

"Sam, you and these men keep them busy, the rest of us we need to get this fire out!" Roberts said as smoke was filling the area.

Sam and twelve men lined the rail firing aimed rounds at the soldiers until they were able to row out of range. The rest of the crew were desperately trying to put the fire out, and just when it seemed that the blaze was too big to handle the blessed rain that Bart had seen coming began to fall and fall hard. What had seemed like a lost cause a few minutes ago had now given the men of the *Charlotte's Fortune* a reason to raise their voices in a cheer. They hoisted their rifles, buckets of water, and pistols in the air and let out loud hails of joy.

Bart looked around at the men left standing. They had lost twenty or so to this fight but would still be able to crew the vessel out to sea. His forehead had drying blood on it from having slammed it into the soldier's nose but overwise he was alive and unhurt. A wonder that no bullet had ended his life during the battle. He and his crooked-nosed mate Francis had been in the thick of it. Bullets flying all around from both sides. It was not his day to die,

Roberts surmised. Those Hawaiians were sure to regroup and return in force once they saw that the ship's fire was out. They needed to escape the harbor.

"Sam, let's get the anchors up and the *Charlotte's Fortune* on her way. Chester, take some men and salvage what you can from those crates and put it in the hold. Collect the guns and ammo then drop the bodies over the side. Clean up my deck. Congratulations, gentlemen. You are all now rich, but we need to escape while we can so that we can live to spend it. Fire up the boilers and let's be off!"

Black Bart Roberts patted a few men on their backs as he headed up the stairs to the pilot house leaving the smiling men to their work.

CHAPTER 20 - A FINE DAY FOR THE PIRATE HUNTER

Edward Thatch spit out a mixture of blood and spit after being struck across the face for the… well, he had lost count of how many times Woodes Rogers had hit him while he remained tied to the wooden chair in the small jail cell. The cell was housed in an old building near the town center. Thatch and Hornigold arrived just before daybreak with their captors. They were roughly thrown into separate cells and Edward was then bound to this chair with rope. He had been alone for what seemed like hours before Woodes Rogers, Jennings, and another man he'd never seen before entered his cell and started questioning him. Questioning and beating him. His eye was beginning to swell shut and he couldn't feel the left side of his face from the many blows the pirate hunter had rained upon it. Jennings stood in one corner near the door beside the short, stocky stranger with a heavy beard that was trimmed to about an inch in length. Jennings was looking on with a smug smile as Rogers rubbed his sore punching hand. Thatch tried to smile to himself, as he joked within his own thoughts that his head was taking a toll on Rogers' knuckles. The smile didn't form as it hurt too much to attempt the feat.

"Come now, you sad demon, tell us the whereabouts of your hideout so we can end your beating," Woodes said as he looked down on Thatch. Thatch only spit again. This time the blood and spittle landed on Woodes' boot.

"You an' your little crew took up with the James brothers didn't ya?" Bill Cooper asked. "We recognized them riding ahead of you. Looks like they don' much care for saving your hide. Didn't even consider turning round to pick you up after your fall."

"No honor among thieves and pirates," said Jennings.

Thatch looked up from the concrete floor at Jennings and said with venom, "Ye no longer callin' ye self a pirate, Jennings? No wonder there, worst pirate sailing was you. Bottom feeder. Spineless. Picking the bones of sunken ships like a vulture."

"The good Captain Jennings took the King's pardon, as the rest of you should have done," Woodes said.

"And I never took an English ship!" Jennings said. "Never committed such a traitorous act. Not like your lot!"

"Traitorous? Once the Crown decided to make peace with the Spanish, they abandoned us all in the Caribbean. No money, no jobs, no more letters of marque! No ways of getting back home. German King George cared not for those in service to England! He sits on his cushioned throne while we bleed, an' slave, an' die for his whims. That pardon was a ruse, meant to divide us."

Woodes suddenly moved his scarred face right in front of Thatch's "And it worked. Pirate Republic. A joke. The idea that the likes of you... deviant, godless men, could form your own nation, absurd. While you and the other captains met upon your evil, stolen ship to discuss your fate, hundreds of cut-throats were signing the pardon on the shores of Nassau.

Your reign is over, Blackbeard. The time of pirates is at an end." The two men stared maliciously at one another for what seemed like an eternity.

"Where were you taking the silver? Tell us where the hideout is and if we capture the James brothers with the silver maybe we don't hang you," Cooper said.

"Go bugger each other, you bilge rats," Thatch hissed.

Woodes backhanded Thatch. "Insolent miscreant!"

"I'm sure we can convince Hornigold to give up the location. He seems a more reasonable man," Jennings said absently.

Thatch turned a glare toward the man.

"Yes, yes. Let's go pay a visit to Blackbeard's old captain," Woodes agreed. "The man is tired and ready for a quieter life. He said as much after he signed the pardon when you brought him to me, Jennings, days before the *Queen Anne's Revenge* arrived in Nassau."

"Liar! Hornigold was the architect of the Pirate Republic, the rightful governor of Nassau! He would never sign that rubbish," Thatch countered.

"Ha! We shall see shan't we?" the pirate hunter said, then led the other men out of the cell, closing the door behind them. Blackbeard struggled against his restraints to no avail and let out a loud scream of frustration that could be heard throughout the hallway.

Woodes Rogers happily washed the blood from his hand in a basin while Jennings, Cooper and several of Cooper's men waited. His own two Royal

Navy sailors were waiting outside for Rogers to give them orders. It was a fine day to have the infamous Blackbeard in his custody. If he could hang him by sundown this day might go down in history as his greatest of all. Woodes really cared nothing of the silver the man and his cohorts stole from that technical marvel they called a train. His only goal was to bring these dreaded pirates to justice, Blackbeard being the one he sought most to string up by the neck. Born a demon, that one. His father should have sent him straight back to hell while he was still a child. *It's in the eyes*, thought Woodes. He could see it plain as day. Woodes dried his hands on a towel and turned toward the men.

"That devil won't talk, any more effort is wasted. We'll get the information we need from Hornigold then I and my men will help you round up the remaining lot of vermin. Once that is done, we will be on our way back to Nassau, with your assistance as promised," Woodes said to Cooper who nodded.

"Nassau? Why not back to England?" Jennings protested. "There could be nothing there for us. It's been one hundred and fifty years. Who knows if anything is left?"

Woodes turned to Jennings, "Good God, man! Why do you insist on speaking the impossible?"

Jennings looked toward the heavens in frustration. "Why do you not understand?" He turned toward Cooper whose face showed his amusement at their argument. "The year is 1873, correct?"

"That it is," said Cooper.

Jennings looked at Rogers to see if this had sunk in. The man only smiled like Jennings was a child.

"It is but a simple explanation, Jennings; many cultures have different calendars than we do in the civilized world. I have sailed throughout the globe, much further than anyone would have thought possible, and I've seen many villages where the inhabitants had no idea of our dates. Some only counted moon cycles, some kept no track at all. It's childish, really, to jump to such fantastical solutions. You've obviously been associated with these uneducated, lesser men for far too long." Rogers put a fatherly hand on Jennings' shoulder. "Come now, Henry, let's go and find out what Hornigold knows then be done with this place."

CHAPTER 21 - AIR VS WATER

Philip watched as a dozen men loaded the supplies he had rented onto the chartered steam-powered tugboat. The captain, a Dutchman named Beekman, had spent the last ten years in the San Francisco Bay working salvage jobs and towing broken down and derelict ships. He had on staff two skilled divers that would descend to the bottom of the bay where the *Queen Anne's Revenge* was said to lie. The tug was now outfitted with two air pumps that would fill two large bladders, the size of hot air balloons, that the divers would place inside the hull of the ship. Once the air was pumped inside it should displace the water and allow the ship to rise. The tugboat could then pull it toward shallow water and the ship could be careened so repairs could be made. He looked over at the two dark-skinned pirates as they walked along the deck of the tugboat, admiring the vessel. Philip was quite surprised when Edward Thatch's first mate Black Caesar showed up with thousands of dollars in silver this morning. Philip had done as he was asked to do, finding, and hiring a salvager that could possibly do the job that Thatch had asked for, but he honestly expected the whole ordeal to be a farce. Now here he was in modern times, standing with two pirates born in the late 1600s, preparing to raise a 200-ton seventeenth-century frigate off the bottom of bay.

Beekman was watching the pirates as well, especially the exotic beauty Charlotte De Berry. He stood on two bowlegs that belonged on a horseman rather than a sailor and leaned against the pilot house entryway smoking an ivory-bowled pipe. He used the pipe to point toward Charlotte. "You, lass, you were in the hold when the ship went down?"

"Aye, that I was."

"How large was the hole that took her down?" Beekman asked, sticking the pipe back into the side of his mouth.

"Cannon size," Charlotte responded dryly.

"Mm-hmm, and you all have a good idea where she lies?"

"We do." Black Caesar handed over a map of the bay with an x marking the approximate spot where the *Queen Anne* had gone down. Beekman looked at the map, then out toward the direction the spot indicated. He then rolled the map up and handed it back to Black Caesar.

"Then let's be off," Beekman said.

"We are waiting for two others and the boy," Philip said.

Black Caesar had sent the cabin boy back for the two pirates waiting in the stable for the rest of their crew. He didn't want to be so greatly outnumbered if they were able to raise the ship with all of Captain Blackbeard's treasure on board. The boy left an hour ago on his errand and Philip had given him an additional stop at the Paris to see if Colette's network of little birds had news regarding the whereabouts of Thatch and the other missing party members. Colette's pretty waitresses were a reliable source of information as men's lips seemed to loosen while in their divine company. It was as if Colette had instructed them on the arts of subtle interrogation, and

Colette being the ever-smart businesswoman knew that information could be the most valuable asset.

It wasn't long before Phillip spotted Charles Vane, Mary Read and the cabin boy striding along the dock toward them.

"A heavy ship without sails you hired, scientist? Going to take hours to move us out there and I'll not be rowing such an ugly beast as this," Vane said after looking the tugboat over.

Philip ignored the comment, figuring the act of sailing the ship would prove its worth better than trying to explain how the steam-powered tug operated to the likes of Vane. Instead, Philip made the introductions of the newcomers to Captain Beekman and the ship was prepared to depart.

The loud coughing and roar of the steam engine as it started up had taken the pirates by surprise. They all flinched and crouched, expecting the boat to explode like it was hit by a heated round shot. They tentatively watched the smokestack in the middle of the ship belch black smoke into the air. Once the engine was running smoothly, Beekman gently throttled the tug away from the dock and motored out past the moored ships and into the larger San Francisco Bay. The pirates were in complete awe at the power of the tug and moved from fore to aft, and port to starboard looking over the side rails, staring at the churning water as the steam-powered screw pushed the tug faster and faster through the cold water.

It took just fifteen minutes for the tugboat to reach the search area where Black Caesar directed them to go. Beekman slowed the boat to a crawl, and they began to search in a grid pattern for a sign of the *Queen Anne's Revenge*. There was a bit of arguing between the pirates as they all had an opinion on where the ship went down. They pointed out landmarks and Charlotte was immediately insulted when Vane accused her of being half-blind and untrustworthy of spotting anything visually beyond a yardarm.

Philip pulled the Chinese boy aside and asked him what he'd found out at The Paris. The boy told him that everyone was gossiping about the train robbery, and it was rumored that the James Gang was involved. Miss Colette told him two men were reported to be captured and held in the city's jail. It wasn't believed that either of the two men were Frank or Jesse James. The two men caught were likely to end up on the gallows since several men were killed during the robbery. Philip complimented the boy and handed him a silver dollar for his work. The boy pocketed the coin and went to join the pirates.

If it wasn't the James brothers in that jail cell and the news made no mention of a woman being caught, then it was definitely Edward Thatch and Benjamin Hornigold they were holding. For reasons he couldn't explain Philip felt a strong desire to help rescue the pirate captains. It could be that he felt a natural kinship to his fellow Englishmen, but it was much more than that. His scientific mind was enthralled by the idea that these men and women somehow traveled through the cloak of time to arrive here. He wanted—no, needed—to find a way to explain it. He was also captivated with the mythology of their lives and being close to them was the most exciting thing he could imagine. He knew that every moment he spent with them was a moment of danger and potential violence but the longer he spent with them the more it was like a drug he couldn't resist.

Philip walked over to the divers' equipment to admire the cylinder air tanks that sat like metal pillows behind their backs. A hose went from the cylinder to the front of the diving helmet to supply breathable air. There was also a hose that went out of the cylinder and up to the boat to supply fresh air by way of a small hand-powered pump. The divers could stay safely submerged for around thirty minutes he was told. As Philip looked over the equipment, his scientific mind was working out a way to improve the performance of the pumps by using a small piston engine that could be powered by electricity. If he could figure out a way to tap into the steam engine to generate the electricity…

"Thar she is!" yelled Mary Read, interrupting Philip's train of thought from the port side of the boat. Everyone rushed to Mary's side to look down upon the *Queen Anne's Revenge*. The dark brown hull and three masts were easily seen from the surface of the water. Beekman powered down the tug and strode over to assess the job he was about to undertake. He chewed on the end of his pipe while he moved along the rail to see the entirety of the sunken frigate.

The top of the main mast was merely ten feet below the surface. The rest of the ship was lying on the port side atop the sandy bottom. If the ship were upright the main mast would have probably broken the surface.

"Amazing. Looks like a pirate ship. What year was this thing made?" Beekman asked.

"1710," Black Caesar replied without taking his eyes off the ship.

"Impossible. She'd have rotted and fallen apart by now," Beekman said.

"Yet there she sits. And in great condition," Phillip replied in a state of awe.

"Besides the hole that be bigger than you," Charlotte said standing beside the petite man.

Philip looked up at her. "Well, we're going to fix that now aren't we?"

They all stared down as the tug slowly drifted over the wreck. The workmen and divers who joined them at the rail watched in silence and one of the men drew the sign of the cross on his chest. No one talked for a moment until they drifted past.

"Let's get cracking!" Beekman said loudly through teeth clenched against his pipe. With that the crew went about anchoring ten yards away

215

from the *Queen Anne*. They then worked on preparing the dive suits and equipment they were going to need to raise her up.

Anne, Jesse, and Frank quietly entered the stable with guns drawn. The only sound was from the horses stirring in their stalls. They each took a direction and searched the building for any signs of their friends. They had ridden hard and fast into the night putting as much distance as possible between them and the posse that had chased them. It was quickly apparent that Blackbeard and Hornigold had been caught or killed. Frank had said that there was a small chance they had just taken a different direction but once they knew their pursuers had given up on them it seemed clear that not all the pirates had gotten away. Anne and the James brothers had eventually stopped to rest their horses awhile before taking an out-of-the-way route back to San Francisco.

"They were here. Their horses are boarded so they're on foot," Jesse said.

Frank was looking over the wagon that they had used in the heist. It was empty of supplies and loot.

"We get God damned double-crossed?" he asked.

"Not sure. At least we know the wagon group didn't get caught," Jesse answered. "You think they made off with the silver?" he asked Anne.

"They are pirates," Anne answered absently. She was looking around the room at the empty bottles of whiskey and signs of eating. Then, moving further into the stable she looked at the tack wall that held assorted bridles, reins, and saddles. Anne ran her hand along a few items then turned toward Frank and Jesse with a scowl. She was about to say something when she noticed a length of rope hanging from a hook on a post near the door. She walked over to the rope and touched the knot that was tied into it by another length of rope.

"You boys seen this kind of knot before?" Anne asked.

They walked over and looked at the rope and shook their heads.

"What is it?" Jesse asked.

"A rolling hitch. Mary taught me how to tie it my first week sailing with her an' Calico Jack. It's a slip knot for transferring weight from one rope to another. Use it on the rigging to stop the tension on a sheet. Can't imagine what use it would be to a horseman."

"What of it?" Frank asked with irritation.

"It's a message. They made it back and are at the waterfront. She's saying she's on a boat," Anne said.

"Alright then, let's search down there. They must have moved the silver, an' used some of it to hire the salvage boat. Come on," Jesse said leading them out the stable doors.

Twenty minutes later those same stable doors burst open, and a dozen armed men surged inside and quickly searched the building before Cooper, Jennings and Rogers followed them in. The stables were empty but for the abandoned wagon and several horses in the stalls. One of Woodes Rogers' navy men picked up a whiskey bottle with an inch of liquid swirling at the bottom and smelled it. He looked at the fancy label and took a sip. Woodes gave the man a harsh look that prompted the soldier to set the bottle back down.

Cooper looked over the wagon and the horses in the stalls.

"Could be the same wagon. Horses look like the ones we'd seen them on, but it was dark, might be mistaken," he said.

"Most likely they were here and maybe they will be back," said Jennings.

"Unless Hornigold lied," Rogers replied. He then looked around the room. He approached the pile of hay in the corner and began to use his boot to move the hay around.

Cooper pointed to two of the Wells Fargo men. "You two, find a spot across the way to keep an eye on this place in case they do return. Make sure you stay out of sight." He turned to Rogers as the man continued to nose around the haystack. "You find something?"

Rogers looked up at Cooper, his scarred face unreadable. "Place has a smell of pirates."

"I just smell horse shit," Cooper snarked.

"What's this?" Jennings said. He made his way to the door. Cooper and Rogers followed to see what caught his attention. Jennings fingered the rope with the rolling hitch on it.

"It's a rope," Cooper said dryly. "Don't have them where you're from?"

"The knot is for a ship's rigging," Jennings said.

"What of it?" Cooper asked.

"It's a knot only a sailor would tie. An' you wouldn't use it here. It's a message," Jennings said.

"What kind of message can you say with a knot?" Cooper asked. Jennings turned toward the Wells Fargo man and knitted his brows.

"The kind a pirate would understand," he said.

"That means they *were* here," Rogers said. "Let's go pay another visit to our good Captain Hornigold."

Beekman's two divers were brothers from Russia, Stefan and Peter. Neither minded the cold waters in the Bay of San Francisco since they grew up in the icy territory of Southern Russia. They both wore insulated suits that kept out most of the water but after ten minutes of diving you could feel the sea creeping underneath the water-resistant material. The two men had found the hole in the hull easily enough. They were able to swim inside the flooded compartment and see the chaos that the sudden flooding of sea water had created through the gloom. Once their eyes totally adjusted to the lack of light in the water-filled hold, they were able to make out the crates and wreckage that would need removal to get the bladders inside to fill with air.

Peter made a note that the beams and structural supports were all in fine shape. This was quite a big job they were undertaking and if the ship's integrity was in question, they would not attempt to bring it up for fear the vessel would crack in pieces. Stefan carefully moved about the area making sure his air tether line was not getting twisted or hung up on anything. Stefan gave a hand signal to Peter that he would swim toward the back to inspect the area. Peter acknowledged and began to reconnoiter the crates and stores. Most of the crates were still intact but a few were damaged with their contents spilt out lying near the container or floating nearby with bits and pieces of wood and cloth. Peter noticed something gleaming in the gloomy light, catching his attention. He swam a bit closer to see that the small amount of sun filtering from the surface through the cracks and holes in the walls was illuminating something that was underneath a pile of boxes. His heart sped up as he neared the wreckage. There, under the pile, was a crushed and broken chest. Scattered around it were a spectacular collection of jewels and shiny coins, the like of which he'd never seen before. Peter forgot all about his tether, and the canister on his shoulders, as well as his brother working a short distance away. He only saw the dimly visible treasure that was just lying for the taking in front of him. He raked his fingers through the pile of coins and picked one up to bring it close to the glass of his face mask so he could see it better. Gold. It was certainly a gold coin. They all were. He was rich, he thought in his head. He ran his hand across the jewelry and precious trinkets. *Richer than the Czar.* Peter's hands fell upon a large diamond-encrusted cross with a golden chain. The cross was the size of his hand that was made from a silvery pink metal. He pulled the cross toward him. The chain suddenly caught on something underneath and he wasn't able to easily loosen it. He wanted that cross and had no patience to move the mess around it to dislodge the necklace. Instead, he just pulled harder. He didn't want to break the chain, but really what did it matter if he did? It was the cross with all its diamonds he was after. That piece would easily bring in a kingsley price. He pulled and pulled deciding that he didn't care if he broke it.

CRASH! The chain didn't break but what was attached to it came loose and triggered the crates, along with a stored cannon barrel, to come rolling down upon him. His face mask took the brunt, and it instantly cracked as he was pressed to the floor by the collapse. The heavy iron cannon barrel rolled to settle on his chest, pinning him underneath the wreckage.

Stefan burst through the surface next to the tugboat yelling in Russian, startling all on board. Black Caesar grabbed the man's arm and pulled him aboard like he was lifting a child. Stefan was shouting and pointing toward the water while everyone gathered around to see what the matter was.

"Slow down and speak English, Stefan!" Beekman yelled at the frantic diver.

Stefan took three deep breaths before speaking. "Peter. He is stuck. Down, in ship. Many boxes, cannon fall on him. Can't move them by myself."

"Does he still have air? Can he breathe?" Philip asked.

"For moment. Yes," Stefan answered, panting.

"We need to get him up before the air in his tank is too stale to breathe. There is another tank and hose but someone strong needs to go," Philip said looking at Black Caesar.

Black Caesar shook his head. "Don't like to be under water."

"You've spent a life at sea!"

"Don't matter, sailors don't trust the water underneath," Charlotte told the scientist.

Philip looked around at all the sailors on board, pirates, and Beekman's crew. They all turned their eyes away. He sighed in frustration. If it was strength that was needed it couldn't be him to go. He looked again at Black Caesar. "It must be you. You're the strongest. It's your ship."

"Blackbeard's ship," Black Caesar said quickly.

"But you know it best," Philip said.

Black Caesar looked off into the water with trepidation, then at the desperate look on Stefan's face.

"Ahhhg!" Black Caesar exclaimed, giving in. "If I drown in this icy bay, know this, little scientist, I will haunt you for your next seven lives."

"Let's get him down there then. Get him one of those barrels of air!" Charles Vane said, slapping Black Caesar on the back.

"You are a strong man as well," Black Caesar growled at Vane.

"Yes, but nothing like the likes of you, my friend," Vane said with a smile.

Black Caesar shook his head as Stefan brought him the spare diving equipment. The suit was much too small for him, so he was left with the weight belt, air canister, and helmet to dive with. Stefan quickly showed him how to breathe through the helmet and the rules of the hose. Black Caesar had no time to practice with the equipment as time was running out for Peter. Stefan jumped into the bay and trod water as he watched Black Caesar ease his feet into the cold sea with a shocked face.

"Think warm thoughts, my friend," Vane said leaning close to him, then pushed him off the edge of the boat. Black Caesar let out a yelp as his body submerged below the surface.

Black Caesar was in a state of panic as he sunk quickly down. He was about to start swimming for the surface when Stefan appeared in front of him. Stefan put his hands on Black Caesar's shoulders and gave him a calming look, nodding his head. Looking up, they could see the hull of the tugboat rapidly becoming a distant shadow. A moment later they touched bottom with a muted thump, as clouds of sand and slit rose around them. They carefully moved out of the cloud, trying not to disturb the bottom any more then was necessary.

Stefan used a hand signal to point out the wreck and the two divers made their way to the sunken ship. Black Caesar forgot about panicking and how cold the water was once he saw the *Queen Anne's Revenge* lying on the bottom only twenty yards away. The ship was massive from this perspective, rising up higher than many buildings. He made his way toward the hole in the side of the ship that had a hose leading out of it and up to the tugboat, Peter's lifeline. He watched as Stefan carefully made his way inside the hole, pulling his own air hose to make sure it didn't kink or tear on the broken wood of the entrance. Black Caesar copied what Stefan did and pulled himself inside the hull. At first it didn't seem that there would be enough light to see by, but then his eyes started to adjust to the murky interior. He could make out the figure of Stefan hovering over a pair of legs sticking out from a pile of wreckage. Black Caesar half walked; half swam to the Russian brothers.

Peter lay underneath debris consisting of wood, cloth, and sacks filled with assorted goods and of course the one thing Stefan was unable to move himself, a twelve-hundred-pound cannon barrel. Black Caesar was able to see Peter's face through the cracked glass plate of his helmet. The Russian's eyes fluttered open which let Black Caesar know the man was still alive. Water was creeping through the crack in the glass and mixing with blood from a cut on Peter's head. The blood-water mixture had halfway filled the helmet covering the back of Peter's head up to his ears. It wouldn't be long before the helmet was as useless as a fishbowl full of water. Stefan had moved everything he could that wasn't being held down underneath the cannon. Now, if they were going to free Peter, they would have to work together to lift the iron barrel.

Stefan went to the opposite side of Black Caesar and wrapped his arms around the cannon barrel, Black Caesar did the same. The two men looked at each other through their face plates and Black Caesar mouthed *go* and they both strained to lift the barrel. Stefan's feet slipped out from under him and sent him thrashing down on top of the barrel causing Peter to struggle in pain with the added weight. Stefan quickly rolled off and regained his footing. They prepared to try again. Both men grimaced through their face masks as they strained to lift the cannon with difficulty even as the barrel was lighter in the water. At first it wasn't moving at all, then Black Caesar tilted his head back and gave a roar that Stefan could hear through the water and the helmet. The cannon lifted an inch, then two, then Black Caesar with a burst of strength lifted it high over Stefan's head. Stefan ducked out of the way as Black Caesar swung the barrel away from Peter and let it fall harmlessly away from the injured man.

Peter immediately put his hands to his chest, holding his ribs and rolling to the side. *The man's ribs must be broken*, thought Black Caesar. They would have to carry him up to the surface. He and Stefan each grabbed an arm and lifted the man to float off the floor of the ship. Something underneath the man caught Black Caesar's eye as it glimmered. He took hold of the item and slipped it into his shirt. When Peter turned his head, they could see his face now was completely under water within the helmet. The man was panicking and began pulling the helmet off his head. Stefan pulled the hose from Peter's tank and bubbles emerged from it. Once the busted helmet was off, Stefan put the hose to Peter's mouth so he would be able to take in a breath of air. The three men dropped their weight belts and swam to the opening in the ship's side. Stefan helped Peter through and started to bring his brother to the surface. Black Caesar pushed his way through next but wasn't paying good enough attention to his air hose. It became caught between the broken joists of the hull. He tried to free it, but it was wedged tight. He was desperate to surface and pulled hard on the hose. Snap! The hose was cut in two by the sharp wood and bubbles of air emerged out of the ends. Black Caesar stared as the air rushed out from the canister strapped to his shoulders. He took in several quick breaths before the water started to rush in. He wiggled out of the harness holding the air tank and ripped off his mask and swam frantically toward the surface.

Stefan broke through the water ten yards from the tugboat and started yelling for help as the crew threw him a rope. He was able to grab hold and the men and women pulled him and his brother toward the boat. The two men were pulled aboard, and they carefully laid Peter on the deck. The man began coughing and spitting up water, but it was a relief that he was alive.

"Where's Caesar?" Tom asked.

"He should be behind us," Stefan said worriedly.

Tom, Vane, Charlotte, and Mary peered over the side, searching the water for Black Caesar. They moved around the railing looking for any sign of the man.

"You left him down there, you bilge rat!" Vane said, turning back to yell at Stefan.

"No, no, he was right behind us," Stefan stuttered out.

The pirates searched the waters, worried looks on their faces. As the crew joined the search, the tugboat gently rocked and all were silent.

BANG! Something thudded against the side of the tug.

"He's here!" Tom yelled out from the bow of the boat. Everyone crowded around as Black Caesar emerged from underneath. Vane extended his hand down to the big man who grasped it, out of breath. Vane pulled and with the help of three other men lifted Black Caesar over the side to roll, waterlogged, onto the deck. He turned over onto all fours and spit out the sea water from his lungs and mouth.

"Cold." Black Caesar shivered as he spoke.

"Get the man a blanket!" Beekman called out and a deck hand quickly brought one.

Black Caesar sat against the rail, wrapped in the blanket as everyone stared at him.

"Stop hovering like a bunch of wet nurses," said he growled. "Did the man Peter live?"

"Aye. Only thanks to you," Mary said.

Black Caesar just nodded his head. Vane knelt on his haunches next to him. "So, you get them bladders in the hold? Otherwise, you got to go back down there, mate."

"Never again. You go."

"The ship is cursed. Leave it to its watery grave," Stefan said standing up. "It almost killed us all."

"Captain Blackbeard wants his ship back!" Tom yelled.

"You gonna go down there, lad?" Beekman asked.

"I go. I'm not scared," Tom said puffing out his chest.

"No one's going down there. Not worth the money, not worth the risk," Beekman said.

Black Caesar got to his feet. He looked down at Peter who was watching everyone and beginning to sit up, holding his ribs in pain. He then looked at the crowd.

"There is treasure down there. He's seen it." Black Caesar pointed at Peter. "Do I lie?" Peter shook his head. "The treasure is Blackbeard's, but I be his first mate and can promise you all an equal share. Help us raise this ship and you will all be rich from this day forward."

The crew all looked to each other, unsure of what to do. Most turned toward Captain Beekman for direction.

"What kind of treasure we talking about?" Beekman asked.

Black Caesar reached into his shirt and pulled out the cross that had almost cost Peter his life and held it up for all to see. The men of the crew, Beekman, even the other pirates practically salivated at the sight of the precious work of art.

"Do we raise the ship? Or do we sail back, safe and sound, but poor?" Black Caesar asked, showing the cross around.

Everyone's eyes were firmly on the prize.

"Aye," said Beekman. "We raise the ship."

CHAPTER 22 – PRISONERS

Hornigold paced the small cell after unsuccessfully trying to get some sleep in the uncomfortable little cot in the corner. It had been hours since he'd been questioned by Woodes and his cohorts. He knew Thatch must be held in another room close by as he'd seen a row of metal doors to the entrance of cells just like the one that he'd been thrown into. Rogers had seemed intent on questioning Thatch first when they were brought into the building. Hornigold had been put into his room and that was the last he had seen of Thatch. He had called out to the man a few times, but no one had answered. The small, barred window in the door allowed him to see a bit of the hallway but nothing more. There were no other windows or features to the brick walls that he was now confined in. He was about to sit on the cot again in frustration when he heard the door's lock being opened and Woodes Rogers, Jennings and the Wells Fargo agent, Cooper, let themselves in.

"The stable was empty," Rogers said.

"Maybe they all didn't make it back. Maybe they found a new place to hide out. I told you the truth. We were all going to meet back at the stable if we were separated. They must have realized Thatch and I were caught."

effort.

"Perhaps, but what was the plan going to be after you divided the treasure?" asked Rogers.

"Were you all going to join the James Gang and rob more banks? Maybe another train?" Cooper asked.

"We just needed money to sail back to England or some other godforsaken place. A few wanted to go back to the Caribbean, but from what I understand we are a very long way from the Bahamas. We had no intention of joining anyone's gang. The arrangement with them was one of convenience that Anne Bonny had initiated. Maybe out of desperation, maybe she was just looking for an opportunity for revenge. One of the James brothers killed poor Jack Rackham and we thought she had gone out to hunt them. But, surprise, she had taken up with them. Never could figure out the minds of women. Also, we haven't seen Bellamy and Roberts since the first night we arrived. Figured those two are just as dead as Rackham, or just gone. Swallowed up by this strange city. I'm sure Jennings told you all this, Woodes. We all just want to go home. We had nothing after the *Queen Anne's Revenge* sank."

"Plenty folks having nothing an' don't take up with gangs of thieves. Lots of work in this city for able-bodied men such as yourselves," Cooper scolded.

Hornigold just stared at the man in his well-tailored suit and manicured beard. This Cooper had the makings of a merchant, ranking officer, or maybe a nobleman of Hornigold's time. It seemed, though, that here in the late 1800s, he was a mere constable.

"Benjamin," Jennings said, trying to reason with Hornigold, "what was the plan and where can we find the rest of the pirates? It's not you they're after. I've explained to Mr. Cooper what a loyal Englishman you are and that you must have been coerced into the schemes of Blackbeard and his like. For

God's sake, you were a privateer with a letter of marque from the Crown at one time. The two James brothers are wanted killers and the good Sergeant Cooper just needs your cooperation to bring them to justice."

"You give us some more information," Cooper said, "information that leads to me catching them, and you may go free when this is all over. Otherwise, if you don't help, you could find yourself swinging by the neck from a tree alongside your friend Blackbeard." He drew out the name Blackbeard threateningly with his accent.

"Yes, you can't help the rest of them evade justice, but surely, you'd like to save yourself," Rogers said. "Mr. Cooper here just wants the James men. He has told us that we are free to do as we wish with the rest of your lot. The King's pardon still stands, Benjamin. A signature absolves all sins. So come now, my good man. Tell us how to find the rest of them."

Hornigold looked at the three men and their stern faces.

"I already told you where to find them, maybe wait around to see if they come back."

Jennings strode right up to Hornigold's face. "Were you going to use the silver from the train to buy a ship? Were they going to the port? Maybe back to that brothel you were so fond of?"

Hornigold returned Jennings' icy stare. "I don't know. Why don't you let me out of here and I'll help you find them?"

Cooper let out a laugh. Then he looked at Woodes and Jennings and saw that that was an idea they were entertaining. "You ain't seriously considering that? He's one of them! He'll warn 'em or just run away."

Woodes and Jennings stared at Hornigold, matching the hard look he was giving them while they decided on their next course of action.

"Gather up your men, Mr. Cooper," Woodes said. "It's time we paid a visit to your city's docks." The men opened the cell door and started to exit.

Woodes turned to look over his shoulder at Hornigold. "Leave him here until he becomes more cooperative."

Hornigold paced the small room again once they left. His mind was clouded with anger. He thought back to the night this all started. If he'd only stayed in Nassau instead of attending that damned meeting on Blackbeard's ship, he would not be in this tiny cell, marooned in a time so distant from his own. He stalked to the door and grabbed the bars on the small square window, his knuckles turning white from his strained grip.

"Thatch! Thatch, are you there, you rotten bastard?" Hornigold yelled. He then heard some loud shuffling and a bit of grunting.

"Aye, I'm here, Benjamin. More in spirit then in body, but I'm here." Edward Thatch said from a cell several doors down from Hornigold.

"Why did you not answer me earlier?"

"Ha, well, might have fainted from fright after laying me eyes on the blighted face of the pirate hunter. Either that or it was his strikes to me head that put me to slumber," said Thatch.

Hornigold let his anger fade some upon hearing Thatch's words. His closed fists relaxed and released the bars. He leaned his head against the door.

"Woodes can be a nasty one," Hornigold said.

"Jennings, that rat as well. Never did like the man, pompous bone picker. Never really lived the life or the code of pirates. Ha, don't know how Vane sailed with him for so many years."

Hornigold never liked Vane much, the man was too cruel even for a pirate. Jennings just used him as a sharp end of a sword. If blood needed to be sprayed, Vane was the man to do it. He had no qualms with slicing off an ear, a finger, or a much larger body part to get what he wanted.

"Those two don't seem to be working together at the moment," Hornigold said.

"No. Vane was never going to give up piracy for that sham pardon written by a counterfeit monarch. It seems all for nought now that we find ourselves stranded here."

The two men were quiet for a moment in the solitude of their cells. Hornigold turned and leaned his back against the door, head next to the window so he could still hear Thatch.

"Woodes is going to see us hanged," Hornigold told Thatch matter-of-factly.

"Aye. Sure, would have loved to see the *Queen Anne's Revenge* sail again. I do love that ship. She's the greatest prize I've ever taken."

"Do you think that little scientist can actually raise her from Davy Jones' locker?"

"I believe, Benjamin. I believe."

CHAPTER 23 - THE ASCENT

It took three men again to pull the exhausted Black Caesar onto the deck of the tugboat. The big pirate was dripping wet and shivering from the cold waters of the bay. Two other divers were helped aboard and in a scurry of activity the crew readied the pumps and pulleys that extended down toward the sunken ship. Charles Vane brought a dry blanket to Black Caesar and wrapped it around the man's broad shoulders. He slapped him on the back good-naturedly.

"If I didn't know any better, I'd say you were born a seal the way you've taken to the waters," he quipped.

"I have no strength left for your jokes, Vane, but once I stop shaking from cold, I may decide to wring your neck and throw you overboard."

Vane laughed and slapped his knee. "Well, let's see if all your efforts will bring back the *Queen Anne* from the deep before you toss me down to join her."

The men and women aboard the tug watched Beekman pace around the railing, looking over the side, inspecting the hoses and lines descending below the water, down to the ship lying beneath them. He checked the pumps and the anchor to see that all were properly readied. Turning to the anxious crew he smiled and nodded to them. "Start the pumps!"

Charlotte watched the hoses inflate as the manually operated pumps sent volumes of air down toward the bladders that were placed inside the hull of the ship. Philip approached and stood beside her watching as the air pulsed through the rubber tubes.

"How long will it take?" Charlotte asked him.

Philip looked at the men working the two pumps, pulling down on the long handles from the seesaw mechanism, one pull after another. He calculated the amount of air pressure that was created by each motion and then applied that to the number of pulls each man accomplished per minute. He then calculated the amount of air each of the two bladders held. "Twenty-eight minutes should be enough to inflate each bladder, but we should start seeing results in around twenty minutes. First the ship will start dislodging itself from the bottom. The lines attached to the lanyards can then be used to right the ship and guide it up as it starts to float to the surface."

"The wonders of this age," Charlotte reflected.

"Indeed. The age of man conquering the world through the use of science is upon us. Nothing is out of our reach; our technology must seem like magic to someone from your perspective," said Philip.

"I was never one to believe in magic or sorcery. Even in my homeland the superstitions seemed pointless but only to warn small children of spooks and dangers. My fellow seamen remain a naïve lot with the many myths of the waters they sail upon, but mermaids and nymphs... I have yet to see such things. Then again, here I stand, swallowed, and spit out by a storm of time. One hundred and fifty years passing by in mere moments." Charlotte gazed down at the ship resting at the bottom of the bay. "Maybe we'll find a beautiful woman with the tail of a fish living in Blackbeard's cabin."

Philip stared at the profile of the dark-skinned woman. What an unusual beauty she was, and an immeasurable intelligence lurking behind those tan eyes that shone bright with flakes of gold.

"Do not stare so fervently at me, scientist, lest I cuff you on your bulbous head."

Philip smiled but took the hint and wandered over to Beekman to watch the blurred vision of the ship below.

"Once it starts to rise, I will need you to be my eyes while I start the engine and maneuver the boat to keep abreast of the ship."

Philip nodded and the two men watched and waited.

Mary Read and Tom stood at the stern of the tug watching the scene below. The main mast could be seen below the water standing at a forty-five-degree angle. Tom had never spent much time around the waterfront. It was a dangerous place for a young boy. He had heard stories of boys being hijacked and forced to work aboard ships, never to return home. This was the first time he was ever on a boat or for that matter on the water. He looked up at the pretty woman with red hair that was now his friend, Mary. He had begun to have a heavy crush on the lady after dancing with her at the saloon. He knew she'd say no, but he wanted to ask her to marry him. He was far too young but in about eight or ten years he had decided he would propose to her. His eyes turned to the distorted image of the captain's great ship lying below. He wished very hard for the men and women around him to be able to raise the ship so that he could sail around the world on fantastical adventures with Captain Blackbeard and his new friends. If only the tugboat captain could make this dream come true for him.

Tom's sharp young eyes were the first to spot movement from the drowned ship.

"Look!" He pointed.

Mary peered down at where the boy was pointing. She could see the mast rising and then falling as the ship below shifted its weight on the bottom of the sandy bay. They were quickly joined by Black Caesar, Beekman, Philip, Vane, Charlotte, and several crew members.

Beekman watched as the ship slid toward the tugboat. He then began to call out orders as he went to start the engines. The boat quickly became a flurry of activity as crew members rushed about doing their jobs. The lines from the lanyards and winches began to go taut as they were ratcheted to control the movements of the ship below.

"Where is she?" Beekman yelled at Philip from the pilot house.

Philip watched as the *Queen Anne's Revenge* moved slowly toward starboard.

"Starboard side!" Philip called.

"Stand where she is!" Beekman yelled back.

Philip moved his body to where the *Queen Anne* was and then shuffled along the rail so that he was staying in front of it. Beekman gently throttled the tug to keep it lined up on the side of the ship that held the winches stretched over the water.

"Keep pumping!" Beekman told the men working the air pumps. They didn't need the encouragement as they were caught up in the excitement and any sore muscles from the nearly half-hour of exertion was quickly forgotten.

Philip looked at his pocket watch to see that more than twenty-three minutes had passed since they started to inflate the bladders. Five more minutes and they would be near full and by all calculations the ship would rise. The pirates and crew were crowded around him as the tug and ship struggled against each other. He was unable to move his body with the people pressed against him so he couldn't correct the location for Beekman to see where the *Queen Anne* was.

"Move, people! I need room," he said loudly and waved his arms at them. Once they realized they had been caught up in the excitement and needed to give way, they quickly complied.

Philip watched with studied interest while he moved around the deck, keeping pace with the ship. It was now rising, and the main mast was going to break the surface soon, but its course was directly at the tug. If they didn't switch sides, they would either break the mast or it would punch a hole in the tug.

"Hold!" Philip yelled. "Stop pumping! Hold!"

The pumping stopped and Beekman changed the thrust of the boat to remain stationary.

"The mast is coming straight at us; we need to be on the other side," Philip called to Beekman who nodded he understood.

Beekman expertly throttled the engine to bring the tug in a half circle as Philip gave him directions. Once they were on the other side of the *Queen Anne's* mast Philip gave the go-ahead to continue pumping air into the bladders.

"Give a little slack to the lines!" Philip called over to the men minding the winches and the lanyards who quickly adjusted the tension. Philip watched as the mast slowly emerged to crest the surface. The pirates stealthily gathered around him again as the *Queen Anne's* ascent brought it from a blurry outline to lucid detail. Flotsam and debris slid from the deck of the ship as it rose at a listing angle toward starboard, but what a sight it was. Philip couldn't take his eyes off it. A real-life pirate ship, Blackbeard's pirate ship, a 200-ton frigate was being raised right in front of him. The second mast now crested the waters, and he could see the massive deck and sides lined with closed, ported doors where at one time cannon barrels would have been pushed through to give fright or fight to any oncoming ship. He took note of the reefed and torn sails swaying in the water. There were several swivel guns mounted fore and aft as well as one each on the starboard and port rails. Rope and fabric hung over the sides from all areas of the ship and its masts. It was at once a wreck and a thing of beauty as the deck neared the surface.

Philip hardly heard all the shouting of orders by Beekman as he guided the tug with his hands on the wheel and the men with his voice to keep their distance and stabilize the ship while raising it. Philip watched as the wooden rails reached the air and water began to cascade off the port side as the deck emerged. The ship's bell, now clear of the water, swayed back and forth sounding its deep-toned gong with each rise and fall. Loud cheers erupted from the pirates and the crew alike. Black Caesar lifted Tom up and onto his shoulders and the travelers in time danced around each other cheering. Beekman ordered the men at the pumps to cap off the hoses leading to the bladders as more air at this point would not bring the ship up any higher. The listing *Queen Anne's Revenge* let out low creaks and groans as water gave way to air. The two waiting divers made haste to submerge and swim to the hole made by the cannon barrel that had sent the great ship to bottom of the bay. They would install planks of wood to temporally hold the water back after the bladders were capped where the hoses entered the ship. The tug would then slowly pull the ship to a cove where it could be careened and repaired.

Philip felt the large hand of Black Caesar lay upon his shoulder. He looked up at the man who still had young Tom on his shoulders.

"The captain would be proud. I wish he was here to see it," Black Caesar said.

It was a rare moment that found Philip without words, but now was such a moment. Before him was the beautifully constructed wooden vessel that had housed hundreds of pirates, the quarterdeck standing many stories high, the ornately designed forecastle looking freshly painted in red and black. The water-soaked wood was sparkling in the sun, and he blinked his eyes again and again as the sails began to snap in the wind, sending a salty spray of water droplets floating in the tug's direction. The rest of the pirates and crew were silent while the ship rose and fell with the small swell that moved throughout the bay. He saw Beekman stare at the ship, open-mouthed, letting his pipe fall into the water without a care for it. He looked again in awe at the *Queen Anne's Revenge*, his smile frozen on his face.

CHAPTER 24 - FRIENDS IN LOW PLACES

Colette flipped over a playing card with a six on its face adding to her hand of fifteen to total a winning twenty-one. She held in a smirk as the loud groans of the two cowboys sitting across from her caused the three men at the poker table next them to look over in curiosity. "Sorry, boys. Seems the cards are running cold for you today."

"Pleasure watching you take our money, Miss Dallaire," one of the cowboys said. "Come on, let's find ourselves a drink at the bar." They both stood up from their chairs.

Colette pulled the winnings in front of her and skillfully stacked the chips, coins, and cash. She gathered the cards and shuffled the deck, looking around the hall. The late afternoon crowd was just thirsty she could tell, as most of her gambling tables were empty. The bar was crowded and the tables surrounding the stage were filled with men eating and drinking after a hard day's work. Her piano player was sticking to the lively tunes Colette required for this time of the day. The somber pieces were to be reserved for the late night, closing-time hours so that the men's mood would be mellowed as they left The Paris. Hopefully the calming music would keep the men from being riled up and going out to cause trouble on the streets of San Francisco. Her goal was to keep her customers out of jail cells so they could work the next day and return to spend their money in her establishment.

The front door opened and a familiar-looking, slight man wearing a bowler hat stepped over the threshold. Philip Edward Albert smiled as his eyes found Colette and he scurried over to sit at her table, his soft boots making no sound on the hardwood floors.

"Good day, Miss Dallaire," he said taking off his hat and setting it on the table.

"Have you taken up sailing, Mr. Albert?"

Philip raised his eyebrows in response.

"Your scent is of the ocean rather than the mixture of sandalwood and vanilla I've become accustomed to smelling when in your presence."

"Ah, well today I have been toiling aboard a working man's tugboat, such that my own specially blended cologne, which I make myself, has been overpowered by the scent of the saltwater bay and dare I say the sweat of my toil. Forgive me for my offense."

"There is no offense. Just an observation. I would love to hear about your shipboard experience. Would you like a drink and a few hands of cards?" Colette nodded to one of the pretty waitress girls to bring two drinks to the table.

"That would be just the thing to relax the body and the spirit, dear lady," replied Philip.

Colette smiled and shuffled her deck of cards then nodded her head to Philip. He returned her smile as he got her intent and pulled his billfold out to place several bank notes on the table. Colette collected the money and exchanged it for the house chips. Philip placed two chips in front of him, and she began to deal out a hand of twenty-one. Two glasses of amber-colored liquor arrived, and Philip took a tentative sip. His face displayed delighted approval of the whiskey.

"Kentucky bourbon."

"Our last bottle. The distributor had some… issues en route, hence we will not have more coming in for quite a while."

"Most unfortunate. It will be difficult to enjoy the usual gut rot that is for sale in this city."

"Philip, you insult The Paris and me as well calling our spirits gut rot," Colette replied with a tisk, tisk.

"My apologies. I seem to just have a more discriminating palate then your usual customers."

Colette dealt Philip a hand of twenty, then turned her cards over to reveal an ace and a ten, twenty-one.

"You see what happens when one says something derogatory about our saloon? Their luck is swept away."

Philip chuckled and placed his bet for the new hand.

"So, what had you working on a tugboat today?"

"I have been tasked with raising a sunken ship from the bottom of the bay. A task that has been completed with unprecedented success; I might add. I'll appreciate your discretion with this information. It would not do to announce our efforts as many ears would be interested to know the ship's whereabouts." Philip's eyes darted furtively around the room.

"That sounds very exciting, Mr. Albert. I would be delighted to see such a ship with my own eyes."

"It is a must. Truly a work of wonder for such a ship to survive after all this time." Philip smiled at Colette and continued with the card game for a moment.

"Any word on our friends Edward and Benjamin?" he said suddenly.

"They are locked away and to be hung shortly, I'm afraid. The docks are being searched for the rest of them including the James brothers," Colette replied.

Philip kept his eyes on his cards, thinking it was lucky they had careened the ship in a distant cove, out of sight from the main port. It had been a far walk back to town for him but at least it kept him out of the eyesight of the Wells Fargo men and the English pirate hunter.

"It would be a shame to let our new friends meet their end at the gallows," he said, raising his eyes to see how Colette felt about the situation. Would she be receptive to helping him and his pirate associates? Philip was certain that Colette was at the very least amused by the pirates and seemed to have an interest in Blackbeard in particular. He was a good judge of the wants, needs and intent of others. He was a man who paid close attention to details, it was important in his line of work. The slightest variation when dealing with chemistry and combustible items could create disastrous results. That same skill worked on people as well. He could predict reactions after studying one's personality, where their eyes met, their body language and how the tones of their voice would change with each person they spoke with. As a trained scientist and chemist, Philip knew with certainty that there was chemistry between the lovely Colette in front of him and the rogue Edward Thatch.

"Yes, it would be a great shame," Colette said as she took another hand from Philip.

"Could I persuade you to assist in implementing my plan to spring the two forementioned pirates from their captors?" Philip asked conspiratorially.

Colette looked at the scientist for a long moment with a curious expression.

"A jail break?" she asked with a slight smile.

"Indeed."

"Well, that does sound exciting. Will it involve danger? Guns? I might have access to some firearms if necessary."

Philip looked at her with a jolt of surprise. Her eyes were intense with thrill. He slowly looked up to the large native behind the bar who was watching their exchange like he could read their lips, or maybe their minds. Philip had forgotten for a moment that a woman such as Colette could be just as dangerous as any man. A woman running such a business catering to such wild and sometimes wicked clientele would have seen her fair share of violence and most likely been forced to participate on occasion as well. The mountain of a barkeep would keep most men in line but as Philip looked around at the working girls moving about the hall, his intuition began to tell him that Colette and her pretty waitress girls would be a formidable foe if one had the misfortune to cross them. He re-engaged his eyes with the pale blue ones staring eagerly across the table at him.

"It will be quite exciting, and will certainly be dangerous, but guns? No guns. Not for your part."

"What would my part be then?" Colette asked with a tone of disenchantment.

"I need someone to deliver baked goods to Edward and Benjamin," Philip said sheepishly.

"Baked goods? Biscuits, muffins, cakes, and the like?" Colette said with sarcasm.

"It's not something I could do myself. Besides, these baked good would have a few... special ingredients."

"Special ingredients? Well, I'm beginning to like the sound of that. I might have some... baked goods options in the kitchen," Colette said with a smile.

The harbor master pocketed five percent of the bank notes that the merchant paid for the use of the dock to unload his shipment of whale oil from the Pacific Northwest. The rest of the money would go to the port of San Francisco. He knew not to take any more than five percent as being too greedy with his skim would have him winding up with an anchor tied to his ankle at the bottom of the bay. In his line of business, government work, everyone skimmed. You just needed to keep it at a level that no one above you thought you were taking more than they were taking. Leave enough so the one above you could take their share was the law of the land in government work. He would have loved to take seven or maybe even ten percent of every dock fee as his expenses at home had gone up. He had recently married a woman almost half his age and was only now becoming aware of the financial demands of matrimony. The new two-bedroom house needed to be furnished and a lady's wardrobe needed to be filled. Empty spaces made this new wife an unhappy companion. He sighed and pulled his flask from his jacket pocket to take a long pull. He noticed a group of men approaching him on the wooden dock. They had the look of government and navy types. Nervously he capped the flask and stored it back in his jacket.

"You the harbor master?" Cooper said as he, Woodes, Jennings and their associates walked up.

"I am. Name's Stilwell. Who might you be?"

"We're here on business for the mayor's office. You been on duty all day?" Cooper asked.

Stilwell looked at the barrel-chested man and then at the men with him. He was right about them working in government and the others were Navy but not ours. *Probably British* he thought from the colors of their uniform. The one navy officer had deep distorting scars on one side of his face. Next to him was a stern-looking fellow in old-fashioned clothing that he couldn't quite place.

"Aye, been here since dawn," Stilwell answered.

"We're looking for some wanted criminals, we think they might have been here at the port, looking to buy or maybe steal a boat," Cooper said as he unfolded a piece of paper. He handed the paper over to Stilwell to look at. It was a wanted poster with a hand-drawn picture of Frank and Jesse James.

"Jesse James," Stilwell said quietly with a sense of awe. "He really in these parts? Some rumors say they robbed the Wells Fargo bank couple of days ago."

"Those ain't just rumors," Cooper said.

"Well, ain't them cowboys? Wouldn't think they'd be interested in sailing."

"We think they've taken up with pirates," Cooper replied.

Stilwell let out a snorting laugh. Then noticed the stern faces staring at him. The scarred man approached him.

"Pirates, thieves, robbers are all the same vermin. This would be an unusual lot to your eyes, Englishman with long hair and a sour disposition, large African man, a wench with wild red hair, a dreadlocked African woman along with those two cowboy men," Woodes Rogers said.

Stilwell rubbed the stubble on his chin in thought. He recalled seeing the two Africans this morning, truth was it was hard to miss them in a crowd. The man was extremely large and broad with several tribal designs tattooed into his thick arms. The same was true for the African woman that he had noticed as they passed by him on their way to board the tugboat captained by that Beekman fellow.

"Aye, I seem them. They was working on a tugboat. I don't recall seeing Jesse James or his brother but maybe I missed them."

"A tugboat? What is such a boat?" Jennings asked.

"Not a seaman eh? Tugs push or pull boats that can't navigate on their own. They pull derelicts and the like as well."

Woodes turned to Jennings. "What would they want with such a boat?"

"Possibly to dive the wreck of Thatch's ship," Jennings said.

"The thieving bastard probably has treasure in the hold that they just can't let go. We can catch them while they are picking the bones clean." Woodes turned to the harbor master. "We need to commandeer a ship with armaments. Show us to such a vessel."

Stilwell turned to Cooper for some sort of explanation or support of the request by this scarred-face foreigner.

Cooper sighed inwardly. These Englishmen were a demanding lot. He was resigned to continue working with them though. They seemed to be able to track these pirates and Cooper was sure they were all working with the James brothers at this point. If he wanted to catch those two bank robbers, it was best to pursue the group as a whole with the assistance of this Woodes fellow and his navy men. They were at least able to catch the two men they had in jail cells who were part of this pirate gang. The James boys were a dangerous pair, and he liked his odds better with the four extra men on his side.

"Do we have any armed navy vessels in the harbor, Stilwell?" Cooper asked.

"Just that ironclad, the *Comanche,* she's got two fifteen-inch guns."

"What is an ironclad?" Woodes asked.

"She was built in 'sixty-five, six-inch iron hull, eighteen hundred tons, does about seven knots. She was at Mare Island for years but now she's sitting off near Sacramento Street, along Central Wharf," Stilwell told them.

"I know where that is, let's go have a look," Cooper said.

Stilwell watched the stern-looking group head back down the dock. He took his flask back out and sipped the gin that was held inside. *The James brothers partnering with pirates? Seems like the stuff of dime store novels*, he thought as he then decided to pick up one such novel on his way home. He'd seen one in a store with the title "Jesse James, The Outlaw." *Imagine that, Jesse and Frank James might have walked right past me today on this very dock. What a story that will make tonight at the saloon.* Stilwell felt a surge of excitement well up as he fingered the banknotes stuffed in his pocket. His new wife's clothes would have to wait, or maybe he'd double this money at the saloon playing a few hands of poker.

Anne Bonny stood with one booted foot against the wall watching Jennings, Woodes Rogers and his associates exit the docks and walk further up the street toward another wharf. She had pulled her long red hair up into her cowboy hat and tipped it low over her brow to prevent her from being recognized by them. Jesse and Frank stood on the opposite side of the road from her street corner view to stay out of site of the men. Lucky for them,

Anne had spotted Jennings and the other men heading toward the docks and the three of them had followed staying well behind. Anne looked across the street and she could see her reflection in the window. She smiled to herself as she liked what she saw. She felt comfortable and mobile in her tan dungarees and loose-fitting blue shirt. Her sleeves were rolled up as she had seen Jesse do, just above the elbow. She had on a brown waistcoat made of leather with black stitching that hugged her torso in all the correct places. Her hand lay on the butt of her pistol, holstered on her belt that was also held in place with a strap tied around her thigh as Jesse had shown her how to do. That way when she ran the holster would not bounce against her leg. She crossed her arms across her chest as she watched Jennings and Woodes make their way down the street. She nodded to Jesse and Frank, and they began to follow again at a distance.

"They're lookin' for your friends, ain't they?" Jesse said as he and Frank caught up to her. The three of them walked down the crowded street on the opposite side closer to the shops then the bay side. Carriages, wagons, horses, and pedestrians wove themselves through the streets near the wharfs where a heavy amount of commerce was taking place. Fisherman, merchants, and vendors were everywhere.

"They are, and it seemed they got some information from that man working the docks," Anne replied.

"They do seem like they are walking with purpose," Frank said.

Anne set her hand out onto Jesse's chest to slow them down as she saw Woodes and Jennings turn up another wooden dock full of ships. Anne recognized the spot as she had been by here days ago with her pirate friends. It was the dock with the odd iron ship that sat squat in the water with a large turret in the center supporting two enormous guns that could turn 360 degrees pointing the two 15-inchers in any direction.

"I'd seen one of them in a river during the war. Iron's so thick you can't sink 'em. Imperviable to rifles, fire, or cannon," Frank said.

Anne watched as the pirate hunter and that Wells Fargo man talked with the sailors on the ironclad. The captain of the vessel came up from below and after handshakes, was handed papers from the Wells Fargo man. While he read the papers the captain gave an order to one of his crew and the man doubletimed it off the ship, down the docks and into the crowd on his assignment.

The captain led the men down into the belly of the ship and Anne turned to Jesse. "We need to find them before Rogers does."

"We don't know where they are."

"I do. I remember where Blackbeard's ship went down. It was dark, but I could find it. We need a boat." Anne walked back toward the other dock and began moving along the bayside of the streets. Her eyes searched for something that would be work for her plan.

"Either of you do any sailing?"

Frank and Jesse looked at one another. "No, ma'am." Jesse answered.

A few minutes later Anne spotted what she was looking for. They casually walked down a low-trafficked dock and Anne stopped in front of a twenty-six-foot sloop, painted white and blue. It looked as if it had been built within the last couple of years with a wide mainsail and jib. It looked sleek and fast. Hopefully Jesse and Frank were fast learners as she would need some help to operate the craft. Anne untied the rope from the mooring and stepped aboard. Frank and Jesse exchanged a look and followed her onto the ship, rocking it some and the two men stumbled as they lost their balance by the sway of the ship. Anne smirked as she noticed their lack of sea legs.

"Use that oar to push us off," Anne called to Jesse as she quickly accessed the equipment of the sloop.

Jesse took an oar and used it to push the ship away from the wooden dock.

"Frank, take this line and pull the main up to the top, then tie her off," Anne ordered. "Jesse, come take hold of the tiller." Jesse hurried over to her in the stern of the sailboat. She held her hand over his and moved the tiller in the direction she needed. It was the first time they touched in this way. She looked up to his handsome face and smiled.

Jesse's heart was beating fast. He had never sailed before and now here he was stealing a boat with this crazy strawberry-haired filly. Her hand remained on his as she guided him to where the tiller should move to. Her face was so close to his and he noticed the sun freckles that speckled her pretty face. She was smiling at him with a siren grin, and he was completely absorbed by it. *Is she going to kiss me? Damn, this woman is the boldest I've ever met.* Jesse had never met such a woman. She was dressed like a man, yet he was completely drawn to her physically. She was excitingly dangerous, and he had felt out of balance since he'd met her. He held her gaze and moved his head closer to hers, his focus darting between those lips and her dancing green eyes.

"A little help here!" called out Frank, breaking the mood.

Anne looked back at the snapping sheet that was the large main sail. "Keep her here," she ordered Jesse, who nodded back. She made her way toward the main to move the boom and noticed a man running toward where they just vacated the dock. He was shouting and waving his arms. Seemed the owner or whoever should have been watching the boats just noticed their bit of thievery. She waved back at the man, and he paused in confusion then shook his fist at her. She laughed and then went back to giving orders to the two green cowboys so that they could get properly under way. She moved the boom, the breeze caught the main, and with a gentle lurch the ship gained speed cutting through the waters of the bay. Her spirits were high, she was captaining her first ship, a small crew of men were under her command and an adventure was afoot.

Charlotte De Berry opened the barn door with a flourish. Holding the reins, she then led in the horse-drawn wagon packed with four barrels of gunpowder that she had purchased from a supply shop. Once the wagon was inside, she closed the barn door. She looked around the room to be sure no one was inside then she went to stand before a large mound of hay in the corner. She took a hay rake from the rack of tools and began tossing the fodder to the side as she dug underneath. In a few moments several open crates containing silver bars were revealed.

Outside the barn two Wells Fargo men that had been waiting a very long time for someone to return began to stealthily move forward. They had watched the well-armed African beauty move her wagon inside the building and close the door. They had been told not to engage, only to watch and report back but that was so long ago and their patience for action had waned. The barrels loaded in the wagon had the markings of gunpowder and that demanded immediate action in their minds. They pulled their pistols as they approached the door. One man stood to the side as the other wrapped his hand on the door handle. He mouthed his count of one, two, three then threw open the door.

Charlotte dived for cover when she heard the door suddenly open and drew her new revolver.

The two men entered, guns leading the way as they saw a flash of Charlotte darting behind a crate. The horse harnessed to the wagon spooked and moved forward and back, rocking the wagon.

"We've got you! Now come out with your hands up," one of the Wells Fargo men called out.

Charlotte spun around the crate bringing her revolver to point at one of the crouched men. BLAM! BLAM! BLAM! BLAM! BLAM! BLAM! She emptied the chamber in seconds as she was unaccustomed to having so many rounds at her disposal. The effect of the loud rounds being expelled had a further frightening effect on the horse bound to wagon as well as on the several other horses constrained in their stalls. They reared and whickered. One man was knocked back by the startled horse and his pistol went tumbling away. The other man rushed behind a beam for cover and returned fire at Charlotte.

Charlotte moved like a cat, leaping over a half wall and pulling two throwing knives from her belt. She knelt with her back to the wall, a blade in each hand, listening to the sounds of the men moving. She needed to pick through the notes and tones of the chaos that reverberated throughout the barn as the horses bellowed and stomped. She could pick out the sounds of the men she stalked creeping around, attempting to gain the upper hand. She heard someone searching the ground on all fours behind the wagon. Then the click of a pistol hammer being pulled back sounded to her right. She popped up, spun, and threw her knife with incredible precision at the man peeking around a structural wood beam, pistol looking for its target. THUNK! The knife sunk into the flesh of two of the digits holding the gun, severing them from their hand.

The man let out an agonized cry as his fingers and the pistol clattered to the ground.

Charlotte again leaped over the wall and rushed toward the man with her other blade. In a surge of adrenaline, the Wells Fargo man dodged to the right, narrowly avoiding Charlotte's slash. He then pulled his Bowie knife from his hip with his uninjured hand. Charlotte and the man circled each other, knives lashing out. Charlotte cracked a smile at the competitiveness of the situation. This was clearly not the man's first knife fight. His right hand was damaged and unable to wield a weapon, but his left seemed to be competent and skilled with the blade. She could hear the other man scratching the hay-covered floor, searching for his lost pistol. Charlotte needed to finish this one before the man was successful in his pursuit.

The knife-wielding man stabbed forward at Charlotte then executed a back slash as she dodged left. She swiped after him, again and again, putting the man on the defensive. They moved around the barn until the man had his back against the wall racked with tools. He grabbed a hammer and threw it at Charlotte's head, missing only because of her quick reflexes. Charlotte flipped her knife from handle to blade and hurled it, and it sank into the man's shoulder. He grunted, but ignored the pain, taking his turn, flinging his knife at her. She again dodged the deadly blade as it passed her to stick in the far wall.

The man ignored the knife protruding from his shoulder, all but forgotten in the melee. He pulled a sickle from the rack and swiped it several times at her as she backed up. Charlotte unsheathed her kukri and spun the 12-inch curved blade to meet the oncoming sickle. She ducked underneath the reach of the man as their blades clanged together. She shot up using her shoulder and momentum to throw the man over her head, sending him rolling to the ground in front of the other Wells Fargo man. Charlotte stalked forward as the sickle-wielding man gained his feet. Hate and deadly contempt written on his face, he met her with a wide slash of the sickle to her face. She ducked under the blow and used the kukri to block it away from her. The man started to initiate a back swing when Charlotte spun, leading with her razor-sharp curved steel sword. There was a sickening sound as her kukri sliced through flesh and bone. The left arm wielding the sickle dropped to the floor, severed from the man's elbow. Sinking to his knees the man dropped, holding the shortened arm in his three-digit hand. "Bitch," he growled at her. Charlotte nodded in agreement to the man at her feet and struck once more, ending the man's life.

The other Wells Fargo man had watched in horror. He was unarmed and scared for his life in the face of this sword-wielding she-demon. He broke for the door as Charlotte looked up toward him. He crashed through the doorway and out into the yard. Charlotte started to pursue but as she exited the barn, she saw that there were several townsfolk across the street. She watched as the man cut around the corner to disappear into the city.

It was time for her to go. She hurriedly loaded the silver into the wagon and covered it with a tarp. She led the horse back and out of the barn. There were several onlookers watching, no doubt curious from all the gunfire and commotion. They were content to keep their distance so as to not become involved in the violence occurring within the barn. She climbed into the driver's seat and cracked the reins, driving the horse and wagon away from the deadly scene.

CHAPTER 25 - BISCUITS & BOMBS

It took some searching but within an hour the Wells Fargo man that escaped from the barn finally found Cooper and the Englishman. They were about to set out on the ironclad named *Comanche* to search for the James brothers and the pirates attempting to dive the wreck that brought them here. He told them about the gunpowder and the wagon as well as the crates of silver bars he was able to see. If the African girl pirate was still in the town maybe more of them were as well. Cooper worried the gunpowder had something to do with a plot to free the two men they held at the Broadway jailhouse. It was decided that the on-the-water search be delayed until they dealt with the prisoners. Woodes Rogers was in favor of hanging the two men right away. They loaded up the horses and carriage and made haste back to the prison.

Basket in hand, wearing her Sunday-best dress complete with frills of white against a lovely light blue fabric, Colette walked up the steps to the door of the Broadway jailhouse. It was a brick three-story building with a solid stone basement on the corner of Broadway and Pinkney Alley. The first floor had no windows, and the entrance was on the second floor via a stairway up to a landing with an iron railing. The back of the building had a walled-in yard that was for giving prisoners some time in the sun and fresh air as well as having a permanent structure for the gallows that had seen much use these past several years. The sheriff was keen on inviting hundreds of townsfolk to attend the morbid events. In addition to the throngs of people that would crowd the yard to watch the spectacle of men hanging from the neck there would be many more that would watch from the windows of other buildings and even from faraway hills that had views of the walled-in prison yard.

A sheriff's deputy exited the door as Colette's hand reached for the knob, and she jumped, startled, perhaps feigning it a little.

"Pardon me, ma'am. Let me get the door for you." The deputy held open the door for Colette to enter.

"Thank you, kind sir."

"Quite welcome," the man said and waited for her to completely enter before closing the door.

The interior office of the prison was drab and sterile. Gray walls with wanted posters lined one side and several desks and chairs crowded the narrow room. The far wall had a large shelfing unit that was covered with a metal grated door revealing a collection of confiscated weapons. Colette spotted the cutlasses that belonged to Thatch and Hornigold among the rifles, pistols and ammunitions. There were three men in uniform gathered around one of the desks and they all turned to watch her walk in. A balding man with an overgrown mustache stood up from his chair and walked over to greet her as she stood holding the basket with both hands in front of her.

"What can I do for you, darling?"

"My dear uncle has been arrested and I was hoping to see him. You see, he's fallen in with some bad men and went and got himself into some trouble. He's really a sweet fellow just, well, misguided. I fear that the poor man might fall into a horrible state of despair and if you would be so kind as to allow me to see him, spend a few moments with him to… pray for his salvation than maybe I could ease his troubled soul." Colette spoke with as much southern charm and innocence that she could muster.

"What's in the basket?"

"Oh, I thought I would bring these cakes and muffins as a gesture of goodwill. I baked them this morning for you all." Colette opened the basket, and the other two men came to take a look at the treats. There were some fancy sugared ones as well as a plain biscuit-looking roll.

"These for us, ma'am?" asked a skinny fellow with stringy blond hair.

"Why yes. Please take two, you could use a little eating, sweetie."

The skinny man's hand hovered over several treats before picking two coated with sugar.

"Which one is your uncle?" said the mustached man.

"His name is Edward. He has a heavy black beard that he likes to tie in braids."

"That one looks like the devil himself. Hard to believe you two have any relations."

Colette smiled at the man. "Oh, he may look dangerous but really, he's sweet as can be. You know, it was me who started braiding his beard and hair. When I was a little girl, he'd sit and let me fix his hair as we was too poor to buy me a doll. I think his stealing might be because of me. Other kids made fun of me and one day he came home with the most precious little doll that seemed brand new. When I think back now Uncle Edward must have stolen that doll just to please me. Bless his heart."

The men looked entranced at her, buying everything she was selling. The man with the mustache shook his head and said, "I think a few minutes wouldn't hurt no one. But one of us has to stay in there with you the whole time. Keep you safe."

"Of course. That would be fine."

"Kenneth, you think you can handle this?" asked the mustache man of the skinny one.

"Sure thing. Follow me, ma'am," Kenneth said, taking a set of keys and starting for the back door. Colette, basket in hand, started to follow. The mustached man grabbed her arm.

"Hang on. Leave the basket here."

Colette stopped and looked down at the basket for a moment. "But maybe Uncle Edward is hungry. He does love my baking," she said and looked up at the deputy. He stared at her, considering for a moment. He looked down in the basket and picked out the plainest, hardest roll.

"Why don't we leave the rest here? You can bring this one to your uncle." The mustached man handed her the roll and she looked down at it, then nodded her head.

Colette followed Kenneth through the door then down a stairwell to the basement where all the cells lined the hallway. Each door had small, barred windows cut into the metal and a slot lower down that was used to slide in a tray of food. There was a guard sitting in a chair reading a newspaper next to the stairwell. He nodded to them as they passed by, eyes glued admiringly on Colette. Then he noticed Kenneth eating one of the cakes.

"Where did you get that sweet cake, Kenneth?"

"The lady brought 'em. Better go get one before they're gone."

They continued walking down the hall while several prisoners cat-called and whistled as Colette passed by. Kenneth used his club to smack the bars of the windows as he passed to shut them up. He stopped at the last door at the very end of the hall. Kenneth looked through the small window.

"Stand to the back of room, mister. I'm opening the door; you've got a visitor."

Colette waited while Kenneth found the right key and she heard the loud click as the lock was disengaged. With the club in one hand, Kenneth swung open the door. She could see Edward Thatch standing against the far wall watching, one hand twirling a twisted braid from his beard, a glint of surprise in his animated eyes. His dark features were made even more so by bruises and lacerations around his eyes and cheeks. He was dirty and scruffy even though he wore the suit of a well-to-do gentleman. She couldn't help but feel the rise of a tingling sensation as his eyes bored into her as she entered the room. He was leaning casually, one shoulder against the wall and a smile forming on his lips.

Colette quickly started the conversation to uphold the ruse she had created. "Oh uncle, I was so worried for you. Thank goodness you are still alive!" Colette hurried over to embrace him. Thatch was quick to return the hug and wrapped his long arms around her.

"Now hang on! There's no touching," Kenneth yelled out and pushed the billy club into Thatch's shoulder then pulled Colette away. The two parted and Thatch held his ground while Kenneth raised the club threateningly.

"I'm sorry, deputy. You'd said nothing about that," Colette said.

Kenneth backed up a bit and lowered his club as Thatch remained against the wall. "Well, I was distracted. Talking is fine but no more touching."

Colette looked over Thatch's wounds as he stood there. "Deputy! Did you beat my uncle? Where is the justice in that?"

"Not me, ma'am… not me, it was the Wells Fargo men and that scarred Englishman," Kenneth stuttered out, not wanting to incur Colette's ire, even though they'd just met.

"I'm well, considering… dear niece," Thatch said. He and Colette looked at Kenneth. He took the hint and went to stand in the doorway and pretended to not listen in.

"Is your friend Benjamin well? He's here too?"

"Aye. He's fared better than me. Seems Woodes Rogers has a distaste for my handsome face and wishes to beat it until it more resembles his own."

Colette smiled at him. "Well, it does seem like he's close to succeeding. Such a shame."

"It is good to see your lovely face, wasn't expecting such a treasure before they hang me from me neck."

The two looked at each other, then Colette glanced back at Kenneth who dodged her glare and kept his eyes lowered.

"Well, not without a trial, this is a civilized city for heaven's sake," Colette said.

"Civilized or not, the pirate hunter has neither the time nor the patience to wait for a judge to find me guilty. But please inform me on more pressing matters. What has become of our endeavor to rescue… poor Anne from the waters?" Thatch asked in choice coded words.

"You will be most pleased to hear that Anne was found and rescued. She is being tended to this very day. I haven't seen her myself, as she was spirited away to recuperate somewhere so she can have some privacy. Caesar and the others are attending to her. The scientist was most helpful, and he wanted me to let you know that he has offered you his help in your current predicament." Colette smiled at him. "Which reminds me, I do know that you love my baking and I imagined that they have neglected to feed you well while holding you, so I brought you a biscuit." She handed Thatch the plain-looking bun. He turned it over in his hand, glancing at Kenneth who raised his eyes to him. Thatch pulled a piece from the side facing him and put it in his mouth. He smiled and looked back down at the biscuit, his eyes remaining a moment on the treat.

"It is as delicious as I remember your baking to be, dear niece."

"You gonna pray for him, ma'am, because I think the time is almost up," said Kenneth.

Colette got on her knees and held her palms together in prayer.

"Dear Lord, please look after Uncle Edward. Allow him to see your light, let him search his pockets and his soul for that light. Let him take your bread and burst the bonds that trap his soul in the realm of the devil. Please remove from his mind the weapons of destruction that our good and moral deputies had removed from his possession and locked away in the office upstairs. Bless these fine keepers of the peace and bless my dear uncle who underneath that crusty exterior beats a heart that longs to be gold. Amen."

Colette rose and smiled at the smirking Thatch.

"That was real pretty, ma'am," said Kenneth. "Now let's get you back up top and out of this foul basement before you are soiled by all the stench." He held the door ajar for her. Colette turned and walked out, followed by the deputy who gave a last glare at Thatch before closing the cell door and engaging the lock.

Thatch strode to the door and was able to see a quick glance of the two as they walked out of sight down the hallway. He went and sat on the cot and looked down at the biscuit in his hand. The piece that he'd torn off and eaten revealed a bit of wool wire and wax. He broke the biscuit in half and pulled out a small amount of coiled wire, as well as a narrow wax rod with something inside. He looked closely at the rod, intrigued. It had a small, bored hole on one end that was capped with a small metal piece. Thatch unrolled the spool of wire and saw that the wire fit perfectly in the hole. The setup reminded him of a cannon, where you would light the wick protruding from the barrel. He gently squeezed the wax, and it molded underneath the pressure. He played back Colette's prayer to him and recalled the coded detail about searching his pockets and soul for light. The pirate hunter had made sure that all his pockets were emptied as well as being thoroughly searched for hidden weapons. He stood and put his hands in his pockets one by one. His fingers found a small box made of hardened paper. He pulled it from his waistcoat pocket and saw that it was the same box of matches that Philip had shared with him the night of their first meeting when poor Jack Rackham had been killed in the duel with Jesse James. Colette had slipped the box into his pocket when they embraced. The woman proved to be even more astounding each time their paths crossed. She had just completed an ingenious performance of acting in front of the deputy and picked his pocket better than any tramp in London could have done—well, in reverse in this case, placing the matches in his waistcoat. She was also able to tell him where his armaments were stashed right under the nose of the dense jailer. He decided to wait to use his gift until he was sure Colette was far away from the jail. *I do not want to put that angel in any danger me escape attempt my cause.* He settled back on the cot with his back against the wall and finished the biscuit.

Tom looked over at Philip the scientist standing next to him holding a large satchel and watching the front of the Broadway jailhouse from a block away. The man was thin, pallid, and just a few inches taller than Tom. He held his cigarette in slender, delicate fingers as his sharp eyes darted around the streets missing nothing. The scientist was so different from Blackbeard and the other men. Their strength and aggression visible and felt when in their presence while the scientist projected an ever-present superiority of the mind. Tom longed to grow into the image of those pirate men, especially Captain Blackbeard, but he was beginning to like Philip very much as well. Maybe he could learn, develop and become a formidable combination of the two types of men.

"Ah, the mistress of intrigue emerges with the look of success on her exquisite features," Philip said as he watched Colette leave the prison and casually walk toward them. A satisfied look on her face gave him confidence that all had gone according to plan. He surveyed the street to make sure none followed her, nor anyone paid undo attention as she approached.

Philip dropped his cigarette and ground it underneath his booted heel. He moved a few paces down the walkway to sit on a bench under a store window with Tom following him. Colette sat down on the bench between Philip and the young Chinese boy.

"How was Captain Blackbeard?" Tom asked, looking up at her worriedly.

"He's fine, young Tom. Fit as a fiddle."

"Did everything go as we had hoped?" asked Philip.

Colette nodded. "How did you know the jailers would take all the sweet buns and leave the biscuit for Edward?"

"I'm a student of human nature as well as the sciences. They were certainly going to deny the captain a treat but would most likely look to please you, the entrancing figure that you are, by allowing you to feed an unadorned, crusty morsel to their prisoner. The jailers eating the sweet cakes was never in doubt, but the rest of the plan's success remains to be seen. Do you think Captain Thatch will be able to grasp the use our gift?"

"I watched him take a bite of the biscuit and see the contents. I believe I was able to convey the use of your improvised device through my recited prayer."

"Your prayer?" Philip raised an eyebrow.

"You take the opportunities that are given to you," Colette said, smoothing the hem of her dress.

"How long do we wait?" asked Tom glancing through the window of the shop they sat in front of.

Philip turned and looked at what the boy was eyeing. In the window of the shop were displays of candy and other sugared treats. Philip reached into his pocket and pulled out a coin purse. Opening it, he took several coins out and leaned over to hand the money to the boy. "Something for the lady and me as well, my boy." Tom's face expressed a rare wide smile, and he leaped up and hurried into the shop. Colette and Philip smiled at each other then turned to watch the front of the prison. Philip knitted his brows, stood, and gazed far down the street. Colette rose alongside him and looked at what caught his attention. There were about a dozen men on horseback riding next to a carriage many blocks away. Even from this distance she could recognize the group as the Wells Fargo men. She looked worriedly at Philip. He slowly sat down again on the bench, setting his satchel next to him, arm lying atop the brown leather bag, slim fingers absently drumming against it.

"What do we do?" Colette asked.

"You might want to consider your newfound talent of prayer."

Colette slowly lowered herself next to Philip and the two of them settled in, waiting for the oncoming violence.

Thatch knelt in front of the keyhole on the metal door that opened out toward the hallway. He carefully molded the thin wax rod to fit inside. He pushed the wax with what looked like sawdust within through the thin hole trying to get as much of the small explosive into the lock mechanism as possible. He then threaded the fuse into the metal ring on the end of the rod that he assumed acted as a type of blasting cap. He stood back looking at his work. The fuse protruded six inches from the lock. He wasn't sure how long it would take to burn up to the explosive, but he wasn't able to move that far from it anyway in the cramped cell. He figured the blast would be small, with just enough force to disable the lock. Thatch looked through the barred window to see if anyone was near. With the coast clear, he pulled the matches out and struck one. He watched as the flame caught then held it under the fuse. It ignited immediately and Thatch quickly moved to the far corner. He turned his face to the side and covered his ears.

BLAM! Smoke, debris, and bits of metal exploded from the lock. The sound was loud and echoed through the small room, bouncing off the concrete walls. Thatch hurried to the door that was still lodged in place. He pushed to open it, but it only moved a little. Some of the lock must still be holding it from opening. He put his shoulder against the door and shoved his weight against it, but it still held. There was yelling and hollering from outside his cell. *It's now or never!* he thought. Thatch took a step back and gave the door a kick. He saw that it budged a little more. He backed up a few feet then charged the door. WHAM! He slammed his shoulder into the door, and it finally gave way, swinging wide and clanging against the outside wall. Thatch was barely able to stay on his feet from his momentum and caught himself against the opposite wall.

He looked down the hallway expecting guards to be running toward him but only saw a man slumped in the chair near the stairwell, unresponsive to all the noise. He started toward the exit as the other prisoners whooped and hollered at him. He saw Hornigold's face in one of the barred windows as he was passing.

"You're free, mate!" Hornigold shouted.

Thatch paused and put his hand on Hornigold's that was fisted around the bars. "Aye! I'll find a key and come back and set you free."

He made his way cautiously to the unconscious guard. There was drool running down the man's slack face, but Thatch saw that he was still breathing. There were crumbs scattered in his beard and on his shirt from a sweet cake. He searched the man and found a key ring as well as a billy club. He took them both then made his way back to Hornigold's cell.

"How did you do it?" Hornigold asked.

Thatch opened the man's cell and Hornigold looked around the hallway in confusion.

"The lovely Miss Dallaire and our little scientist friend whom you wanted to kill upon first meeting."

"Well, luck has it that I didn't," Hornigold said.

"Indeed." Thatch led the way down the hallway as the rest of the prisoners pleaded for them to open their cell doors. He stoically ignored them as they reached the stairwell believing that stealth was of the essence in their escape. He cautiously ascended the stairs to the top where a closed door blocked the way to the upstairs office. He looked back at Hornigold to see if the man was ready for whatever came at them upon opening the door. He pushed the handle and eased the door open, leading with the billy club as he entered.

The room was quiet, and he saw that there were three men slumped unconscious, two of them at their desks, and the one that came in with Colette leaning his head against the wall where he must have slid to the floor. Thatch eyed a basket that still contained three sweet rolls.

"What happened to them?" Hornigold asked.

"I'd say Miss Dallaire's baking didn't agree with them."

Thatch wondered for a moment if all the baked goods had been laced with some kind of sleeping poison. The one he ate was clearly meant for him, so he put the thought aside. He looked around the office and his eyes stopped on the cabinet holding all the weapons. It took only a moment to find the right key on the ring to open it. Hornigold stood close by as Thatch retrieved his pistols and cutlass. He handed Hornigold his armaments as well.

"Shall we?"

"Aye," Hornigold said as they made their way to the door. The two pirates stepped out into the late afternoon sun to gaze upon the crowded streets. Thatch led the way down the stairs and out onto Broadway with Hornigold next to him. Just at that moment a dozen riders and a carriage pulled up in front of them. The riders surrounded the pirates in a semi-circle and pointed their pistols and rifles at them. Thatch looked up to see the faces of the Wells Fargo men taking aim at him. Thatch already had his cutlass and a pistol in his hand and pointed it at them, from one horse rider to another. The door of the carriage opened to reveal the pirate hunter and Jennings. The two men stepped down from the carriage and Woodes approached Thatch and Hornigold to a distance of six feet. The horse rider's guns remained trained on Thatch.

"Aren't you a resourceful fellow, Edward Thatch," Woodes remarked.

"Come any closer and I'll put six more holes in that scarred face of yours, Rogers."

"Don't be a fool, Thatch," Jennings hissed. "Drop your weapons. You have no chance of escape."

"I should have never let you step aboard the *Queen Anne's Revenge*, Jennings. You soil her with your treachery. Pirate turned pirate hunter; the world has known no greater scum," Thatch said, keeping careful watch on all the enemies in front of him. "To think you were once part of the Pirate Republic, you be a traitor among traitors."

Jennings laughed aloud at Thatch's words. "Pirate Republic? The grand illusion sung by a tired, old, drunk man without the heart to tell his disciples of the true ruse. Did you really expect all the miscreants and scoundrels you sail with to live within the rules of a republic?" Jennings scoffed. "While the very architect himself works to dismantle and deliver the killing blow in return for the pardon and favor of the Crown."

Thatch stared at Jennings and then saw the pirate hunter smirk within his disjointed jaw. He looked over at Hornigold whose eyes were averted from him. Thatch's mind reeled. Had Hornigold worked against his own republic? Could what Jennings be referring to be true?

"Lies!" Thatch yelled.

"Come now, Captain Blackbeard," Woodes said smoothly, "who do you think led us to your secret meeting on board your ship? All the pirate captains on one ship, below deck. Who would have had us cut your anchors? And ask yourself who would have told us about the details for your train robbery so that we would be there to catch you? We know about your plan to dive the treasure of the *Queen Anne* and before long, we will find that wreck, your crew, and hang the rest of your pirate republic." Woodes spit out the last two words with distaste.

Thatch couldn't believe what he was hearing. Could his old captain and friend have been betraying him all along? He looked over at the man. Hornigold's eyes finally met his and Thatch saw the shame and culpability behind them.

"You wouldn't listen to reason. You, Vane, and others were harassing and taking prizes of English ships! Targeting the Spanish, the Dutch, French… but our own homeland? We were sailors in the Royal Navy, you and I." Hornigold pointed an accusing finger at Thatch. "I told you this wouldn't stand; we had gone too far. Take the pardon I said. The risks were too high."

"You were going to give your governorship up to Woodes? You built Nassau! How could we give up the capital of the republic?" asked Thatch with anger.

"The pirate captains could never be united. It was plain to see. Criminals from all over the world, English, French, African, Irish… loyalties always divided. It was a fine idea for drunken talk, but it would never have worked. I couldn't convince you of this, but it was doomed to fail." Hornigold shook his head.

"We had as many ships as all of them put together. Thousands of men. An army!"

"There was no king to lead them! They were all doing as they wished. You'd expect them to pay taxes to Nassau? To unite under a single commander?" Hornigold lashed out.

Thatch stared with cold eyes at Hornigold as Jennings and Woodes chuckled.

"So, you helped them end it did you? You were like a brother to me. You'd see me hang then?" Thatch's grip on his sword tightened. He pointed the sword at Hornigold. "Your old first mate and dear friend Blackbeard hanging from a noose while you sail away into the night." Thatch turned to look at the men surrounding him. He dropped his pistol and the belts that held the other weapons. He held his cutlass in front of him then turned to Hornigold. "Draw your sword, Benjamin."

Hornigold looked at Thatch with confusion, then glanced at Woodes and Jennings who were smiling and enjoying the show.

"Parley is over. It is time to solve this matter over swords, traitor," Thatch growled.

Hornigold looked again at Woodes, unsure of himself.

"Rid the world once and for all of this demon and your freedom is assured, Captain Hornigold," Woodes said.

Cooper, watching the scene unfold from his horse, motioned his men to lower their guns and give the pirates room to fight. They backed up their horses as the growing crowd and stopped traffic converged toward the spectacle. Cooper had seen knife fights before, but sword fights were out of the norm in the wilds of the western territories. It seemed like something from the books of English knights and princesses. Maybe there was some truth in the stories of these men being born more than a century ago. He was

271

intrigued enough to let the action play out in front of this crowd and his own eyes.

Hornigold unsheathed his sword and swatted it around, loosening his arm. The two pirates circled each other, watchful for the one who would make the first move.

"You should have taken the pardon, Blackbeard," Hornigold said. "It would have saved your life. Instead, your ego has brought us all to this hellish Earth, marooned in time." He suddenly thrust his sword at Thatch.

Thatch moved left and parried, and their swords clanged together with the sound of steel striking steel. The duel had begun.

Thatch moved aggressively into an attack, using his long arms to slash toward Hornigold's left, then right side, driving him back. Hornigold's years of fighting experience kicked in. Anticipating Thatch's next swing, he dodged right and executed a back slash that caught Thatch off guard. Blackbeard hastily adjusted his stance, bringing his sword up and across his chest just in time to deflect Hornigold's swing.

The two men traded blows for blows, pressing each other back and forth in front of the cheering crowd.

Blackbeard lunged in for an overhead strike which Benjamin blocked, staggering back, and their two swords locked together at the hilts, their sweat-beaded faces inches from each other, fixed in masks of fierce scowls. Blackbeard raised his boot and kicked Hornigold in his gut sending him stumbling back into one of the Wells Fargo riders. The man's horse spun back and away from the melee, knocking several onlookers to the ground. One man was unfortunate enough to have a hoof driven into his leg, breaking it with a loud snap and cry of pain from the man.

Hornigold recovered quickly and paced a circle around the panting Thatch. He could see the evidence of the many beatings Woodes had delivered to Thatch. Those wounds were taking a toll on the winded, lanky man. He pressed his advantage with quick slashes of his cutlass from the right side along with several thrusts that drove the man back toward the wooden walkway that paralleled the street. Thatch in his defensive retreat stumbled backwards as he reached the raised sidewalk. He landed hard on his back and Benjamin took the moment to deliver an overhead strike down toward Thatch's head. Blackbeard rolled desperately to the left at the last second and Hornigold's cutlasses sank into the wood inches from Thatch's face. He then spun away and put a few feet of distance between them.

Hornigold tugged on the cutlass and found it stuck in the wooden planks of the sidewalk. He looked down at the steel embedded in the wood and saw that underneath it was the remains of one twisted black braid from Thatch's beard. He put his boot next to the blade and used the leverage to pull it loose. Hornigold turned toward Thatch and spun his sword about his wrist in a show of swordsmanship. He rushed forward to give the man no quarter and the two swords clashed with ringing cries. They danced around within the circle of onlookers as the duel progressed with Hornigold seeming to have the upper hand.

Thatch was once again on the defensive as Hornigold backed him up against the carriage that Woodes and Jennings arrived in. With another lunging attack deflected by Blackbeard, Hornigold was pressed up against him, both men locked with the swords over their heads, both hands gripping their hilts.

"You befoul the code, knave," Thatch hissed.

Hornigold brought his knee up to strike Thatch's groin but connected with his hip as Thatch pivoted to avoid the debilitating blow. Thatch twisted underneath Hornigold's arms, spinning around to lock his sword arm underneath Hornigold's chin as he now was behind him. He held Benjamin's wrist with his other hand that was wielding the cutlass. Thatch applied as much pressure as he could to Hornigold neck. Hornigold in a desperate bid to free himself from Thatch's grasp launched himself backwards, causing Thatch to slam his back against the carriage. Hornigold felt the pressure on his neck release some and bent his knees, then shot up again, forcing Thatch to bash once more against the wood and metal carriage.

Thatch's grip on Hornigold's wrist slipped and Hornigold ripped his arm forward, then sent his elbow back, smashing into Thatch's nose. Blackbeard's eyes watered, and he saw stars as Hornigold broke from his grasp and turned to face him, sword raised above his head. Blood gushed from Blackbeard's nose as he bent over, sword gripped haphazardly in his hand as he reeled from the pain.

"To hell with you, Blackbeard," Benjamin said before swinging his sword down in a strike to remove Thatch's head.

Blackbeard lunged in a blaze of speed up and under the hovering Hornigold as the sword came swiping down to the spot where Blackbeard had been only a split second before.

Hornigold choked in wild-eyed horror as Blackbeard rose, underneath him, his sword embedded in Hornigold's gut. The two men once again stood against each other, faces dripping with sweat and blood mere inches apart. Hornigold looked down at the hilt of Blackbeard's cutlass protruding from his insides, then his eyes rose to meet Thatch's. There was a fire dancing in those stormy eyes like an image of a burning ship out at sea. Hornigold let his cutlass slip from his grasp, the strength to hold it leaving his hand.

"You broke me heart, Benjamin," Thatch said and pulled his sword from his old friend's dying body.

Hornigold slumped and landed with a thud on his back, arms wide apart, blood pooling from the wound. The street was silent, and Thatch was incognizant of the crowd around him. A deep sadness overcame him and mixed within the blood, dirt, and sweat, a tear rolled down his bruised and battered cheek.

"Hang that man!" screamed out Woodes Rogers.

Seconds later without any fight left in him Blackbeard's arms were being held by two men and he was surrounded by several others from the Wells Fargo company. He allowed himself to be shoved and led up the stairs of the prison while the crowd chanted for his hanging and screamed their excitement of the proceedings. The guards pushed him through the door, and he was vaguely aware of the scene inside the office as he was dragged out another doorway leading to the back yard of the prison. A twelve-foot concrete wall surrounded the area and in the far-left corner stood the wooden gallows, noose hanging at the ready.

Hundreds of people thronged into the yard. Woodes and Cooper shouted at their men to keep the rowdy crowd back as they half pushed, half carried Blackbeard toward the gallows. Two Wells Fargo men hauled him up the steps to stand underneath the rope. Woodes and Jennings had followed behind with stern faces but excitement dancing in their eyes. Jennings tied Thatch's hands behind his back while Woodes pulled the noose over Blackbeard's head and tightened it around his neck. The great black beard was caught inside the noose and Thatch twisted his head around uncomfortably, attempting to dislodge it.

He looked out to the crowd, taking notice of the hundreds of people who were pouring into the yard. There were smiles and shouts of excitement at the lynching that was about to take place. His lynching. He searched the crowd for a face that he recognized but none surfaced. He laughed in spite of himself as he realized that in all the world, he only had a handful of people he could claim as friends, and he'd just killed one of them. He was a stranger here, a forgotten character from another time, another place. He had lost everything in a matter of days. His ship, treasure, his mates, all swallowed up in the sea of time and now his life would end by the dread hand of the pirate hunter.

"Last words, Edward Thatch?" said that scarred face as it appeared in front of him.

Ironically, none came to mind as Thatch stared out at the mob. He had spent his life priding himself as an orator, skilled at inspiration as well as intimidation should the situation warrant it. He had easily led men into battle with his words and charisma. Now, the cat had caught his tongue, or maybe it was the noose constricting his neck, depriving him of thought and imagination. He could think of no words to utter at his end.

Woodes was not of the same mind. He relished this moment of triumph. He turned to the crowd and raised his hands for their attention.

"This fiendish man before you, Edward Thatch... known throughout the Caribbean and the Americas as Blackbeard the pirate, will hang before you by order of the King of England, George the First. I, Woodes Rogers, hereby pass sentence on Blackbeard, wanted for murder, mayhem, debauchery... long sought for piracy, and all manner of depravity to hang from the neck this very day until he be dead, dead, dead!"

"You're going to kill me three times or are you just a stutterer?" Thatch asked loudly, finding his voice to taunt Rogers at the last. To this the crowd gave a laugh and Woodes turned his distorted face toward Thatch. He looked down at the trapdoor on which Thatch stood and strutted over to the lever that would release the latch holding it in place.

"To hell with ye!" Woodes took hold of the wooden lever and as the crowd roared, he forcibly pulled it back.

CHAPTER 26 - THE PIRATE LIFE

Frank James let out a low whistle as they spotted the careened *Queen Anne's Revenge* in a lonely cove a few miles from the main port.

"An' here I thought you was yarnin' the hours away about this pirate ship," he said to Anne as she adjusted the tiller to take them closer to the large frigate. The ship was listing only slightly now as the tide was coming in to fill the cove. Anne knew that it was necessary for the damaged hull to be out of the water so the repairs could be made. From where Anne sat, she could see that a patch of new wood was already in place and once the tide came all the way in, by moonrise the ship would be able to free herself from the shallow bottom. She shielded her eyes from the low sun and visually inspected the condition of the *Queen Anne*. The masts and rigging were still intact and the reefed sails most likely would function with just the short time the ship had been under water. The cleanup would be extensive, but she was confident the ship would sail.

Frank and Jesse gazed admiringly at the vessel. The craftmanship and artistry that went into the construction of such a ship was difficult to comprehend. The ornate paneling of the three-story-high aftcastle called to mind the most beautiful architecture that they'd seen in paintings of European churches and castles. Frank took in the extensive and confusing web of rigging, yardarms, booms and masts that stretched out well past the structure of the ship and possibly over a hundred feet high. He could see narrow decks that circled the beams of the masts at variable intervals. He knew from books that the topmost deck was called the crow's nest, a place so high that one would be able to see for miles in all directions. The two men couldn't take their eyes from the ship as Anne steered their craft toward it without their novice hands to assist.

Several rifles were trained upon them as they approached until Mary called out to Anne, recognizing her from the deck of the ship. A few of the tugboat men had stayed behind to work on the repairs and cleanup with the promise of high wages. The tug captain and crew were well paid with a share of Blackbeard's treasure and were sworn to silence on the threat of death that would be delivered by Black Caesar and Charles Vane should they go flapping their lips.

Anne was able to sail up to the side of the *Queen Anne* and tie their small craft to the rigging. Mary rolled a ladder down for them to climb aboard. Jesse and Frank followed Anne up and over the rails to greet Mary. The two women embraced.

"I'm so glad you got away. You saw my message at the stables?" Mary asked.

"I did. Clever girl with the knot," Anne said.

"So, this ship was really at the bottom of the bay?" Jesse asked.

"Aye, and the repairs are going quick. Just one hole really. A really big hole but still, just about patched," Mary said.

"So, she'll sail again?" asked Anne.

"With the moon if necessary and if the tides allow," Mary answered.

"Well, it's nice to see our investment in this endeavor is about to pay off," Frank James said.

Anne looked around the chaotic deck. Linens and supplies lay about everywhere, drying out and in various stages of repair. A shirtless Vane and Black Caesar emerged from below decks, dirty and oily from their repairs.

"Ah, cowboys and mermaids board our ship, Caesar," Vane said with a 'cat ate the canary' grin.

"Blackbeard's ship," Black Caesar answered.

"We have all earned our share and a new crew deserves a new vote as to who will captain it," Vane said placing a battered and drying tricorn on his head.

"Skeleton crew we have here. Unless these two landlubbers Anne has conscripted know anything about sailing, we are going to be hard pressed to get the *Queen Anne* out on the open sea," Mary noted.

"What of the captain?" Black Caesar asked.

"We've heard nothing. But the more pressing matter is that we saw Jennings and Woodes Rogers commandeering that iron beast with enormous cannons that sat in port with navy men aboard," Anne said.

Vane, Caesar, and Mary remembered the low iron ship with the deadly turret in the center.

"Where's Charlotte and Blackbeard's cabin boy?" Anne asked.

"The black powder was all ruined from the sea water. She went to purchase more an' stop by the barn to bring the rest of the silver from the train. The boy went with the scientist to rescue Captain Blackbeard and Benjamin," Black Caesar said.

"That damn silver was in the barn the whole time?" Frank asked.

Black Caesar nodded.

"Just a boy and that namby-pamby are going to spring those two men? Wish I could be there to see that," Jesse said.

Anne looked around the ship and up at the rigging. "Then we are off with the tide?" she asked.

"Aye," said Black Caesar.

Anne turned to Jesse and Frank. "You boys want a tour?"

"I'd like to see the treasure I was offered a share of, for following all you odd sticks in this adventure," Frank said.

The large main hold was mostly cleaned out of the broken crates and debris that had littered it after the sinking. The air still smelled of the rank sea water and growing mildew, but the hole made by the cannon barrel was patched and tarred to be waterproof against the bay. The wood floors still gleamed wet but were free of standing water. Several oil lamps illuminated the space as the group stood before four large chests that Mary Read opened one by one to reveal a horde of gold and silver coins, precious artifacts, silver and porcelain finery, and ornamental weapons inlaid with gold and jewels. Mary pulled a wet sack made from embroidered purple fabric and hefted it in her hand before tossing it to Frank. He opened it with curiosity and his eyebrows arched. He poured a handful of gold dust from the bag into his palm, whistling low once again.

Frank then looked over at the looming Black Caesar. "Deal still stands? Equal share of this treasure?" he asked, and Black Caesar nodded.

"If you ain't gonna kiss this crazy filly you got us hooked up with, I will," Frank said to Jesse and then gave a hearty cowboy 'yeehaw!'

Jesse took up the charge and yelled as well. That brought the rest of them into a small celebration of smiles and back pats. They all went searching through the chests, admiring the rarities and fineries. Caesar pulled a crate over and sat down to watch. As the ship's quartermaster he would need to record the dividing of the shares of treasure to keep the accounting fair for all parties. With only a dozen or so shares to divide his job wouldn't be difficult. Usually, the crew numbered in the eighties, or on occasion hundreds, making the accounts more onerous. He decided to let them enjoy their party of spoils before he took to writing down and recording each sailor's take. He fingered the large diamond cross that now hung around his neck. He was happy they were successful so far but worried over the fate of his captain. The *Queen Anne's Revenge* would sail again but would it do so with Blackbeard at the helm? He was having trouble pushing the dark thoughts aside as he sat watching the happy crew try on jewelry and run their fingers through piles of golden Spanish coins.

"Mary, where is that bottle of rum you found floating intact?" Vane asked as he slipped several rings onto his dirt-covered fingers.

Frank busted up laughing as the woman pulled the rum bottle from her flowing shirt. She uncorked it with her teeth and spit out the stopper. She handed the bottle to Vane after taking a swig herself, then the bottle was passed to Frank who took a long pull and wiped his mouth with his sleeve as he grimaced.

"Whoo wee. That is strong." Frank looked at the bottle's crude label. "Jamaica '14. 1814?" he asked Mary.

"1714," Mary answered with a snort. Frank looked again at the bottle and shook his head, then took another drink.

Jesse was admiring a golden ring with a green sapphire when he caught the eye of Anne Bonny. She was testing the weight of an ornate hilted dagger by balancing it on two fingers, then one. She tossed the blade into the air, and it spun twice before landing perfectly on the back of her hand, then she flipped it again to land in her palm. Jesse approached her holding up the ring in his thumb and forefinger. He moved himself into her space standing very close, and she held her ground with a curious, yet challenging look on her face. He brought the sapphire ring up between them, and the light reflected off it, illuminating her green eyes.

"I'm not sure which jewels are more lovely," Jesse said, staring into her eyes. Anne cocked her head to one side watching him. "What I mean is, your eyes are like jewels." Anne smiled at the man's awkward advance.

"Are you offering me this ring or are you looking to take out my eyes?" Anne smiled a devilish smile.

"The ring is yours if you'd like it," Jesse said, inching closer.

Anne inched closer herself, looking up at his handsome face.

"Why don't you kiss me like your brother advised?" Anne brushed her wavy strawberry colored hair to one side revealing her bare neck and shoulder. "Best do it before I change my mind and stab you with this exquisite dagger."

Jesse put his hand on hers that held the blade, bending that arm around her back so that he could pull her closer still. The other hand caressed her neck, reaching up to the back of her head, fingers combing up through her hair. He tilted her head up toward his as his lips descended down to meet hers. Anne closed her eyes and wrapped one arm around Jesse's waist to pull him against her and then kissed him long and passionately. For a moment all the world melted away, the only sound they heard was their own beating hearts. Gone were the noises of their friends as they drank and enjoyed the spoils of the moment. Anne and Jesse were only mere steps away from them but seemed worlds apart as they wrapped each other in a kiss and embrace that shielded them in a cocoon of intense desire that seemed impenetrable. Slowly, gently their lips parted, and Anne opened her eyes to see Jesse's closed lids. She moved her hand that still held the dagger up to his face and caressed his cheek with the back of her fingers. He slowly opened his eyes, a look of love-struck awe on his face. Anne smiled gently and kissed his lips once again, short and sweet.

Jesse looked over at her hand against the skin of his face that still clutched the dagger.

"Am I in danger?"

"Oh yes, most assuredly… but not today," Anne said pushing him away but taking his hand in hers. She led him back over to the treasure trove. "How 'bout that rum, Mary?"

Mary laughed and nodded at Frank who took one more swallow before handing it to Anne.

Anne held the bottle in the air with one hand, the other held Jesse's. "To the pirate life!" She took a swig, and then cheered with the rest joining in.

CHAPTER 27 - A SHORT TRIP TO HELL

BOOM! With a deafening blast the concrete wall exploded into the prison yard with such force that the entire gallows were blown over as well as everyone around it, standing upon it and hanging from a rope attached to it. To the detriment of those underneath, Edward Thatch was saved from hanging by the neck as he and the wooden structure he was attached to landed upon the spectators gathered around to see him executed. The concrete from the wall rained down upon the entire yard and its inhabitants along with wood, metal, and rocks. After the echoes of the tremendous detonation faded, the prison yard was awash with silence as those still conscious existed in a daze while the ringing in their ears dominated their shocked minds.

Thatch rolled in pain as his hands were still tied behind his back and were useless in helping him gain his feet. Several people that were lying beneath him moved and groaned as he tried to disengage himself from the pile. His ears buzzed and his vision was blurred. Someone under him pushed him away and his shoulder lit up in agony and he was rolled once more onto his stomach. He felt hands on him, attempting to turn him over. He pivoted onto his side and his vision started to clear. He became aware of someone holding his head. He laughed a tortured cackle when a young, fearful but eager Chinese face came into focus above him. His cabin boy Tom was holding his face in his hands and shouting at him but all he could hear was the ringing in his ears.

Tom pulled a knife and stepped behind the prone Thatch. He cut his hands loose from their bonds and then loosened the noose and removed it from his neck. The boy helped Thatch sit up and then get to his feet, allowing him to lean heavily on his shoulder.

Smoke and chaos filled the area. Men, women, and children were dazed and battered. Some continued to lie on the ground unconscious or dead, Thatch couldn't tell which. He stumbled to his knees and was caught by a woman, an angel in blue. He looked up at her face and his mind was lost for a moment, he felt like he was at the bottom of the sea, weightless, floating just above the sandy floor. There she was, floating as well, blonde hair moving with the currents surrounding her perfect face. Someone grabbed his other arm, and the vision was gone as he screamed out in pain.

Philip quickly let Blackbeard's left arm fall after the man almost fainted from the agony. He saw that that arm hung unnaturally at the man's side. He knew immediately that it was dislocated. He moved to the other side of the man and helped Colette and Tom guide the staggering Blackbeard out through the jagged hole made by the explosion that Philip had quickly rigged to breach the prison wall. He had packed the TNT hastily, but the desired result was obtained even though it was a bit more force than he would have wished. He looked up to see several law enforcement officers regaining their wits and felt sure the two pirate hunters were among the frenzied crowd. He stopped and pulled another device from his satchel. This was a new item that he had been perfecting for a few months. It was a round gray ball with the texture of hardened clay. He struck a match while Colette and Tom continued with Thatch through the blast hole in the wall. He lit the wick protruding from the device and waited for it to burn close to the end. He tossed the bomb a few feet back toward the crowd and when it hit the ground it began to discharge a thick cloud of brown smoke that also had a very foul odor to it. He smiled to himself as this smoke would cover their escape for the time being without any more loss of life or limb.

Exiting through the hole he caught up with the others and they stopped along the far end of the enclosure.

"Lean him against the wall," Philip said.

Thatch leaned back in pain against the concrete. Philip took his billfold from his pocket. "Bite down on this."

Thatch allowed the leather billfold to be put between his teeth and watched as the little scientist looked over his limp arm. He put one hand on Thatch's chest and with it, pressed his back flat against the wall. Philip took Thatch's left wrist in his other hand, then counted two, before yanking on the limp arm, painfully snapping it back into place. Thatch let out a sudden tortured scream when it happened, but relief washed over his sweating and bloody face as the pain quickly subsided.

Thatched leaned over to catch his breath. He rubbed his hand on his neck that was sore to the touch. Colette moved in front of him and took his face in her hands. He looked up at her and she smiled at him. "Are you okay?" she asked.

"Aye. Never better, lass," he said. "How do I look?"

"Like any other vagrant after a wild night at The Paris," Colette said with a smile.

"We need to go," Philip interrupted.

They all nodded and followed him around the front of the prison to Broadway where several dazed and battered people were filing out of the prison building. The streets were a mayhem of activity as some fled the scene and others went to lend aid.

Philip pointed toward the carriage that still waited on the street where Woodes and Jennings had left it. Hornigold's body was being carried to the other side of the street by a few Good Samaritans.

Tom spotted Blackbeard's pistol belts and weapons lying in the mud and muck near the sidewalk and hurried over to pick them up. Just as he reached the weapons, he came face to face with the Chinese baker that hit him over the head the day he met Thatch. The aproned man stood only steps away from him with a shocked look on his face as he recognized this smartly suited boy as the street urchin that had stolen rolls from him time and again. The man's intentions were clear that he was going to take the weapons before Tom had arrived. The boy narrowed his eyes at the man and moved his jacket aside to display his holstered derringer. The baker's eyes went wide as he saw the pistol. He quickly turned on his heel and hurried off, glancing back in fear that the boy was about to shoot him in the back.

Tom let a half smile slide across his face as the man ran from him then he gathered up the stash and rushed to join the others.

Colette and Philip helped the exhausted Thatch into the carriage and Colette rode inside with him. Tom dropped Thatch's armaments into the cab and climbed up to the driver's bench with Philip and sat down next to him. Philip grabbed the reins and snapped them with gusto, cajoling the two horses to pull the vehicle into motion.

Inside the leather-lined carriage Colette ripped a portion of the hem from her dress to wipe away the blood and dirt from Thatch's face.

"You saved me, life," Thatch said.

"You ran up a large tab at The Paris. Just wanted to make sure you're alive to make good on it," she said as she carefully cleaned his wounds while the vehicle bounced and jostled.

"Is that the why of it eh?" he said.

"Why else would I help such a wretch?"

"I think you've become smitten with me." Thatch smiled then winced as Colette rubbed hard at dried blood on his bruised cheek.

"Smitten with you? Such imaginative tales you tell. Pirate ships, time travels, now a fantasy about me having feelings for you. I dare say you've been knocked dense."

Thatch took her hands, stopping the cleaning. "I may have been beaten senseless, but me heart is still beating. It quickens when I see you. Me skin tingles from your touch. Your voice is like music to me ears and your eyes… draw me like the sea."

Colette stared into Thatch's eyes, his strong hands holding hers. *Why does this rogue intrigue me so? There is intelligence, and humor behind this devilish façade.* The moment was thick with attraction and the crackle of electricity between them. He slowly moved toward her, still holding her hands.

THUMP! SLIDE! The carriage bounced and sharply turned a corner sending Colette and Thatch crashing against the door.

"What the devil is going on out there!" Thatch yelled.

"We're being pursued!" yelled Philip from the driver's bench.

Thatch looked out the window and saw several men on horseback pursuing them, guns pointed in their direction. Upon seeing Thatch's head lean out the window one of the men took a shot at him that sent him ducking back inside. Thatch saw the armaments that Tom had picked up and placed inside the cab. He pulled a pistol from its holster and leaned out the window again, firing back at the riders. The speed and reckless driving of the carriage caused his aim to be poor and he emptied the chamber without hitting any of the pursuers. Colette handed him another loaded pistol and took the empty one from him. He watched her for a quick moment as she started to reload the spent pistol thinking he was truly, completely, smitten with her as well.

He leaned out the window again and… BAM! A rifle fired a round so near his head that the bullet whizzed by his ear. He turned back to see Tom leaning around the carriage firing at the horse riders. Tom had one eye squinted as he sighted down the barrel that was much too long for him to control on the jouncing carriage.

"Damn it, boy! Watch where you aim! You almost blew me ear clean off," he yelled at Tom.

"Sorry, Captain," Tom said, then turned in his seat to lean over the roof of the carriage so as not to hit Thatch as he fired back on the riders.

The horsemen were gaining on them, and their aim was improving as they continued to fire at the carriage.

"Faster, man, faster!" Thatch yelled at Philip.

Philip grimaced as he snapped the reins, urging the foaming horses to speed up. He knew the single riders were going to catch them eventually. He needed a new plan if they were going to get away. Looking ahead Philip could see a wagon up ahead carrying a load of barrels going in the same direction as they were. He wasn't sure what was in those barrels, but it gave him an idea. The man driving the wagon looked back at the sounds of gunfire and commotion that were rapidly approaching him. He snapped his reins to speed his team to get away from the coming maelstrom. Philip steered the thundering carriage toward the wagon, coming up alongside of it. He could see the driver's ghost-white face of fear as they raced side by side. The two vehicles bumped and clattered against each other, the barrels bouncing dangerously in the back. Philip began to take a lead as the man tried to slow down his team to let the chaos pass him by.

As an intersection quickly approached, Philip further turned his carriage into the wagon, banging against the side and sharply cutting the man off as he skidded around the corner to the right. The awkward momentum caused the wagon to lose control, the right-side wheels coming off the ground. Philip's carriage made the turn, but the wagon wasn't so successful. The tongue of wagon broke free as it twisted and the horses raced ahead without their burden, leaving the tilted wagon behind. The wagon spun and crashed, a dozen barrels spilling into the street, the driver, thrown to the ground, rolling forward as his momentum carried him yards away from the splintered wreck. The horsemen reined in as the blockade appeared in front of them. One of the riders was thrown from his horse to smash into the obstruction of barrels and wagon parts that littered the street. Philip looked back to see the pursuers fall far behind. He took a left turn at the next street, slowing a bit so as not to wreck his own carriage and means of escape.

Once they were many blocks away Philip slowed further so they would cease attracting so much attention speeding through the crowded streets. Blackbeard leaned his head out the window to see they had lost the pursuers and turned to Philip. "Where to now?" he asked.

Philip took a quick glance back at Blackbeard. "I shall deliver you to your ship, dear Captain."

Woodes Rogers strode through calamity ignoring the cries for help and assistance. His forehead was bleeding and somehow a nail was protruding from his arm, just below the elbow. He looked down at it in distaste. Without stopping he pulled the nail out and discarded it among the rest of the rubble littering the ground. Smoke still bellowed in wandering clouds around the prison yard. He stepped through the gaping hole made by the explosion that occurred just when he was about to end the life of that wretched Edward Thatch. He looked down the long concrete wall toward the next street. All that could be seen were civilians in various states of shock and confusion.

His ears still rung with the sound of loud bells, but something sounded underneath the ringing that caused him to turn around. Jennings was staggering up behind him calling his name. There was a large gash in the man's bald head but otherwise he looked unharmed. He couldn't hear what Jennings was saying with the damn ringing sound in his head from the blast. In moments Cooper and several of his men met up with him. They walked out to the street and his hearing started to clear.

"He got away," Jennings said as he held the empty noose and rope.

"I'm aware, you ingrate!" Woodes said in frustration.

Cooper looked around at the streets as bells from a fire brigade could be heard in the distance.

"We're gonna need more men. We need to kill these bastards, or the mayor is going to have my head on a platter," Cooper commented as Woodes' two remaining navy men ran up with only a couple of Wells Fargo men.

"They'll be taking him to the ship if they were successful with their dive," Jennings said.

Woodes looked at Jennings then at Cooper. He paced, curling and uncurling his hands into fists. He strode up to Cooper and pointed his finger at him.

"The boat, the tugboat or whatever it was called, the one the harbor master said was boarded by the African pirates. We need to track the captain down and question him. He'll know where the wreck is. Find the wreck and we them," Woodes said.

"I know where the harbor master drinks," said one of Cooper's men.

"Then let's go buy the man a drink and get some information out of him," said Cooper.

Harbor master Stilwell had a crowd of six men around him at a saloon called Red's. It was a long narrow pub with a bar that ran almost the entire length of the establishment. Red's was one block away from the docks which is why it was frequented by sailors, fishermen, dock workers and cops alike. A real working-class place with cheap drinks and greasy food. Below the ever-present odor of beer there was a persistent underlying smell of salt water and fish that permeated from the patrons' boots and clothes. Stilwell sat on a stool holding court while he polished off a mug of warm beer poured from a wooden keg behind the bar.

"Word is these pirates are in league with the James Gang," said a young man with the sunken eyes of an opium addict.

"That's what I've been trying to tell ya. I seen these two Africans walking on the docks side by side with Jesse and Frank James," Stilwell said, telling his exaggerated story and wiping beer foam from his lips.

"How'd you know it was the real James brothers?"

"Them two's wanted poster's up all over town and that strange crew of government men showed me their picture," Stilwell said. "It was definitely them. And let me just say, they had the hard look of killers."

"You said they went out on Beekman's tug?" the barkeep asked.

"That's right, and if he were here, he'd vouch for every word I'm saying," Stilwell said, looking around to see that Beekman wasn't in the bar tonight.

"He's usually here by this time," the barkeep said, looking at his pocket watch.

"Maybe Jesse James kilt him," the sunken-eyed man said.

"What business would the James Gang have with a tugboat?" another man asked.

"Yes, what business indeed?" Woodes Rogers said upon overhearing the conversation as he entered the pub with Cooper, Jennings, and several other members of their group.

Stilwell stared, a bit startled, at Woodes' scarred face.

"You'd told us you didn't see Jesse James last time we spoke," Cooper said, putting a heavy hand on Stilwell's shoulder. "Now I hear you telling he was walking alongside the two African pirates. So, which is it?"

Stilwell looked around nervously as his bar mates faded from his side and the group of men surrounded him.

"I... I said I didn't think I saw Jesse James with them, but maybe he was there."

"'Maybe' he was there?" Jennings asked with malicious undertones.

"Yeah... well, I might have just seen them from the back is all."

"That's not the story you were just telling your friends," Jennings said.

"Well... see... I had time to think, an' reflect on the memory and I think I can say with high probability it was them James brothers boarding the tug alongside the Africans."

Cooper looked hard at Stilwell, deciding if the man was telling tales or not. He looked at Woodes who seemed dubious as well.

The door of the pub opened, and an upbeat Beekman entered with his two divers, Stephan and Peter, in tow. The men were smiling and backslapping each other as they headed toward the bar. The men had just pocketed several years' worth of pay on a single job with a cut of gold from the pirate ship they helped raise. The happy planning on how it was going to be spent prompted the men to enjoy a celebratory drink at Red's tavern. Their good fortune even colored the near-death experience that Peter had had while diving on the *Queen Anne's revenge*.

Stilwell's eyes lit up when he saw Beekman enter and he happily pointed the man out to Cooper and his group.

"There's the man you're looking for! Not me... there's Captain Beekman," he said.

Beekman turned to see the group of stern men approaching, and if his face wasn't so sun-darkened it would have turned white as a sheet.

"You Beekman?" Cooper asked.

"Yeah. Who wants to know?" he said as the group surrounded him and his two divers, blocking the way back to the exit.

"You the one in league with pirates and bank robbers?" Woodes Rogers asked.

"I don't know what you're talking about," Beekman said, then turned away from the group to motion to the barkeep. "Bring us some beers, Red."

Cooper unfolded the wanted poster with the Jesse and Frank James drawing on it and slapped it down on the bar in front of Beekman.

"You took these two men on your tug to dive a shipwreck?" Cooper asked.

Beekman looked hard at the poster. "Jesse James? What the Dickens would Jesse James be doing on a tug? An' what makes you think I'd be aligned with a wanted killer and bank robber? I've been working this harbor many years, making an honest living, mind you."

"You took two African pirates and probably several others out on your boat in search of Blackbeard's treasure," Woodes said, inching his face real close to Beekman's.

Beekman, annoyed, pushed Woodes away. "Get your ugly mug out of my face!"

The two divers stood up from their stools to back up Beekman, but then Cooper and his men pulled out their pistols, as well as Jennings, and the navy men with Woodes. Beekman slowly raised his hands as the serious nature of the situation sunk in. Beekman had never found himself with so much firepower pointed at him before. He decided that keeping secrets wasn't worth the cost of his life. Besides, he, Stephan and Peter had already hidden their treasure in a safe location. Giving up the pirate's location would not include giving up their loot, at least that was what Beekman hoped.

"Look, we just came in for a drink. We ain't looking for no trouble," Beekman said slowly as he watched Stilwell slip out of the bar.

"You're going to be in a whole world of trouble if you don't start telling us what we want to know. Understand?" Cooper growled.

Beekman sighed and nodded his head.

"Good," Cooper said.

"Now then," Woodes said as he pulled out a nautical map of the San Francisco Bay and flattened it out on the bar. "Where is the location you took those pirates to?"

CHAPTER 28 - STRIKE THE COLORS

Philip steered the wagon off the dirt road and slowly followed rutted tracks that were difficult to see in the dark of night. The crescent moon was low on the horizon and failed to give much light, but the soft glow of an oil lamp that was held on a long pole in front of the horses helped to keep the carriage on the path. They were descending a ravine toward the bay, but their view was blocked by a rocky rise in the terrain. The going became very bumpy and Thatch stuck his head out the window.

"We nearly there, Mr. Albert?" Blackbeard asked.

"Yes, Captain," Tom answered for Philip as the boy remembered the way.

"You say 'Aye', young Tom. That ways you sound like a sailor, not some banker or priest."

"Aye, Captain," Tom said with gusto.

"That's a good lad," Blackbeard said then sat heavily on the seat across from Colette.

"What's she like?" Colette asked.

"The *Queen Anne's Revenge?*"

Colette nodded her head.

"Ah, she's like you, dear Miss Dallaire. A prize worth dying for." He gave a wolfish grin. Colette only smiled and shook her head.

"She was a slaver we happened upon in 'seventeen near Martinique. Two-hundred-ton beauty built in Nantes by the French in about 1710. A frigate with twenty-four cannon and full rigging, more than a hundred feet of length she is. An' fast for such a big girl, swift like the wind. Those poor slaver bastards never stood a chance when we found her. She'd been struck by a storm, the men rampant with scurvy. Only a quarter of their crew left aboard alive. Some twenty slaves out of the three hundred remained in her hold. She gave up without a fight. We careened her near Martinique and sold the cargo, made some modifications, and brought her cannon to forty. She'll stand against any ship, even a ship of the line. The French had named her *La Concorde*, but we struck our colors, an' I named her the *Queen Anne's Revenge*." Blackbeard's eyes had taken on a distant look.

"Why *Queen Anne's Revenge*?"

"Because she would take her vengeance against the house of Hanover, the despots that wrenched the throne from the Stuarts when they laid dear Queen Anne to rest."

"A queen reigns again in England—Victoria," Colette said.

"Aye, the little scientist has said as much, but with her, the Crown still remains in the House of Hanover," Blackbeard said with a heavy sigh. "Maybe the *Queen Anne* and I are here to set the world right again. Another chance to correct the direction of my homeland."

Colette let out a good-natured chuckle. "Why, Edward, you do have a grand view of your place in the world."

Blackbeard looked darkly at the woman.

"Captain!" Tom shouted from the front of the carriage as they slowed to a stop.

Blackbeard opened the carriage door and stepped out into the cold night air with Colette following him. They stood on a rocky rise above a sandy cove. Blackbeard's white teeth showed against his dark-haired face in the starlit night. There, moored in the small cove, was the majestic wooden ship lighted by oil lamps that hung along the railing and masts. The ship looked perfect in the nightscape just as she did when they arrived in the Nassau harbor more than a week ago in life, and a hundred and fifty-five years of history ago. Thatch's heart was beating hard as he gazed upon the *Queen Anne's Revenge* floating proudly, upright with the high tide.

"She is indeed a treasure. The most beautiful ship I've ever laid eyes upon," Colette said softly. Blackbeard looked down at her face to see the awe that swept over it.

Philip and Tom approached to stand next to Edward and Colette.

"You swabs going to lend a hand or just stare with your mouths agape waiting for a fly?" Charlotte De Berry asked from the shore thirty yards away.

They all turned to only now notice the small skiff being loaded on the shore near a banged-up wagon. Charlotte and Frank James were finishing the transfer of the barrels of gunpowder and the silver bars to the *Queen Anne's Revenge*. The group carefully made their way down the rocky gradient to assist in the final transfer to the ship. It took two short rides across the water to bring all on board. The final trip was made by Blackbeard, Tom, and Colette.

Black Caesar was there as Thatch climbed aboard his precious ship, his eyes taking in every inch, the rigging, masts, decks, the black flag gently moving with the wind. He stared hard at the lone white skull painted on it, and just below it flew the flag of pure deep red that would send shivers down any sailor's spine should they see it encroaching on their wake.

"Welcome aboard, Captain." Black Caesar said holding out his hand. Thatch grabbed the man's large palm in his and gave it a hearty shake.

"Well done, Caesar, well done! I trust she's seaworthy?"

"Aye, Captain. Our crew is small, but we can manage," Black Caesar said.

Thatch noticed the large silvery pink diamond-crusted cross hanging from Black Caesar's neck.

"Become a Christian have ye in me absence?" Thatch said.

Black Caesar's hand touched the strange metal. "I've taken a shine to its theatrics."

Thatch smiled and raised a brow at the man, then padded his back.

"It complements you, my friend. You've kept a good crew, Caesar. My heart soars stepping back aboard me ship."

Charles Vane approached with Anne Bonny, Mary Read, Jesse James, Charlotte De Berry, and several of the men hired from Beekman's crew.

"Crew? My thinking is that now is the time for us to parley. We stand here with many of us captains in our own right. We should put to vote what man should be elected to captain this ship," Vane said as he stepped up to Blackbeard.

"Or woman!" Anne Bonny said.

"Aye, no reason the vote should be in favor of a man when Mary, Anne and I stand aboard, capable as any here, more so than some," Charlotte said.

"Blackbeard is captain!" Tom said.

"Not without a vote. It is the law of the Republic. The pirate way," Mary scolded the boy.

Thatch looked around at the many different captains that stood before him. It was true that they had all once captained their own vessels, but the

Queen Anne was his and he knew only death could keep him from commanding her.

"Where's Hornigold?" Mary asked.

"The pirate hunter killed Benjamin," Thatch said steadily. Mary looked at Anne, then Vane.

A quiet settled over the crowd as they took in the news of Hornigold's death. Philip gave a curious look to Colette, and she matched it but kept silent. Tom's face was unreadable as he stood watching, hands stuck in the pockets of his coat.

"You saw it?" Vane asked.

"I did, and we will avenge him one day, sending Woodes and your old captain, Jennings, to lie in Davy Jones' locker," Thatch said.

"This ship sails nowhere until a vote is taken. I didn't risk my neck raising the beast to be conscripted without a say in the captaining of it," Vane said.

"Aye then, it's a vote we shall have," Blackbeard said. "Let's have it so we can be on our way. I make the assumption you throw your name in the hat, Charles?"

"Aye," Vane said stepping forward.

"Mary?" asked Blackbeard.

Mary stepped forward.

"Charlotte, Anne, you stepping forward?" Blackbeard asked. The two women did so. Thatch turned to Black Caesar. "You stepping forward, Caesar?"

He shook his head. "My vote is with you, Captain."

Black Caesar looked over the rest of the crew, Philip, Tom, Colette, and the several men from Beekman's ship that Blackbeard had not met.

"Then five candidates stand before you, each vying for the captain's title. You standing here must decide. The fate of the *Queen Anne's Revenge* rests with your vote. I remind you, though, it's my treasure that fills your pockets. My generous nature to offer you a share of the plunder from the toils of meself and Caesar. No man—nor woman—knows this ship like I. How she sails, her speed, abilities and quirks are well known to me like she is a part of my soul."

"Please, can we dispense with the theatrics and get on with it?" Charlotte said with a sigh.

"Aye. Cast your vote then." Blackbeard pointed at Black Caesar.

"Blackbeard is my captain."

Thatch then pointed at each of the new men from the tugboat, three voting for Vane, one for Thatch as they had only known these men and women one day. The three voting for Vane seeing him as strong man with leadership skills, the fourth voting for Thatch merely out of fear from the figure of the man.

Vane nodded to the men and Thatch continued with the vote.

"What say you?" Thatch pointed at the James brothers.

"Anne," said Jesse with a smile to Anne.

"I've seen Miss Bonny sail. The woman is unlike any I've ever met, tough as a man, clever as a fox. I'll put my trust in her, besides if I didn't, I think I'd need to sleep with one eye open for the rest of my years," Frank said to a round of chuckles.

"These men are not sailors. Why should they get a vote?" Vane protested.

"They are part of the crew now! They risked their lives for us," Anne said.

"An' we risked our money. Never could have done that train job without our investment," Jesse said.

"Their votes shall stand," Thatch said. He then turned to Philip.

"What say you, scientist? Like the James brothers you are a member of the crew. You sail with us and have a vote."

Philip's heart rate quickened. He couldn't believe that he was standing on this seventeenth century pirate ship with Blackbeard asking him to vote as a member of his crew. He felt dazed and lightheaded as he looked into the intense eyes beneath the thick dark brows of the pirate. The Edward Thatch was asking him, Philip Edward Albert, graduate of the university of London, a man seeped in science and education, to be a pirate on the *Queen Anne's Revenge*.

"You have my vote," Philip said as his voice cracked. Vane rolled his eyes, as did Charlotte upon hearing Philip squeak out his vote.

Thatch set his eyes on Colette. She felt her temperature rise when he did and chastised herself silently for the blush.

"Whom do you cast your vote for, Miss Dallaire?"

"Now this is too much!" Vane bellowed. "The woman is not part of the crew; she is no more than a serving wench, a whore working—"

"You bite that tongue," Thatch exploded at Vane, "or I'll carve it from your mouth and serve it to the rats!" Thatch held his dagger inches away from Vane's neck. Vane held his hands up, leaning away from the knife.

Colette approached the two men and set her hand on Thatch's arm, lowering the blade.

"I am no wench, nor whore, Mr. Vane," Colette warned him in a calm but malicious tone, "and if you so much as infer such ideas again I will be the one to cut out your tongue as well as other appendages you might be fond of."

Vane looked down at her and sheepishly nodded.

"Aye, I do apologize. It wasn't my intention to sully your reputation. I just think this vote is getting muddled," Vane said.

Colette nodded and put her hand on Thatch's chest to calm him down. He took his murderous eyes away from Vane and looked at Colette and his anger began to subside.

"I am not sailing with you," she said to Thatch. "I have my saloon to run and I'm not part of this crew. You can give me a tour of the ship once this business is decided then I must take the carriage back to The Paris. I shall not cast a vote."

Thatch nodded and turned to the group. "Where were we?"

"Seems tied. Three votes Vane, three votes Thatch and two votes Miss Bonny. Guess we must revote, or do you break a tie with a duel?" Frank said.

"That's not necessary. There's still one vote uncounted," said Thatch. He then turned to Tom, standing there largely unnoticed by everyone.

"The Chinese boy gets a vote?" Vane said exasperated.

"He's the cabin boy. A member of the crew. He gets his vote," Mary said with a smile down at the boy. She knew the young runaway had a crush on her. She had received no votes thus far and felt that she could at least count on one vote from the lovesick boy.

Young Tom smiled at Mary and looked around proudly as all eyes were on him. Living on the streets for months with no family and few friends had taken a toll on him. His heart filled up with the joy of belonging. He had never believed there would be anything good again in his life, but here he was, with a whole group of new friends. Adults that treated him with respect and saw that he had value. His life was now full of adventure and dare he think it... family. He looked again at Mary, her pretty face and beautiful red hair, his future bride.

"Who do you cast your vote for, boy?" growled Vane.

Tom puffed up his chest. "Blackbeard!"

Blackbeard smiled at his cabin boy. "It's decided."

Mary whacked Tom on the back of the head and he looked at her in confusion, wondering what he'd done wrong.

Blackbeard held his arm out for Colette to take. "Your tour, lass?" Colette smiled and hooked her arm in his and he led her toward the aftcastle, pointing out details along the way.

Mary passed the bottle of rum to Charlotte who took a swig and handed it to Anne. The three-woman watched in dim moonlight as Blackbeard and Colette said their goodbyes on shore next to the carriage. The crew was making last minute arrangements for departure from the cove. Black Caesar was teaching Jesse and Frank the basics of the rigging and finding jobs they felt comfortable performing. The plan was to sail out of the bay and into the Pacific to make their way down the coastline toward a land the James brothers called Mexico. Once there they could take on more crew and supplies to make the trip around Cape Horn and back toward the warm Caribbean waters.

"These ignorant men, with their self-importance and pride, will never see a woman as an equal. They've all proven themselves to be of poor character and dim intelligence," Anne said.

"At least you received two votes. I and Mary were snubbed by all," Charlotte said with a shake of her head.

"The attractive one is certainly sweet on you," Mary said with a shoulder knock to Anne.

"He is handsome, isn't he?" Anne said turning to watch Jesse with Black Caesar working the rigging. "I think I might be sweet on him as well."

"If I had a cared for Rackham, I'd put up an argument about killers and lovers, revenge and all that nonsense… but never much did, so I hope you both will marry and have many children, or maybe you'll kill each other before the morn," Charlotte said, then took a swig of the rum and roughly slapped the bottle into Mary's chest. She then walked off toward the forecastle.

Anne looked darkly at the African pirate as she walked away.

"Oh, don't mind her," Mary said. "She's just jealous. Hasn't had a man near her since Black Bart Roberts disappeared."

"What do you think happened to Roberts and Bellamy? Think they died somewhere or just made off on their own?" Anne asked, turning back to watch the shoreline.

Mary finished the last of the bottle of rum and tossed it into the water.

"Don't know. Don't care. We are surrounded by enough of these so-called pirate captains. Couldn't stomach one more of them."

"Maybe find you a nice cowboy. I may know an older brother of Jesse that might be to your liking," Anne said, elbowing Mary in the side.

Mary looked back at Frank James coiling rope while Black Caesar watched with his arms crossed over his chest. "He is a fine-looking bloke. Kind of old though."

"There is always the cabin boy who looks at you with hearts in his eyes," Anne said, and the two women shared a good laugh.

Blackbeard took Colette's hands in his. They had been talking for a good while and it was time for him to return to the ship and her to her saloon. He was anxious to sail away from this cold-water port and back to Caribbean seas. The *Queen Anne's Revenge* had a hold full of treasure waiting to be spent and he wanted to put as much distance between him and the pirate hunter as he could. He could still feel the pain and bruises from the noose that had been tied around his neck. He had no desire to tempt fate by remaining in San Francisco, no matter how his feelings for this wild yet elegant beauty grew with each delicious gaze he cast upon her.

"If you ever fancy a hand of twenty-one you know my table is aways open to you."

Blackbeard laughed. "An easy way to fill your pockets and empty mine, your little game is." He pulled out a bagful of gold coins that he'd filled for her while on board the *Queen Anne*. "I want you to have this share of the loot. You were part of our plots and risked your life and business to save mine."

He set the bag on the floor near the driver's seat of the carriage. She only smiled at him and smoothed her dress.

The two utterly different people stared at one another, both wanting the other to stay or join them but unable to utter the words, each knowing that their lives were on different paths and only by random acts of fate had their tracks collided. Colette, a woman of her times, was striving to make a name for herself, the desire for independence strong in her. Edward, a man from a distant past, was lost in time, hunted and out of place, yet confident in his knack for survival and success. They each knew not to expect the other to give up their trajectory as it would only end in disaster. This moment, this moment alone was all that was left for them.

Edward slid his hand to Colette's cheek and moved her blonde hair away from her neck in a caress. Colette in turn stepped toward him and with both hands pulled his bearded face to hers. She stood on her toes as his lips came down to meet hers and her breath was taken away by the kiss they engaged in. It was the first time she understood what the term *swoon* meant—the feeling of the world melting away, for one moment, while kissing another. Edward lifted her from her feet in his strong arms before the embrace ended. His eyes were closed as he lowered her back down to the ground. When he finally opened them, they were met with the sparkling pale blue of Colette's. They let the moment stand as they both fought the urge to say something that would make the other stay with them. Thatch looked back at the darkened form of his ship resting in the cove, then back to the beautiful woman in front of him.

"You should leave, dear lass, before I carry you away to my quarters and abduct you for all eternity," Thatch said heavily.

Colette smiled and squeezed his hand. "Goodbye, Edward." She turned and stepped up to the driver's bench of the carriage. She smiled back at him one last time, then looked away down the rutted trail. She cracked the reins and the horses lurched forward, beginning their trek back to town.

Blackbeard watched the carriage until it disappeared over the rise then made his way to the skiff. He pushed it back in the water and hopped aboard. Taking hold of the oars he started rowing back to his ship. The water was calm and the night air cool and quiet. He felt something he hadn't felt in quite a long while. He felt happy. With a chuckle he chastised himself for being such a sap. A song came to his mind, and he began to sing.

My love she does wait on a lady so fair,
And I do belong to a stout privateer,
Rich prizes I've taken since the wars did begin,
From the lofty monsieurs and brought them all in.

And now of these riches my love shall have share,
For she shall be dressed in rich silks most rare.
With ribbons and rings my jewel I'll deck,
And a fine chain of gold to hang round her neck.

And before that my money begins to grow scant,
I'll away to the sea, for my love shall ne'er want,
And boldly we'll make the loud cannons to roar,
And bring home rich prizes as heretofore.

You pretty young maids who have sweethearts at sea,
Pray take this advice and be ruled by me,
Slight not a bold sailor while he's ploughing the main,
Most richly he'll clothe you when he comes home again.

CHAPTER 29 - THE CROSSING

A thin layer of fog held its fingers to the waters of the bay. It took most of the night to set the rigging and prepare the *Queen Anne's Revenge* for the voyage, but now they were finally under way. The winds were beginning to dissipate the fog layer and supply a helping push to the sails. The slow start was giving a chance for the sparse crew that now incorporated two land-raised cowboys to get their sea legs under them. The James brothers were so green on the ropes that Black Caesar needed to be ever watchful so that they didn't hurt themselves or others as the booms swung port to starboard. The sun had yet to fully rise but the bay traffic was beginning to pick up with the multitude of fishing boats heading out for their early start to the day. They had passed several of the trawlers with the fisherman staring and pointing in awe at the seventeenth-century frigate that was crewed by the eclectic band of pirates. It had taken all hands to get the ship under way and now Blackbeard stood on the aftcastle manning the wheel, watching the incoming clouds, and changing weather. He had wanted to escape this bay and be out on the open waters but if a storm was coming, they would need to wait it out in the protection of this large inlet.

He watched the traffic to see if any boats reversed course after hitting the ocean water, but it was probably too soon to judge. He had no map of these waters to help him navigate and anticipate the next cove or inlet that would grant his safety on their journey south. The scientist was moderately helpful as he knew several of the larger harbors they would encounter on their way to Mexico, but he had only seen them from land. Blackbeard's worry was that they would leave the safety of the bay, encounter a storm, and not find another cove before the ship would be wrecked once more, this time splintering to kindling against rocks or reef.

Blackbeard had hoped to pass the San Francisco harbor in the cover of night or blanket of fog but now it seemed the best course was to move swiftly under full sail past the busy port. He knew from Anne and the James brothers' report that Woodes Rogers had a ship of war at his disposal. That low-profile iron ship with its revolving turret of twin guns was now inducing nightmares in Thatch's thoughts. Charlotte was able to supply the fresh black powder for the *Queen Anne's Revenge*'s forty cannon, but Philip had advised him that they would be but a mere nuisance to the thickly plated ship. It was just as well since they had barely enough crew to man the rigging, let alone load and fire cannon. The *Comanche* was the moniker of the vessel, he was told. It was taken from the name of a fierce native tribe that had ruled the middle territories of the Americas. Blackbeard's only hope was to outrun the beast on the open waters. If this were a true approaching storm the *Comanche* would suffer in rough seas with its deck a scant eighteen inches above the surface. The *Queen Anne* under full sail with brisk winds would be able to best the ironclad's maximum speed of seven knots from its steam-powered single screw.

Tom felt his stomach lurch as the giant wooden mast moved with exaggerated motion under the rise and fall of the ship. From his perch, high up in the crow's nest, he could see further than he ever had in his young life. *This must be what it feels like to be in one of those balloons that carries people up into the sky*, he thought to himself. He had seen balloons filled with hot air attached to people-holding baskets rise in the sky at a celebration near the City Hall of San Francisco. It seemed like magic until he overheard two adults explaining how it operated. Tom's pride peaked as he had neared the top of his climb after Captain Blackbeard assigned him 'look out' and pointed to the nest at the highest spot on the ship. His hands had gripped the rope and netting with knuckle-whitening strength as he hastened up the tallest mast. Once he reached the top, he had looked down with a thundering heart to see his captain nod his head, confirming his trust in the newly recruited cabin boy. His sharp eyes now looked out on the dark blue bay, watching as the crowded San Francisco harbor emerged into view.

Tom was tasked with alerting the crew of any oncoming obstacles either under the water or on top. He needed to anticipate where the ship would travel under its current course and let the crew know if any adjustments needed to be made to keep the ship on a safe trajectory. He listened to the bellowing voice of Black Caesar as the big man called out orders. In return the sailors called back their affirms that they heard the order and were following the directions. The voices of Mary, Anne and Vane traveled loudly up to his ears. Jesse and Frank were gradually getting the hang of their positions and their voices were sounding more confident as they cranked winches and tied off lines. He glanced down at the scientist as he moved around the deck with a spyglass, searching for danger. Tom would have liked to have had one of those devices as well, but the item was denied him for fear he would drop the valuable instrument from his perch.

He watched as the harbor grew near and marveled at the many different vessels that crisscrossed one another on the water or sat moored at the docks that stretched out from the shoreline. Tom called out ships that could have the potential of crossing the *Queen Anne*'s path as they entered the waters around the port. Those ships easily maneuvered to sail clear of the frigate as they were well versed in navigating the crowed harbor. His heart was starting to ease as no one had spotted any danger from the other ships. It seemed they were viewed as just another vessel, though antiquated, on its way to the open sea. The captain steered the ship to port and around the rocky point that led to the channel where the bay emptied out into the Pacific Ocean. The wind grew stronger here, and the water's chop increased. He could see the high cliffs marking the narrowest part of the passage in the distance. Soon they would be free of the congested bay.

He looked down at the scientist peering intently over the fore railing, his feet braced against the rise and fall of the bow. It seemed the slight man had something that piqued his interest from his view through the spyglass. Tom followed the line of sight from Philip's stare and used his strong young eyes to spot the vessel they all feared encountering. The long narrow form of the *Comanche* caught his eye as the ten-foot cylinder turret slowly rotated, searching for a target. The *Comanche* had parked itself in the center of the bay in that narrow channel. It was sitting low in the water, watching, waiting, threatening, as several men stood mid-deck looking for their prey.

Philip peered through the spyglass and confirmed the crew of the *Comanche* consisted of the pirate hunter Woodes Rogers and his dour associate Henry Jennings. In his view he saw Woodes point toward the *Queen Anne* and bark out orders. Woodes and the men on deck all filed below as the ironclad and the turret began to turn in their direction.

If Thatch had felt a sense of relief after passing the harbor unharassed, there was a new concern rising in his gut as the early-morning boat traffic started heading back from the Pacific after venturing out to sea for just a short time. Now that they were in sight of the open ocean the wind was blowing stronger and they were forced to tack aggressively in hopes of emerging from the bay. The horizon was full of dark clouds to the west and the sunrise to the east was creating a glorious painting of colors across the foreboding sky. He longed for a larger, more experienced crew as he noticed Charlotte rushing over to help one of the cowboys work the rigging.

Shouting suddenly broke through the sound of the sheets snapping, and the bellows of orders from his first mate. It was coming from the cabin boy, high up in the crow's nest, but the message was getting lost in the wind as well as being difficult to decipher on account of the boy's Chinese accent. He looked up at the boy and as the sheets moved and jerked, Thatch could see that the boy was pointing fore. Thatch looked down the deck and saw the little scientist was frantically making his way toward him shouting as well. Without having to hear their words clearly, he knew they were about to encounter the ironclad ship and its enormous twin guns. Philip's head broached the top of ladder to the aftcastle and the sound of both his voice and young Tom's combined in the same instant to ring out distinctly '*Comanche!*'

"Man the forecastle gun!" Blackbeard shouted out.

"It will do no good, Captain, it's skin is too thick with iron, too tough," Philip said.

"Maybe we get lucky, Mr. Albert, make her think twice, just enough for us to get past her," Blackbeard said through gritted teeth as he was finally able to make out the distant form of the ironclad from the starboard side as they tacked port.

Both Anne and Vane ran to the swivel gun mounted on the forecastle railing.

"I'll man her," said Vane.

"I'm the better shot."

"Bullocks you say!" Vane said, insulted.

"I've seen you shoot when we's both on the *Lark*. Remember whose shot was more true that day we took a run at the *Phoenix*?" Anne said as she loaded and primed the small cannon. Vane stared at her and then at the approaching small target that the ironclad presented. He did remember that day where the HMS *Phoenix* blocked their escape from Nassau harbor and Anne and Mary far outshot the other crew members including himself allowing, in part, their escape.

"I'll load you so we can be quick about it. Aim for that tower sticking out of the water," Vane said.

"Aye, just like shooting the member off a nude man floating in a lake," Anne said, straight-faced.

Vane slapped her on the back.

"Anne, you are the right woman for the job," he said with a chuckle.

Thatch paid little mind to the traffic oncoming from the sea in the direction of the bay. He needed all the speed and maneuverability the *Queen Anne's Revenge* could offer. Those other ships and boats would have to steer clear of his course as he would not yield way. He also tacked to the outside of the other vessels placing them between the *Queen Anne* and the *Comanche*. He hoped the pirate hunter's bloodlust wasn't so strong that he would open fire with innocent ships in the way. Thatch saw a steam vessel quite a bit larger than his traveling out to sea off his port side. On his next tack he planned to put it in between him and the ironclad.

BOOM! The *Comanche* blasted a shell from one of its guns toward the *Queen Anne's Revenge*. The shot was high and sizzled past in a blink of an eye to explode into the rocky shoreline in an eruption of rock and dirt. All hands turned toward the destruction the single shell caused and in unison back to the guns of the *Comanche*.

KABOOM! The second gun fired and was wide, landing behind them in shallow water with an enormous splash sending water thirty feet in the air. The crew of the pirate ship was frozen in panic by the sheer power of the guns.

"Come about!" Blackbeard shouted, bringing his brethren back to life. He spun the wheel, and the crew worked the sails to erratically turn the ship to port. The wood groaned deep in the keel as the *Queen Anne* listed heavily into the turn.

"Tom! Come down, boy!" Mary shouted below the main mast at the cabin boy hanging on for dear life high in the crow's nest. The top of the mast was now almost at a forty-five-degree angle, extending out far over the water. If the boy fell from there, he might survive but would be lost in the cold waters of the bay. Tom could do nothing but cling to the rope railing of the perch while the ship made its turn trying to escape the fire from the ironclad.

BOOM! Another round came at the *Queen Anne* but luckily the turning ship was creating a smaller, faster moving target. Thatch held the turn as they crossed the center of the channel and once they were on the port side of the steam ship he spun the wheel to straighten the trajectory. The ship rocked in the opposite direction and Tom was sent higher in the air as the mast rose up under the deck then pivoted starboard before righting itself to its natural ninety-degree angle. Tom had his eyes shut tight and both arms wrapped around the rope rails. He opened one eye to see the steam ship in between the *Comanche* and them. Mary's voice rose to him, shouting for him to come down. He looked below at her, nodded, and untangled his arms from the rope then with shaking legs and arms started his descent.

Blackbeard ordered his crew to spill the wind from the sails, slowing their speed to keep pace with the steam ship. He wanted the *Comanche* to have no line of site with them as they passed. The steam ship's crew were running the decks in confusion, men pointing in both directions. They were now close enough for Thatch to hear their shouts and see the fear in their faces. The steam ship's captain had several choices he could make: he could slow down, speed up, or move starboard closer toward the *Comanche*, but Thatch would give no quarter for the ship to come further to port. He wanted to keep the vessel right where she was until they passed the ironclad and could race out to the sea.

Thatch saw the steamer's men looking at him in fear, shouting questions. Thatch pointed out to sea. The two ships were close enough now that their shouting could be heard.

"Keep us steady, Mr. Albert," Thatch told Philip, giving him the helm.

Thatch climbed down the aftcastle and strode quickly to the starboard rail, his beard and hair blowing in the wind looking like a black lion's mane. Several men from the steamer were at their railing and listened as Thatch's voice boomed across to them.

"Make for the sea or we'll blow you too bits!" Thatch yelled as he loaded a starboard deck cannon and held a lighted linstock. "Faster you swine!" he screamed at them.

"She's hiding behind the steamer, Commander," called out the first mate of the *Comanche* from his position watching from the view port in the forward position. The ironclad had an armored box that rose above the main deck about three feet tall for viewing. Using a ladder from below deck the sailors could look out and navigate in the safety of the box with several portholes that could be closed for protection from small arms fire, artillery, and water flooding the inside. Jennings hovered near the first mate, watching through the portholes as the *Queen Anne's Revenge* disappeared from view behind the larger steam ship.

"Blackbeard will use that ship as cover. We should come around behind them," Jennings said.

"We could lose them if they get too far ahead. Their ship will be faster in these winds, and we are already at a disadvantage with this chop in the bay," said the *Comanche*'s commander, Charles McDougal. He had been told by his superiors that he was to assist in the capture or death of the James Gang and these pirates who had robbed both a local bank and a train, killing federal and local law enforcement officers in the process. This was the first time since the *Comanche* was launched in '65 that it was seeing action and he needed this mission to be successful. Blowing the antique frigate from the waters would be a shame but if he was the man who ended the James Gang's run then he would be awarded a fistful of commendations and finally make the navy rank of captain.

"Move to keep pace with them. We don't want to be left flat-footed when they pass," McDougal ordered.

The *Comanche* throttled to intercept the ships as they rapidly approached the south side of the channel.

Woodes, Jennings, Cooper and McDougal crowded the porthole to see what the intent of the steamer was going to be. *If the damned ship would just slow down to let the pirates pass, we would be in a position to sink them with one shot*, thought McDougal. Frustrated from his crowded low view he hurried up the ladder to the turret deck. The other three men followed him. The turret deck was located inside the ten-foot tall, fifteen-foot-wide rotating cylinder. It was manned by four men working the rear-loading smoothbore guns with explosive shells. The turret also had narrow portholes through which to see outside. The twin guns continued to track the two ships sailing side by side, the pirate ship hiding behind the large steamer. They were all quick to see the steamer was not going to yield way and slow, instead she noticeably increased her speed to head out to sea with the pirates hiding in her shadow.

"Bloody hell!" Woodes exclaimed. "They're going to get away!"

"Max speed!" McDougal yelled down below deck.

"Max speed," came the reply from the helmsmen.

The *Comanche* was now on a parallel course with the two ships, though she would be slowly falling behind as they reached the mouth of the bay.

"Fire at that ship!" Woodes screamed.

The four men manning the guns looked unsure of themselves and stared at the lieutenant commander for orders. McDougal hesitated. If he fired on the innocent ship, would he be committing murder? If he didn't do something the odds were greatly in favor of the pirate ship escaping. The main deck of the steamer completely obscured the pirate ship hiding on its port side, not even the masts of the vessel were visible. McDougal turned from the porthole that he was watching from to come face to face with the scarred English captain.

"Blast the top of that ship and it will send it careening into the pirates," Woodes growled at him.

"I can't risk the lives of the…" McDougal got out before Woodes slapped the man in the face. McDougal bent over more in shock then pain and looked up at the pirate hunter looming over him. "How dare you!" he said standing up. Woodes grabbed the man by the shirt collar and shoved him into the bulkhead. Cooper grabbed at the two men and separated them, pushing Woodes back.

"Enough!" Cooper said, pointing at Woodes. "Enough, both of you!" He then pointed at McDougal. "Our orders were to capture or kill these murdering thieves by any means necessary." He let that statement sink into McDougal's head. Cooper approached the commander and got right in his face. "By any means necessary," he repeated.

McDougal stared at Cooper then at Woodes to see the seriousness of the men. He then turned to his gunners and said, "Open fire on that steamer. One volley."

The gunners stared at the commander in shock.

"I said fire, damn it. Now!" The gunners immediately went to work, sighting the steamer and calling out the position and firing orders. BLAM! BLAM! The noise and the concussion from the 15-inch guns was deafening and rocked the men on their heels. A split second later the sound of the rounds hitting the mix of wood and metal from the steamer rocked the turret as well.

Jennings stared out the porthole as the mid-castle of the steamer erupted in a burst of debris and fire, the force of blast pushing the vessel to port along with all the splintered projectiles that had once been the pilot house of the steam ship.

Mary screamed as the sound of the guns and explosions from the starboard side rocked the *Queen Anne's Revenge* with shrapnel and debris from the steamer. Tom was still twenty feet up the main mask when the *Comanche's* guns blew apart the middle section of the steam ship. Her scream resonated in horror as the young boy lost his grip and fell from the dizzying height. The boy's arms and legs pumped the air as he grappled with the nothingness, falling toward his doom. Mary could do nothing but watch, her hand over her mouth. Suddenly the mighty arms of Black Caesar were underneath him, catching him before the boy's body could smash against the solid deck of the ship.

A split second later the ship was rocked as the wake of the steamer being forced to port crashed into them, followed by the two ships banging together then separating as the steamer veered starboard, away from them. The shock wave from the crash sent the entire crew slamming into whatever was near them. Vane and Anne held onto the swivel gun for support, waiting for their chance to fire a 3-inch round shot at the portholes of the ironclad. Jesse and Frank had held their ground with the help of the rigging and stood again with little more than a few scrapes. Charlotte threw off a stretch of sail that had been torn from the fore top-mast and fallen to envelop her. She looked up and saw the remaining length of the sail blowing useless in the wind.

Thatch made his way back up the aftcastle ladder, calling out orders to whoever could hear them.

"Full sail! Fifteen degrees starboard!" he yelled as he hurried over to help up a struggling Philip. The man had a gash on his forehead and didn't quite have his wits about him yet. Thatch knew they would need to tack alongside the veering steamer to keep it between them and the ironclad. He got the scientist to his feet and looked over at the out-of-control steam ship. The pilot house was gone and what was left underneath was aflame. He saw that it was turning sharply into the line of travel the ironclad must be sailing. That should give him a moment to put some distance between them. He took the wheel and gained control of the *Queen Anne* as the wind caught the sails and the crew began to make them full.

Black Caesar was lying underneath the young cabin boy when Mary arrived to take Tom into her arms. The frightened and trembling boy clung tightly to her, and she soothed his pounding heart. She took his shoulders and held him in front of her. "Don't ever scare me like that again, you hear?" she said and the boy nodded, close to tears. She hugged him again quickly. "Anything broke?" The boy shook his head no. Black Caesar patted the boy on the back then rushed off to help with rigging the sails for the chase.

"You stick by me and do as I say," Mary told the boy, then the two of them made off to assist where needed.

Charlotte reefed the useless sheet so it would do no more harm to any of the nearby rigging. She expertly moved across the deck inspecting the damage that the shrapnel from the blast had done. If they weren't racing for their lives, she would have little concern as the damage was minimal. As it was, the smallest tears in the sails would slow them down and if the pressure on them became too great, those tears would enlarge until the sail would become useless. She found a sheet off the fore mast flapping futilely due to a severed line. Looking out at the slowing steamer, she expected the ironclad to emerge at any moment. Charlotte took a running leap and latched onto the netting of the mast and with the dexterity of a cat ascended up to the topsail yard, forty feet above the deck. She inched her way out on the yard, trying to match her balance with the motion of the ship. She reached up while holding the yardarm to grab the hanging end of the rope. She was inches away from grabbing it when she looked down to see the ironclad sailing into view. Her time was short and the need for safety had passed. It was do or die. She let go of the yard and leaped up to grab the rope. Her hand clenched it, and her feet came back down to the narrow yardarm only to slip, and she began to fall from the mast.

Charlotte still held her one-handed grip on the rope, pulling the sheet down with her as she fell. The effect was that the sheet caught the wind as it lengthened into place, slowing her descent, and she grabbed another yard with her other hand as she passed it, hanging from it while the sheet tried its best to pull from her grip. Charlotte wrapped the rope around her wrist so it would not fling from her grasp. She pulled her legs up to wrap around the yard, further securing her to the precarious position. Hanging underneath the yard she was able to tie off the sheet so that it would not come loose. BLAM! Charlotte almost lost her grip in fright from the sound of a cannon blast. She looked down to see smoke escaping the three-foot swivel gun being manned by Anne Bonny.

"Take that, you scarred-face dog!" Anne shouted as Vane reloaded the barrel. Her shot was fired just as the turret became visible from behind the steamer. The ironclad's nose was pointing starboard to escape running into the damaged steamer, which put some more distance between it and the *Queen Anne's Revenge*. Anne had heard and seen the round shot hit the iron plating of the wide turret, but she knew that it had barely scored the flesh of the beast.

"Aim for the eyes!" Vane shouted.

"What do you think I'm doing?" Anne shouted back.

The turret was turning to take aim upon them, and Anne lined up her shot at one of the gun ports in hopes of blasting through the small opening.

"Hard to port, fifteen degrees!" Thatch cried out from the wheel. The order was loudly repeated by Black Caesar.

Anne felt the ship lurch and turn sharply. This caused her aim to be off. BLAM! She fired again but the shot went wide. It was just as well, she thought, as the *Comanche* had fired right after she did. KABAM! The shell would have most likely hit them if Thatch hadn't turned the ship at that moment. The man was smart, she'd give him that. He knew the ship and what she could do better than anyone. As the *Queen Anne's Revenge* turned away from the ironclad and the safety of the steamer's shadow, she lost the line of sight with this fore-mounted gun.

"Let's get to the aft cannon!" she shouted at Vane as she ran toward the rear of the ship. Jesse's eyes met hers as she ran past. There was a mixture of fear and excitement in those eyes as she passed him.

"Give 'em hell, Annie!" he called as she leaped over the ladder of the aftcastle. She couldn't help but smile at his call of encouragement to her. She and Vane reached the gun a moment later and the two of them worked together to load and prime the weapon with more speed than either thought possible. It was like instinct kicked in and their hands worked as if they were attached to a single body.

Anne lined up her shot as the ironclad sailed into view, waiting for the rise and fall of the ship to create the perfect arc to her target.

BLAM! Her iron round shot out of the cannon and a second later connected with the *Comanche*.

Jennings saw the incoming shot as it streaked through the air toward him. He ducked down just in time as the 3-inch iron ball slammed into the 4-inch wide slit in the turret he had been staring out of. BAA-CLANG! Pieces of the iron ball burst through the hole sounding like bees as iron shards ricocheted around the metal room. Jennings had his eyes closed and his arms wrapped around his bald head. His ears continued to ring long after the noise of the shot dissipated.

He slowly opened his eyes and removed his arms. Blood seeped from his forearm where a piece of metal shrapnel protruded from a wound. If he hadn't covered his head this projectile would have been sticking out of his forehead. He looked around, realizing that he had been the lucky one. The lieutenant commander lay prone on the floor, eyes open but seeing nothing. A pool of blood was growing underneath his head. Cooper had taken a grazing shot to his cheek and one to his collar. The Wells Fargo man took out a handkerchief and pressed it to stop the bleeding.

Woodes Rogers looked around the room at the dead man on the floor then at the gunners who were standing unharmed. He strode over to Jennings and took his arm, helping him stand up. His face was inches away from Jennings'.

"Go below and take charge," Woodes said then ripped the shrapnel from Jennings' arm. He then turned to the gunners. "Don't just stand there like cod fish! Fire on that ship!"

Vane let out a cheer as he saw the smoke and crack in the porthole appear after Anne's shot had hit its mark.

"That porthole where you were aiming?" Vane said with a knowing snicker.

"Close enough don't you think?" Anne said as the two worked together to reload the cannon.

"A finer shot I've never seen," Vane said, shaking his head and squeezed her shoulder with his hand once the cannon was ready to fire.

BLAM! Anne fired another round. It slammed into the turret, giving it a good dent but otherwise doing no further harm.

Lightning flashed and the crack of thunder echoed over the water as rain began to fall. The fast-moving storm had arrived to deliver stronger winds as they sped toward the open ocean. The boat traffic was giving the fighting ships a wide berth as they came back into the bay to escape the gale. The *Queen Anne* was tacking aggressively as it continued to slowly outpace the ironclad. The *Comanche* had no need to tack as its powerful screw pushed the beast straight ahead at a consistent five knots. Normally the calm bay would allow its speed to reach seven or even eight knots but the swells and chop from the storm were battering the low-profile vessel quite badly.

Thatch called back to Anne for a report on the ironclad.

"She's falling behind and I gave her one right in the eye!"

"Well done, lass! Keep harassing her 'til she's good and bloodied," Blackbeard called out.

Jennings went below to the lower deck where the operations of the ironclad took place. The crew of sixteen men went about their work keeping the ship in the chase. Woodes' two navy men tried to look helpful, but they were completely out of place on the ship operating on only steam power. The four Wells Fargo men sat with their prisoner toward the bow of the ship where the crew bunks were kept. It seemed useless for the men to hover over their captive as there was nowhere to escape to.

"The commander has become a casualty of this war. It is an unfortunate turn of events that will not deter us from our mission of bringing these pirates to justice or kill them in the process. Captain Woodes Rogers of the Royal Navy has assumed command of the vessel. I am now the acting first mate. If there is any dissention it will be dealt with swiftly and violently as we are now under wartime orders." Jennings slowly looked around the room to see the expression on the faces of the navy sailors. These men were more frightened then angry over the change in leadership. He nodded at Woodes' navy men, and they took position around the room along with Cooper's men. The sailors aboard the *Comanche* were not armed at the moment so Jennings felt confident that they would not mutiny.

"Let's give chase to these bastards and make them pay for the murders they've done!" Jennings called out. With only a second of indecisiveness the crew went back to their jobs and took up the call to action. The now former first mate came up to Jennings with a worried look.

"Sir, the pumps are falling behind, the sea is swamping us and filling the bilge. It's slowing us down and the boilers are in danger of flooding."

"Are all the pumps being utilized?" Jennings asked.

"Not the manual ones. We'd need additional sets of hands."

Jennings snapped his fingers for two of the Wells Fargo man to come help.

"Take these two men and get them working the pumps, we need to keep this iron pot afloat," Jennings said. He then strode over to the ladder leading up to the armored porthole box that protruded above the top deck. He took caution as he leaned to look through, not wanting to meet another round shot coming straight at his eyes again. He could see the *Queen Anne's Revenge* tacking on the starboard side now as she made her run for the open water. The horizon was a frightening site from his vantage point just mere feet from the roiling waters. BOOM! BOOM! The twin guns sounded from behind his protected metal box. He winced as they echoed throughout the hull of the ship. He watched as the shots went wide, both hitting the water much closer to a terrified fishing trawler rushing in from the heavy seas then Blackbeard's ship.

The guns of the *Comanche* could fire a great distance, more than a mile, but as with all naval warfare, hitting a moving target while you were in motion as well was never an easy task. Jennings watched as the *Queen Anne* reversed tack and made its way to port, and out from the shelter of the bay. They were going to catch a wind now and would be able to avoid the need to tack, easily riding the wind southward. Jennings let out a sigh as the chase was now over. BOOM! BOOM! Went the *Comanche*'s guns again, more out of frustration then the promise of success. Jennings could only imagine the dark scowl that must be covering Woodes Rogers' face right now.

Thatch felt the deep rise and fall of his well-built 200-ton frigate as it cut through the growing swells. He watched as water splayed out in great splashes as the forward end of the hull crashed down through the heavy sea. A smile grew from his lips as saw and felt the sails fill to their maximum density of air as the wind pushed the ship to the speed of almost ten knots. There was a cheer from the crew as Vane yelled a curse at the ironclad as it fell behind. The scientist, with his feet set far apart, peered at the *Comanche* through his spyglass.

"She's not built for these seas; they do risk disabling or sinking her if they follow us," Philip commented.

"Woodes won't give up so easily, Mr. Albert, though I would love to see that beast go down to a watery grave with the pirate hunter inside."

Philip kept his eye to the glass and said, "You're right, Captain, they are not straying from their course. You just might get what you desire if they continue to get swamped by the sea."

Jesse James spun the winch as the boom passed over his and Frank's heads, swinging from one side of the ship to the other. The trial by fire of learning seamanship had allowed the brothers to learn the ways of the rigging in record time. The two men were in sync with each other as they worked with Black Caesar and Charlotte to keep the ship's sails filled with wind.

"She's bucking like a wild bronco, Jesse!" Frank said as he allowed his feet to slide on the rain- and sea water-soaked floor. Their boots slid on the slick surface, but each was already accustomed to the feeling and let the natural tilt of the ship bring them to the position they needed to be in. Both men were in fine shape and quite dexterous from a young age, roping and riding their way into adulthood.

"I'm getting the hang of this sailing, but what I'd give to be on a horse galloping over dry land instead of this," Jesse said as he worked to tie off the rope holding the boom in place.

"Not bad, cowboy," Charlotte said as she looked at his knot. She was on the continued hunt to solve problems as they arose.

Black Caesar pointed at a slack line and shouted to Frank, "Shore up that line!", and Frank hopped quickly to the task.

Jesse heard the snapping of a loose rope and the clanging of an iron ring. He searched for the source of the sound. He looked along the sheets of the main mast and saw that the one in the middle was flapping about more than it should, the wind not being held inside creating slack in the line. He moved around the circumference of the largest mast on the ship to get a better look at the sail.

"That ain't good," he said audibly to himself. He looked up to see a tear in the sheet that was quickly growing as the wind billowed through.

"Reef that sail!" Charlotte called out.

'Reefing a sail' was a lesson neither James brother had been taught and in seconds the entire length of the sail was split and flapping useless. The streams of the shredded sheet beat against the one below it and a loose line whip-slapped that sail as well. Charlotte shouldered the cowboy out of the way and began to unloose the rigging to reef the troubled sail. Her efforts were too late as the sheet below developed a rip that quickly traveled its entire length, rending the sail useless.

Charlotte looked at the other sails and more tears were visible. It must have been the shrapnel from the steam ship that poked holes throughout the assembly of canvas. Only now under the strong winds and heavily enveloped air that pushed the ship forward were the holes becoming tears and larger rips. If they continued at this pace many more sheets would become useless before long.

"Spill the wind!" yelled Charlotte.

Black Caesar heard her command and looked up to see the sails developing holes. *Damn!* He thought to himself. They were almost free. He called out the order to spill the wind and he, Mary, Charlotte and the two brothers let the wind out of the sails to slow the ship down.

Edward Thatch heard the order as well. He was about to rescind the call to keep up their speed but from what he could see when he looked at the *Queen Anne's* sails Charlotte was correct. They needed to reduce speed, or their sails would be ripped apart and then they would become an easy target for the ironclad.

Jennings watched as the *Queen Anne's Revenge* slowed down. She'd lost two sheets in less than a minute due to the strong winds. The fabric must have been damaged while it sat on the bottom of the bay or by some scrap or debris blasted from the steam ship. Whatever the cause, the tide just turned in his favor. He jumped down from his perch at the porthole and made his way to the turret-level ladder.

"Keep with it, men! We almost have her. Helmsmen, stay your course," Jennings called out to the crew.

He emerged from below to find Woodes turning toward him with a rare smile on his face.

"The demon is losing sails; he can't outrun us now," Woodes said.

"Aye. These seas are heavy though, more than this vessel was built to withstand. I fear the elements more than Blackbeard. I advise caution," Jennings said while water continued to pour into the ironclad through the open gunports as the ship was swamped by each swell.

"I will not be denied, Henry! God is with us, and we will prevail." Woodes grabbed Jennings' shoulders. "Our journey is almost at an end. We will send them to their waiting graves, then you and I will sail home, heroes once again."

Jennings' stomach sank either from the jolting rise and fall of the awkward vessel or from Woodes' denial of their real quandary from being lost in time. Woodes turned away to watch through the gunports as they closed the distance to the frigate. Jennings descended the ladder shaking his head at the fact Woodes still believed God was going to return them to 1718 once they killed all the pirates. There was magic at work here, but he couldn't follow the idea of God's hand being behind their time travel. He also didn't believe Blackbeard had any part in the mechanism of their journey as he had once thought. He resigned himself to just accept his fate, finish this war with Blackbeard and Woodes, then find his way back to Bermuda to live out his days.

"Status, helmsmen?" Jennings inquired.

"The gunners should be able to make short work of her in a few moments. She's slowed to an estimate of three knots. We're making up ground, sir."

"Good. Let's close the distance, blow her out of the water and then escape this storm." Jennings went back to stare out the porthole box to watch the end of Blackbeard the pirate.

CHAPTER 30 - THE CRASH

"Tell me where her guns are pointing, Mr. Albert!" shouted Thatch as he fought the twelve-foot swells, rain and wind, his big hands gripped tightly on the wheel. He wanted to make the *Queen Anne's Revenge* a difficult target for the *Comanche* to hit. Steering into the troughs and using the swells to hide the bulk of the ship were his best option as the ironclad slowly gained upon them. Philip stared through the spyglass giving Thatch the location of the enemy so that he could quickly make adjustments to their course.

"Steer hard to starboard!" Philip called out to be heard over the storm. He watched as the ironclad struggled through the churning sea, waves swamping over the low deck of the ship. *If only our sails had held*, thought Philip, *we would have easily escaped them on the open ocean*. The advantage the ironclad had was that its engines would consistently push the ship through the sea and the turret would be able to train in on its prey no matter which direction they were facing. He lost sight of it as the *Queen Anne* dipped into the deep trough of a swell and Thatch rode in between the waves for as long as possible. When at last they crested the next swell, he saw that the *Comanche* was cresting at the same moment, it's turret well placed to fire at them.

"Hard port!" Philip screamed out.

KABOOM!

The *Comanche*'s guns blasted at them. Thatch turned the great wheel to bring the ship to port. The first shot from the ironclad ripped straight through a sail on the aft mast, shredding it to bits as the wind roared through the sheet. The second shot was wide, making a great splash into the water behind the ship. The sudden turn Thatch executed brought them crashing into an oncoming wave, sending a great surge of water up and over the bow, slowing their momentum. Philip surged forward, barely staying on his feet, holding onto the railing with one hand. He looked back at the *Comanche*, no longer needing the spyglass to see the turret clearly and his stomach dropped as the guns flashed again.

BOOM! Another sail was ripped away to the wind. BOOM! went the aft gun manned by Anne and Vane. Philip saw that their return fire went harmlessly into the water.

"Full sail!" Thatch commanded, desperate to bring more speed to the ship. He knew he risked shredding the sails, but they were now sitting ducks left with no other option as the *Comanche* gained on them.

"Full sail," Black Caesar repeated, and Mary, Charlotte, Frank, Jesse, and the few new men left aboard from the salvage ship helped to adjust the sheets to fill with wind.

Tom appeared next to Thatch to look up at the man with fear in his eyes. Thatch stared down at the boy and his gut twisted with regret. He could very well have caused the end of the kid's short life by bringing him aboard the *Queen Anne's Revenge*. Tom was shivering in the cold rain, his arms wrapped around himself. *Damn that Woodes Rogers*, Thatch cursed to himself.

"Don't let them see your fear, boy!" Thatch pulled one of his revolvers and handed it to Tom. "Take good aim and shoot them in the eye."

Tom looked at the heavy pistol in his hands then looked up into the dark, wild-eyed face of Blackbeard. The shiny metal barrel was cold and slick with rain in his hand. Tom looked over his shoulder at Philip watching the *Comanche* from the aft railing next to Anne and Vane loading the swivel gun for another shot, then he turned back to his captain. "Aye, Captain Blackbeard," he said. Tom strode confidently, head held high, unflinching from the storm as the *Comanche*'s guns sounded again. His eyes set on his target, he reached the railing and stood next to Philip. Philip looked questioningly at the boy as he lined up the pistol using a gunwale as a brace for the weapon.

BOOM! went the cannon next to him, followed by the clanging sound of the round shot hitting the armor of the turret. Anne and Vane cheered even as their shot merely dented the thick iron paneling. The two pirates went back to the task of loading the cannon for another round. BAM! BAM! BAM! Tom fired off several controlled rounds at the turret. Metallic plinks could be heard over the storm as each shot found its mark against the *Comanche*'s armor.

"Ha! This young pirate's got the dead-eye aim, Miss Bonny!" called out Vane.

"Aye, a finer shot I've never seen!" boasted Anne. "Keep at 'em, Tom, give 'em no quarter!"

Tom, with a determined face, continued to fire at the ironclad as its turret swiveled to take aim at the *Queen Anne* once again.

Cooper watched from the porthole of the turret as the *Queen Anne's Revenge* struggled to gain momentum in the raging seas with half her sails in tatters. The salty, cold waters of the Pacific flooded and frothed through the openings of the turret as the low deck was swamped with each wave that crested. *This God damn tin can wasn't meant to sail these waters*, Cooper thought as the deluge of sea swirled around his boots before draining below deck to be siphoned from the struggling bilge pumps.

"We've got these bastards now, they're dead in the water," Cooper said to Woodes and the gunners.

Jennings hurried up the ladder to emerge into the turret and look out the porthole. "Had to close the hatch down below, too much sea flooding in."

"Better view to watch the end of the pirate Blackbeard," Woodes said with conviction.

"An' those damn James brothers. To hell with them!" Cooper said, wiping away the blood and salt water that was stinging one of his wounds.

Woodes watched through the gap in the turret that the barrels protruded from. The *Queen Anne's Revenge* was cresting a swell, emerging right in their line of sight.

"Finish them!" Woodes ordered the gunners.

The turret suddenly filled with the blasting sound of a ship's air horn blare.

"What the devil?" came from Woodes.

Jennings looked out the porthole on the starboard side of the turret. "God in heaven."

The air horn sounded again louder, closer this time. Woodes rushed over and shoved Jennings out of the way. His disfigured jaw dropped as he saw the bow of an enormous ship racing at them.

"Guns to starboard!" shrieked Woodes.

The gunners spun the turret at the oncoming vessel. Their eyes went wide as they saw how close it was to crashing over them.

KABOOM! KABOOM! Both 15-inch barrels fired at the bow of the oncoming ship, easily finding their mark over the short distance. The two blasts exploded through the towering hull but did nothing to slow its momentum. The gaping holes revealed the damaged structure of the giant vessel, its skin peeled back to show its insides.

"Brace for impact!" Woodes yelled out and watched as the heavily damaged ship rose to dominate the entire view from the turret.

The deep-hulled bow of the ship slammed into the rear of the ironclad, causing it to be pressed deep under the water with the front of the *Comanche* rising out of the sea to stand almost straight up. The entire crew was thrown back toward the aft of the ship, slamming into bulkheads and machinery. The oncoming ship's hull was further cracked down the side as the *Comanche*'s screw continued to turn and chew up its underside as it passed. The two gaping holes in the bow of the steam ship were now flooding rapidly with sea water.

The ironclad's bow came crashing back down to the surface of the water and everything including the crew rolled forward to settle in a shambles of bodies, broken equipment, and flotsam.

Bart Roberts sighed with resignation as he watched the chaos of his crew aboard the *Charlotte's Fortune*. Chester had the men readying the lifeboats with as much treasure from the hold as they could carry. His beautiful prize was going to sink under the cold waters of the Pacific in a matter of minutes. It was a difficult decision that he had had to make within seconds when he came upon the *Queen Anne's Revenge* being fired upon by the low-profile iron ship with the enormous guns. Sam had whispered suspiciously to him that it was only a ghost ship, as they had been aboard Blackbeard's frigate when it sank only a short time ago. Through his spyglass he had confirmed that the pirate was indeed alive along with others trying desperately to escape the devastatingly dangerous naval vessel.

The *Charlotte's Fortune* still had no cannon to fire upon the other ship, so he was left with only two choices: leave his fellow pirates to their fate or use his giant steam ship to ram the iron beast. His eyes had found Charlotte working the rigging while looking through the spyglass and his decision ultimately was made. The havoc of the storm and their seemingly single-minded focus of destroying the wooden frigate had allowed him to bear down on the enemy vessel without them becoming aware until the last seconds. Roberts had only decided to blow the loud air horn once he realized he was going to arrive a hair too late. *The sound must have shaken the crew of the ironclad to their core,* he thought. Unfortunately, blaring the horn before they were able to ram them gave enough time to turn those big guns on the *Charlotte's Fortune*, blasting big holes into its hull.

Bart watched as Sam flew up the stairs two at a time to run into the pilot house where he stood watching, dry, sheltered from the storm.

"She's lost, Bartholomew. The lower decks are already flooded, engine power is gone. Chester said maybe forty, forty-five men made it out."

"Let's be done with it then," Roberts said. "We want to be away when she pulls under. Abandon ship, Sammy." Sam handed him a long rifle from a weapons store near the instrument panel and took one for himself. They needed to be prepared to return fire from the iron ship if it survived the blow they had dealt it. The two pirates made their way down the stairs and to the hoists that were lowering the treasure and weapon-laden lifeboats into the water. Four had already been launched in the churning seas that were becoming worse with each passing minute. The fifth boat was being lowered on the starboard side where the pirates had gathered as the ship gave out a huge groan and began listing heavily to port. The boat being lowered beat against the hull of the ship and Sam, Bart and the remaining men held onto the rail as the angle of the incline was enough to send them sliding to the other side of the deck if not for their grasp.

"We're out of time!" Bart called out. He then pulled himself over to the controls of the hoist and released the hanging boat to fall into the water. He watched with bated breath as the boat landed on its side, spilling most of the contents into the sea, then it settled upright and began to float away from the sinking ship. Bart climbed over the railing to hang off the side.

"Follow me to meet Poseidon, boys!" With that he used the listing ship's hull as a slide, cascading down the structure toward the water. He used his feet just before the hull curved inward to launch himself out and into the cold dark sea.

Sam looked at Chester and the three other waiting men. He shook his head and muttered, "Into the deep we go again." He leaped over the rail and mimicked Bart's slide and followed him into the water. Sam's heart skipped a beat when the cold water hit him, drenching his clothes, and clutching his skin with its icy fingers. His head broke the surface, and he swam toward the bobbing lifeboat. Amazingly he still clung to the long rifle he'd had when he jumped. He was about to abandon the gun approaching the boat as it was difficult to swim with it when Bart's hand emerged in front of him to assist him aboard the vessel. Sam rolled over the rail and onto all fours, spitting out the sea water that had got caught in his lungs. Bart then helped Chester and the other three crew members climb aboard.

Only three oars had remained on board when the boat fell into the ocean. The three crewmen used them to row the boat away from the sinking steamer through the heavy seas and toward the four boats waiting a hundred yards away for their captain to join them. The *Queen Anne's Revenge* and the ironclad were not visible beyond the sinking *Charlotte's Fortune* as they both lay to the port side of the doomed vessel. Bart, Sam, and Chester worked to dislodge the water from their firearms and prepare for any upcoming battle that would take place.

The crew of the *Queen Anne's Revenge* couldn't help but stop what they were doing and stare at the aftermath of the clash of the two ships. One, seemingly indestructible, flat, iron-armored ship being rammed by a second, enormous, steam-powered vessel. The wooden frigate rose and fell in the swells as the pirates all watched from the railing of the aftcastle. Thatch put his hand on the shoulder of the young cabin boy. Tom looked up at him with a confident smile. The mood had become almost jovial beneath the dark storm-ravaged sky that hid the sun completely, as if it had never risen.

"Let's hope that was the end of the pirate hunter Woodes Rogers. Lie with Davy Jones, you pious bastard," Thatch said then spit out to the sea.

"Who the devil rammed that ship into them to save our skins?" Jesse asked.

"Don't know but I could kiss them right here, right now," said Mary.

"Roberts," Charlotte said.

"What?" asked Charles Vane. "What makes you think that?"

Charlotte pointed out the name of the ship written above the aft hull: '*Charlotte's Fortune.*'

"Oh, he's got it bad for you," Mary said with a chuckle.

"Who's Roberts?" Jesse asked.

"I told you about him and Sam, the ones that went missing that first night we's landed here," Anne said.

"The other colorful characters with the monikers of Black; Black Bart, Black Sam, Blackbeard, Black Caesar..." Frank said then looked up at the huge dark man that stood next to him. "No offense."

Black Caesar looked down at him. "None taken."

They stared out at the broken and damaged ships while the rain continued to pour down on them. The ironclad was visible with smoke billowing from several portholes. It seemed dead in the water, rising and falling with the swells, moving but not under its own power, pushed by the whims of the sea.

"The ironclad still a danger, Mr. Albert?" Thatch asked Philip.

He was looking at the *Comanche* with the help of his spyglass. He noted that the turret was not damaged but also not turning in search of a target. The ship's engines were surely damaged when the steamer rammed them. Philip knew that the turret would only turn under the power of the steam engines, still it was possible the gun could still be operational if anyone survived inside the ironclad's belly.

"I believe, dear Captain, if we stay away from the business end of those guns, we will be okay. They may be able to fire them, but the turret will not turn."

"Aye." Thatch slapped Charlotte on the back and started back to the wheel. "Let's go rescue our love-struck brethren."

Mary smiled slyly at Charlotte and knocked her hip against hers.

"Man the rigging, come round one-hundred-eighty degrees, make way to retrieve passengers," Black Caesar called while starting to unfurl the operating sails.

Philip stood with his precious spyglass watching the ironclad. The smoke had lessened, and the ship still rode with its deck a mere foot off the surface. He considered their predicament for a moment. The ship was not built to traverse the ocean as its design was meant more for rivers and the calm waters of the bay. Sailing under steam power in these seas, it would be easy for the deck to be swamped continuously by the high swells but inert as it was, she could ride the rise and fall without too much trouble. If there was flooding inside, hand pumps could help to drain the water from sinking the ship, provided there were no holes in its hull and men still alive to work the pumps. It didn't seem likely that she would escape without a breach after the beating it took from the massive steamer, but she wasn't listing to any degree.

He slowly moved his field of view over the deck to the turret. The guns were facing west, away from him and slightly to the right of the sinking steam ship that had struck them. As he watched, the hatch on the mid-deck swung open. A moment later a man in a navy uniform pulled himself up to sit on the edge of the opening. He gazed around before calling down below. Philip watched him stand carefully on the deck as it rolled in the rough seas. He put his hand down the hole to help someone climb out. Even from this distance he recognized Woodes Rogers emerging from below. Philip lowered the spyglass and stared as several more figures emerged, armed with rifles.

The *Queen Anne's Revenge* lurched forward and steered toward starboard to intercept the rowing lifeboats. Philip hurried from the rail to alert Blackbeard that Woodes still lived.

Jennings followed up several armed men to the deck of the *Comanche*. The two-hundred-foot craft was rising and falling with the stormy swells. The falling rain and ocean spray kept the surface of the deck slick as glass. His attention turned for a moment to the sinking hulk of the ocean-going steamer. It was listing heavily, and the main deck was nearly at the water line. It wouldn't be long before the seas claimed her completely. He looked east at the five boats packed with men and supplies, the survivors of the steam ship. Jennings couldn't understand why the captain of that ship would intervene, risking his ship and crew to ram the *Comanche*. It seemed unlikely that they had hit them by accident since they had been in a gun battle for many minutes before. Surely the captain and crew had heard and seen the conflict taking place. The boats were rowing toward the slowly moving *Queen Anne's Revenge*, so they had plainly picked a side.

Cooper arrived from below, more bruised and battered then he was even before the crash. He was raging and looking for blood. He and Woodes were cut from the same cloth. He carried with him a long rifle and was shoving bullets into the chamber as he strode to the edge of the deck where Woodes and several naval men stood sighting their own rifles and began firing rounds at the five lifeboats. Jennings cautiously approached them as the men on the escaping boats, not content to be picked off by the pirate hunters, were firing back at them. The boats were less than a hundred yards away but were not grouped together to make the shooting easy. There were at least a dozen men in each boat except the last one in which Jennings counted only six. That was the closest one to them and as Jennings focused on those men, he noticed some of their features looked familiar.

"Ha!" Jennings let loose a laugh. Woodes and Cooper looked at him like he'd gone mad. He shook his head and pointed at the near boat with the six men. Two of them were dressed in the same outfits as he'd last seen them. One had long curly black hair, wet from the rain, but a mane that would have any woman green with envy. "Black Sam Bellamy and the dreaded Bart Roberts". So those two weren't lying dead in some opium den or drunk in some tavern. They had lived up to their reputations by taking an enormous prize and continuing on with their pirate endeavors. Too bad the pair had chosen a ship without cannon.

Two naval men set an open crate packed with extra rifles and ammo next to the crouching shooters. Jennings took one of the rifles and loaded it as he watched the two pirates aim and shoot at them. Neither crew was having an advantage over the other. The storm and swells made hitting your target an act of extreme luck rather than skill. Jennings attempted to time the wave motion as he took aim on the two pirates who he now felt took a good portion of the blame for his circumstances. He had spent the last weeks focusing solely on holding Blackbeard culpable, but the rest of these miscreants are just as guilty. Rage built inside him as he took stock of his predicament. He fired his rifle as each vexation entered his mind; lost in time, homeless, marooned on a dead, sail-less ship, penniless, and conscripted to Rogers for God knows how long. He prayed for his shots to land true for if they didn't, he would turn this damn rifle on himself.

Bart, Sam, and Chester crouched low in the lifeboat using the gunwale to steady their rifles as they returned fire at the men huddled on the low deck of the iron vessel. The men rowing didn't have the luxury of crouching down as they pulled hard on the oars to increase the distance between them and their enemy. Thankfully the giant guns on the ironclad's turret were pointing away from them and Bart hoped they were damaged enough to be unable to fire. He wasn't sure who these men on the iron ship were, but he didn't want to wait around for an introduction. He glanced at the *Queen Anne's Revenge* heading toward them and hoped their cannons still operated. None were easy targets in this turbulent sea, but a few broadsides would send those bastards running for the belly of their iron beast.

Sam was glancing at Blackbeard's ship between firing shots at the navy men.

"How is it that Thatch raised that ship from the deep?" he asked.

"Don't know, maybe the same magic that brought us to the future, Sammy. The man is a mystery and I've heard many a rumor that he be the devil in disguise."

"Not such a good disguise, most take him for the devil at first sight," Sam said firing off a round at the iron ship.

"Can't wait to meet this devil we just sacrificed our ship and treasure for," grumbled Chester sarcastically.

"Looks like you won't have to wait too long," Bart said with another glance, as the *Queen Anne's Revenge* began to tack on a course to intercept them.

Blackbeard spun the wheel to bring the port side of the ship to bear against the ironclad. He smiled as the turrets still faced away from them without power to operate. There were a dozen or so men on the deck firing at the longboats launched from the sinking steamer. He would pound those bastards to the bottom of the sea in a moment.

"Give 'em a broadside, Miss Bonny and Mr. Vane!" Thatch yelled out.

Anne and Charles were now located on the gun deck. They couldn't hear the order directly, but Tom was standing in the stairway ready to repeat any order the captain gave.

"Give 'em a broadside!" yelled out the cabin boy.

"Let me, Anne, you've had all the fun so far. I just want to give 'em a scare first, see 'em run like rats," Vane said.

"Aye, take your shot," Anne said, giving up the gunner's position.

Vane took the linstock and fired the cannon. The concussion of the blast sent the big iron barrel rocketing back against its rope restraints. Smoke billowed out the discharged cannon and Anne and Vane looked out the gunport. The bar shot pounded the deck of the ironclad with a loud clang before ricocheting off into the sea. The effect was enough to send a few of the rifle men scrambling below in fear.

"Ha! Look at 'em go!" Vane laughed.

"Let's load it up so I can take a turn at 'em," Anne said with a devilish grin.

"Aye, what a lady wants a lady gets" Vane said, helping to load the cannon for another round.

The first lifeboat arrived at the side of the *Queen Anne's Revenge*. Jesse and Charlotte tossed them a line to tie off and dropped the rope ladder. The seas made it difficult to keep the boat from bashing into the frigate. The first man to climb the ladder shook Jesse and Charlotte's hands. His nose was crooked from being broken at some point in his life. The man looked to be in his mid-twenties with the callused grip of one who labored since a young age.

"Thanks for coming to our aid," he said.

"Couldn't let you drown after you saved our asses. What's your name, sailor?" Jesse said.

"Francis."

"Bart Roberts aboard your ship, Francis?" Charlotte asked.

"He's our captain."

"He make it off alive?" Charlotte asked, hopeful.

"Aye, he's in that last boat," Francis said, pointing at the furthest lifeboat that was taking the most fire from the remaining men on the ironclad.

"Get your men up and cast the boat off," Charlotte said.

"Not before we get them boxes up," Francis said.

"We don't have time to hoist them up," Charlotte said, looking at the crates crowding the boat.

"What's in 'em that's so important?" Jesse asked.

"Treasure."

The current was bringing all the boats closer together, Woodes realized. The first broadside from Blackbeard's vessel had sent several of the *Comanche*'s navy men to safety below the armored deck. His men, Cooper and Jennings continued to fire at the last boat. Jennings had hit one of the rowers in the arm, slowing their progress down. He looked over at the other boats lined up alongside the frigate taking on their men and cargo. He cursed them with all his being. This damn weather, that damn steamer captain, and that damn demon Blackbeard, may they all die a blighter's death. He wanted to at least kill these laggards in the lifeboat before they boarded the ship. Woodes and his crew kept firing as a lone cannon from the *Queen Anne* continued to send round shot, grape shot, and anything else that might put a dent in the iron ship at them.

The churning sea worked against both parties, neither side was able to hit the other with any accuracy. That would change as they drifted closer, and the advantage would go to the frigate and its bigger guns.

"Woodes!" A deep voice sounded across the wind and water. Woodes looked over at the ship. Standing atop the aftcastle against the railing was Blackbeard the pirate. Woodes could see him clearly in all his devilish glory. His long black hair blew wildly in the wind. His long-braided beard smoked and smoldered, lit aflame in spite of the rain that fell. The pirate hunter had heard rumors of this very sight but seeing it with his own eyes caused his mouth to drop agape and nervous sweat to bead his forehead, mixing with the water from the heavens. Woodes Rogers had sailed further around the world than any man of his time, seen tribes of natives that would eat you alive, and yet this ghastly beast that taunted him from the majestic ship was sending shivers of fear up his spine. It didn't matter that just days before the man sat tied in a chair that allowed him to strike him repeatedly as he saw fit. Now, on the open sea, it was like facing Poseidon himself, a god of the deep, or rather, in Thatch's case a devil.

"Woodes, I have enjoyed our games," Blackbeard said, walking along the deck. "It's time for me to leave you, but I don't want you to be cold on these Northern waters… So, I shall send you some of my flame." Blackbeard stood and set both hands on the railing, leaning his lanky frame forward, one of the cannon gunports directly below him. "Fire!"

The cannon fired from below Blackbeard's feet. A heated shot, aflame with oil, sailed into the side of the ten-foot turret sending fire and debris around the deck. Woodes, Jennings, and Cooper flinched as the round made contact. Woodes grabbed Cooper's shirt in his fist and pulled the man close.

"Get the prisoner," he growled.

Cooper ran to the hatch and disappeared down inside.

Blackbeard took a rolled cigarette and lit the end with an ember from the tips of his beard. He placed it in his mouth and set his hands back on the rail. The cigarette glowed red each time he inhaled a puff. Smoke from his beard continued to circle his face like a dancing mane of fog. Thatch watched as Woodes straightened himself and strode closer to align himself directly across from him. He pulled a pistol from his belt and checked to see the load. He then held the gun at his side.

Another heated shot was fired, and it pounded the aft of the ironclad's deck with a fiery blow.

"Fire another round and you risk scorching something very precious to you, Blackbeard," yelled Woodes across the distance.

"I have all I hold precious right here, pirate hunter," Thatch said.

"Not everything," said Woodes.

Blackbeard heard a scream and saw Cooper emerging from the lower deck with a handful of blonde hair. The hair was attached to a fighting, and frightened Colette Dallaire. Cooper pulled the woman up from below by her tresses and then dragged her over to Woodes. With a smile on his scarred face, Woodes pulled the woman forward to stand next to him. Her hands were tied together in front of her, she was bleeding from a cut on her cheek, and her clothes were torn.

"Hold your fire!" Thatch hissed to his crew before another round from the cannon could be shot.

He tossed his cigarette into the roiling seas and paced back and forth. He looked down as the last of the lifeboats connected to the ship and saw Black Sam and Bart Roberts looking up at him ready to climb the ladder. Seems he would owe those two pirates a debt of gratitude should they survive this day. He motioned his cabin boy over.

"Tell Caesar to hold that longboat, we may need it," he said, and Tom rushed off to deliver the message.

He turned back to Woodes.

"Are ye looking for a trade?" he yelled over the water.

Woodes smiled in his broken, malicious way. "The wench for you, Captain Blackbeard," He practically spit out the last two words.

Jennings looked at Woodes questioningly and asked in a low voice, "What makes you think that scoundrel cares for this woman more than his own hide?"

"Hornigold said there was a strong bond between the two, she risked her neck for his. We shall see won't we?"

"You should be begging for mercy rather than taunting him. He will destroy the whole lot of you!" Colette said.

Woodes slapped the woman's face with a backhand while holding her with the other. Colette stomped on his foot and continued to fight before Cooper and Jennings each grabbed an arm and held her tight. Woodes cocked the pistol he was holding and held it to the side of Colette's head.

"Damn you, Woodes! Harm her and I will burn you alive!" Blackbeard screamed at the pirate hunter.

"You see, even the devil can fall in love," Woodes said to Jennings without looking at the man, eyes never leaving the figure of Blackbeard.

Blackbeard began his way over to where the men from the steamer had boarded his ship. There were maybe forty or fifty of them, milling about with their boxes and crates, all armed to the teeth. Bellamy and Roberts had found themselves an up-to-the-mark crew since he last saw them on the first night this adventurous nightmare began.

Charlotte was there to greet Bart as he was climbing up the ladder. She looked down at him with a slight grin, her deadlocked hair, impervious to the rain, framed her attractive face and Bart climbed faster to reach her, leaping up to the deck. He stood before her and took her hands in his. They stared for a moment to drink in each other's presence.

"*Charlotte's Fortune*?" she questioned slyly.

"Aye. But now I hold the real prize."

"A prize, am I? For the taking?" she said with a raised brow.

"My tongue speaks without thought, because my heart races and takes my breath away in your company."

"See me as your equal and there might be a future for us."

"I've thought of nothing else since seeing you last," Roberts said, moving closer to her.

"We shall see then, Black Bart Roberts," Charlotte said with a hint of seduction.

They were interrupted as Black Caesar, Charles Vane, and the other pirates arrived to greet them.

"This seems no different than when we last boarded the *Queen Anne's Revenge*," Bart said as he shook Black Caesar's big palm. "Your welcoming hand, the pirate hunter on our heels, and a storm raging around us." Bart then saw the identical necklace hanging on Black Caesar's chest. He put his hand on his and held it up. "Where did you acquire that?"

Black Caesar held his own cross and looked at Bart's. They brought them closer to each other. "It was in our hold, booty from a French ship we raided."

"Mine was from a French ship as well," Bart said in wonderment. The two held the crosses inches from each other. As Bart gazed at the two large ornaments made from the strange metal his eyes narrowed. "What the devil?" he said and watched as the falling rain stopped and hovered in mid-air in between the crucifixes. It was as if he was staring at a painting, frozen on a canvas. *How is that happening? What kind of magic is afoot?* His thoughts were interrupted as Blackbeard strode up and slapped him and Sam on the back. Black Caesar stepped back and let his cross fall back against his chest.

"Welcome aboard, you right bastards!" Thatch said with a grin of white teeth. The wind was beginning to howl, and he had extinguished his smoldering beard. The rain was arriving in sheets, and the lines from the reefed sails snapped and pulled loudly against the rigging. "You do bring the weather, don't you?"

"Here we were going to lay blame on you, Thatch," said Sam.

Thatch laid his hand on Bart's shoulder. "I'll be borrowing your little boat to parley with the pirate hunter, but I leave the *Queen Anne's Revenge* in your charge. Just don't change her name while I'm gone." He winked at Charlotte.

"Hold on. Why's he taking charge? He's been aboard five minutes?" Vane spoke up. "It should be me." He looked around at the other pirates. "Or at least one of us."

"He's in charge because he arrived with a crew of fifty who will follow his orders. We need men to man the cannons and bring the *Queen Anne* to full complement. We are at war and as captain, I have full authority to make decisions without a vote. Are we clear, Mr. Vane?" Blackbeard said staring at the fuming man.

Vane looked up and down at Bart Roberts. The man was as impressive as ever. Dashing, handsome, full of self-assuredness. Roberts' old crew had told stories of him being impervious to bullets and blades when such talk would happen in the taverns of Nassau and Havana. *Should have known the bastard would show up again*, Vane thought. He looked back at his company of men; they were a work-hardened, sturdy sort as far as he could see. Thatch again had made a wise choice; didn't mean Vane would have to like it but his argument against it was quickly at an end.

"Aye," he said, keeping his eyes locked on Thatch's just so the man knew his decision was not made because he was cowed. Thatch nodded to him in understanding.

"Caesar, Sam and four of your men, Bart, can row me over to Woodes. Then they'll bring Miss Dallaire back safely here while I deal with the pirate hunters." Thatch handed his weapons one by one to Tom, leaving only his cutlass on his waist. "Keep these in good form for me, boy."

Tom nodded his head and then took his Derringer out. He handed it secretly to Thatch, who smiled at the boy and stuffed the small pistol up his sleeve. He ruffled the boy's hair and descended the ladder to the waiting boat.

CHAPTER 31 - THE TEMPEST

The wild seas worried Thatch as he watched the *Queen Anne's Revenge* rise and fall in the growing swells. She would need to be under way to shelter soon. His own little boat was becoming swamped by the treacherous sea as they struggled to row the short distance to the ironclad. The *Comanche*'s deck was now being battered by the waves as they struck from the breaking swells. Woodes, Jennings and the other men hung onto ropes that were rigged between the turret and other points on the deck. Thatch could see that Colette was soaked to the bone holding the lines with tied hands to keep from being swept into the sea. He desperately wanted to get to her, save her from Woodes and this tempest. He looked back at Black Caesar, Sam and the other men rowing heartily with their weapons stowed next them. He was grateful for them willing to risk their lives in his quest to save this woman he'd only known for mere weeks but who had captured his heart like none other.

"Faster, men. The sea's looking to swallow us whole," he urged them on. They crested a twelve-foot swell and sped down the back side finding the *Comanche* just in front of them. Their momentum brought them clanking against the low deck and Thatch leaped aboard, swinging over the rope railing. He then tied the boat off to the ironclad and turned back to Black Caesar.

"Don't let my sacrifice be in vain, whatever happens keep Colette safe."

"Aye, Captain. You have me word."

Thatch carefully walked the slick deck toward the waiting pirate hunter. The smugness of the scarred man's face amplified his overwhelming desire to put his fist through his nose. He looked at Colette who wore a look of foreboding that was as heavy as the seas.

"Let her go, Woodes. I'm here," Thatch said, stopping several feet away. He looked back at his men in the boat. All had their guns at the ready.

"Don't trust him, Edward. He's a snake," Colette told him.

"On your knees and she will walk slowly to the boat," Woodes ordered. He nodded at Jennings who released Colette's bonds and pushed her on her way, as Thatch went down to his knees. Thatch locked his eyes with Colette's as she let go of the rope that offered security from being swept overboard.

"Be quick about it, lass. Those men will keep you safe," he said encouragingly.

Colette carefully started across the drenched and slick deck toward the waiting boat. She met Thatch's eyes as she passed him. "Don't you dare die on me," she said in a low voice.

"I will find you when I'm done with these scourges," he said in a voice for her alone.

As Colette was walking toward the boat the ironclad was hit by a large wave causing the starboard side to rise, tipping the occupants abruptly toward port. Colette lost her footing and slid across the deck, headed to be dumped in the sea.

"Colette!" Thatch shouted and leaped to grab her hand. He was unsuccessful and she rapidly, uncontrollably, slid to the edge.

Colette screamed as she was pitched toward the water, but at the last second the big hands of Black Caesar snatched her from her doom. He pulled her inside the boat with the other pirates. Their boat was violently jostled by the wave and the line holding them to the ironclad snapped and came loose. They were quickly lifted and spun away by another set of waves.

Thatch spun on all fours to see the boat being swept away, Colette safely on board. The distance quickly grew as the swell now pushed the vessels apart. He looked back to see Woodes pointing a pistol at him, as were Jennings and Cooper, their aim wavering in the torrent. The deck was rocking back and forth continually now, and Thatch wrapped a line around his wrist to keep him from sliding off the side. He was still on his knees when a wave washed over the deck, drenching his heavy clothes.

"We need to get inside," Cooper said to Woodes.

"Your reign is at an end, Blackbeard. God is speaking. Do you hear his wrath?" Woodes said, stretching his arms out and looking into the storm. "He is condemning you today, the demon that you are."

Blackbeard gave a hearty laugh. "This storm is for you, Woodes! It's my doing! I bring it here to bury your bones and flesh beneath the sea, to be picked apart by crabs and the fish. This… this is all for you Woodes!" Thatch continued to laugh a haunting laugh at Woodes whose face was a mix of anger and horror.

The ship was now getting repeatedly battered by foaming and crashing waves, making it difficult for the men to remain standing, let alone keep their pistols trained on Blackbeard as he slid from side to side at the end of his rope.

Woodes fired his pistol at Thatch, who intentionally rolled about the deck to escape the bullets. Woodes kept pulling the trigger until the chamber was empty, never hitting his mark. Cooper was first to abandon the cause.

He opened the hatch and climbed his way down. Jennings grabbed Woodes' arm and pulled him toward the opening.

"We must go! Now!" Jennings screamed at him over the howling wind. Woodes took Jennings' pistol from him and fired it back at Blackbeard as he was dragged into the lower deck, again unsuccessful in his quest for vengeance. Once they were inside Jennings locked the hatch closed. He looked over at the soaked and distraught pirate hunter and grabbed the man by the shoulders.

"The hatch is locked. He is dead out there. There is no hope for him in those seas. It's over, Woodes. You've won," Jennings told the wild-eyed man who could only nod his head back at him.

The longboat banged hard into the side of the *Queen Anne's Revenge*. The men and women above were shouting down at the occupants to make haste up the ladder. Black Caesar pushed Colette up first, following her so that she did not get dislodged by the pounding waves. Charles Vane's rough hands grabbed Colette's arm and hoisted her to the deck. Sam and the rest of the men climbed aboard after Black Caesar. They were unable to secure the lifeboat and it disappeared into the storm.

Colette pressed herself against the rail hoping to see the ironclad and Edward Thatch, but it and he were lost from sight.

"Edward! Edward!" Colette screamed out to the sea. A wave crashed into the side sending a spray of cold ocean water to wash over her. She looked down to find Tom pulling on her arm.

"We must get below!" he yelled at her. The ship rocked and men ran and stumbled about to work the rigging. They were trying to get the sails up to give them some control over the frigate rather than being tossed by the storm. She turned and let the boy lead her down below the aftcastle deck. She remembered the location from her tour with Thatch. Tom hurried her to the room in the back, the largest quarters on the *Queen Anne's Revenge*. They entered the ornately furnished quarters of Blackbeard the pirate. Tom left her to sit on the carved oak bed while he made sure the windows and shutters were secure against the storm. Colette looked around at the beautiful artistry of the paintings that hung on the walls, and the eclectic collection of antiquities that decorated the chamber. This room was the most resistant to the motions of the sea as it was the topmost place above the stern, even so, articles slid from the desk and shelves. Colette rose to help the boy store the items for safe keeping.

Above deck, chaos engulfed the crew of the ship. The few working sails were no match for the twisting currents that threw the ship this way and that. Bart Roberts fought the wheel as a little man named Philip that he had met moments before, called out their direction as he watched his compass spin.

"I can't get this to give us true north," Philip exclaimed.

"Just tell us where the shore is," said Vane as he stood looking for the shadow of the coast.

"I can't unless I know where north is, damn you," said Philip.

"I will not be captain of two sinking ships today," Roberts said more to himself than the men and women around him as he struggled to steer the ship into a coming wave.

The wave caught the port side and pushed the ship from where Bart intended. He worked to correct their position. The wind changed direction and the sails lost their air. He looked up, waiting for them to catch the wind again, but something seemed wrong.

"Why are you sailing us backward?" shouted Mary from her position with the James brothers and Anne by the aft mast.

The wind was now at their backs it was true but the cause of it seemed other-worldly. The ship's motion was in reverse, and its speed was increasing. It was as if the frigate was being pulled from behind or flowing down a river stern first. The crew gave up the rigging and gathered around the aftcastle. Roberts could no longer work the wheel, as the keel was caught solidly in place. The wind and speed increased and the sea to the port side rose higher than the starboard side. The water was crested higher than the deck, yet it did not crash over the top of them. It was a colossal whirlpool a mile across that they were caught in. They could do nothing but watch as they were pulled round and round, faster into the vortex.

With a tremendous groan the ship swung to face the direction of the spin, bow forward as it was meant to sail. The violence of the motion sent the crew bashing into the rails, masts, and deck walls. It was a wonder none were lost over the side. Now that the ship faced the right direction its speed increased even more as it sailed lower with each turn into the whirlpool, whose circumference was shrinking the deeper it went.

"Look!" cried out Anne, pointing across the water.

The *Comanche* was caught as well in the vortex directly across from them. They could see a man on the deck, struggling to pull himself along by the end of a rope. It was Blackbeard using all the strength in his arms to pull himself to the turret. Hand over hand he inched his way to the armored spire. The wind whipped his hair and beard behind him. Upon reaching it he took hold of each porthole and pulled himself around the fifteen-foot circumference to find the gunports. They watched as he tried to squeeze himself into one of the holes.

"Hold on!" screamed out Sam Bellamy as the water on all sides began to come crashing in on them. The gray of the sky faded, and the darkness of the deep sea enveloped the entire ship. A sound as loud and roaring as thunder assaulted their ears and darkness closed in on them as they were swallowed by the sea.

Charlotte was the first to stir. Her face felt warm on one side and cold on the other. She was lying with her head pressed against the rain- and sea-soaked deck, but she could feel the sun's warm rays on her other cheek. She struggled to open her eyes and squinted at the bright sunlight. The storm was gone, and she awoke to the brightness of a cloudless afternoon. She pressed her hands on the cool wooden floor to push herself up. She got to her knees and looked about the cluttered deck. She saw Mary near her, moaning, lying on her stomach. Charlotte moved closer to roll Mary onto her side. Her red hair covered her face like that of a sheepdog. Charlotte brushed the tresses aside. Mary's eyes rolled into place to focus on Charlotte.

"Was it all a dream?" Mary asked, befuddled.

"A nightmare maybe," Charlotte answered, helping the other woman sit up. She then looked around at the rest of the stirring bodies that littered the deck.

"Charlotte! Charlotte!" She heard her name being called out.

"Here!" she answered.

A worried and unsteady Bart Roberts found her and wrapped her in his arms. "Thank the Lord," he said softly. "I thought I lost you."

Charlotte took his face in her hands and kissed him long and hard on the mouth, the brush with death prompting her to waste no time and take what she desired.

Jesse held out his hand to help Anne stand up. They too embraced. Jesse, not wanting to let go of this young woman he'd fought alongside and found such great adventure with over the past week, held her close and kissed her lips. Frank stood next to them looking around at the ship and the clear horizon, marveling at the luck to have survived the tempest.

Sam and Chester walked to the railing. Philip followed, limping from a bruised leg. Looking out from the starboard side they were met with a view of a tropical island densely dotted with houses and buildings. A long broad port stretched out from the harbor with moored ships of unimaginable size even when seen at this distance of several miles. The sea was calm and blue, the sun warm, as well as the air. There was heavy humidity in the atmosphere, almost like what you'd find in the Caribbean.

Bart and Charlotte came to stand at the rail with Sam and Chester. Vane and the others slowly crowded around them to gaze at the fantastical sight. Colette and Tom emerged from below deck to join them, neither speaking a word but staring off at the majestic coastline and unusual harbor. Tom held Colette's hand as they stood next to Black Caesar. The big man laid his palm on Tom's shoulder and patted it. Tom looked up at him and gave a half smile.

"The isle looks familiar…" Bart said, his voice trailing off.

"It's… Hawaii," said Sam.

"Aye, but not the one we left days ago," remarked Chester.

Bart shook his head. "It can't be."

The drone of several engines could be heard from behind. They turned to see what sort of ship was coming toward them, but none appeared on the water. The sound grew louder and louder until they realized it was coming from the sky. They looked up as four gigantic metal birds flew over them a hundred feet above the top mast with a deafening roar of engines that caused them to duck and flinch from the sight as they roared overhead. Philip was the only one who stood, back straight, and stared, awe-struck. His face turned up a smile while watching the four contraptions fly by. As they passed, he saw the goggled face of a man perched inside the glass lid of the beast. The man turned back to look at him and saluted with a leather-gloved hand as he continued his flight toward the coast.

To be continued…

ACKNOWLEDGEMENTS

I would like to start by thanking my amazing wife, Janina. She was the first to read the novel and offer her feedback on the characters and story. She has always been a voracious reader since childhood and though our genres of choice don't always align, I trust her opinions and taste more than anyone I know.

My daughter Ava was also my confidant as I worked out the original story and she was always there for me to bounce off ideas of. Those two wonderful women in my life continue to be the backbone of any success I have, even though they have humorously made endless fun of me for my pirate obsession. "Yo ho!"

Robin Seavill edited this novel and is owed a debt of gratitude for his guiding hand and intriguing notes during our collaboration. His wit and humor endeared me to him from our first written exchange. He added his unique Bristolian perspective on the many English characters and dialog throughout Pirates of the Wild West. To you my friend I give a mighty "Huzzah!"

I'd also like to thank my buddy Danny for always encouraging me to keep writing, as well as keeping me in stitches as we continue to pursue all our entertaining side projects.

Thanks to my friend and business partner Brent for always being there to support the entrepreneur spirit and dreams of everyone around him. There is no one else I'd choose to stand with me and face the sharks.

A LITTLE ABOUT ME BEFORE YOU GO

I grew up with a fascination and love of pirates and cowboys. Born in Miami, so close to the Caribbean, pirate themes were everywhere. I was influenced by their history, legends, and mystique that was portrayed in books and films. Later in my youth my family moved to Tucson Arizona where I developed my love of the cowboy genre. My adolescent mind was so enthralled with both pirates and cowboys that I would often find myself oscillating between the two, resulting in a peculiar ensemble of cowboy boots, shorts, a holstered plastic revolver and an eyepatch that obscured my vision while riding my trusty steed (a Huffy bicycle with a banana seat). I would energetically wave my plastic cutlass at parked and passing cars, lost in my own vivid imagination.

When I started thinking about a story where pirates are unwillingly transported to another time, I imagined what effect it would have on them. What if they went into the future but not far enough that the world would seem magical and confusing to them. It's not until the industrial revolution that daily life dramatically changes for humans. The 150 or so years that our pirates travel have only minor advancements to the eyes of the pirates. There is nothing that would seem otherworldly in 1873 like cellphones, the internet, or space travel. I felt that the wild west would give them a bridge to the coming future they might later experience in other books. On that note, book two, as you have most likely noticed, will have them transported to an age where humans have accomplished the marvel of plane flight.

I hope you have enjoyed this book as much as I have in writing it. If you'd like a taste of what is to come in book two, please sign up for my newsletter on my website and I'll send you the first chapter.

www.bryancantrell.com

You'll also find more about me there, my other projects and passions. I also host the www.piratefanclub.com there. It's a place for pirate history, merchandise, stories, and news.

If would like to do a pirate a huge favor, please leave a review for Pirates of the Wild West wherever you happened to acquire it. Content lives or dies by reviews these days and I would love for this book to not be condemned to lie in Davy Jones' locker. Thanks Matey!

Printed in Great Britain
by Amazon

24428114R00212